Praise for the novels of
Don Donaldson

"Full of twists and turns, and brimming with chillingly authentic medical details . . . takes the reader on a lively ride."
—Tess Gerritsen

"A wonderful tale that will remind readers of the best works of Cook."
—*Midwest Book Reviews*

"Donaldson . . . excels here at balancing a credible rendering of the workings of medical research and the day-to-day life of doctors with intrigue and treachery."
—*Memphis Commercial Appeal*

"Streamlined thrills and gripping forensic detail."
—*Kirkus Reviews*

"Genuinely heart-stopping suspense."—*Publishers Weekly*

"The autopsies are detailed enough to make Patricia Cornwell fans move farther south for their forensic fixes."
—*Los Angeles Times*

"Donaldson combines an insider's knowledge of modern technology with a real flair for making the reader's skin crawl."
—*Booklist*

"Sheer pulse-pounding excitement."
—*Jackson Clarion-Ledger*

Medical thrillers by Don Donaldson

DO NO HARM
IN THE BLOOD

IN THE BLOOD

Don Donaldson

BERKLEY BOOKS, NEW YORK

IN THE BLOOD

A Berkley Book / published by arrangement with
the author

PRINTING HISTORY
Berkley edition / March 2001

The Penguin Putnam Inc. World Wide Web site address is
http://www.penguinputnam.com

ISBN: 0-425-17878-1

BERKLEY®
Berkley Books are published by The Berkley Publishing Group,
a division of Penguin Putnam Inc.,
375 Hudson Street, New York, New York 10014.
BERKLEY and the "B" design
are trademarks belonging to Penguin Putnam Inc.

PRINTED IN THE UNITED STATES OF AMERICA

10 9 8 7 6 5 4 3 2 1

Acknowledgments

I'm indebted to many people for providing assistance with this book. Foremost among them is John Oncken, who showed me the ropes of dairy farming in southern Wisconsin and helped me understand that part of the country. I was also greatly aided in this by Steve Yttri. My decision to set much of this book in Wisconsin came from discussions with Dr. Carol Everson, who opened many doors for me, including an introduction to her delightful mother, Helen, and sister, Diane, without whom I would never have met John Oncken or been treated so well during my visit to Edgerton. I couldn't have done without the help of Dr. Mark LeDoux and his explanations of the diagnosis and treatment of seizure-presenting disorders, and am grateful also to Dr. Curt Dohan, with whom I spent several hours discussing the features of prion diseases and looking at slides of patients so afflicted. Important contributions were additionally made by Dr. Bob Burns, Dr. James Womack, Dr. Malinda Fitzgerald, Dr. Liz Wilson, Dr. Steve Kritchevsky, Dr. Alessandro Iannaccone, Cantor David Julian, Chad Lindley, Corey Mesler, Lee Merrick, and Phyllis Appleby. My apologies to anyone I should have mentioned and didn't.

Prologue

Chester Sorenson expertly attached the pulsators to the third Holstein in the row of thirty animals standing at an angle on the tiled floor above him. He didn't like working for a corporate dairy farm, partly because the milking parlor was so sterile . . . everything tiled and smelling of antiseptic . . . nothing like a small dairy barn where the odor of alfalfa hay and manure mixed with lime on the walkway and stale milk that had leaked from cows too full to hold it in made a man feel really alive.

He didn't plan to be a mere dairy hand for the rest of his life. One day he hoped to own his own farm with his brother, Buddy. So he saved every penny he could. There were some small farms in the area whose owners were getting old and whose kids had moved to Milwaukee to become bankers, or write software, or sell clothing. But when they were ready to sell, would he have enough put away? It was a question that worried him.

As Chester moved to the next cow, he saw something he didn't recognize on the floor by the animal's hind legs. Puzzled, he leaned in for a closer look.

Chester had grown up with cows and knew just about everything there was to know about them. He knew that if a cow tolerated another cow mounting her, the mounted animal was in heat. He knew that when cows lie down on a hillside, their heads always point uphill, and if a cow falls so that its legs end up with the feet pointing to the sky, it will die.

But with all he knew and all he'd seen, he had no idea what this was on the floor. There was some ropy-looking stuff that reminded him of one thing, but nothing else about it fit.

He moved around to get a look from a different position and began to think that what he believed was a single object, might in fact, be more than one. He wanted to shift the thing around a bit, but didn't want to touch it.

"What have you got there, Chester?" a voice said from behind him.

Chester had been so interested in the object that he hadn't heard his supervisor, Peter Dobbs, come up behind him.

"Damned if I know," Chester answered.

Dobbs took a quick look, then said, "I can't tell what it is either, but it doesn't belong in here. You go on with your work. I'll take care of it."

Before departing, Dobbs said something to the milker working the animals on the other side of the parlor and then practically pulled the guy from the room. Reluctantly, Chester left his discovery and returned to his duties, his mind still on that object.

Dobbs sent the other milker to the main office to straighten out some problem with his time card. Dobbs then went to his desk and made a phone call.

"No, he didn't seem to know what it was," he said.

He listened carefully to the lengthy response then said, "I'll take care of it."

As Chester was fitting the pulsators to another animal, Dobbs returned with a black plastic bag and a wide aluminum dustpan. Producing a metallic screech that startled the cows, Dobbs scooped up the object and put it in the bag, leaving behind only a slimy spot on the tiles.

A short while later, while Chester was cleaning things

up between milking sessions, Dobbs approached him with a white envelope in his hand.

"I need for you to take this down to motor pool storage and give it to the guy who's waiting there. He's the contractor for some renovation work scheduled for that building and this is the signed contract. So don't lose it."

Though rankled at Dobbs's suggestion that he was a moron, Chester didn't let it show. "Why can't he come up here and get it?"

"When you're in charge, *then* you get to decide how things are done. It shouldn't take more than ten minutes. So you won't get too far behind here. Take your car."

Yeah, right. Like I was planning to walk all the way down there, Chester thought as he headed for the exit.

The dairy was situated on rolling land just inside the corporate limits of the little town of Midland, Wisconsin, about thirty-five miles from Madison. The motor pool storage building sat in a valley so that when you were there, all you could see of the rest of the farm was the incinerator smokestack. As Chester pulled onto the asphalt apron in front of the building, he saw a car, but no driver. The big metal overhead door was open. Figuring that the contractor was inside, Chester parked and went to find him.

Going inside, Chester edged past the four-wheel-drive truck with the big blade in front they used to keep the dairy roads free of snow. In the back, past an old hay baler, he saw a man wearing a bright clean pair of blue coveralls that made him look more like a newly minted garage mechanic than a contractor. He was standing with his hands in his pockets, butt against a workbench on which there was a galvanized washtub.

"Good morning," the man called out.

Then Chester recognized him: a guy he'd seen around for a couple of years, mostly in the Lundstrom brothers' café, where he was always in a shirt and tie. They'd exchanged enough "how are you's" for Chester to feel he knew him, but he'd never heard his name.

"I didn't know you were a contractor," Chester said.

"And I didn't know *you* worked *here*," the fellow said, grinning.

"Fair enough," Chester replied. He extended his hand and introduced himself.

The man responded in kind.

"Here's the contract," Chester said. "What are you gonna do with the place?"

The man put the envelope in his pocket. "Move that wall over there out about thirty feet," he said, gesturing beyond the hay baler and a tractor on the other side. "Say, Chester, let me ask you something. You ever see anything like this?" He pointed into the galvanized tub.

What, again? Chester thought. *Two oddities in the same day?* He eagerly walked up to the tub and looked in. But he saw only a foot and a half of clear water. He turned to the contractor. "It's just water."

"No . . . I mean what's swimming in it. You have to look closely."

Chester bent and stared into the water.

Suddenly, there was pressure on the back of his head, forcing his face into the water. In his surprise, he inhaled, flooding his lungs.

He struggled hard, but not for long. As he passed from this life into the next, he briefly saw himself riding proudly on a brand-new, bright green John Deere tractor.

Back at the main complex, Peter Dobbs led the cow that had been closest to the strange object on the floor out of the barn. It followed him docilely, until about ten feet from their destination between two huge silage bunkers, the cow's legs buckled and it went down. It then began to kick wildly and mucus bubbled from its nose and mouth.

Dobbs was bewildered at what was happening, but it made what he had to do easier. Walking to the animal's head, he lifted the .45 caliber pistol at his side and fired a shot into its brain.

1

"Here's the chart for room three."

Holly Fisher accepted the clipboard and scanned the existing data on Ralph Hanson, a fifty-three-year-old real estate agent, who had been referred by his regular physician following a nasty discovery during his annual physical. Satisfied with her grasp of the details, Holly opened the door of room 3 and went inside. Her patient got off the examining table and stood when he saw her.

"Mr. Hanson, I'm Doctor Fisher."

Other than being about thirty pounds overweight, he didn't look sick, which of course, he wouldn't. She could see the fear in his eyes and when she shook his hand it was like gripping a moist sponge. At her request he returned to the examining table. "What's this about?" he prompted, one dangling foot beating out waltz time.

"Part of your recent physical included a quantitative analysis of the various kind of cells in your blood," Holly said. "It was found that you have an unusually high number of the type known as lymphocytes."

"Which means what?" Hanson said.

This was the point where she'd have to use the word and his life would never be the same again. Even now, after having uttered it to so many patients that their faces were lost to her, it still set off an internal fire alarm. No surprise there, considering . . .

"It means you have leukemia."

The blood drained from Hanson's face and the bounce went out of his foot. Holly hastened to tell him the rest. "Chronic lymphocytic leukemia, to be precise," she said. "The key word here is *chronic*. If you have to get leukemia, that's the kind to get."

"It's not . . . terminal then?" Hanson said.

"I have a patient who was diagnosed eighteen years ago and in all that time, she's only had to treat it for a two-week period."

Hanson's color brightened.

"Your lymphocyte count is only about four times normal. That's not terribly high. In all likelihood, this condition will not create any problems for a very long time. And when it does, we'll treat it."

"And the treatments are effective?"

"Yes."

"How long before I'd have to worry?"

"Let's put it this way. When your time comes, chances are slim that this will be the cause. But I do need to give you a short physical exam."

As the referring physician had noted, Holly found no enlarged lymph nodes, and though it was a bit difficult palpating Hanson's spleen through his extra weight, it too felt normal in size. They talked for a few minutes after the exam, during which Holly told him to return in three months for another blood study.

It was now nearly four o'clock, almost time for her to hit the gym for a little workout. But first she had to do a total white count and a differential on some preparations that had come up from the lab just before she'd seen Mr. Hanson. Normally, she'd have let a med tech handle the counts, but this was a very special case.

Returning to the office, she sat in front of her binocular microscope, where two Wright-stained blood smears and a sample of the same blood in a solution that dissolves red cells were waiting for her. She set about performing the total white count by drawing a small amount of the sample into a tiny tube fitted into the cap of the container holding the sample. She filled both chambers of a counting slide with blood from the tube, then put the slide on the scope. After a few adjustments, the white cells came into view, standing out like shiny ghosts against the vague debris of the dissolved red cells. She made the count quickly and plugged the result into a standard formula that yielded the good news; seventy-five hundred cells per cc, right smack in the middle of normal.

She replaced the counting chamber with one of the blood smears. A couple turns of the coarse focus, then a tweak of the fine, brought the tiny embalmed blood components to sharpness, revealing a punctate landscape as familiar to her as the furnishings in her home. Technically, the slide was excellent; the erythrocytes nicely separated from each other and spread evenly over the slide, the white cell nuclei just the right shade of purple, the various granules specifically tinted orange or azure.

She'd always enjoyed looking at blood smears, finding beauty even in the disturbed and immature shapes that spelled trouble for the patients they came from. But these cells were perfectly normal in appearance and in a few minutes, when she'd completed her diff count, she saw that the number of the various components were all within normal limits. This pleased her immensely because this blood was from a woman who, seven years earlier, while a student in medical school, had faced a death sentence from acute myelocytic leukemia ... not the relatively benign disease Mr. Hanson had, but a fire-breathing dragon. And now, after treatment, she'd been in remission for more than six years. This continued evidence that the woman could look forward to a long life filled Holly with a joy that couldn't be put into words, for the slide had been made from her own blood.

To treat her, her doctors had taken a sample of her bone marrow and purged it of the outlaw stem cells causing her disease. They had then given her drugs to kill all the stem cells in her remaining marrow. The purged marrow was then injected back into her with hopes that those cells would begin producing only healthy progeny. And they had.

But until today, Holly had not fully believed she was cured. She'd worried that the chemo they'd given her to kill the renegade stem cells in her body or the method they'd used to clean up the marrow sample they'd reinjected had missed one or two that had merely gone into hiding . . . that one day they'd mount a suicidal coup and she'd be in the obituary column before she'd really lived. That fear was one of the reasons she'd decided on a specialty in hematology . . . to know the enemy. But now, with these good results she suddenly felt free of all that. She *was* cured, really and truly.

She picked up the phone, entered the number of Grant Ingram's pager, then waited for him to call back, which he did barely two minutes later.

"Hi, I need to talk to you. Can I come up?"

"Sure," Grant replied. "What's the topic?"

"It's a surprise."

As she passed the small room that housed the practice's phlebotomist, or vampire, as Rena liked to call herself, Holly leaned in. "When you get a chance would you dispose of that blood sample in my office and clean my hemacytometer?"

"Will do," Rena said, keeping her attention on her patient's arm, where she was searching for a vein. "You off to take out your aggressions on some gym equipment?"

"Actually, I'm on my way to propose to Doctor Ingram."

This got Rena's full attention and she looked at Holly, her face beaming. "A frontal attack. I love it."

Cured.

Was there any more magical word in the world?

In the years since her disease had gone into remission, Holly had tried to live a normal life. And for the most part, she had. For weeks at a time, she wouldn't even think about the possibility that someday her leukemia might return. But even then, the specter was always there, lurking in the shadows at the edge of perception. Several times a month she'd see it clearly, often enough to remind her not to make any long-range plans or commitments.

But that was in the past.

Waiting for the elevator, she felt reborn; fresh and new, her life an uncluttered highway, stretching away to a distant horizon that held mysteries and wonders she longed to experience. So as the crowded elevator arrived and she stepped on, she began to hum a lullaby for the child she was now free to think about, caring not at all about the curious glances the other passengers were giving her.

Two floors up, Holly found Grant in the hallway of his practice area scribbling in a chart.

"Remember, somebody else may have to read that," she quipped.

He looked up, his brow furrowed. "I write legibly."

"It was a joke," Holly whispered in his ear.

"Oh." He gave her a smile with no heart in it and motioned with his head. "Let's go to my office."

In college Grant had been a champion swimmer and his office was filled with the trophies he'd won. Now he was one of the city's brightest young internists, and his blond hair still looked as though he'd just popped out of the pool and toweled it dry. He sat behind his desk, put his feet up, and cupped his hands behind his head.

"I'm yours for the next five minutes."

"I just looked at my blood. Everything's still fine," Holly said.

"That's great, babe."

"For the first time I feel as though I can plan for the future . . . like I'm going to be around as long as anyone else."

"I never doubted that."

"I did. So when do you want to do it?"

"Do what?"

"Get married. Start a family."

Grant took his feet off the desk and rocked forward. "Slow down, babe."

"What do you mean? I've *been* slowed down. I couldn't even think of having a child when I didn't know if I'd be around to raise it. But I'm sure now that I will." Holly stared at Grant's strained expression. "I don't understand. I thought this was something you wanted too, and that you were just being considerate and supportive by not pressuring me to do something I felt so strongly was wrong."

"That's not entirely correct," Grant said. "I don't recall ever saying I was ready for that responsibility. I'm only thirty-three years old, my practice is just beginning to take off, I'd like to travel . . . "

"You son-of-a-bitch," Holly said. "You only stayed with me because I was safe. As long as I was afraid my leukemia might return, you knew I wouldn't pressure you for any kind of commitment. I was just a . . . vagina with no strings attached."

Grant shot to his feet. "Now that's pretty nasty."

Holly crossed the room and snatched a framed photo of Grant accepting some swim medal off the wall, lifted it over her head, and impaled it on one of his trophies, sending glass everywhere. "No," she said. "*That's* nasty."

Fighting back tears, Holly returned to her own floor.

"When's the date?" Rena asked as Holly steamed past.

"He'd rather travel," Holly said, leaving the words trailing behind her.

In her office, Holly grabbed her coat and headed back to the elevators, ignoring the receptionist, who tried to hand her a message. Feeling utterly betrayed by Grant and stupid for allowing that to happen, Holly claimed her car from the parking garage next to the medical arts building and pulled onto Madison Avenue.

Last year in Memphis, the terrible summer heat carried all the way into mid-October, irritating the inhabitants and making many of them, Holly included, wonder why they remained in a place where summer lingered so long. This year, in a turnaround that would help make the average temperature for October match the benign numbers put out by the weather service, the city had been experiencing record lows each of the last two nights. With the temperature now hovering around thirty-four and a low of twenty-nine expected, it would only be a matter of hours before the light mist speckling Holly's windshield would turn dangerous, a rotten day for aimless driving around.

But that's what Holly did, finding herself an hour later, in Mississippi, forty miles down I-55. In truth, the trip hadn't been worthless, for she'd made a decision. She didn't need Grant to have a child. She didn't need *any* man. Well, at least not one she'd ever have to look at. It was too late today to call the clinic, but first thing in the morning . . .

"Hello, this is Doctor Holly Fisher. May I speak to Doctor Morrison please."

There was a moment of silence, and then the woman on the other end said, "Did you say Holly Fisher?" as if Holly were some kind of celebrity whose call was a big surprise.

"That's right."

"I'll get the doctor."

Now that the moment was almost here, Holly felt apprehensive . . . not so much about her decision, but whether the whole thing would work. For most women, to conceive through the use of a sperm donor was a relatively simple matter; pick the donor, show up at the appropriate time of the month, and wait for results. If it doesn't take, you try again.

But with Holly it was different. Warned that the chemo she'd be given to kill her bone marrow would probably also destroy all the eggs in her ovaries, Holly had delayed treatment until Doctor Susan Morrison at Fertility Associates had induced her to superovulate eleven mature eggs. For seven years those eggs had been sitting in liquid nitrogen at the clinic waiting for Holly . . . eleven tiny spheres, hardly big enough to see with the naked eye, let alone hold a woman's future. And now their time had come.

"This is Doctor Morrison."

"Hello, Doctor. Holly Fisher here. Seven years ago I had some of my eggs stored there while I underwent chemotherapy . . . "

"Yes, Doctor Fisher. I remember that very clearly."

"I'd like to make an appointment to discuss plans for fertilizing those eggs and implanting them. I know it's short notice, but I just decided to do this and I'm free today. Could you possibly see me?"

"Yes. I most definitely think we should get together at the earliest moment."

The clinic was two hundred miles away in Jackson, Mississippi, where Holly had been living when she was diagnosed. Since it was one of the best anywhere, she'd never considered moving her eggs to a Memphis clinic. But that meant . . . "It'll take me about three and a half hours to make the drive."

"Would two o'clock work for you?"

"Perfect. I'll see you then."

It was only after hanging up that Holly reflected on the odd phrasing Morrison had used when she'd agreed to an appointment today. She'd actually seemed eager for them to meet, as if the clinic needed the business, which, considering its reputation, didn't seem likely.

Thinking that it was probably just her imagination, Holly turned her mind to the things she'd have to do before heading for Jackson.

The waiting room for Fertility Associates was more like a drawing room in someone's home than a doctor's office: a muted floral carpet, comfortable upholstered chairs, Impressionist-style paintings of children at play in gardens bursting with flowers. The presence of six other women waiting for their appointments showed that business was in fact as good as Holly had believed.

Holly stepped up to the receptionist, a pretty olive-skinned brunette behind a carved English desk, and gave her name. Hearing it, the girl inhaled sharply, then practically lunged for the phone. She announced Holly's arrival in a breathless voice.

What on earth is going on here?

A nurse appeared in the doorway to the clinic area. "Doctor Fisher, please . . . come on back."

Holly followed the nurse to an unoccupied office with furnishings that continued the theme from the waiting room.

"Doctor Morrison will be with you very shortly," the nurse said, leaving Holly alone.

On the credenza behind Morrison's desk was an assortment of pictures—a couple of kids, most likely her grandchildren; a young man wearing a graduation robe and mortarboard; a teenage girl in a prom dress; and one of Morrison herself in camouflage fatigues, a shotgun tucked under one armpit, the opposite hand holding up a fistful of limp ducks.

"Doctor Fisher . . . so good to see you."

Morrison came over and clasped Holly's hand in both her own as if they were dear friends.

Though Susan Morrison had to be nearly sixty, the years had not found their way into her eyes, which retained the glow of youth. But there was also something else in there . . .

Still holding Holly's hand, she said, "I hope it wasn't wrong of me to ask you to make such a long drive, but . . ."

While Holly wondered why Morrison was apologizing for arranging an appointment Holly had asked for, a terrible thought took shape. The odd things she'd been noticing in talking to Morrison and the receptionist . . . Maybe it was because . . .

Oh my God.

"I just didn't feel right about saying this over the phone," Morrison continued. "The eggs you left in our care . . . they're gone."

2

"What do you mean, *gone*?" Holly moaned.

Morrison released Holly's hand and pulled the other chair in the room around so it faced her. She sat and folded her hands in her lap. Then, her eyes on the carpet, she began shaking her head. Finally, she looked at Holly. "In May of last year, a man who said he was your lawyer came here with your death certificate and a copy of your will in which you gave instructions that in the event of your death, he was to take possession of the eggs we were holding for you and arrange for their disposal."

"And you *gave* them to him?"

"I know. Looking back it seems foolish, but at the time, well . . . I had no reason to question any of it. When you first came to us, you were gravely ill. So it all seemed reasonable . . . that you hadn't made it."

Holly was wracked by emotion. In the dark hours while battling back from the chemo and then later, fighting off the pneumonia that had settled in her lungs before her purged marrow could restart her immune system, she'd been sustained by the thought of those eleven eggs, safe from everything her doctors and her disease could do to her, believing that one day she would claim those eggs and fulfill her destiny, not through adoption, not with another woman's genes, but with her own, the mystical continuity of life unbroken. Her leukemia was not an inherited disease, so there was no reason to fear that she would transmit a defective genome. There'd just be a son or daughter to carry on, to go forward. Now, all that had vanished, leaving behind a white-hot anger that threatened to consume even the chair she sat in. And then she remembered . . .

"What did this lawyer look like?"

Morrison searched her mind. "He's hard to describe because he wasn't distinctive in any way; mid-fifties, relatively short brown hair, average build, maybe a little on the heavy side, average height."

Holly shook her head. "No, that's probably not the guy I'm thinking of. But I'll bet the two work together."

"Then you know about all this?"

"Maybe . . . Last year I was approached by a slightly built man with a neatly trimmed mustache and goatee, who was part of a research team doing an NIH-funded study on enzyme levels in human oocytes. He said they were trying to determine if certain physical traits in women could predict that their eggs contained high levels of several key enzymes associated with fertilization and implantation."

"I've never heard of any study like that."

"As he told it, this research group believed their work would ultimately help in the management of infertility. He said I possessed the traits they were looking for and he offered me five thousand dollars to participate in the study."

"So they could induce you to superovulate and collect some of your eggs . . ."

"Exactly. Of course, because of the chemo I'd had, I couldn't have accepted even if I'd wanted to, which I didn't. To me, oocytes aren't just cells to be played with and then discarded." Anticipating a reaction to this last comment from Morrison, Holly quickly added, "I know . . . If everyone felt that way *you* might not possess the skills I wanted you to use on my behalf. Okay, so I'm a hypocrite."

"I don't think that. You told this man about your medical history?"

"Not in any great detail, but too much to be telling a stranger."

"Did you mention this clinic?"

"The bastards must have figured it out . . . somehow learned I was living in Jackson when I was diagnosed, took a chance, and showed up here."

"That would explain why the lawyer took your eggs away in a small container of liquid nitrogen. I wondered about that at the time. If you'll pardon my skepticism, I find it difficult to believe that any group funded by NIH would do something like this."

"Lots of money at stake. No results—end of grant. But I'll tell you this, if they think they can meddle with me and destroy my future and nothing's going to happen to them, they're too stupid to have a grant. Considering how much time has elapsed, it's probably futile to hope they haven't used what they took yet. But I'm still going to track them down and I don't care how long it takes."

"I can't help but feel responsible."

"Don't. You were tricked."

"I take my responsibilities to my patients very seriously. And this situation makes me sick. I shouldn't have just handed your eggs over without checking further. I'm embarrassed and I'm angry. And I want to help find these people."

"I guess you don't still have the lawyer's card."

"I don't think he gave me one."

"So where do we start?"

"By going through a listing of all reproduction-related grants currently funded by NIH. I have the data at home, but as you saw when you came in, I've got a full schedule the rest of the afternoon and it'll take a while to go through it. How about I give you a call as soon as I've done that? And we'll decide then what to do next."

They exchanged home phone and pager numbers and Holly left to make the long drive back to Memphis. Stopping only for gas and a visit to the rest room in a nearby McDonald's, she reached the Memphis city limits a little after six o'clock angrier than when she'd left Jackson. By then it had occurred to her that as slow as the government works, if this research grant they were looking for was a relatively new one, it might not appear in Susan Morrison's database. Needing to do something herself to find the creatures who had so thoroughly loused up her life, she did not go home, but drove instead to the public library, where she had to cruise the lot three times before finding a parking space.

It didn't seem likely that the man who'd tried to enlist her in the study had come to Memphis just to court her. More likely he was here on a general recruiting trip and had just seen her by accident, which in turn meant that they might have tried to find other donors through an ad in the personals section of the paper.

Inside, the library was overrun with kids . . . standing at all the computers, occupying all the chairs at every table, filling the place with youthful energy that made Holly feel her loss even more keenly than before.

The children did not have much interest in the microfiche records of past newspapers, so after Holly obtained the files for March, April, and May of the previous year, she had no trouble finding a viewer.

About forty-five minutes into her search she found the ad in the April twelfth edition:

EARN UP TO $5,000

Women wanted to participate in federally funded research project. If you are healthy and between the ages of 18 and 35 and are willing to provide scientists with a small number of eggs from your ovaries, call . . .

•   •   •

She spot-checked later dates and learned that the ad ha
run about a month. Harvesting eggs was something yc
couldn't do in a motel room. They would have neede
a significant amount of equipment, which meant they ha
either set up a temporary clinic or had made an arrang
ment with a local medical practice to use theirs.

Holly made a copy of the ad, returned the files, an
headed for the pay phones. Her subsequent discovery th
every phone had a kid attached to it sorely tested h
love for children. Trying hard to remember that long cha
with friends they'd seen just a few hours earlier was a
important as oxygen to kids, she waited for her turn wi
exemplary patience.

This virtuous behavior though, was not rewarded, fo
after two rings, a recorded message informed Holly th
the number in the ad was no longer in service.

Finished at the library, she returned to her car. As sh
pulled onto Peabody and headed toward the river, she sa
an aged West Highland terrier plodding along the sidewal
The dog stopped and looked back, apparently waiting fo
its owner, an old man moving at a glacial pace, to catc
up. Driving on, Holly wondered what would happen to th
dog if the old man died. Would it find a good home fo
its remaining years? Or would there be no one to ca
for it? Holly had long wanted a dog, but until she cou
be sure her leukemia wouldn't return, she hadn't felt
would be right to buy one. Just another example of ho
even though she was still alive, her disease had robbe
her of life.

By now, her blood sugar had fallen to a level th
could not be ignored, so before going home, she stoppe
by the Bayou Bar and Grill for some red beans and ric

Holly lived in a multi-story apartment building wher
except for the time when three monkeys got loose fro
the nearby zoo and took up residence for two days c
the building's balconies, life was uneventful even fo
those who were not sure they had much of it left. Du
ing the drive to Jackson earlier in the day, she had thoug

that with a child, she would need more room, perhaps a small house in one of the historical neighborhoods. But with her hopes stolen, it now seemed likely she would remain where she was.

As Holly opened the door to her apartment, she heard the phone. Dashing to catch it, she found herself hoping it was Grant.

"Holly, this is Susan Morrison. I didn't find any listing for that research study. It's possible though that it just hasn't made it into the records. Tomorrow I'll call a friend at NIH and ask about it."

"An hour ago I thought I had a lead here," Holly said. "For a month last year, around the time *I* was approached, the Memphis paper ran a classified ad trying to recruit egg donors for a federally funded research project."

"That *has* to be them," Susan said.

"I called the number listed hoping it would turn out to be a clinic they'd tapped into for its equipment, but the phone's been disconnected."

"It's possible the paper still has a record of who took out the ad. The phone company too. I don't think they install phones without knowing who they're dealing with, even if they paid in advance."

"Those are great ideas." Holly said. "I'll look into them."

"So I guess this group we're looking for just set up their own temporary operation."

"That had to be a lot of trouble."

"Expensive too."

"What kind of scientists would do what they did to me?"

"Maybe we'll find out tomorrow."

"You'll let me know as soon as you learn anything?"

"I'll give it top priority. And Holly . . . I want to apologize again for not being more careful."

3

The next morning when she had a couple of free minutes, Holly called the classified desk at the newspaper. The clerk who answered thought they probably had a name on file for whoever had taken out the ad, but it sounded like a court order would be needed to get it. Same with the phone company. With patients waiting, she didn't have the time to ponder her next step, but it seemed clear that whatever crime had occurred had taken place in Mississippi, not Tennessee. That alone would surely complicate any effort to force the paper and phone company to release their records.

At ten forty-five, while Holly was with an AIDS patient she was treating for anemia, there was a knock on the examining room door.

"Come in."

It was Debra Demetrius, the receptionist. "You've got a phone call from a Doctor Susan Morrison . . ."

"I'll take it in my office."

Holly excused herself and went quickly to the phone. "Hi, Susan. What have you learned?"

"NIH is funding no such study. Neither is NSF."

"Then who the devil are we dealing with?"

"Wish I knew. What about the paper and the phone company?"

"They have a name, but won't give it up."

"Maybe you should hire a lawyer to get it. I'd be glad to share the expense."

"Is there any legal basis to expect we'd succeed? The fraud took place in Mississippi."

"Didn't you tell me yesterday the ad that ran there said they were recruiting donors for a federally funded project?"

Seeing her point, Holly said, "That would be fraud too, wouldn't it?"

"Anyway, those are issues for a lawyer. Lay out the situation for them, see what they say."

"Right now I can't think of any other way to go."

Wishing she had time to mull this over, Holly hung up and went back to her patient.

A quarter after twelve, Holly headed downstairs to the food court and got in the Subway sandwich line. The only lawyer she knew was a friend of Grant's. And lawyer-client confidentiality aside, she wasn't going to call *him*.

Grant . . .

With a little time having elapsed since her blowup in Grant's office, enough dust had settled to permit some scrutiny of the circumstances leading up to it. How had she been so misled about his intentions? Had she read more into their relationship than had really been there?

Of course she had. But whose fault was it? Had he ever actually expressed an interest in marriage and kids?

She thought back . . .

Yes.

It was a night around three months after they'd started sleeping together. They'd had dinner at Owen Brennan's, that New Orleans–style place with the jazz band out east. They'd left the restaurant and were greeted by . . .

"Snow," Holly said. "How beautiful."

It almost never snowed in Memphis, so this was an indescribable treat; big soft flakes falling steadily into

*the glow of the parking lot lights, frosting the asphalt
like powdered sugar. Holly stepped from under the restaurant's portico, spread her arms, and turned her face to
the sky. "It tickles," she said. "Like . . . the tips of an-
gels' wings."*

*Not given to such displays himself, Grant went into
the snow and watched her with his hands in his coat
pockets. "Okay, Eskimo girl," he said after less than a
minute. "We better go before you get run over."*

*Reluctantly, Holly followed him to the car, took a last
look at the heavens, and got in. Feeling moisture on her
face from the melting snow, she turned on the overhead
light and checked her makeup in the mirror. What she
saw made her howl with laughter.*

"What's going on?" Grant asked.

"Look at me."

*She turned and faced him so he could see how her
mascara had run down her cheeks. "Trick or treat." She
returned to the mirror and howled anew.*

*Her laughter was contagious and Grant joined in.
"You're nuts, you know that?" He reached for her. "But
you're* my *nut."*

Then they were kissing. . . .

She could recall it now with the utter clarity of an event
just moments old, the urgency of their embrace, the feeling of being lost in him, surrounded and protected.

*Inexplicably, at that moment, the specter of her illness
whispered, "Don't get too happy, kid, cause it ain't over
yet."*

*The day she'd first been diagnosed, she'd cried end-
lessly. But then, deciding that giving in to it that way was
like being dead already, she'd toughened and hadn't wept
since. But for some reason, that little whisper in the car
cut right through her.*

*In the flash of another car's lights, Grant saw the
tears on her face and realized it wasn't melting snow.*

"What's wrong? I thought you were happy."

"I was. But then I remembered . . ."

"Remembered what?"

She hesitated, not wanting to say it aloud. But finally, the burden was too much to carry alone. ". . . that I might have no future, that I may die without ever having a family, that I'll never wake up in the morning next to someone I can make breakfast for and tell my troubles to and know that it's not just for a day or a week or a month . . ." Now that the gates were open, her fears galloped through them. ". . . that I'll never see the look on my children's faces when they open their gifts at Christmas or show them how to color eggs for Easter, never see their report cards or help them tie their shoes and blow their noses, never feel their arms around my neck."

Grant pulled her close. With his cheek against her hair and his mouth next to her ear, he breathed "Holly, whenever you're ready, just tell me and we'll make all those things happen."

He'd said that. And there was no mistaking the meaning. But maybe she'd overreacted in his office. Wasn't it possible he'd just been taken by surprise—that by now, he'd realized what he'd done?

But even as she spun this web of self-delusion, it began to tear.

"Hi, Holly."

She turned and saw that she'd been joined in line by Elaine Miller, the new addition to the pediatric practice on the sixth floor. They'd met a few months ago when they'd shared a table here and had done so numerous times since. She was a dark-haired, curvaceous beauty with huge brown eyes and a perfect smile, facts that made women of lesser stature dislike her on sight or at least distrust her. Though Holly was a different type—blond, green-eyed, and lean from the rigorous exercise regimen she'd adopted to give her body every chance to fight off any remaining leukemic cells in her marrow—she too was a head turner. So the two women were able to interact as equals.

"I heard you and Grant have broken up," Elaine said. "Is that true? I'm not trying to pry into your private life, but . . . well, it's something I need to know."

"He asked you out, didn't he?"

"Frankly, yes. He told me you two had separated, but I just wanted to hear it from you."

This blew away the last remnant of the fictional Grant Holly had been imagining a moment earlier, and her anger at him came back in a rush. Editing what she really wanted to say about him, Holly replied, "Obviously I can't recommend him to you, but if you'd like to see for yourself what he's like, go to it."

"I'm not sure I should. I mean, he's asked me to go skiing with him in Denver. That's kind of a big deal for a first date."

Denver.

The word gave Holly an idea that pushed her anger aside. "I just thought of something I need to do. I'll see you around."

Holly's next patient was scheduled for one o'clock. That gave her barely thirty minutes. Memphis isn't the kind of town where you can step outside and hail a cab. You can stand on the curb for hours and never see one. So Holly found a pay phone, looked up taxis in the Yellow Pages, and had one sent.

It showed up twenty minutes later smelling like bathroom deodorizer.

"World News," Holly said, getting in. "One twenty-four Monroe."

"You call cab just to go one mile?" the driver asked. He was Asian, Vietnamese maybe. "Bus go there. Make no money on such short trip."

"You get to bring me back too, and wait for me while I do something."

"Need nice tip too," he said, pulling into traffic.

About the time she became accustomed to the cab's odor, they were there.

"I'll only be a few minutes," Holly said.

"Can't stay here. Must circle block."

"Just be sure and come back."

"Have to come back. You owe money. This no trick to avoid paying, right?"

"It's no trick."

Holly went into the newsstand and gathered up every out-of-town newspaper she could find, a cache that included the *Dallas Morning News,* the *New York Times,* the *Philadelphia Inquirer,* the *Chicago Sun-Times,* the *Cleveland Plain Dealer,* and the *New Orleans Times-Picayune.* She came out of the newsstand considerably lighter in the wallet, with a cumbersome armload that made her hope her cabby hadn't just passed.

Two minutes later he turned the corner and picked her up. As they started back to her office, the driver looked at her in the mirror. "You know, many lies in newspaper. You read all that, you think you informed, but many lies. Even here."

Presumably by *here,* he meant the United States. "I'll keep that in mind."

"What you do?"

"I'm sorry?"

"To make living."

"I'm a doctor."

"Very fine occupation. You must be very smart lady. My son want to be doctor. You have son?"

"No."

"Daughter?"

"No."

"Children much problem, but also much pleasure . . . when not screwing up."

By the time they arrived back at the medical building, Holly had decided that despite the driver's initial irritating remarks, she rather liked him. So he got his nice tip.

She didn't have time to look at the papers until later that afternoon when one of her patients was a no-show.

Though it had been many months since she'd been approached about selling her eggs, it seemed possible that the people who had stolen her future might still be running ads in *other* cities looking for donors. But was it likely she'd find them in one of the papers in front of her? Who knows? To find out, she pulled the *New York Times* off the pile and began hunting for the classifieds.

Twenty minutes later, as she put the *Philadelphia Inquirer* on the pile of papers she'd already checked and reached for the *Dallas Morning News,* Debra Demetrius informed her that her last patient of the day had arrived.

"Bring her in."

Hurrying, Holly flipped through the paper to the Dallas classifieds and ran her finger down the personals column.

Looking for chess partner . . .
Single? We can change that . . .
Need someone to share purchase of a bass boat . . .
Adopt . . .

Holly's eyes lingered on this one.

A lifetime commitment. We can offer a special life to a child. Love, happiness, and financial security. Expenses paid. Please call . . .

Adopt.

Was this the answer? Was it better to have someone else's child than none at all?

Damn it.

She shouldn't have to confront this. At least not yet. Right now she should still have eleven chances of bearing her own child. Even if the odds were long against success, she should still have that hope. With her anger freshened, she moved down the column.

Then a boldface heading caught her eye.

EARN UP TO $5,000

Women wanted to participate . . .

4

The clapboards clothing the north side of Ronnie Johannson's house on the outskirts of Midland, Wisconsin, were so rotted they just *had* to be replaced. At least that's what he'd been hearing daily from his wife, Skye, for nearly six weeks. It was a lousy time of year to be taking on that kind of job, but he'd gotten the distinct impression that installation of the new siding might lead to resurrection of certain bedroom activities that had lately been in short supply.

He'd considered assigning the task to Dennis, his goofy brother-in-law, who had been staying with them until he could "get on his feet." But then, believing that Dennis would probably just end up driving a nail through his hand, Ronnie became resigned to doing the job himself. Dennis was sure as hell going to help though. Certainly the whole thing would go faster with the pneumatic nailing gun Ronnie now held in his hand.

"It's not only faster than a hammer with that little gem," Shell Phillips, the owner of the hardware, said as if reading Ronnie's mind. "But the nail goes in so fast, there's less chance of the wood splitting." He was called

Shell because of the shell collection in the glass case by the door.

"Yeah, I like the idea," Ronnie said. "But I don't have a compressor to run it."

"Might be I could rustle up one you could rent," Shell said.

Suddenly, Ronnie's thoughts of clapboards and nailing techniques were toppled and carried away by a flood of memories, released by the smell of rubber and perfume that had just engulfed him. He'd been unfaithful to Skye only once in their twelve-year marriage: two years ago, with a woman he'd met having a battery put in her car at the BF Goodrich store.

While he'd waited for them to install new shocks on his pickup, they'd sat in front of the store's TV and talked. She'd laughed at his jokes and looked deep into his eyes like the girls in high school used to when he was an honorable mention all-conference receiver for the Midland Brahmas. He wasn't cruising for any action, but that look of availability, that moment when he realized he could have her, made him forget he drove a truck for a living and had no future. Once again, he was Flying Ronnie Johannson, a football cradled in his arms, the crowd on their feet, calling his name. Who could blame him for wanting that rediscovered moment to last as long as possible?

Skye, that's who.

Afterwards, he'd felt such guilt he was almost sick to his stomach. And he was afraid . . . afraid they'd been seen, that she'd try to contact him, that Skye would find out.

But he'd never heard from the woman again, or even seen her anywhere. And now she was standing right behind him. He was sure of it.

Heart tripping, he turned and saw . . .

No one.

Relieved and perhaps a little disappointed, he realized that if she *had* been there and had been wearing the same perfume, he shouldn't have smelled rubber too. That had come from the tires all around them at the BF Goodrich store.

So what *was* the origin of that smell?

Then, Ronnie's vision frayed and blurred at the edges. As he turned back to look at Shell, the diameter of the tunnel Ronnie seemed to be looking through grew smaller and smaller . . .

The store began to rotate . . .

Behind the counter, Shell saw Ronnie's eyes roll upward until the colored part almost disappeared. For a moment Ronnie seemed to stiffen, then his left arm began jerking rhythmically the way he used to do after scoring a touchdown. But then he dropped to the floor and his right arm joined the beat, his legs also bucking.

Having no earthly idea what to do for someone having a fit, Shell ran for the phone.

"And now, ladies and gentlemen, our benefactor, the founder and CEO of Bruxton Pharmaceuticals, Doctor Zane Bruxton."

The medical director stepped aside and the man of the hour took the podium. Five rows back on the left side of the small hospital auditorium, Richard Heflin was still marveling at how old Bruxton was. From his reputation, Richard had expected a tornado of a man, but Bruxton didn't look as though he could blow the fluff off a dandelion.

He was wearing a dark blue suit that contrasted so much with his luminous pink complexion he seemed to have a lamp on inside him.

"I know you're all very busy, so I'm only going to say a few words," Bruxton began in a surprisingly strong voice.

Behind him was the projected image of the MRI scanner he'd donated to the hospital, a major gift for any facility let alone a small operation with only forty beds. The gift had been made possible by his company's newest product, Vasostasin, a substance that reduced the size of tumors by denying them a blood supply and also made the residual cells more sensitive to conventional chemotherapy. Because of Vasostasin, remission rates for many types of cancer were skyrocketing.

True to his word, Bruxton spoke about five minutes, then stepped away from the podium to more-than-polite applause. As the crowd filed out of the auditorium to the hallway, where there were coffee and cookies, Jessie, Richard's sister, who headed one of Bruxton Pharmaceuticals' R&D teams, spoke from behind him.

"Well, Richard, what did you think?"

"I expected him to be bigger."

"That's all you can say after what he's done for this hospital?" Jessie replied, letting her irritation show. "You know you're one of those who will benefit most. I'd think you'd be grateful."

Jessie was right. As the area's lone neurologist, he and Dean Goodman, the only orthopod around, would probably be the MRI's primary users.

In the hallway, Jessie pressed her point.

"Because of him, you're going to be able to give your patients much better care."

"Not to mention what his company's stock has done for your portfolio," Artie Harris said. Then, seeing the look on Richard's face, Harris said, "You didn't buy any? Richard, I told you that when Vasostasin got FDA approval their stock would go ballistic."

Artie was a better insurance agent than stock picker. Before his Bruxton tip, every one of his recommendations that Richard had acted on had promptly headed south. For Jessie's sake—for some reason, she was in love with the guy—Richard chose to ignore the bait and not ride him over his dismal record. Instead, he responded to Jessie.

"My comment about Bruxton wasn't meant to be critical. I couldn't be happier over what he's done for the hospital. It was a very generous act."

"Yeah, but considering the dough his company's raking in, he could afford it," the director of the critical care unit said, entering the group with a cookie in one hand

and coffee in the other. "Do you know how much it costs to treat the average cancer patient with Vasostasin?" Without waiting for a reply, he answered himself. "Five hundred and sixty K."

"I realize that their healthy bottom line is a major reason why Bruxton could give us such an expensive instrument," Richard said. "But come on, half a million dollars?" Failing to notice Artie's hand signal, he went on. "I can't help but wonder if it really *has* to cost that much."

"Actually, it does," a voice said from behind Richard. He turned to see the medical director with his face pinched into a look of disapproval. Beside him was the man who'd spoken: Zane Bruxton.

The director managed to unclench his teeth long enough to introduce Bruxton to everyone except Jessie, whom of course he already knew. Bruxton then continued his response to Richard's comment about the cost of Vasostasin.

"To bring any drug from conception to the marketplace is a hugely expensive endeavor," he said. "Many millions of dollars. To be able to engage in that kind of developmental activity, a company has to establish an R&D set aside from the sale of its existing products. That money doesn't go in anyone's pocket. It's plowed back into the creation of even better products that ultimately benefit the sick. Now I'm sure I haven't just said anything all of you didn't already know. But in the case of Vasostasin there's a special problem that has a significant impact on its cost. We're able to obtain the parent protein by recombinant technology: the insertion of the gene for its production into bacteria, which then manufacture prodigious quantities at relatively modest cost. But bacteria are not capable of adding sugars to proteins. Unfortunately, the parent protein devoid of its sugars is inactive. It is therefore necessary to add those sugars by a patented process one of our scientists developed several years ago. And *that,* my friends, is *very* expensive.

So, Doctor Heflin, the pricing of Vasostasin is not as capricious as you might have imagined."

"No, I see that now," Richard replied, sheepishly. Feeling his pager vibrating in his pocket, he excused himself and went to the nearest house phone, where he was summoned to the hospital's west wing to see a new admittance. After the hole he'd dug for himself with Bruxton, he was glad to have an excuse to make a dignified getaway.

Reaching the room where he'd been directed, Richard found a man about thirty years old having a generalized seizure in his bed. Under the direction of Tom Faulk, one of the doctors who staffed the ER, the patient had correctly been placed on his side and allowed to ride out the seizure with no other interference.

"Hi, Tom. What do we know here?"

"Guy had a seizure in a local hardware, then slipped into a coma. He just started that one after we paged you."

"Any history available?"

"We called his home, but there was no answer."

"Any medical information on him?"

"No."

"What's his name? Do we at least know that?"

"Ronnie Johannson. One of the medics who brought him in said he was a big high school football star around here."

As they talked, the seizure, which involved all of the patient's limbs, began to subside.

"Did you see this seizure start?" Richard asked.

"Yeah. It began in his left arm, then spread."

This was a big clue, as seizures that begin focally and then generalize are usually acquired rather than genetic. Considering that Ronnie was once a football player, it seemed possible that an old head injury might be behind this. Richard turned to the nurse standing by. "Let's get him started on Dilantin, forty megs a minute up to a total of . . . " Richard guessed Ronnie's weight at around one sixty. Drawing on numbers he'd stored in his head from years of treating epileptics in Boston, he settled on . . . "thirteen hundred megs." While the nurse set about preparing the Dilantin, Richard enlisted Faulk's help in getting Ronnie onto his back. Before beginning his examination, Richard said to Faulk, "We can't raise anybody at his home——how about trying to find some other relative?"

"Do you have any idea how many Johannsons there are in the phone book?"

"It's a small town. Start with the hardware store where he was picked up. See if *they* know anything."

Ronnie was now lying quietly. Richard leaned down and called his name.

"Ronnie, can you hear me? Ronnie . . . "

No response.

"Ronnie Johannson . . . Can you open your eyes?"

Still nothing.

Richard lifted Ronnie's right eyelid and checked that pupil with his penlight. The green disk of Ronnie's iris closed down. The other eye was equally reactive.

In any sudden onset of neurologic symptoms in an otherwise healthy individual, stroke has to be among the first things considered—either a burst vessel producing a clot that presses on the brain, or a clot within a vessel, denying blood to the region of the brain the vessel serves. Because patients with a bleed don't usually present with seizures, Richard didn't believe that Ronnie had blown a vessel.

Could it be the other kind of stroke? Richard didn't know. And because Ronnie was unconscious, he couldn't conduct the kind of neurologic exam that would help him find out. Actually, the seizures were Richard's primary concern at this point. Even though Ronnie's only movements at the moment were the rise and fall of his chest as he breathed, it was possible that his brain was still showing the wild spiking of epileptiform electrical activity. If so, the Dilantin Richard had ordered might not be sufficient to get this under control. Aware that the longer Ronnie's brain was allowed to misfire, the harder

it would be to stop it, Richard put the MRI scan he'd be
wanting on the back burner and called the EEG lab.

"Ray . . . it's Richard Heflin . . . Can you take a patient in about three minutes? Good. We'll be there
shortly."

Before taking Ronnie to the lab, Richard conducted a
quick neurological exam in which he discovered that
when he rolled Ronnie's head from side to side, the eyes
compensated correctly in the opposite direction, suggesting that at least the brainstem was intact. This was
supported by his observation that when he stroked either
of Ronnie's corneas with a wisp of cotton, there was a
brisk blink reflex on the stimulated as well as the un-
stimulated side. But when he stroked the soles of Ronnie's feet with a tongue depressor, the toes on both feet
lifted and splayed, indicating a dysfunction in both cerebral hemispheres.

As soon as the nurse got Ronnie's IV started they all
headed for the EEG lab, where Ray Charles Collins, the
medical instrument tech, was fiddling with the rainbow
assortment of spaghetti wires that made up the twenty-
two leads he'd attach to Ronnie's head.

"Looks like this one won't be appreciatin' my rapier
wit," Collins said.

"Unlike the rest of us, you mean?" Richard said, entering into banter he didn't feel. "Let's get him trans-
ferred."

Richard and Collins moved Ronnie from the gurney
onto the EEG table.

Even with his new laid-back lifestyle here in Wisconsin, Richard couldn't bear to just hang around and
watch for the twenty minutes it would take for Collins
to get Ronnie wired. He could put that time to better use.
"He's been having seizures," Richard said to Collins. "So
we've got him started on Dilantin. If he should have another one while you're hooking him up, call Gloria here."
He turned to the young nurse. "If Ray calls you, get right
down here and give the patient two megs of Ativan and
page me. Okay?"

They both agreed and Richard wrote his instructions in Ronnie's chart. He then went into the next room and called his office, which was in a small medical building attached to the opposite wing of the hospital.

"Hi, it's me . . . I'm in the EEG lab, but I'm going to make a quick run over to the Gustafsons' and check on the Mrs. I should be back in twenty minutes. How's my schedule for this afternoon?"

He learned that the single appointment on the books when he'd left to hear Bruxton had increased by one: a woman suffering from migraine headaches.

"Okay, thanks."

On his way out, he told Collins, "I should be back by the time you're ready to start. If I'm not, just go ahead."

A minute later, Richard stepped into a gorgeous autumn morning with air as sharp as Baccarat crystal and so sweet it hurt. He thought briefly about Ronnie Johannson and how unfair it was for anyone to fall ill on such a day.

But when was life fair?

The months since he'd moved to Midland melted away.

"Doctor Heflin?"

"Yes?"

"I'm afraid I have some bad news for you. Your wife has been involved in a carjacking."

Richard's blood congealed in his vessels and his heart tried to escape through his mouth.

"There's no good way to say this, but she's been . . . "

"Hurt?" Richard said, hoping that by filling in a lesser word he could control what was happening.

"Doctor, she was shot . . . fatally, I'm afraid."

A lousy phone call.

The cops hadn't cared enough to send someone to tell him personally. She was just another entry in their records for the year, half a percentage point, a keystroke on a secretary's computer, a call to be made and forgotten. To this day, no one had been charged with her murder.

He'd never forget their callous treatment and would never forgive the city for spawning her killer. With that one phone call, less than a minute out of his life, everything changed, and he'd become filled with hatred, not just for Boston, but for himself and the practice he'd worked so hard to make one of the most successful in the city, the practice that had consumed him, stealing time he could have spent with Diane . . . his beautiful Diane. Even now, nearly two years from that phone call, the memory of it all caused his eyes to blur.

Reaching his car, he got in and sat for a moment, reflecting on how Jessie had saved him, suggesting that he leave Boston and come here where they needed a neurologist and life was simpler.

Simpler indeed . . .

Where once he saw as many as twenty-five patients a day, he now saw four or five. And here he was making a house call, to a woman slowly recovering from a stroke that had left her partially paralyzed so she had trouble coming to his office. Might not even get paid for the visit . . . part of the reason why his income was about a third what it had been.

Five months ago he'd been approached about finishing out the term of the newly deceased county coroner. The job required the officeholder to investigate all deaths in a long list of categories and arrange for autopsies when there were legal implications or there was any question about the cause. If it wasn't a homicide or suicide and there were no suspicious circumstances surrounding the case, it would be autopsied locally. The others would be sent to the forensic pathologist's office in Madison for a complete workup. This sounded like more work than he could handle and still maintain his practice, slim as it was. There was also his little girl, Katie. He couldn't be on call at night and leave her alone. When it was explained to him that the office averaged only five calls a week and there were two deputy coroners who regularly took night call and another who could be pressed into service to cover for him if he was with a patient, he reconsidered.

After some reflection on the proposition, he'd accepted, partly because the extra money, which wasn't much, would help him provide for Katie. In addition, after what had happened to Diane, the thought that he might, in some small way, be responsible for keeping his new home free of crime appealed to him even though the county had a murder only every ten or twelve years. Then two months ago, he'd taken the call for Chester Sorenson, a dairy worker found drowned in a farm pond, clearly murder, though that had been kept under wraps. So far, there were still no leads on the killer. So much for his high hopes of being an instrument of justice.

But if you didn't factor that in, or his modest financial picture, he was flourishing. Despite the flashback he'd just had, he was coping well with Diane's death. He'd always considered himself a compassionate physician, but there was something about these people here that made him feel close to them—so that his concern for their welfare came more from his heart than his head.

He'd adapted so well to the community that, like many of its inhabitants, he kept a garden. In it he'd grown a pumpkin that weighed forty pounds. He knew how big it was because he'd taken the bathroom scales out and weighed it. Oddly, he was as proud of that pumpkin as almost anything he'd ever done.

It turned out that Richard was wrong about not getting paid for visiting Sara Gustafson, because when he left her home, she insisted that he take three jars of homemade strawberry rhubarb jam with him.

He was welcomed back to the EEG lab by the sound of an air blast as Collins dried the adhesive holding an electrode to Ronnie's scalp just behind his left ear.

"What do all great comedians and all great doctors have in common?" Collins asked.

"Tell me," Richard said.

"Timing." Collins grinned at Richard's look of incomprehension. "That was the last electrode," he explained.

"So maybe we should go on the road together."

"Okay, but you'll want separate rooms, 'cause frankly, Doc, I fart like crazy in my sleep."

"I hear all great comedians do that."

"What about great doctors?"

"They don't. How's he been?"

"Completely zonked, but he hasn't had another seizure."

"Good. Maybe the Dilantin's got him stabilized."

The two men went back into the next room, where the hospital's Nihon Kohden EEG machine sat against a wall with a big window in it so they could see the patient while recording. Looking at the old Nihon war-horse made by a company that had gone out of business years ago, Richard thought briefly of Zane Bruxton and how if he ever felt another surge of generosity, he could buy the hospital a Nicolet Bravo, one of those state-of-the-art digital jobs.

Collins sat at the machine and turned it on, sending a wide tongue of lined paper sliding under the recording pens that clattered for a moment like knitting needles before settling down to work. Collins ran a few calibration pages, then a few more that proved the instrument was functioning properly.

Collins hit a button and the pens began tracing sixteen lines representing Ronnie's brain waves, each line corresponding to the area of cortex between two of the electrodes on Ronnie's scalp. The machine was capable of being set in a variety of patterns, or montages, combining electrodes in different ways so that the entire brain could be mapped. The analysis they'd be conducting consisted of six montages. With eighteen pages of recordings needed for each montage, Ronnie's case would generate a hundred and eight pages of ink scrawls.

As the first tracings rolled past, Richard noted with relief that Ronnie's EEG was showing no evidence of wild epileptiform activity; so far so good on that count.

On the other hand, his brain waves were slower than normal and of lower amplitude, nothing terribly diagnostic, but considering that it had now been long enough since his last seizure for his brain to be showing a normal pattern, this wasn't a good sign.

All the succeeding montages showed the same thing—slow waves of low amplitude—and Richard saw no evidence of asymmetry in this pattern, no region of the brain that seemed to be the focal point of the problem.

So maybe it *wasn't* a stroke. But what was it?

Then they set the instrument on montage four. With the pens clattering and the instrument churning pages into the box on the floor, Collins got up and went to Ronnie's side, where he took Ronnie's left thumb and pressed hard on the nail with a reflex hammer.

Back at the Nihon, Richard drew a slash mark and the letters LT on the recording.

Collins then repeated the maneuver on Ronnie's right thumb. Again, Richard marked the recording as it flew past.

Collins did that entire routine once more, then clapped his hands three times next to Ronnie's left ear.

Richard marked the recording.

After three claps at Ronnie's other ear, the entire clapping routine was repeated. Collins then leaned down and called Ronnie's name loudly three times in each ear. This too, was repeated. When Collins returned to the Nihon, he found Richard slumped in his chair, for Ronnie's tracings had not shown the slightest response to any of the stimuli Collins had provided. Since it was now long past the time when Ronnie's brain should have ceased to show any residual effects from his last seizure, this was extremely worrisome.

"I didn't see any physical response at all," Collins said. "How'd he do on paper?"

"Lousy."

The phone rang and Collins took it.

"It's for you."

Harboring a very bad feeling about this case, Richard accepted the phone.

"Heflin."

"This is Faulk. We located Johannson's wife."

"This isn't going to be a good day for her," Richard said.

"You can say that again. She's down here in the ER in a coma."

5

Holly made her way through the passageway from the plane and stepped into the Dallas–Fort Worth airport, where she spotted Susan Morrison standing by a small piece of black luggage.

"How was your flight?" Susan asked when Holly reached her.

"Quick and uneventful. Yours?"

"The guy sitting next to me threw up."

"Doesn't that entitle you to triple frequent flyer miles?"

"You're certainly in good spirits," Susan said.

"Nervous actually."

"When's your flight home?"

"Four o'clock tomorrow."

"I'm out at five." Susan picked up her bag and gestured in the direction of the terminal. "We'd better get moving if we're going to be there by two. I hear they're doing a lot of work on the interstate that's really slowing traffic. And I've got to pick up something in the baggage claim area before we leave."

"You checked a bag? We're only going to be here a day."

"It was something I couldn't take on the plane with me."

"What?"

"My Beretta."

"Isn't that a . . . "

"An automatic pistol."

"Now I *am* getting nervous . . . if you think we need to be armed."

"It's just a precaution."

After finding the ad in the Dallas paper, Holly had called Susan to discuss what to do next. In that conversation they'd come to realize they had very little to offer the Dallas police to get them involved, particularly since the new ad wasn't worded exactly like the one in Memphis. Where in Memphis they had used the phrase "federally funded research project," the Dallas ad said "major research project." This not only removed the possibility of bringing fraud charges against them in Texas, but also created some doubt that they were the same people.

So the two women decided to visit the clinic and see what they could learn. Holly had then called the number in the Dallas paper and passed herself off as a prospective donor, receiving a two o'clock appointment for the following Monday and instructions on how to find the clinic.

From the airport, Holly and Susan took a shuttle to a National car rental office. A few minutes later they headed for their appointment with Susan behind the wheel of a Buick Century.

"I saw that picture in your office of you with the shotgun. How is it you're so familiar with guns?" Holly asked.

"My mother and father were both hunters. It was just something I grew up with. And I was in the Israeli army. Not by choice, of course. Everybody has to serve." Answering the question on Holly's face, Susan added, "My maiden name is Kaplan. My husband, Walter, was kind of a problem for my parents at first, but they came around."

"Did you see any action in the army?"

"They try not to put women in combat situations, but I chose the division that builds and maintains the *kibbutzim,* the settlements on the country's borders. From time to time, we had Arab invasions and sometimes I had to defend myself."

"Did you ever shoot anyone?"

"Like I said, I had to defend myself. So who are *you,* Holly?"

"What do you mean?"

"Draw me a picture. What gets you riled?"

Holly shrugged. "Rap music, humidity, people who spit on the sidewalk . . ." She thought a moment. ". . . and men who mislead you."

"Sounds like someone's shining knight fell off his horse."

"Big time."

"It's a huge planet, Holly. They're not all like that."

"Maybe you got the last good one."

"Walter was a find, true enough, but it's dinosaurs that are extinct, not good men."

"What does Walter do for a living?"

"He teaches paleontology at Southern Miss."

"Hence the dinosaur reference."

Susan smiled. "You're on to me."

As they drove toward Plano, a Dallas suburb, Susan broached a new topic. "I'm sure we discussed this when you first left your eggs at the clinic, but we haven't talked about it since you came for them. You do realize that the small number of your eggs we had to work with and the fact that they'd been frozen were significant obstacles to success."

"I know. But there *was* a chance and now . . ."

"Do you remember that case a while back where, a year or so after these two women had given birth in the same hospital, it was discovered they had each been given the other's child by mistake?"

"Vaguely."

"What do you think they did?"

"I don't know."

"Both women decided to keep the child they'd been given."

". . . to avoid traumatizing the kids, I guess."

"And because both women loved the child they had."

"I don't believe I could have done that."

"You may not know yourself as well as you think."

The clinic in Plano was in a modern, three-story, brick professional building with a parking lot landscaped with stunted pine trees. In fact, the whole city seemed unable to produce a tree of any size, probably because of too little rainfall, Holly concluded.

They left the car in the parking lot and went inside, where they took the elevator to the second floor and located suite 206.

Holly paused at the door and looked at Susan. "Ready?"

"Let's go."

The waiting room was small and not particularly well decorated, but it had the necessities: a half-dozen chairs, a couple of nondescript end tables bearing cheap lamps, and a rack on the wall offering multiple copies of *People* magazine. The only other person in the room was a young woman with straight brown hair and a gold ring in her left nostril. She nodded vaguely at their entrance and went back to her magazine. Holly and Susan crossed the room to the counter in the far wall, behind which they could see a nurse in white with her back to them.

"Hello, I'm . . ." Holly paused. Jesus . . . what name had she used when she'd called? Then she remembered. "I'm Carol Lewis. I have an appointment."

The nurse turned and came to the counter. She had a pale pinched face that wasn't flattered by her short blond hair, which curled under on each side so it perched atop her head like a parchment scroll. She reached to her left and picked up a clipboard holding a form and a small pencil with no eraser. "Please fill this out and return it to me," she said, handing it over.

Behind Holly, Susan shifted her position to get a better look at the rest of the room beyond. All she saw was a desk, a computer workstation, a microwave, and a coffeemaker. Holly took the form to a chair and began work on it while Susan sat next to her, alertly watching and listening for anything that would be useful in proving that these were the people they were after.

The form was mostly a standard medical history. Holly lied liberally as she worked through it.

Suddenly, the door to the clinic opened and a young woman who looked too normal to be selling her eggs came out, walked quickly through the waiting room without looking at anyone, and left. A few seconds later, the door opened again and the nurse called for Nan Shivers, the girl with the ring in her nose. When Holly finished the form, she put it on the counter and returned to her chair.

Now the chase got dull as she and Susan waited to be seen. Fifteen minutes passed like a funeral procession, and then Nan Shivers came out looking no different than when she went in. She hadn't been gone long enough for them to have collected any of her eggs, so this must have been either a reconnoitering visit or she was in some stage of preparing for her collection. She, too, left without comment.

There was another short wait, presumably while Holly's form was reviewed, and then she was called to the back.

"Hope it's okay for my friend to come too," she said to the nurse. "You know, for moral support."

"That's for the doctor to decide."

Holly and Susan followed her past a room with an examining table and other medical equipment, to an office, where they were met by a reasonably attractive older woman with her dark hair pulled severely back from her face in a bun. She extended her hand.

"Hello Carol. I'm Doctor Sartain. It's nice to meet you."

Holly shook the woman's hand then introduced Susan. "This is my friend . . ." Having not made up a name for

Susan and failing to see how it could do any harm, Holly just used her real name. "I'd like for her to hear about this too, if you don't mind."

"Not at all."

When everyone was seated, Doctor Sartain said, "Carol, from the information you've provided us it appears that you're an ideal candidate for our program. But I'm curious. Why have you come to us?"

Though surprised by the question, Holly could see only one reason. "The money."

"So you have no problem with this?"

"Exactly what will you be doing with my eggs? You won't be creating embryos with them, will you?"

"I can assure you the eggs will never be fertilized."

"Then I have no problems."

"But you should realize that once you commit to the program, there will be a fair amount of inconvenience. We'll have to draw blood numerous times and there will be a significant number of hormone injections to stimulate your ovaries to yield more than the single egg they normally produce each month. As the time for collection draws near, you'll have to come in a couple of times for ultrasound examinations of your ovaries so we can closely monitor how they are responding. On the day of collection, you'll be given some medication through an intravenous line to make you drowsy. The entire collection procedure will only take about thirty minutes, but you'll need someone to drive you home."

As Dr. Sartain outlined their procedures for Holly, Susan noted that there were no medical degrees on the wall.

"Think you can handle all that?" Sartain asked.

"I'm sure I can. Where will the study using my eggs be conducted?"

"We prefer our donors not know that."

"Why?"

"For the same reason adoption agencies maintain anonymity between the birth mother and the people with whom the child is placed."

"This hardly seems like a similar circumstance."

"Certainly there are significant differences, but the board that oversees our work believes in the policy and insists we observe it."

"So the research won't be done in Dallas. You're just a collection agency."

"That's correct."

"And you travel from city to city?"

Though Susan wanted very much to know the answers to the questions Holly was asking, she was becoming uncomfortable at how they might sound to Sartain.

"Forgive me for saying so, but I think we're drifting a bit from the purpose of this meeting," Sartain said. "Do you have any other questions involving *your* participation?"

Holly thought a moment; then, to appear legit, asked, "If I decided to participate, when would I begin?"

"As soon as possible."

"I guess that's it then. I *will* need a little time to think it over."

Sartain got an odd look on her face. "Don't you want to know about the money?"

Holly threw her hands up in a "dumb me" gesture. "How could I have forgotten that?"

"We pay two thousand dollars just for signing up. Then, for each egg we collect, you get another five hundred, up to a total of five thousand. If you complete our entire protocol and for some reason, we obtain no eggs, you still get the two thousand. But you must complete the protocol. How does that sound?"

"It seems fair."

Sartain rose out of her chair. "Then we'll wait to hear your decision."

On the way out, Susan glanced into the room with the computer workstation and saw the nurse conferring with a man in a gray suit. Neither of them looked at Susan, but when Holly passed, the man turned his head in her direction.

In the hall, Holly let out a held breath. "Whew. I'm glad that's over. But I don't think we learned much."

"On the contrary," Susan said. "Did you notice the man talking to the nurse as we left?"

"I saw him. So?"

"He's the lawyer who took your eggs."

6

Holly reached for the door to the waiting room, intending to go back and confront the man Susan had seen.

"Hold on," Susan said. "I don't think we ought to reveal ourselves to them yet. Let's go down to that little refreshment stand in the lobby, get a cup of coffee, and think this through."

Somewhat reluctantly, Holly nodded. "Okay."

Downstairs, Susan bought two Colombian mocha lattes and they took them to one of the small tables nearby.

"You were right to stop me up there," Holly said. "I was just so mad, I wanted to get my hands on him. But we should probably just go to police headquarters, wherever that is, and tell them everything."

Retreating into thought, Susan lightly cradled her coffee with one hand while the fingers of the other tapped on the side. Then she said, "Our only real piece of evidence connecting them to what happened is that guy. If he should disappear . . . Oh-oh." Susan looked down and supported her forehead with her hand, shielding her face. "There he is, about twenty feet behind you. He knows me so I can't watch where he goes."

"He's heading for the front door," Holly said, following his progress with her head turned slightly his way. "Okay, he's outside."

Susan shot to her feet, turned, and went after him. "C'mon. We don't want to lose him."

When the two women stepped from the building, the lawyer was about fifteen yards ahead on their left, entering the first parking bay in the lot.

"He's going to his car," Susan said. "Stay with him. Get his license number if you can. I'll pick up our car and come back for you."

Susan set out at an angle toward the far side of the lot.

Needing to get closer to the man, Holly picked up the pace.

About halfway down the parking bay, he went to a tan car and got in. Positioning herself at the rear of a vehicle six cars away, Holly pretended to search her bag for her keys. When the man backed out, she got a clear look at his Texas plates.

Just as he disappeared around the cars at the far end of the bay, Susan pulled up beside her.

"You get the number?" she asked as Holly got in.

Holly recited the number and Susan gave chase.

At the highway he turned toward Dallas. Susan could have entered the highway right behind him, but instead let a few other cars get between them.

"Just because he has Texas plates doesn't mean he lives here," Holly observed. "That could be a rental car."

"All the more reason for us not to lose him."

For several miles they encountered no problems; then, as they approached a large intersection, the tan car slowed and the right turn signal came on. Instead of turning onto the intersecting street, the lawyer went into the Exxon station on the corner, where he pulled up on the near side of the cashier's building.

Thinking quickly, Susan went past the station, made a right at the corner, and entered the station from an access on that side, where the lawyer couldn't see them.

Intending to park next to the air hose, which would give them a clear view of the tan car when it left, she made a wide loop and came back hard against the curb on the outside of the pump island.

On the opposite side of the station, the lawyer had found that both 87-octane pumps were out of order. If he'd chosen to reach the island on the other side of the station by going around behind the store, everything probably would have been fine. Instead, cell phone to his ear, he circled back to the front and came at it so that he passed Susan and Holly with barely two feet between his car and theirs.

When the lawyer saw Susan, it was obvious he recognized her. Then he looked at Holly. Hitting the accelerator, he shot past them and fishtailed onto the street, where he poured on the gas and barreled into the intersection against the light.

Holly saw it coming as if in slow motion . . . another car approaching the intersection at a high rate of speed from the right. She winced and her hand went to her mouth. The oncoming vehicle hit the tan car on the side, dead center, filling the air with a sickening cacophony of contorting metal and breaking glass that Holly could hear even inside their closed car. With the force of the impact, the driver's door flew open and the lawyer's body was thrown into the air. Still as if in slow motion, Holly saw the body tilt in the air and hit the pavement head first.

Moved by the horror of what she'd seen, Holly had no thoughts that he'd received the punishment he deserved for what he'd done to her. There was only her racing heart and the image of the frightening damage such a fall can inflict. Then objectivity set in. She was a doctor and there were people who needed her. She and Susan left their car and headed for the crash simultaneously.

"I'll check the lawyer," Susan said as they ran. "You see about the driver of the other car."

Holly's assignment turned out to be a redhead in her twenties. The deployment of her airbag had saved her life, but she was dazed and confused.

"What happened?" she moaned. "I can't remember . . ."

The engine of the car had been pushed backward, but it didn't appear that her legs were injured. The right sleeve of her blouse was soaked with blood, though.

"Everything's going to be fine," Holly said. "You just sit here and try to relax."

Holly ran around to the other side of the car, wrenched the door open, and climbed in. In better position now, Holly could see what was obviously arterial blood welling up rhythmically through the fabric of the woman's sleeve. Trying not to think about the possibility that the woman's blood was carrying HIV, Holly took hold of the redhead's upper arm and slid her fingers along the inside surface, searching for the brachial artery. .

There . . . Feeling a strong pulse, Holly pressed hard, expecting that this would shut off the blood flow. But it kept coming, undiminished. She adjusted her grip and tried again. And still it came. Holly couldn't press any harder and she was certain she was on the brachial artery. Of course if the bleed was being fed from an anomalous vessel, it wouldn't matter how hard she pressed. Whatever the reason, if the woman continued losing blood at this rate, she'd soon go into shock.

Holly looked around the car for something she could use as a tourniquet, but there was nothing.

Then a trucker who had seen the accident and stopped to help stuck his head into the car. "There's an ambulance on the way. Anything I can do here?"

"Give me your belt," Holly said.

"My belt . . . Why?"

"So I can stop her bleeding."

"Okay, sure." After he'd stripped it off, he looked at the woman's arm and hesitated. Apparently anticipating that his belt was going to get blood on it, he removed the silver-dollar buckle before handing it over. "I don't need it back."

Holly wrapped the belt twice around the redhead's upper arm and pulled it tight, holding the two free ends in her hand. The bleeding slowed to a trickle then stopped. Through the cracked windshield she saw Susan come around the lawyer's car and hustle toward the open door on the injured woman's side.

"How's the situation here?" she said, bending down and looking in.

"Under control. What about the lawyer?"

Not wanting to upset the girl who'd hit him, Susan simply shook her head.

"I want to go home," the redhead said.

Susan took the girl's left hand and patted it, taking her pulse at the same time. "This won't last much longer, dear."

Even though Holly relaxed the tension on the belt periodically to prevent tissue damage below the tourniquet, her hand was aching by the time the ambulance arrived. While the paramedics loaded the redhead onto a gurney, Holly joined Susan to watch a patrol car, approaching fast.

"We'll have to tell them what we saw," Susan said. "But this isn't the time to get into all the rest."

"Why not?"

"Those are merely patrolmen. They wouldn't know how to handle it. For now, our story begins when he passed us in the gas station."

"As eyewitnesses we'll have to give them our names and addresses," Holly said. "They'll want to know why we're in Dallas."

"No they won't. That focuses on us. They've got other things to worry about."

"What if they ask?"

"Then we're here on personal business."

"That's pretty vague."

"Precisely. I'd rather not lie to them."

Seriously doubting the wisdom of Susan's position, Holly agreed to go along with her plan. And it unfolded just as Susan had predicted. The cops never asked why they were in Dallas.

Holly had managed to help the injured woman without getting any blood on herself. Even so, she washed her hands thoroughly in the gas station's restroom. Returning to the car, where Susan waited, Holly got in and made a suggestion. "We could use the phone here to call the police and find out who we should contact to tell our complete story."

"Not just yet," Susan said, starting the car. "There's something we need to do first."

"What?"

"I'll show you in a few minutes."

Susan left the station and headed toward Dallas, quickly leaving the crash scene behind. She drove until they came to a small shopping strip, where she pulled into a parking space well away from any other cars.

She then reached into a pocket of the light jacket she wore and withdrew a man's wallet.

"Oh no," Holly groaned. "That isn't . . . You didn't . . ."

"It was lying beside him. I didn't take it off the body."

"This is *not* good. I can't believe you did that. Now the cops won't even know who he is. How will they notify his nearest relative of his death?"

"We're not going to keep it. I just didn't want us to be totally dependent on the police for information. They have a way of keeping everything to themselves. If it should happen that they don't respond in an effective way to our story, which is highly possible, we'll at least have whatever we learn from this."

"You sure don't think much of the police."

"I just don't like being left in the dark. Now, let's see who that lawyer really was. Have you got something in your bag to take notes?"

While Holly looked, Susan started going through the wallet.

"All right," she said quickly. "According to his driver's license, his name is Palmer Garnette and he lives in Madison, Wisconsin. Are you writing?"

"How do you spell Garnette?" Holly asked, her ballpoint poised over the back of a grocery receipt supported by her own driver's license.

Susan spelled the name and recited his address in Madison. She then turned the license over. "He didn't check the organ donor box. Pity."

She put the license back in the slot where she'd found it and looked further.

"We're not going to just march into police headquarters and hand over the wallet when we're through with it, are we?" Holly asked.

"That wouldn't be wise. Ah, here's his AARP card . . . Palmer Garnette, same as before. So that's probably who he really is. It's funny, I never think of old crooks belonging to AARP. But I guess they don't have their own retirement organization."

"If we're not going to admit we picked up the wallet, shouldn't you be wearing gloves when you're handling all that stuff?"

"You're worried about my fingerprints?" Susan said incredulously. "They're not going to give that a thought. They don't even look for prints when somebody ransacks your house. It's like they have to pay for that black powder themselves, out of their paycheck." She pulled an insurance card from another slot. "He left a Chrysler Sebring back in Madison. State Farm. Guess they insure anybody."

The wallet subsequently produced a small cache of credit cards, a video rental membership, a couple of business cards from antiques shops in Madison, a Blue Cross/Blue Shield ID, and a wad of receipts from Dallas restaurants. Then Susan noticed a scrap of paper tucked into a slot so just a tiny edge of it showed. She took it out and unfolded it.

"What's that?" Holly asked.

"A phone number. Write this down . . ."

She recited a phone number with no area code and Holly entered it on her grocery-receipt dossier.

Now it was about time to contact the cops.

7

Zane Bruxton stopped abruptly at the door to the lab, the pain almost more than he could bear. Knowing what was happening, his personal aide, Phillip Boone, steadied him.

Unwilling to live in the twilight existence that pain medication imposed, Bruxton was left to fight back with only the force of his will. And he exerted it now, shutting the door that had let the demon in. He gently pushed Boone away. "I'm all right now."

When he'd first been diagnosed, the irony of the situation had fed his anger. Pancreatic cancer—one of the few malignancies unresponsive to Vasostasin. The first round of chemo had sent the disease into remission. But it had returned, stronger. His doctors had fought back, changing drugs, trying different combinations, and once more they had driven it off. Then, three months ago, it had stormed his gates, overwhelming the chemicals deployed against it. And now he was dying.

Had he been a man of limited means, he might have gathered what resources he could and traveled to a place he'd never seen. But he'd been everywhere. Or he might have mended broken relationships or made amends for offenses he'd committed. This too was denied him because he'd done nothing he was sorry for. Moreover, his heart and mind were as cold toward religion as they ever were. There was no God and there was no Hell and he couldn't even hedge his bets by giving lip service to the possibility. Not only would that be hypocritical, it wouldn't work.

His vast fortune, recently augmented by the six hundred million dollars he'd made by selling ten percent of his stock in Bruxton Pharmaceuticals, had turned from a comfort to a problem. Business was war, and money was the spoils of war. It belonged to victorious generals. Inherited money was a curse, dulling the spirit of the beneficiary and killing incentive. A person who isn't able to figure out for himself how to make a fortune wouldn't be capable of handling one given to him. The money his two ex-wives were enjoying had been taken from him unwillingly. *And look at them. What have they done with it? Nothing. They consume, but don't create. It has damaged them.*

So he had decided that his fortune must go to institutions, as with the MRI he'd given to the hospital. Eight million dollars for a plaque on the wall with his name on it. A high price to pay even for posthumous virtue. So he would use his money for a library at the University of Oklahoma, a park in Harlem, a children's museum in Houston, an athletic field in Toledo.

As for his disease, until the day came when he could function no more, it would be doors open as usual. No quarter asked, none given.

The pain shut out for the moment, Bruxton entered the lab and looked around for Henry Pennell. Though the place was fairly neat by most standards, Bruxton's forehead wrinkled at what he perceived as a sloppy operation. A scientist's habits should be as meticulous as his mind. It was all attention to detail. And that being so, he wondered once more whether Pennell was capable of delivering.

Bruxton found Pennell in his office, his back to the

door, reviewing tables of data on his computer. Back to the door . . . so trusting . . . a child who'd spent his life suckling at the academic nipple. Well, he was in the real world now.

"So you're here," Bruxton said loudly, intending to startle, to show Pennell how vulnerable he was sitting like that.

Pennell turned and shot to his feet, his discomfort at being in Bruxton's presence already in full bloom. To make him even edgier, Bruxton stood in the doorway without speaking, staring into Pennell's eyes.

Pennell was a long-faced man with eyes too bright, a chin too long, and hair too short; a fellow who probably looked out of place in his own home, a self-conscious man whose very essence shouted *social misfit* so loudly that even if he'd been wearing a suit by Bruxton's personal tailor instead of khaki pants and a wrinkled white shirt with the sleeves rolled up, anyone could still spot him for what he was. Finally, Bruxton said, "Sit down."

Pennell sat gingerly in his chair as though while he'd been standing, someone had booby-trapped it.

Bruxton could have summoned Pennell to the main office during the day to have this talk, but surprising him in his own space after normal business hours was far better, for it showed him that there was no haven from the Bruxton reach.

Growing tired, but being careful to hide that, Bruxton sat in the chrome-and-leather visitor's chair and crossed one leg over the other. "I came by Saturday morning and the place was locked."

"I ah . . . had something important to do. And I *was* here until at least ten o'clock every night last week."

"Doctor Pennell, do you remember what you told me when I interviewed you for this position?" Bruxton asked coldly.

"I said I was the man for the job."

"And I believed you. But what has my faith produced?"

"I *am* making progress." He gestured to his computer. "This table . . ."

"Progress? Doctor Pennell, this isn't an NIH-funded project where progress is a satisfactory achievement. Do you have any idea what your delay is costing this company? No, of course you don't, because you think that's not your problem. But you're wrong. It is very much your concern. And every day that you fail to deliver what you promised me drains the life from this company."

"If I don't understand that, perhaps it's because I've never been told what use the company will make of the techniques I'm working on. May I know what the large goal is?"

"You may not. Just do your job."

"I *will* accomplish what I said I would, Doctor Bruxton."

Though the pain had begun to creep under the door Bruxton had shut against it, there was no evidence of this on his face as he rose from his chair. "See that you do."

A few moments later, in the car, on his way home, when the pain was once more banished, Bruxton's thoughts returned to Pennell. Of the twenty men he'd considered for the job, he still believed Pennell had the best chance of succeeding. So he had no intention of firing him. But he'd seen in Pennell's face that the man had felt humiliated by their conversation, and even though he was earning far more with Bruxton Pharmaceuticals than he could anywhere else, he was likely weighing his alternatives, wondering if the job was worth it.

All men become addicted to their income level, acquiring habits and tastes they are loath to give up. But Pennell was so important to Bruxton that he didn't feel he could rely solely on that to keep him in line.

"Boone, the phone please."

After he'd been handed the phone, Bruxton activated the sliding glass panel that separated him from the front. Then he dialed a number in D.C.

"Eli . . . Zane Bruxton. Sorry to call you at home, but I need a favor. Wednesday when your committee is considering whether to give FDA approval to that engineered

blood vessel from Histogen, I'd like the decision put off
so the company can gather more data on its performance . . . No, no. You're not listening, Eli. I don't want
you to disapprove the application. Just delay it a while,
say . . . for two months. Then we'll see. That's right. So
how's the missus? . . . I'm glad to hear it. And Marjorie,
she doing all right in medical school? . . . Well, everybody there is bright. They can't all be at the top of the
class. But I'm sure she'll make you proud."

Bruxton hung up and reflected on what he'd done.

Pennell had been hired after the Vasostasin-fueled explosive increase in the price of Bruxton Pharmaceuticals
stock. He had therefore missed that boat. From the firm
Bruxton employed to keep tabs on certain key people in
his organization, he'd learned that Pennell was holding
a heavy position in Histogen, and stood to make a killing
when their stock increased in price, as it surely would
after it gained FDA approval for its artificial vessel. And
this just wasn't a good time for Pennell to start feeling
independent. As Bruxton lowered the window and handed
Boone the phone, the pain once more demanded his attention.

Henry Pennell sat staring at his computer screen, but not
seeing it. When he'd signed on with Bruxton, he'd been
convinced he could produce the technological advance
that was called for. Now, after six months on the project, he wasn't sure *anyone* could do it.

With Bruxton in his face like that, threatening him,
he'd had to put up a confident front. But now, alone with
his doubts, he began to fear for his future. If Bruxton
fired him, what would he do? Go back to academics?
With his lousy reputation as a teacher? Not likely. Sure,
maybe he could catch on at some half-assed community
college making a third-world salary to teach students who
didn't have a clue. But a job at a real school? Pee-wee
Herman had a better chance of being appointed Lucasian
professor of mathematics at Cambridge. And there was

no way he'd get a recommendation from Bruxton for another industry slot.

All that made it absolutely imperative that the feds okay the Histogen vessel for clinical trials. Then he could unload his stock and live happily ever after and Bruxton could go screw himself. Otherwise, he'd have to think harder about Micky Hardaway's proposal: a fat finder's fee and a lifetime job at Calgene. And all he had to do was deliver the protocol for the way Bruxton was coupling sugars to the parent protein for Vasostasin. A little corporate espionage.

It wasn't something he wanted to do . . . and wouldn't do, unless he was backed into a corner. Then, Bruxton would have only *himself* to blame.

8

"So you believe this fellow recognized you at the gas station and in trying to get away ran the light at the intersection?"

"That's correct," Susan said.

They were talking to Detective Jack Newsom of the Fraud and Document section of the Dallas police department. In looking down the list of the department's various offices, that had seemed the likeliest place to start. And so far, Newsom's actions hadn't indicated otherwise.

About a half hour after they'd gone through Palmer Garnette's wallet, they'd put it, along with an anonymous note explaining where it had been found, in a padded envelope addressed to the traffic investigative division. They'd then dropped the envelope off at a branch post office a few minutes before closing. Susan believed that if the police were any good at all in Dallas, the fact that it wouldn't arrive for a day or two shouldn't create a significant problem in looking into the case she and Holly would present to them.

After mailing the wallet, the two women discovered that all the Fraud and Document detectives had gone home for the day. Since both Susan and Holly had planned on an overnight stay in Dallas, this delay created no hardship.

Detective Newsom had sandy hair and bore more than a passing resemblance to the TV reporter Ted Koppel. He stared briefly at his coffee mug, which declared that he was the "Best Dad in the World," then looked up. "I have to tell you, this is a new one."

"When will you be going to the clinic?" Holly asked. "I don't know about you, Susan, but I'd like to go along."

Newsom raised both hands, palms out, as if fending off an attacker. "Whoa . . . it doesn't work like that. I've got a lot of background checking to do before I talk to anyone over there."

"How long will that take?" Holly asked. "We can only stay for another few hours."

"I suggest you just go on home. It could be a few days before I let them know they're being investigated."

"Will you keep us informed?"

"Give me a call day after tomorrow. I'll bring you up to date."

After Susan and Holly left, Newsom pulled the phone over and set about making a few calls to Memphis and Jackson to see if he should file the information they'd given him in the drawer with the alien abduction cases.

"What do you think?" Holly asked on the way back to their car.

"About them doing anything? We'll see."

One ring . . . two . . .

"Detective Newsom, please."

"I'll transfer you."

"Newsom. What can I do for you?"

"This is Holly Fisher. Susan Morrison and I—"

"I remember."

"What have you learned?"

"The fellow who was killed in the wreck was named Palmer Garnette. He wasn't from Dallas. He lived in Madison, Wisconsin."

Well, score one for the post office and one for inter-departmental police communication, Holly thought. She waited for more, but Newsom didn't continue. "And?" Holly prompted.

"And when I went over to the clinic this morning, it was out of business."

"How do you know it wasn't just closed for the day?"

"All the equipment was gone."

Anger and frustration waged a pitched battle in Holly. If Newsom had moved faster, this wouldn't have happened. *Now what?* She said it aloud. "Now what?"

"I don't mean to be insensitive, but this is no longer a problem that concerns our department. Even if the operators of this clinic *were* violating some local or state ordinance, and it's still not clear that was the case, the issue is resolved."

"So I guess then that your interest in bank robbers ends as soon as they leave the building."

"That's hardly the same thing."

"Theft is what were talking about."

"Maybe so, but not in Dallas."

"Your sense of justice overwhelms me."

"I'm not paid to police Jackson, Mississippi. According to your story, that's where the theft took place. I'm sure the Jackson police would love to help."

Seeing this was getting her nowhere, Holly swallowed her anger and shifted to another tack. "Were you able to locate Garnette's next of kin?"

"We don't think he was married. At least no one answered the phone at his home address. We've got the Madison police looking for relatives."

"Did you try . . . " Holly was about to ask if they'd checked out the phone number on the scrap of paper Susan had found, but realized that then they'd know who mailed them the wallet. "Has it occurred to you that if you'd hadn't let an entire medical clinic slip away right under your nose, you might have learned who to contact from the people who worked there?"

"Do you find that this righteous indignation approach

generally works for you?" Newsom said. "Because it sure does nothin' for me. Now I've got work to do."

Holly hung up and sat for a moment reflecting on the situation. The clinic had fled Dallas, the operators apparently unnerved by Garnette's death. But why? The rest of them couldn't have known what had led up to the accident . . . unless that's who Garnette was talking to on his cell phone when he'd seen her and Susan. He could have told them then what was happening. Was it possible after this that they'd appear in another city, run an ad there? And if they did, how would she know? She only had access to papers from a few places.

She opened her bag and located the grocery receipt bearing the things she'd written down while Susan had gone through Garnette's wallet. On impulse, she pulled out the phone book and looked up the area codes for Wisconsin. Turning to the phone, she punched in 1, then 6-0-8, the code for Madison, and added the number from the scrap of paper Susan had found.

"Midland Dairy," a cheery female voice said.

Forging ahead on pure hope, Holly requested the manager.

While waiting, her mind raced, trying to figure out what to say next. At this point, she just wanted to find out if Garnette had any real connection to this dairy . . . not that she could see how that would relate to the clinic he was involved with. But if the dairy was part of this somehow, they probably wouldn't admit knowing him.

"Hello, Don Lamotte."

"Mr. Lamotte, I have a collect call from Mr. Palmer Garnette. Will you accept the charges?"

"Is this a joke?" Lamotte said angrily.

Heart pounding, Holly hung up.

Not only did this guy know Garnette, but he was obviously aware he was dead. And the police hadn't even tracked down Garnette's nearest relative to inform them, which could only mean the people who'd fled Dallas had told him.

Though she was very much in the dark about the big picture here, Holly believed she'd learned something significant.

Her next call was to Susan, who came to the phone within seconds after her receptionist let her know who was on the line.

"I just talked to the Dallas police," Holly said. "They blew it. By the time the detective got over there, they'd closed the clinic and apparently left town, taking all their equipment with them."

"Damn it," Susan said. "I don't understand why criminals should be more organized and responsive than the cops."

"They got the wallet, but haven't done much with it. Haven't even found Garnette's nearest relative yet."

"The successes just keep piling up."

"But I think I've got a lead. I called the phone number from that scrap of paper you found in Garnette's wallet, and reached a *dairy*, of all places. Instead of asking the manager if he knew Garnette, I pretended I was a long distance operator and asked if he'd accept a collect call from him."

"Inspired idea," Susan said. "What did he say?"

"He got angry and asked if this was a joke."

"So he knew Garnette was dead. And the cops hadn't even told his relatives yet."

"There has to be some connection between the people at the clinic we saw and the dairy."

Susan grew silent.

"Susan . . . are you there?"

"You know what I think?"

"What?"

"We need to pay this dairy a visit."

9

"Think hard, Dennis," Richard Heflin urged. "In what ways did your routine at the house differ from Ronnie's and Skye's?"

When Richard had received Faulk's call in the EEG lab, he'd been reluctant to believe that Ronnie and his wife had contracted the same illness. It just seemed too unlikely. But five minutes after he'd begun to examine her, she had a seizure that began in her right arm and spread, so that Richard had to face the truth. And just like Ronnie, her brain had not responded when Collins tried to stimulate it with pain and sound.

Ronnie had died first, several hours after his blink and gag reflexes deteriorated and he was put on a ventilator. Skye followed Ronnie the same afternoon. And Richard had no idea what had damaged them so horribly.

Neither of them had shown any abnormalities when their brains were scanned with the MRI Bruxton had donated. Nor did the differential cell counts on their blood reveal anything. Their spinal fluid contained the usual amount of protein, no red cells, and only a few white cells. The chem 24 results on their blood were likewise normal in all respects. Nor was anything found in their

drug screens. Samples of blood and spinal fluid had been
sent out for bacterial and viral cultures, but Richard was
certain they'd grow nothing.

That seemed to leave only one possibility: Ronnie and
Skye had been killed by some sort of toxin. But Dennis,
Skye's brother, who lived with Ronnie and Skye and who
was now sitting across from Richard, looked perfectly
healthy.

The circumstances had required that the bodies be taken
to Madison for a forensic workup. Neither the autopsies
nor the toxicology analysis of either victim's blood had
produced anything useful. One phase of that examination,
however, was incomplete. Because the brains would have
to harden in formalin for at least a week before they were
cut, the neuropathology findings would be significantly
delayed.

Richard had sent the bodies to Madison because his
job as coroner had dictated that he do so. But he had believed from the beginning that it was unlikely to be a
forensic case. Even so, he would have wanted the information that kind of scrutiny provided, for he felt that he
had failed Ronnie and Skye Johannson so badly when
they needed help that he couldn't just close the books on
them and move on, as the cops in Boston had done with
his wife. He *had* to find the cause of their illness . . . for
them, for himself, and for the community, where others
might be at risk.

Since toxicology screens are designed to look for certain classes of relatively common substances, they can
miss things. That negative report, therefore, hadn't
changed Richard's opinion that a toxin might be responsible. But where had the toxin come from? And why had
Dennis survived?

"What about meals?" Richard said to Dennis, trying
to get Dennis's mind working. "Did you all eat together?"

"Just breakfast and dinner," Dennis replied. "But not
lunch. 'Cause Ronnie and Skye were at work then."

Dennis was in his late twenties, but his chubby face
with ruddy cheeks, smooth complexion, and soft brown

hair, which he wore long, made him appear much younger. When seen on the street by someone who didn't know him, he could have been mistaken for an overweight young woman.

After talking with him for just a few minutes, Richard found it obvious that what he'd heard about Dennis was true. He was moderately retarded, a condition that seemed to blur the death of Ronnie and Skye into an abstraction for him rather than reality.

"Did Ronnie and Skye take their lunches from home or buy them?" Richard asked.

"Almost always took them. Ronnie said it costs too much to buy."

"What did they usually take?"

"Leftovers from dinner . . . when there was some."

"Did they ever eat at restaurants?"

"Almost never."

That line of questioning seemed to rule out the possibility that the toxin had been acquired in food. If it had, Dennis should also be ill.

"Any exterminators been in the house lately?"

"No."

"Did Ronnie use anything to keep the bugs under control?"

"Once in a while Skye would use a red can from the cupboard."

"Has the house smelled differently in the last month or so?"

"Same as always, which is to say, no smell I ever noticed."

"Did Ronnie or Skye have any hobbies in which they used chemicals of any kind?"

"Ronnie's hobby was watchin' TV. And Skye's was . . ." He shrugged. "Cookin' and cleanin', I guess."

"Are there any pets in the house?"

"Skye has a parakeet."

"Is it okay?"

"Hard to tell with birds. But it's still eatin'. I know 'cause I been feedin' it."

"How long has she had it?"

"Ever since I been there."

"How long is that?"

"Six months."

"Did Ronnie and Skye do drugs?"

"Uh-uh. They thought it was stupid, somethin' losers did."

"Dennis, what are *you* going to do now?"

"What do you mean?"

"Where will you live?"

"I dunno. My folks are dead. And Ronnie's parents . . . they get to decide what happens to the house. They said they're gonna sell it. So I gotta move out soon as I can. A lady from the Lutheran church is tryin' to find me a place and a job. She said I'll be gettin' some money when the house sells, but it probably won't be a lot on account a there wasn't much somethin' built up. I don't remember the word."

Richard had thought while he was explaining to the Johannsons why an autopsy was ordered on their son without their permission, that they seemed like hard people. Their treatment of Dennis confirmed it.

"I know this is difficult for you, but maybe you wouldn't want to stay there even if you could."

"Why not?"

"We don't know what caused Ronnie and Skye's illness. It was a very unusual sickness, and to have two people in the same house get it at the same time suggests that something in the house may be responsible. So until you find a new place to live, you shouldn't change any of your usual routines. By that I mean don't do anything different than you did when Ronnie and Skye were there."

"Or I might get sick too?"

"I don't know that the house is the source of the problem. Your good health suggests it's not. But just to be on the safe side, take my advice."

"Okay."

"In the meantime I'd like to go over there and look around."

"When?

"How about right now?"

Exposure to the putative toxin that had killed the couple could have occurred either through cumulative or acute exposure. The former would be the most difficult to pinpoint. But even if it was the latter, Richard knew the odds were very long against him finding the answer. Dennis had come to Richard's office from home on his bicycle. For the trip back, Richard loaded the bicycle in the trunk of his car so Dennis could ride with him.

The Johannsons lived in a small one-story house in a neighborhood of similar dwellings where individuality was achieved by the owner's choice of yard statuary. For their statement, Ronnie and Skye had chosen three waist-high Holstein cows standing on a bed of pea gravel enclosed by a ring of white painted bricks.

Dennis unlocked the door and Richard followed him into the living room. Contrary to what Dennis had said, the place did have a smell. But it was merely a faint, musty odor that set off no alarms in Richard's head. Considering Dennis's limited mental capacity and the fact that he had been living alone for a couple of days, Richard expected to find the house a mess. But it was actually quite tidy.

The furnishings had the look of things that had been in the family for a long time, probably inherited from Skye's parents: overstuffed, upholstered pieces draped with antimacassars on the backs and arms; an assortment of small tables of yellow oak with lots of doilies. The top of one table was covered with a collection of crystal balls that make snow when shaken. Except for a framed rectangular piece of lacy fabric with "God Bless Our Happy Home" embroidered on it, the ivory walls were bare. Between the area rugs, the oak flooring matched the tables. An integrated decor . . . harmonious . . . that is, if you didn't see the big-screen TV with the large black eye and sleek dark chassis . . . Janis Joplin appearing with Lawrence Welk.

Richard's prime objective was the medicine cabinet.

With only one doorway off the living room, he didn't
bother asking Dennis for directions.

Beyond that doorway there was a bedroom on each
side of the hall, one distinctly smaller than the other. Just
past the smaller one Richard found the bygone-era theme
in the front of the house repeated in the bathroom, where
there was a claw-foot tub and a commode whose tank
was an oak box mounted high on the wall. Among the
usual items in the medicine cabinet, Richard located a
prescription vial labeled Synthroid, with Skye's name on
it. So she had apparently been hypothyroid.

He looked inside the vial at the tiny yellow pills. Were
they really Synthroid? Could they be something else?
Sharing of medicine was not unknown between couples.
Ronnie's feeling tired . . . he decides to take some of
Skye's thyroid pills . . . But they're not really Synthroid.
Or maybe they're contaminated with something toxic, like
that tryptophane was a few years ago. Richard recapped
the vial and showed it to Dennis.

"I'm going to take this with me."

"Sure, go ahead if you want."

Richard slipped the vial into his pocket and pulled out
a drawer in the oak vanity. There, among a clutter of disposable razors, combs, toothpaste, bobby pins, tweezers, and
bandages, he found a small snap-top plastic container of the
type commonly used to store leftover food. Inside was a
cache of gelatin capsules containing a brown powder.

"Do you have any idea what these are?" He held the
container so Dennis could see inside.

Dennis shook his head.

"Have they been in there a long time?"

"A few weeks maybe."

"I'll need to take these too."

"Go ahead.

Richard went from the bathroom to the kitchen, which
was pleasantly decorated with a red-and-green floral wall-
paper and a simulated-brick floor. The sink was full of
dirty dishes.

"I'm gonna clean those up today," Dennis explained.

"You shouldn't blame Skye. It's my fault. If she was here, she wouldn't have let me get away with that."

Richard stepped to the refrigerator, opened it, and looked inside, a bit disappointed that he didn't immediately detect the odor of spoiled food. When he took the plastic wrap off a dish of tuna he found on the middle shelf, he smelled only a faint hint of fresh fish. A zip-top bag of shaved ham likewise seemed fresh. But next to the ham, there was a block of cheddar cheese spotted with green mold. He added this to the items he was taking.

In his rummaging through the refrigerator, he noticed that the Johannsons were big fans of tofu. It wasn't anything he would eat, but that didn't mean it was the source of the toxin that had killed them. And he couldn't take *everything*.

"Hey Dennis, do you eat this tofu?"

"All the time."

So it *wasn't* that.

Under the sink, Richard found a spray can of Raid. Though he knew the active ingredient couldn't produce the symptoms he'd seen in Ronnie and Skye, he added the can to the cheese and the container of gelatin capsules he'd put on the kitchen table.

Across the rear of the house was a small sunroom with wicker furniture and a couple of hanging ferns. Here, Richard found the parakeet, chattering away at its reflection in a small mirror in the cage. In one corner, only partially concealed by a bamboo screen, stood an upright freezer. Richard moved the screen, opened the freezer, and glanced briefly at what were obviously packages of meat wrapped in butcher paper. He then closed the door and put the screen back in place.

He spent a few minutes in Ronnie and Skye's bedroom, but found nothing to take. He didn't bother with Dennis's bedroom.

He then went to the basement, which was accessed through a door in the kitchen. Beside a workbench littered with tools, he saw a set of plastic shelves bearing some canned goods, a container of Peter's Plant Food, another of Miracle-Gro, and a dozen cans of latex paint with colors he'd seen upstairs, dried on the sides. Nothing to get excited about.

A few years earlier there had been a much-publicized epidemic involving infants in one particular area of Pittsburgh, or some other city, Richard couldn't remember exactly where, in which the kids were coming to the hospital with lung hemorrhages. An epidemiology questionnaire of the affected households had revealed that all had experienced a recent water leak. Subsequent investigation had discovered that the water-soaked area was supporting the growth of a rare fungus that was shedding spores into the basement. The spores were then getting into the heating system and being blown all over the house. Because their lungs were more susceptible to the toxin in the spores than adults' were, only infants were being affected.

With this on his mind, Richard asked Dennis to bring him the flashlight he'd seen plugged into a receptacle by the back door in the sunroom.

When Dennis returned, Richard inspected all the dark corners for fungal growth, but everything was clean and dry.

From the basement, Richard went to the small barn replica in the backyard, where Ronnie kept his lawn equipment. As he expected, there was nothing suspicious there.

"Okay, Dennis. I'm finished. I'll just go back in the house and get the things I'm taking and leave you alone."

"What do you think made Ronnie and Skye sick?"

"That's still a mystery."

As he backed out of the Johannsons' driveway, Richard's hopes, faint as they were, centered on the gelatin capsules with the brown powder.

10

"Hi, Katie, are you having a good time?"

Richard Heflin's daughter was visiting his parents in Arizona. As he spoke to her on the phone, the nearly perpetual frown he'd carried around with him since the death of Ronnie and Skye lifted.

"What have you been doing? . . . That *does* sound like fun. Wish I was with you. You've only been gone a week, but it feels like a month. I'll really be glad when you get back. I love you. . . . Okay, baby. See you soon."

Richard listened until he heard the disconnect, then he hung up, the frown back even before the receiver hit the cradle. He picked up the plastic bag containing the items he'd removed from the Johannson home yesterday and left his office. On his way out, he stopped at the desk where Connie Persky, his one full-time employee, was working on the billing.

"I'm off to Madison. I'll be back by four to see Mrs. Branson."

"And make sure you're on time. I don't want to be sitting here while she stares holes in me because you're late."

Connie was a name that belonged on a sweet young

thing who always deferred to authority—everything Persky was not. Connies weren't supposed to have a sharp tongue and an unwillingness to tolerate anything remotely slipshod. But Richard considered himself lucky to have this one, especially since he could pay her only a fraction of her real worth.

"Since when would being stared at bother *you*?" Richard said, entering into the banter that had become customary between them.

"Actually, it wouldn't, but you've got to be kept in line somehow. And if I have to stretch the truth a little to do it, it's a burden I'm willing to bear. Four o'clock now . . ."

Based on pictures of Synthroid pills in the *PDR*, the yellow tablets Richard had taken from the Johannsons' bathroom appeared to be just what their label said they were. When Richard had spoken to the forensic office in Madison about analyzing those and the other things he'd picked up in the Johannsons' home, he'd been told that without the report from the neuropathologist who would be looking at the couple's brains, it would be premature, and would be using the tox lab not as a diagnostic instrument but a fishing pole.

Unwilling to wait for the remaining path report, Richard was on his way now to the University of Wisconsin campus, where Michael Knox, an old friend in the medical school pharmacology department, had agreed to analyze the four items. He could have mailed them, but Madison was only thirty-five miles away and Richard had wanted for some time to not only visit Michael, but see the campus, which, sitting on the shore of Lake Mendota, was reportedly one of the prettiest in the country.

Forty-five minutes later, Richard eased his car off Langdon Street into a small parking lot at the side of the UW student union. He got out, fed a couple of coins into the meter, and took a reconnoitering look around.

Straight ahead, across Langdon, there was a sparsely populated grassy commons backed by a Gothic church. On a narrow gravel strip between the street and the sidewalk on that side, an open-air entrepreneur presided over a couple of folding tables piled high with clothing. Judging by the amount of business he was conducting, he'd soon need to find a new line of work. Turning to look in the opposite direction, Richard caught a glimpse of the blue-white waters of Lake Mendota just beyond a small stand of trees on the other side of a low cement wall. Wanting a better look at the lake and not feeling up to jumping the wall, he walked around to the front of the union and went inside. He followed his instincts through the Rathskeller, a large, dark-paneled dining room full of empty tables, and went out onto a sprawling patio filled with brightly colored metal tables and chairs.

It was a languid day and soft breezes from the lake rattled the autumn-tinted leaves in the patio's maples, sending little fluttering cascades of yellow drifting onto the tables, gathering those already on the ground at one moment, scattering them the next. Hoping to quell, if just for a few minutes, the profound sense of loneliness he felt even on his best days, Richard had wanted to find a crowd of students . . . hear the music of their conversation, sit among them. But the patio was not even half full, most of the kids who should have been there were apparently blown by the wind to some hidden venue. And those that *were* present were subdued, murmuring to each other in muted tones. The whole scene felt like a poorly attended wake for the passing of summer, so that instead of having his spirits lifted, they sank and he saw once again the Johannsons' twin coffins. Not needing this, he left.

Outside the union, after consulting the campus map Michael had faxed to him, Richard set off toward an ornate old red-brick building a hundred yards away that dominated the end of Langdon Street like a Russian czar holding court. His route to pharmacology took him past the red czar and up a steep hill. By the time he reached the top, he was breathing hard. He'd noticed a scenic overlook on the map, so instead of turning on the street

Michael had marked as the shortest route to his lab, Richard kept walking on Observatory Drive.

He was rewarded a few minutes later by a spectacular view of the lake, wide and blue, framed in the foreground by a strip of forest set afire with fall colors, the opposite shore visible only as a hazy smudge. Here and there, the white triangles of boats with full sails aloft scudded over the water. As he watched the sailboats, each of them seemed to carry away a portion of the depression he'd felt earlier on the patio, so that a few minutes later, when he turned and started back the way he'd come, he felt much better.

He soon found himself walking behind a young couple holding hands. The guy was wearing a green pullover, loose-fit jeans that were six inches too long, and a white baseball cap. She was in baggy denim overalls that failed to hide a lithe and graceful figure. Seeing that couple pulled Richard's mind into the past.

He'd first noticed Diane on a tennis court at the University of Virginia, swinging earnestly at the ball as it came to her, usually returning it poorly, sometimes dubbing it off the wood circling the strings. But where most women at that skill level looked awkward, Diane's every move was so purely feminine it took Richard's breath away. Her long tanned legs, the curve of her back, her ponytail flipping in the sun. She was magnificent.

Richard took his eyes off her only long enough to note with satisfaction that her partner was another woman. Beyond this, nothing about the other person made any impression on him. He'd stood motionless, watching the game for nearly ten minutes, when Diane hit the ball so badly it cleared the fence around the court and sailed over his head. Without hesitation, he lit out after the ball like a trained beagle. When he finally got his hands on it, he threw it back onto the court and waved with far too much enthusiasm when Diane called out her thanks in a sweet voice that made his legs weak.

When the game ended, he made sure he was standing near the only way out.

"You've been watching us a long time," Diane said as she passed. "Should I be worried?"

"No . . . I'm Richard Heflin. I'm . . . okay. I mean I'm not dangerous or anything. I'm a freshman medical student."

Dimly, Richard heard her tennis partner say, "Diane, I'll see you later."

"Your name is Diane?"

She stopped walking and turned to face him. With her standing so close, looking only at him, it felt to Richard as if the sun had been behind clouds all his life and had just come out at that moment.

Ignoring his attempt to learn her full name, she said, "Richard, you stood there for quite a while. Tell me . . . What do you think of my ability as a tennis player?"

Then she waited, her large green eyes unwavering, holding him in her power.

"I . . . ah . . . I think . . ." Richard's mind thrashed around, paralyzed by her proximity. *Answer her.* To his horror, he heard himself blurt out, "You're pretty bad."

To Richard's amazement, she laughed, a soft and musical sound that reminded him of the wind chimes in his parents' backyard.

"I don't know how you do on your med school exams," she said, "but you've just passed this one with a perfect score." She offered her hand. "Diane Landry. I'm in the school of social work. I hear that medical students make rotten boyfriends because they don't have much free time. Is that true?"

"It's a fact they work us pretty hard, but I'd rather spend ten minutes listening to Mozart than two hours with a garage band."

"Ego check," Diane said. "Yeah, it's intact."

"I didn't mean . . ."

"It's okay. You've made your point. Now what?"

"Have dinner with me Friday night. I'll make it. We'll have Cornish game hen with mushroom stuffing, wild rice pilaf, asparagus with hollandaise and for dessert, the best chocolate mousse you ever tasted."

"You can do that?"

"My father is the chef at the Watergate hotel in D.C."

Her flawless brow furrowed. "How were you able to come up with that menu so quickly? Am I just another in a long line of women you've done this for?"

Richard wanted to lie, but having done so well with the truth earlier, he said, "Actually, the line is rather short."

Her face brightened. "Well, okay then. Just so you've had *some* practice. I don't want to waste my time on a novice. What time and where?"

That night, instead of studying like he should have, Richard went out and bought a suit he couldn't afford. Friday, he cut Gross Anatomy and Cell Biology to get everything ready for that night.

Diane appeared at his door at precisely seven o'clock, wearing an elegant black dress and heels, a single strand of pearls setting off her tanned skin.

"You look terrific," Richard said.

"So do you." As she came in, Diane handed him a package wrapped in glossy white paper. "Something for the chef."

"You didn't have to do that."

"Open it."

Richard tore at the paper, shredding it. Inside was a white box that contained a green apron with white lettering across the front that said, "It isn't the size of the ladle, it's how you use it."

Richard felt himself blush. "Thanks. It's great."

Dinner went perfectly; the hens were done, the asparagus was tender, and there were no iron soldiers in the rice. After dessert, they sat on the sofa and talked easily about their favorite teachers, their interests, and what they hoped to achieve in life. All the while, in the back of Richard's mind was that phrase, "It's not the size of the ladle, it's how you use it." Why had she chosen that particular apron? Did she expect him to try to get her in bed?

He got the answer a little after nine o'clock when Diane said, "I love it that you wore a suit tonight. It says you viewed this as an important event. And that's a rare thing in this country. In most restaurants if you're wearing a shirt and shoes, that's good enough. Jeans are okay everywhere. So when is anything special? I love the holidays. You should see my apartment at Christmas. I'm like Clark Griswold in that National Lampoon movie. I've got this fake fireplace I set up and I have open house . . . egg nog, cheese balls, the works."

"You don't go home for Christmas?"

She shrugged. "Don't really have one other than what I make for myself. My parents aren't together and they're too busy trying to figure out their own lives to worry about mine."

"I'm sorry."

"What I'm trying to say here, Richard, is that I put a lot of stock in ritual and symbolic gestures that give life a rhythm and create some peaks to go with the valleys. So don't misunderstand the message on that apron, because I view sex as one of the peaks. I think we're on to something here. So if you feel the same way let's give it a chance and see what happens. Interested?"

Hugely relieved to know where he stood, Richard said, "Let the games begin. . . . But please, not tennis."

They kissed with her still laughing and he filled his lungs with her sweet breath.

Richard had been only a fair student, cruising along at a high C average in most of his classes. But then he began studying with Diane in either her apartment or his. She didn't quiz him or anything; they just worked quietly together on their own classes or she would copyedit a manuscript for the New York publisher she worked for part-time. Somehow having her near sharpened Richard's mind and gave him a sense of purpose he hadn't had before, so that by the end of the year, he was a solid B student in everything, though he was actually spending less time studying than before. It was as if he had been born with some parts missing and had been competing at a disadvantage his whole life. But now, Diane filled the gaps.

As for sex, Richard decided to let her lead the way, not that he had any other choice. One night, two months and three days after they'd met, when he showed up at her apartment to study, he'd barely put his book bag down when, with a strange look in her eye, Diane said, "Come here, Richard. I want you to hear something."

She led him into her bedroom, where in the dim light from a lamp hanging on the tail of a crouching bronze cat, he saw that the covers on the bed had been carefully laid back. Diane turned on a small tape player on her dressing table and Richard soon heard the sound of distant thunder. This was followed a few seconds later by the stutter of raindrops hitting the ground. As the tape built to a downpour, she moved into his arms, pulled his head down, and whispered in his ear. "Make love to me."

Entwined, they moved to the bed where they held a kiss until Richard's head was spinning. Then they were naked and he was pressed along the length of her, her skin hot against him.

When it was over, Diane left the bed and changed the tape to crickets chirping. Then she turned on a projector in the corner that flooded the ceiling with constellations. She returned to bed and threaded herself around him, while overhead the heavens slowly passed in review.

Though they made love several times a week after that, Richard never heard the rain tape or saw the star show again. Once, when he asked for their return, Diane said, "There's an old Greek saying that you can never step into the same stream twice. And even if we could, I wouldn't want to."

For a long time Richard never fully comprehended what she'd meant. Now, with her gone, their first night together remained bright and sharp in his memory, clearer than anything that had ever happened to him. And he understood. Her love of creating special moments in life had given him indelible recollections of their life together that would be with him as long as he lived. And she had given him Katie. In Katie, he still had a part of Diane. Today, for the first time since Diane's death, Richard believed that his future might be worth visiting. And, as he stepped into the medical sciences building, he was now confident that he *would* find the Johannsons' killer.

11

Henry Pennell toyed with his food, keeping an eye on the four Italians who staffed the special projects section. There were three men and a woman. He thought one of the men was named Ernesto. He'd never heard names for the other two. The woman was Donata Marchetti. He knew that for sure because she was the one he'd settled on, partly because she held a degree in microbiology and partly because he was afraid of the men.

He'd seen the four practically every day in the company cafeteria, where they never joined any other group, but always sat together. A few times, when he'd passed close enough to hear their conversation, it was always in Italian. The special projects section was the division that produced Vasostasin, and those four were responsible for producing the parent protein and for coupling the sugars to it.

From her CV, Henry had learned that Marchetti was thirty-two, had dual doctorates in reproductive medicine and microbiology from the University of Milan, and had worked for six years at an Italian pharmaceutical house supervising the production of human growth hormone from bacteria. He had no idea if she could speak English. If she couldn't, then his plan would be in trouble even before it began.

They were leaving. . . .

Henry grabbed his tray and headed across the room on a course that brought him to the woman's side.

"Excuse me, Doctor Marchetti . . ."

She turned to look at him, a neutral expression on her face.

"Do you speak English?" he asked.

"Of course," she replied, apparently offended.

"I'm sorry. I didn't know. . . . Could I ask a favor? I'm having problems with some cell cultures and I think it's bacterial contamination. Would you take a look at one and tell me what you think?"

The skin of Marchetti's face was tight and shiny and she had sharp features. Normally, large eyes softened a woman's look, but Marchetti's had not a spark of warmth in them, so they reminded Henry of something you'd catch in the ocean.

"Bacterial contamination is not difficult to recognize," she said.

Ignoring her thinly veiled criticism of him for needing assistance with such an elementary question, Henry plunged ahead. "Great. Then you'll help?"

"Very well. But I can only give you a few minutes."

"My office is just down the hall from your section . . . right on the way."

She turned and spoke to the men in Italian. From her inflection, it sounded like more criticism, but as long as he got what he wanted, what difference did it make?

Feeling like the pied piper with all the Italians trailing behind him, Henry led the way to his lab and unlocked the door. Marchetti and one of the men had a final rapid verbal exchange and she accompanied Henry into his lab, where he gestured at his inverted microscope.

"Over there. That culture flask on the stage is the one I'd like you to look at."

Marchetti sat, turned on the scope's light source, and leaned into the eyepieces.

Henry had left the scope on its lowest power and out of focus on purpose so it would take her a few seconds to adjust it and see the cell culture he'd intentionally contaminated.

Marchetti's hand floated expertly over the microscope's controls. In less than ten seconds she looked up at Henry. "It *is* contaminated and it's definitely bacteria. To know more you'd have to examine stained samples with oil immersion optics or set up cultures on different growth media. Now I must go."

"Sure, I understand. Thanks for your help."

He saw her to the door and watched her until she went around the corner. Then he returned to the scope, removed the engineered ocular Micky Hardaway at Calgene had sent him by overnight express, and replaced it with a normal ocular.

The failure of the FDA to approve the Histogen vessel had made this decision for him. Even so, at first he had harbored some misgivings. But the more he thought about how hard Bruxton had been pushing him, the less he worried about stealing from him.

And those arrogant damn Italians; too good to sit with anyone else, jabbering in Italian right in front of him to make him feel excluded. Clannish bastards.

To put one over on the Italians sweetened the deal. But he was going to need some luck. He'd roamed through the company's files on the computer and had not found the sugar attachment protocol, so there was likely a hard copy somewhere in the special projects section, maybe even in plain sight, like taped to a refrigerator. In any event, he couldn't make his move until tonight when everybody was out of there.

Henry flicked off the lights in his lab and shut and locked the door in case Bruxton should show up to ride him some more. With the place dark, the old geezer wouldn't wander around looking for him.

After a quick glance down the hall to his left, Henry turned and walked quickly in the opposite direction. The usual way out of the building from the special projects section was past Henry's door. He'd been keeping watch, so he knew that two of the Italians had left at five-thirty and the others at six. But he'd waited until much later to do this to make sure they weren't coming back.

With his heart floating against the top of his chest, Henry turned the corner and was stopped by the locked steel doors of the SPS. The doors were controlled by an iris scanner that read the right eye of whoever wanted in. If the pattern of your iris was in the computer, the lock opened. If not, you took a hike.

To thwart anyone attempting to gain unauthorized entry by holding a photograph of an iris up for the scanner to read, the computer was programmed to accept only images that showed the usual fluctuations in pupil diameter and the movement of blood through the tiny vessels in the iris.

It was generally believed that such a device would in time, pay for itself by eliminating the need for a security guard. This was of course, a mistake, for if anyone could breach the scanner, there was no backup. And Henry had the scanner's number.

Stepping up to the scanner port, Henry reached into his pocket for the ocular he'd taken off the microscope in his lab after Marchetti had used it. To all outward appearances, it was a normal ocular, but in reality, it was also a tiny digital camera that had made a ten-second recording of Marchetti's iris.

Unable to get enough air into his lungs because of his nervousness, Henry placed the ocular over the scanner port and activated the recording. After a short delay, there was a sharp sound of the deadbolt in the lock being withdrawn.

Once he was safely inside, Henry began to relax. Then, hearing a tinkling sound, he tensed. . . .

But it was just the lights in the hall coming on auto-

matically. He didn't view this as a problem, because all
the windows in the section faced onto a vast cornfield.

He was in a wide tiled hallway about twenty yards
long. Halfway down on the left was a door, and beyond
that, at the very end, an elevator that went to the receiving area where all shipments came in. Opposite the
elevator, there appeared to be a cold room. Between
Henry and the cold room on that same side, were two
more doors.

He went to the door on the left and tried it.

Surprisingly, it was unlocked. But after finding the
light switch, he saw that it was just a storage room for
old equipment and extra glassware.

From there, he went to the door immediately across
the hall. This one *was* locked. No matter . . . Henry put
down his briefcase and reached inside it for the pick gun
Hardaway had sent in the same package as the ocular
camera. Drawing on the experience he'd gained in a half
hour's trial on the back door of his home, Henry was
soon inside.

Once again the lights percolated on automatically, illuminating an exceedingly large laboratory of standard
design: yellow oak cabinets with green benchtops against
most of each wall; above the benchtops, cabinets of the
same material with sliding glass doors. Two work islands
extended into the room from the far wall.

On one of the island benchtops was a huge blender,
probably for mixing bacteria with the enzyme solution
used to break them open. The rest of that benchtop and
the one on the other island were taken up with tall plastic cylinders half-filled with small translucent beads.
Each cylinder was equipped with a plastic cooling jacket
through which icy water circulated from a refrigeration
unit. These were obviously columns for Vasostasin purification. Most likely the beads in some of the columns
had antibodies attached to them that would bind the parent protein so it could be separated from the myriad other
things the company's engineered bacteria produced with
the genes it came by naturally. Other columns were prob-

ably dedicated to purifying the fully glycosylated final product, which meant the sugar binding protocol should be nearby.

Ignoring the room's chilly temperature, Henry searched the benchtops of both islands looking for a sheet of paper that would probably be in a plastic protector. But he found nothing.

He searched all the other benchtops, with similar results, then checked the various papers held by magnets to the three refrigerators in the room.

No protocol.

Near the refrigerators his eye was taken by a calendar on the wall with the heading, *V PRODUCTION SCHEDULE*. Two eight-day periods were blocked out, with lot numbers written in the shaded areas. According to the schedule, they were now in day one of the second production cycle for the month. On the first day of each cycle, the word *ARRIVAL* had been written in. On the second day, they'd written *BEGIN COLLECTION*.

Arrival of what? Henry wondered. It was his understanding that the entire production of Vasostasin was carried out in this area.

You're becoming sidetracked, he told himself. *Get moving and get out of here.*

He spent the next five minutes pulling out cabinet drawers.

Then he saw it; a plastic-covered sheet.

But it was just an abbreviated set of instructions for the instrument used to collect solutions coming off the columns.

Where *was* the damn thing?

He remained there a while longer, looking in the unlikely larger storage areas under the benchtops just to be thorough.

There were no file cabinets or desks where he was and no notebooks. So all that must be in the *next* room, which would actually make that a better place to look.

The first thing he saw in the second lab was the huge

stainless-steel fermentation chamber where they grew the bacteria that made Vasostasin.

But something was odd.

Having once worked in a hospital microbiology lab, he wasn't as ignorant about bacteria as he'd made himself appear to Marchetti. In any lab that's growing bugs, there's a certain unmistakable smell that comes from the culture medium. The calendar said the Italians were in the first day of production. So why was there no smell?

Henry walked over to the fermentation chamber and rapped on it with his knuckles.

Hollow . . . There was nothing in it.

How could they begin collection tomorrow with the chamber empty? And what did "arrival" mean on the calendar?

The next things he saw were nearly as puzzling as the empty chamber. The Italians had two fancy phase-dissecting microscopes equipped with little culture chambers and micromanipulators. What the hell did they need those for?

On the benchtop along the right wall was a large tissue culture incubator. Opening it, he saw that one shelf was filled with the same kind of rectangular plastic culture flasks *he* used. Too curious now to resist, he removed a flask and took it to one of the scopes. In seconds he had the contents in focus: a healthy pavement of cultured cells—bacteria free.

Why did they need *these*?

Showing Henry's mind a puzzle was like teasing a schnauzer with a Pup-Peroni. So it was with difficulty that he turned his attention back to his search for the protocol.

As he predicted, off the main lab there was a smaller room containing a computer, a couple of file cabinets, two desks, and some bookshelves. After a quick look through the rest of the main lab, he moved to the other area.

Zane Bruxton's impending death created a problem for him beyond the loss of his life. By arranging for his wealth to be distributed to various "worthy" causes, he had set in motion events that would cause his name to be spoken of with affection and respect for many years after he was gone. *If* he solved this problem that was all around him.

He was in his picture gallery, a large, windowless, interior room housing a collection of old master paintings that would be the envy of many a museum curator had its true extent been known. Rembrandt, Titian, van Goyen, Rubens, Vermeer, Caravaggio, van Ruisdale, and many others filled the walls two tiers high. Some of the paintings had been bought on the open market. But more had not been for sale when Bruxton first coveted them. Those had come to him through Karl Moeller, a German art dealer with a knack for acquiring the unobtainable while keeping the authorities unaware of his activities. Moeller was utterly discreet and possessed a fierce loyalty to his customers that protected them against being offered up as bargaining chips should he be arrested.

Even so, only a fool would believe there was no risk in dealing with him. But when Bruxton wanted a painting he *had* to have it, becoming so obsessed with it that Moeller often remarked that Bruxton must have linseed oil in his veins. Now, with Moeller deceased, the only danger to Bruxton was his *own* mortality. For when he died, all the paintings he'd obtained from the shadow market would come to light and he'd be known as a man who'd bought stolen property. Then, every penny he'd given to worthy causes would have been wasted.

How to ensure that this wouldn't happen? *That* was the problem. He'd considered anonymously returning the "liberated" paintings to their previous owners, but to ensure that it was all handled properly to hide his involvement, he'd need to personally direct the return, which meant he'd have to give them up while he was still able to enjoy them. And that, he could never do.

Vexed by the problem, Bruxton went into his study and casually scanned the TV screens that kept watch over the special projects section.

• • •

As Henry Pennell came back into the hall from the second lab, briefcase in hand, his hopes of finding the sugar-binding protocol were dashed. He'd gone through the two file cabinets, checked all the desk drawers and the notebooks. He'd even prowled through the material on the section's computer, thinking it might be in a file inaccessible from the company network. But he'd seen no protocol.

He had, however, run across some odd material related to Vasostasin that had turned his mind back to the questions he'd had earlier. Now it suddenly struck him that he'd seen no stocks of bacterial growth medium. Was that what "arrival" meant? Was the fermentation chamber empty because their shipment of medium hadn't arrived? But why would they arrange it so the medium always arrived on the first day of each production cycle? Why not give yourself a break and always keep some on hand?

Too curious now about the whole operation to ignore anything, he walked down to the cold room and opened the heavy metal door. Wincing at the frigid air inside, he flicked on the light and took a look around. The low room was only about six by eight feet with a sink on the wall opposite the door. The rest of the perimeter was lined by floor-to-ceiling metal shelves holding gallons of different solutions in big flasks and large glass carboys; nothing even mildly interesting.

As he closed the cold room door, he suddenly heard the hum of the elevator. *Someone was coming up.* And it was only one floor. He'd never make it to the entrance at the end of the hall.

He ran to the door of the storage room, yanked it open, and ducked inside. Afraid that if he turned on the light, it might be seen under the door, he left it dark. But that meant he couldn't see to hide himself. If anyone came in, he'd be standing right there.

He heard the elevator doors slide open. Then the sound of footsteps. Whoever it was uttered something in Italian . . . a male voice. From the inflection, he sounded upset.

The hall lights, Henry thought. *They shouldn't have been on.*

His toes curled and the contents of his stomach turned sour.

Another voice . . . calmer. He heard a squeak, like a turning wheel.

The first voice again . . . also calm now.

More footsteps and again, that squeaking.

Henry braced himself. Then, through the hiss of his own breathing, he heard a clanking noise that could only be the door of the cold room opening. After a brief pause, the door clanked again. Footsteps and more squeaking, the elevator doors opening and closing . . . the hum as it descended. Then silence.

Henry stayed in the storage room for three more minutes, listening hard. Finally, he inched the door open and peeked out.

They were truly gone.

Wondering what they'd done in the cold room, he walked down there and opened the door. Sitting on the floor to the right, where there had been nothing when he'd looked a few minutes ago, was a big plastic drum with a snap-on lid.

Needing both hands free, he put down his briefcase then pulled at the lid on the drum and stripped it off. What he saw inside made him forget all about the protocol he hadn't found. Hardly able to believe his eyes, he leaned against the drum and rocked it, shifting the position of the floating contents.

It was absolutely what he thought it was.

My God.

In a flash of intuition, it all made sense, and he knew why he'd been hired . . . how it fit in.

Oh man, oh man.

His worries about Bruxton were over. Once he told the old geezer what he'd seen, he wouldn't dare fire him.

In fact, it should even be possible to negotiate a sort of finder's fee for his discovery.

Elated at his new prospects, Henry shut off the cold-room light and went back into the hall.

In his study, eyes fixed on the TV screen showing Henry leaving the cold room, Bruxton cursed under his breath, for he knew what Pennell had seen. Of all the people in his employ, why did it have to be Pennell? And what perverse forces made him choose the worst possible time to snoop?

Bruxton now had a decision to make. Actually there could be only one decision, even it if would set the program back at least six months. Bruxton reached for the phone.

As Henry approached the guardhouse at the company gate, the night security man stepped out and waved him down. Henry's first thought was that he'd been caught. He thought about hitting the gas, but then, realizing that he had a bargaining chip that would keep him out of trouble even if someone *knew* he'd been in an off-limits area, he stopped his car.

"Evening, Doctor Pennell. Doctor Bruxton called a few minutes ago and said if I saw you I should tell you he needs to talk to you. He called your lab first, so I guess you just missed him. C'mon in, we'll use my phone."

Henry wanted to talk to Bruxton too, but not in front of the guard. Wondering what the hell Bruxton wanted at this time of night, Henry got out of his car and went inside the guardhouse.

"I'll get him for you," the guard said. He punched in a number, waited a moment, then said, "Doctor Bruxton, I've got Doctor Pennell here . . . yessir, I'll tell him."

The guard hung up and looked at Henry. "He's on another line right now. Said he'd call you back in a few minutes. You're to wait."

Even if he didn't now own Bruxton, Henry would

have been irritated at being ordered around like this.
"You're to wait. . . ." Like Bruxton was God or something. Well, he'd hang around this time, but soon, things'd
be different.

Henry stepped outside and lit up a cigarette.

"I used to smoke," the guard said, joining him.

"What made you quit?" Henry replied, too insecure
to tell the guy to buzz off.

"The poster that showed what your face would look
like if the damage smoking did to your lungs was out
where you could see it."

"You're a better man than I am."

"I wouldn't say that, Doctor Pennell. I mean you're
a doctor and everything and I'm just . . . this."

"What you do to make a living doesn't mean that's
who you are," Henry said, not believing a word of it.

This blather went on for about fifteen minutes until
Henry's irritation at being made to stand around like a
retard waiting for instructions reached the boiling point.
Just when he was ready to take off, the phone in the
guardhouse rang.

Henry followed the guard inside and waited to be
handed the phone. Instead, the guard listened a moment,
said, "Okay, I'll tell him," and hung up.

"Doctor Bruxton said to go on home. He'll talk to
you tomorrow."

Jaw clenched in anger, Henry stalked to his car,
flopped in, and left rubber on the pavement as he sped
off.

As he drove, the knowledge that soon he'd no longer
have to tolerate this kind of crap softened his anger. Then
he realized he hadn't even needed to put up with it
tonight. Just because he hadn't yet told Bruxton what he
knew didn't mean anything. He could have ignored his
order to wait and he would have been home by now.

Missed his first chance to take control of his own
life . . . But then when you've been a toady as long as he
had, it was bound to take a little while to shed that skin. . . .

Wait a minute . . . that's not right, he thought, turning

off the highway onto the county lane that led to his home. Toads don't shed their skin.

He drove the next three miles without thinking, hypnotized by his headlights feeding on the white center line. He hadn't passed a single car since leaving work, which, even though it was late, was a little surprising for the main drag. But the road he was on now, dark and small and lined by mile after mile of dried corn waiting for harvest, was used mainly by farmers moving their combines or whatever from one field to another, so at this time of night it was always deserted. And he liked that, enjoyed living in a remote corner of the county, because people had never brought him anything but trouble as far back as he could remember. And even Lynn was turning against him. She'd always been a self-contained person, preferring books and gardening, and her dogs, to people. But lately she'd been complaining constantly about feeling isolated out here. Pretty damn bad when you can't even find peace at home.

Eyes on the white line, Henry guided his car around a gentle curve in the road and hit the brakes.

Damn . . .

There was a car with its hood up, stalled right in the middle of the road. Would it have been so hard to get it onto the shoulder before it died?

He could see the driver bent over the fender, his head and shoulders lost in the engine, apparently oblivious to Henry's presence. Henry didn't know anything about car repair, but figured he *had* to offer the driver a ride to a phone.

Letting the engine run, he put it in park, got out, and walked to the stalled car. "Hello there. Anything I can do to help?"

The driver took his head out of the engine. "Aren't you Henry Pennell?"

"Yeah, but how did . . ."

The other man's hand came into view, holding something. At practically the same instant that he saw the stun gun and failed to recognize it, Henry was hit by an electrical jolt that dropped him to the pavement. While Henry struggled to comprehend what was happening, the other man grabbed him by the collar and hauled him into the cornfield beside the road, where he rolled Henry onto his stomach and wrapped a thin cord around his neck.

And so Henry Pennell, forty-two years of age, died . . . in full compliance with his belief that people brought him nothing but trouble.

12

Susan Morrison touched up the microscope's fine focus and the first of the developing human embryos in the multiwell dish came sharply into view. Satisfied that it looked perfectly normal and healthy, she checked each of the others.

All four embryos were in the so-called blastocyst stage, in which the future child consists of a small cellular cluster at one end of a hollow ball of cells that will eventually form the fetal part of the placenta. In her long career she had seen many hundreds of developing embryos and she still felt the same sense of awe and respect.

Four potential human lives.

In her dish.

Under her control.

Four embryos. Among them, a world-famous pianist perhaps, a Pulitzer Prize–winning novelist, a network anchor, or a drug-controlled thief. Who could tell?

Maybe in the future, the parents could order the exact child they wanted. But for now, the best Susan could do was give them the boy they wanted along with an assurance that he would be free of the common genetic defects. In the next room, a young woman waited, prepped and ready to receive her son.

A few weeks earlier, a reporter had wanted to do a story on Susan's clinic, but she had turned him down. In the eyes of many, she was playing God—and in the Bible belt that was a potentially dangerous perception for her. In time, the miracles she was capable of achieving would be widely accepted and there would be no danger in her art. But that time was years away.

In most clinics it was accepted practice to introduce the earlier four- or eight-cell stage into the patient. But so few of those implanted, and each attempt was so expensive and emotionally draining for the hopeful clients, that it had become customary to introduce as many as four embryos at a time. Occasionally, this produced multiple births. And while a couple might desire a single child with all their hearts, the birth of two or three was often a far less joyous event. So Susan had begun introducing but a single blastocyst. And her success rate with this modified approach soared.

So which was it to be?

Pianist?

Novelist?

Anchor?

Thief?

She looked up at Eric Taylor, the embryologist member of her team. "Let's use number two."

"It's always been *my* favorite," Taylor joked.

While he got the embryo into the transfer catheter, Susan returned to her patient, Sally Marcum, who was on the examining table, her heels in obstetric stirrups, a catheter guide extending from her womb to the exterior through her vagina.

Susan moved to where she could see Sally's face. "How are you doing?"

"I'm okay."

"We'll be finished in just a few minutes." Susan moved to the foot of the examining table, took her seat between the stirrups, and waited for Taylor, who entered a few

seconds later and knelt at Susan's side. With him holding the syringe attached to the transfer catheter, Susan
threaded the thin tube through the already-installed guide
sleeve. As Susan worked, a nurse watched the ultrasound
screen for the emergence of the catheter from the uter-
ine end of the guide.

"I see it."

Susan carefully advanced the catheter a bit more, then
stopped pushing. "We're there."

Taylor gently depressed the plunger on the syringe
and there was a flash of light on the ultrasound screen
as the medium from the catheter entered the uterus. Susan
then removed the catheter from the guide and Taylor went
back to the lab to verify that the embryo had indeed been
delivered.

He returned a few minutes later and gave Susan the
okay sign.

"Wonderful," Susan said. "Freeze the others."

If for some reason, the embryo she'd given her patient did not implant, they would thaw each of those remaining, one at a time, and try again with the first one
that still appeared healthy. Susan looked at her patient.
"Sally, you'll need to stay right there for an hour. Then
you can go home. You should spend the rest of the day
in bed. Tomorrow, you can get up, but don't be very active."

Susan went to her office to make a few notes in her
patient's record, finishing that task at five after nine.
Plenty of time to get to the airport and catch her flight
to Memphis, where she would meet Holly and they would
go on to Madison together.

Ready to depart, she checked on Sally and then let
the other members of her team know she was leaving.
While she was exchanging a few last words with the
group's geneticist, the receptionist interrupted.

"Doctor Morrison, you have a call."

"Tell them I'm away for a few days. Or let Doctor
Shields handle it."

"They said it was extremely urgent."

• • •

Holly watched the passengers file into the airport from the Jackson flight, thinking that it seemed like an unbelievably large number for such a small plane. But so far, no Susan. They must have put her all the way in the back in one of those seats so close to the bulkhead that it won't recline.

The flow of arrivees dwindled to a trickle, then stopped.

Puzzled, Holly entered the passageway to the plane and went to its end, where she met the pilots coming her way.

"Are there any passengers left on the plane?"

"No, ma'am. Everyone's off."

Susan had missed the flight. And it was only thirty minutes until they were to leave for Madison.

Holly returned to the gate and sank into a chair. While wondering what to do about this development, she heard herself being paged to the Northwest Airlines ticket counter.

She hurried back to the terminal and stepped up to a Northwest agent. "I'm Holly Fisher. You paged me."

The man behind the counter consulted a notepad beside him and said, "Susan Morrison asked us to tell you her husband had a heart attack and she won't be able to go with you."

Holly's first thought was for Susan and what terrible news this was. She longed to know more. How bad was it? It sounded as though Walter hadn't died. But he might be in grave danger of doing so. She considered calling Susan, but realized that she was probably at the hospital.

Then, her thoughts shifted to herself. She'd have to go to Madison alone. Until that moment she hadn't realized how much she was counting on Susan. From their trip to Dallas, she'd seen that Susan always seemed to know what to do when the unexpected occurred. How could she proceed without her?

But then, she remembered why she was going to Madison. This was her battle, not Susan's. She didn't need a committee to give these people what they deserved. Chin up, her eyes flinty with resolve, she headed for the gate where they were already preboarding her flight.

Before Northwest Airlines established a hub in Memphis, it used to be said that you couldn't even go to Hell without changing planes in Atlanta. Even now, with the hub, there were no direct flights to Madison. To get there, Holly had to make a connection in Detroit. On the initial leg of the trip, the plane was not full, allowing the seat between her and the woman next to the window to go unoccupied. A few minutes after they were airborne, the woman closed her eyes and began fanning herself with a motion sickness bag so that about fifty times a minute the sun reflected off its shiny black surface directly into Holly's eyes. Hoping to put a stop to this, Holly reached up, opened the air nozzles above both adjacent seats, and directed them on the woman's face. But the fanning continued.

Ten minutes later, Holly felt like grabbing the bag from the woman's hand and tearing it into shreds. And in the row ahead, across the aisle, obnoxious hard-rock music was leaking audibly from some guy's headset.

Ordinarily, Holly would have borne these intrusions with better grace. Though she was not aware of it, her irritability was rooted in fear. She was off to a strange city to investigate people who might be dangerous, and she was alone. The prospect of what lay ahead would have been far less intimidating with Susan along. In any event, when the beverages were served, the fanning woman put down the motion-sickness bag to accept a cup of orange juice and never fanned again.

In Detroit, when she reported to gate D7 for her connecting flight, as instructed by the concourse monitors, a ticket agent redirected her to C9. Upon arriving at that gate, she learned that her plane's departure would be delayed. It finally took off forty minutes late. Even if they didn't make up the lost time in the air, it would still be possible for Holly to reach the dairy before five o'clock if everything else went right. But with all the problems she'd been having so far and still afraid of what she might confront in Midland, Holly was not in an optimistic frame of mind.

Despite the poor start to her trip, Holly enjoyed this leg because she spent a good part of it affectionately watching the seats across the aisle, where a one-year-old boy in little blue sweat pants, a tiny football jersey with the number 98 on it, and the cutest little white gym shoes was traveling with his mother.

Fifty miles out of Detroit, the boy launched his teething ring into the aisle and Holly returned it. A hundred miles later, a little truck went whizzing through the air, landing under the seat in front of Holly. This too she retrieved and returned. For the rest of the trip, the mother slept with the boy in her lap, his hands playing with her hair. As the plane rolled up to the gate in Madison, the boy celebrated their arrival by bouncing a small car off the cabin roof.

After the crowds in the Detroit airport, the Madison terminal seemed almost deserted. Its small size allowed Holly to find the Avis desk easily and sign the papers for the rental car she'd reserved. Having only the sketchiest of ideas about what she was going to do here, it had been impossible to predict how long she'd stay. To be safe, she'd cleared her calendar for three days and brought the appropriate amount of clothing in her carry-on. She'd had the foresight to check the weather in Madison before leaving home, so when she stepped from the terminal and was greeted by a cold wind that made her eyes tear, she wasn't surprised. As she slipped on the jacket she'd brought, the Avis shuttle pulled up at the curb.

Five minutes later, Holly was staring at the sky through the windshield of a white Honda Accord and seeing nothing but fat gray clouds bearing ugly black stria where the bottoms had been sheared off—a sky that could produce anything. It seemed like another bad sign and Holly wished again that Susan was beside her.

But she wasn't and there was work to do.

Using the Madison map the Avis clerk at the terminal had given her and a less detailed Wisconsin map she'd brought, Holly plotted her course to the small town of Midland, where she felt she would find the heart of the mystery she'd been unwillingly drawn into.

13

As Holly made her way to the southwest on the two-lane state highway to Midland, the clouds that had appeared so malignant at the airport became much less threatening. Eventually, there were stretches of several minutes at a time where she could see the sun.

The land here was gently rolling hills, most of it clad in brown cornstalks. In some fields, green or red machines moved down the rows like great herbivores, consuming the crop in wide swaths and spitting a thick stream of shelled corn into an accompanying truck. There was also a lot of farm machinery on the road and Holly often found herself crawling along for miles behind some mountainous piece of equipment before she could pass.

She had arrived in Madison at three-thirty. Without the hindrances she was encountering, it would have only taken around forty minutes to reach Midland. Now, she wouldn't make it until after five, meaning she'd probably have to wait until tomorrow to visit the dairy. Still no breaks.

At five-fifteen, on the outskirts of Midland, she came upon the Green and White Motel, a line of little individual cottages that should have been called the Faded and Peeling Green and White Motel. Seeing a heavyset woman carrying a stack of blankets from the cottages to the farmhouse used as an office, Holly pulled into the driveway and got out of the car with the engine still running.

"Need a room?" the woman asked, coming over to her. Her breathing was labored and with each exhalation it sounded as though she had a harmonica in her throat.

Though Holly did need a place to spend the night and the Green and White had a vacancy, Holly had stopped merely to ask a few questions.

"I was hoping you could give me some information about the Midland Dairy."

"What do you want to know?" Another harmonica breath.

"When do they close?"

"Six o'clock."

Finally, something was going Holly's way. "How far is it?"

"Nine miles." The woman took another deep breath and added, "Straight ahead about five miles, take a left on Dairy Road."

Though Holly very much wanted to visit the dairy today, the late hour and the possibility that she wouldn't find any other place to stay if she waited made her take a chance on the Green and White. With little time to spare, she went into the office and paid for a room without looking at it.

Needing a bathroom break, Holly got into her car and drove down the gravel drive to the unit she'd rented. She grabbed her luggage from the trunk and went inside to find herself in a cheerless room that belonged in a reformatory. On the wall was a hand-lettered sign: "Why ruin your good name by taking our light bulbs?" She tossed her overnight bag on the metal bed. Cringing at the sound this coaxed from the springs, which were part of the frame, she went into the bathroom.

Oh swell.

The shower stall was in a white metal enclosure with a thin green curtain on rings at the entrance. Without even looking hard, she could see the brush marks on the stall from the last time it was painted. "So I guess a mint on my pillow is out of the question," she muttered.

A few minutes later, she was pleased to see that at least the toilet flushed. She washed her hands and dried them on the roughest towels she had ever felt. After a quick check of her appearance, she headed back to the car.

At five thirty-five, she pulled up at a driveway flanked on each side by a small stand of pine trees. On the right, a sign affixed to a yellow brick wall read MIDLAND DAIRY. Right out in the open . . . as though they had nothing to hide.

As Holly slowly entered the drive, her eyes darted about, trying to take in everything: parking area with a lot of pickups to her left; beside that, a milk transport backed up to a two-story yellow metal building; beyond that, three big metal barns with bars on the side like a prison. There were some things past the barns, but, except for a tall smokestack way in the back, it was all too far away to make out.

On the right, next to the origin of a side road that dipped into a valley, a small sign with an arrow pointed the way to VEHICLE STORAGE. Forty yards beyond the side road, she saw a one-story yellow brick building with another parking lot in front. Drawing closer, she read OFFICE PARKING on a sign at the lot entrance. She left the Honda in the lot and walked to the building it served.

Inside, she found an office staff of three women working at utilitarian metal desks in a large room with no carpeting to absorb the keyboard clatter of their computers. Surmising that the floor was vinyl because cow manure would be much harder to get out of carpeting, Holly approached the nearest desk, which was occupied by a young woman with olive skin and a broad, flat nose . . . probably not from a family that ate lutefisk.

"Hi," Holly said. "Would it be possible to see Mr. Lamotte?"

Without asking what Holly wanted, the girl said, "I'll check." She made a call, then pointed to a doorway behind her. "Through there, second office on the right."

Holly found Don Lamotte at his desk, which was also metal and no better than those she'd already seen. He motioned her into a chair.

"I must be doing something right to rate a visit from such an attractive woman," he said.

Lamotte was a thin fellow wearing gold wire-rimmed glasses with egg-shaped lenses. His hairline began on the crown of his head but he had a nice smile and was rather appealing in a favorite-math-teacher kind of way.

Behind him, much of the wall was taken up by a huge aerial view of the dairy with each building identified on little white rectangles. Under that hung a half-dozen pictures of Holstein cows: the milking hall of fame. Holly decided to get right to it.

"Mr. Lamotte, How do you know Palmer Garnette?"

Without a hint of concern on his face, he said, "Palmer is . . . was our company lawyer. Why do you ask?"

"Because he was involved in the theft of some property from me through the use of fraudulent documents."

"I'm sorry, did you tell me your name?"

"Holly Fisher."

No reaction.

"If you're trying to find Mr. Garnette, I'm afraid you're going to be disappointed," Lamotte said. "He was killed last week in a traffic accident."

"Were you aware that he was involved with a traveling clinic that went from city to city enlisting women as egg donors in a research project supposedly funded by the government?"

"This is the first I've heard of that. But then I didn't know the man well. Only spoke to him a few times a year. And that was usually by phone."

"Then how did you know he was dead even before the police had located his family?"

"What makes you think I knew that early?"

"Before any of his relatives were informed, I called you pretending to be a telephone operator with a collect call from him. And you became angry, asked me if the call was a joke. So you obviously knew he was dead."

His face flushing, Lamotte shot to his feet. "This discussion is over. Please leave."

He followed her into the main office and watched her all the way to her car. He was still there as she pulled from the lot. She wished now that she'd explored the property before confronting him. Now, with him aware of her presence, she'd lost that opportunity.

In the aerial view of the dairy in Lamotte's office, Holly had seen a road in the rear that ran out of the picture. Curious about its termination, she made a left at the highway and followed the chain-link fence that surrounded the property until it turned and ran along a poorly maintained intersecting road barely wide enough for two cars. Eventually, this took her to a rear gate secured with a big padlock.

After finding no road that would allow her to explore the back property line and wanting another look at the place, Holly retraced her route. With daylight now fading, she passed the dairy's main entrance as the vehicles of employees who had just punched out for the day poured onto the highway.

Lamotte's reaction to her questions left no doubt in her mind that there was a connection between the dairy and the traveling clinic. But what was it? And how do you investigate something like this? Deciding that there was nothing further she could do here, she made a tight U-turn opposite the dairy's eastern fence line and joined the procession of workers heading toward town.

A few minutes later, three cars ahead of her, a pickup truck from the dairy flicked on its right turn signal and pulled into the crowded gravel parking lot of a tavern called the Lucy II, which looked as if it had been assembled from parts of other buildings. Some aluminum siding, a little stucco, a couple of porthole windows, a Victorian cupola serving as a second-floor porch . . . It was a structural Frankenstein.

Maybe that's what happened to Lucy I, Holly thought. *Villagers with torches and a sense of architectural outrage burned it down.* On impulse, she followed the truck into the parking lot, where she hurriedly got out and locked her car so the two men from the pickup wouldn't get inside before she did and disappear into the crowd.

The noise and the music didn't stop when Holly walked in, but she definitely felt like a stranger in a strange land, for the place was a totally male bastion. The only other female there was a life-sized poster of a blonde in a slinky black dress holding a bottle of beer. Most of the back wall was occupied by a Green Bay Packers football schedule. A lot of the noise was coming from a bank of pinball machines against the left wall. Through a doorway decorated with tinsel, the more athletic of the brethren were stalking the balls on a pool table.

At the bar to her right, every stool was full, as were most of the tables. From the way it appeared, it must be a state law that every male will don his baseball cap upon arising and wear it indoors and out until such time as he returns to bed.

While one of the men from the dairy claimed an empty table, the other ordered at the bar. At this point there was no way of knowing who was in on what was going on and who might be out of the loop. Figuring that she had to start somewhere, Holly walked over to the man at the table, a young guy with chapped skin and sandy hair.

"Hi, I'm Holly Fisher," she said, extending her hand.

"Curtis Larson," he replied shaking her hand. "And that's Gene Whitten." He gestured at his dark-haired friend, who was returning with two beers. Gene put the beers down and Holly shook his hand too.

"Mind if I join you?" Holly asked.

"Heck no," Curtis replied.

"I sure wouldn't mind," Gene added. "Can I get you something?"

"I'm okay, thanks. You two work at the dairy, don't you?"

"Yeah, I'm a milker," Curtis said. "And Gene takes care of the herd. You see, it's an intelligence thing. Your higher-IQ employees don't have to walk in manure."

"No," Gene said. "They just spread it in bars after work."

Out in the parking lot, a man crept up to the side of Holly's car and slipped a Slim Jim between the window and the frame. In just a few seconds, he had the door open.

"How did you know we worked at the dairy?" Gene asked.

Holly certainly wasn't going to tell these guys why she'd come to Midland. Instead, she tried a truncated version of the truth. "I saw you come out at quitting time. Have you worked there long?"

"Quite a while," Gene said.

"Since before the new people took over," Curtis said.

"When was that . . . the change-over?" Holly asked.

"Little over two years ago," Curtis said.

"Why did the previous owners sell?"

Curtis shrugged. "Can't really say. Maybe they got tired of the hassle."

"Who owns it now?"

"I heard that Don Lamotte, he's the manager, has a piece of it. Beyond that, I think it's a conglomerate based in Milwaukee."

"Has anything changed from the way it used to be run?" Holly was pursuing no plan in her questioning, but was just gathering information, hoping to stumble onto something pertinent.

"They replaced all the cows," Gene said.

"Why? Are the new ones better in some way? Do they give more milk?"

"The overall yield is less," Curtis said. "Some of the new animals are as good as the previous ones, but a lot aren't. About a third of the old herd were such good producers we'd milk them three times a day instead of just twice, so we used to milk practically around the clock. Now, we only milk from early in the morning until 6 P.M., which has cost some of my friends their jobs. And I'm not too happy about that."

"Just talk right into the mike," Gene said, holding his closed hand in front of Curtis. "I'll see that Don gets a complete transcript of your views."

"If the new owners are willing to accept a drop in yield, there has to be an upside," Holly said. "Are the new animals more efficient at turning their food into milk?"

Gene took a sip of his beer and said, "I don't have any figures to back this up, but it doesn't seem to me like they're eating less than the others."

"Could be it's easier to get them settled," Curtis said.

"Settled?" Holly repeated.

"That means to get pregnant. The goal in a dairy operation is for each cow to produce one calf a year, because if they're not kept pregnant, they'll eventually dry up."

"So the herd produces a lot of calves," Holly said.

"That's another way the dairy makes money," Gene said. "Selling the calves."

"Or they send them somewhere to grow up, then bring them back to replace old cows or augment the herd," Curtis added.

"*If* they're female," Holly observed.

"Males aren't worth much to anybody," Curtis said.

After her recent experience with Grant, Holly had a ready response to that, but didn't feel this was the place to express it.

•　　•　　•

Outside, in the rear of the parking lot, as far into the deepening shadows as he could get his car, the man who'd broken into Holly's Honda spoke into his radio. "Number two, this is number one. Come in."

"Number two here."

"How are you doing? We can't expect the weather to stay this favorable all night. It could change at any moment."

"If it holds for another fifteen minutes, we'll be fine."

"So there are never a lot of calves around," Holly said.

"You have to wean them fast and get rid of them," Curtis said. "'Cause they just get in the way."

"I'll say this for the new owners, they do that a lot faster than the old ones," Gene said. "Before they took over, earliest I ever heard of a calf being weaned was three weeks. But three days after a birth cycle, like clockwork, the transport truck takes 'em away. Tomorrow at five in the afternoon, that ol' truck'll be at the back gate."

"Birth cycle?"

"Normally, you let a cow dry up two months before calving. You can't have the whole herd dry that long, so the cows are divided into groups and the calving is staggered. All cows these days are artificially inseminated, which not only ensures that the calves will be good producers, but allows the time of conception to be controlled. Then when the calves of a group are due, the vets inject the cows with a hormone to induce delivery and the whole group can be dealt with at the same time. Usually that's all done at night so it doesn't interfere with the other work. They got it planned so every two weeks there's a cycle."

"How many cows are in the herd?"

"Seventeen hundred."

"That's a lot of animals."

"Don't I know it."

"Can you think of anything else unusual that's happened since the new owners took over?"

"Couple months ago had a guy die," Gene said.

"Oh, yeah, Chester Sorenson," Curtis added. "That was really weird."

"He was found floating in Rucker's pond," Gene said. "Nobody knows what happened. That's his brother, Buddy, over there in the green cap, at the bar."

Holly looked that way and saw a young guy staring at his beer.

"He's taking it pretty hard," Curtis said. "They were real close."

"What did Sorenson do at the dairy?"

"He was a milker," Curtis said. "One day he just walked off the job without telling anybody anything. Next afternoon, Virgil Rucker found him dead."

"Was there an investigation?"

"I expect so. But nothing ever came of it. Least I never saw anything in the paper. Some say it was a suicide, but you don't want to say that around Buddy."

"Not that this ranks with Chester's death," Gene said. "But I just thought of something else. The new cows don't have any personality. You work with a group of animals a while, you usually get to know them individually. That's not true with these animals. About the time I think I've come to know one, I realize it's not the one I thought it was."

"And with his social life, that's a real loss," Curtis said.

"I guess you can tell Curtis is probably the cleverest milker the world has ever seen."

Out of questions, Holly suddenly felt hungry. Behind Curtis there was a blackboard with the dinner special listed.

"How's the food here?"

"Actually, not too bad," Gene replied. "If you want something you have to order at the bar. I'd recommend the creamed chicken."

In the parking lot, number two still hadn't arrived.

• • •

Twenty minutes later, having learned that Gene's food recommendations were not trustworthy, Holly got in the Honda and closed the door. Still thinking of the lumps in the mashed potatoes and the metallic taste of the gravy, she reached for the seat belt. But as she pulled it across her chest, it came loose from its attachment on the floor.

Great.

Having a grand time in Wisconsin. Wish you were here.

After such a lousy meal, the prospect of returning to her spartan quarters at the Green and White were bleak indeed.

She'd gone about a quarter of a mile when she noticed lights coming up fast behind her, some kind of truck maybe.

Her mind turned to her conversation with Gene and Curtis. About the only thing of much interest was the guy, Sorenson, who'd died. And maybe the fact that the new owners had replaced all the cows. What was that all about? Especially since they weren't better milk producers.

For the first time since she'd left the Lucy II, the road was devoid of traffic save for the truck behind her. Taking advantage of the opportunity to pass, it now picked up speed.

As the distance between them closed, Holly saw in the mirror that the truck was equipped with a huge angled blade, like those used to move dirt or snow. Trying to make it easier on its driver, Holly edged the Honda toward the right shoulder.

With its engine laboring hard, the truck swung out into the left lane, wider, she thought, than was really necessary. Suddenly, it swerved sharply so the big blade was heading right for her.

Holly's mind screamed for her to respond, but there was nowhere to go . . . no way to evade it . . .

At the moment of impact, the blade began to rise,

lifting the tires on Holly's car off the pavement. Bulling its way into her, the truck kept coming. Under the force of the onslaught, the Honda went over onto its side and kept rolling . . . tires in the air . . . then down the fifteen-foot embankment, still rolling.

14

"Otto, any idea what happened to that guy who worked at Bruxton?" Artie Harris asked. "What was his name?" He looked at Richard Heflin's sister, Jessie.

"Henry Pennell," she said.

"Yeah, that's it."

Otto Christianson, the county sheriff, shook his head. "Car just sitting in the middle of the road, lights on, engine running. Somebody abducted him is my guess."

"You think he's dead?" Artie asked.

"If it'd been a woman, I'd say it's almost a certainty. But a man . . ." Otto thought a moment, then said, "Could be he'll show up somewhere, but I haven't been able to find any reason why he'd *want* to disappear. So I can't be too optimistic about the outcome."

In addition to enforcing county laws, Otto's office bore responsibility for making sure the citizens of Midland, the county's only town with more than three stoplights, observed its ordinances. He'd grown up in Midland and served as sheriff for three decades. When he was a young man, his big ears and wide chin had made him homely by most standards, but having reached his sixties, he had

settled into his face so its excesses were no longer no-
ticeable. He'd never been the brightest cop in the world,
and now that he was getting old and fat he didn't even
have agility working for him. But he was as widely liked
as ever and still possessed the most important quality for
a cop: a dogged inability to put a crime out of his mind
until it was solved.

Otto, Richard, Jessie, and Jessie's boyfriend, Artie,
were having dinner together at Arneson's, their favorite
restaurant, a Midland landmark for the last twenty-seven
years.

"You worked with Pennell," Otto said to Jessie. "What
was he like?"

"I didn't actually work *with* him. His lab was on a
different floor from mine and he kept pretty much to
himself. I don't think he had any friends there. I don't
even know what his job was."

"I heard he tested products under development to see
if they were toxic," Otto said.

"How?"

"He put them in dishes where these cells were growing . . ."

"Who told you that?"

"Zane Bruxton. Why? Is that wrong?"

"He ought to know. But Pennell didn't have any lab
help. Maintaining cells in culture is very labor intensive.
He must have been working his tail off."

"I believe he *was* there most nights."

"I'm not surprised."

"What gets me," Otto said, "is that we rock along for
years around here with nothing much happening out of
the ordinary, then boom, we get Chester Sorenson, then
the Johannsons, and now Pennell."

"What did you ever conclude about Sorenson?" Artie
asked, picking up on the opportunity to probe Otto yet
again about what had become one of Artie's favorite sub-
jects. "You think it was a suicide?"

Being by nature a garrulous man, one of Otto's great-
est faults was talking too much about investigations in

progress. Usually, since the crime itself was relatively inconsequential, this rarely did significant harm. Lately, though, at the urging of his wife after the Sorenson death, he'd been trying to be more careful about this. Certainly, he didn't want to say publicly that the forensic office in Madison had reported that Sorenson's lungs contained tap water, not water from the pond where he'd been found. So, in addition to its petty thieves, squabbling couples, and a few other folks who wandered a little off the path from time to time, the county harbored a killer. And it didn't take much imagination to wonder whether Henry Pennell's disappearance had anything to do with the Sorenson case. From Artie's question, it was obvious that if Richard had told Jessie about the forensic findings, she hadn't mentioned it to Artie.

"That one's still a puzzle," Otto said, not actually lying to Artie. He turned to Richard. "Speaking of puzzles, do you have any idea what killed the Johannsons?"

"Thought I might have found a possibility in their home last week . . . some brown powder in gelatin capsules, but it turned out to be St. John's Wort and quite pure at that."

"St. John's what?" Otto asked.

"Wort. It's an herbal supplement that's supposed to modulate . . ." Remembering who he was talking to, Richard defined *modulate*. ". . . even out a person's moods."

"Does it work?"

"Some of my patients think so."

"Maybe I'll get some for Frannie."

"Whatever killed them might not even be in their home."

"Because Skye's brother is okay?"

"Yeah. It's a long shot, but tomorrow the state health department is putting out some culture plates in the house to see what grows on them."

"Like germs?"

"Fungus or molds."

At that point, Otto's radio crackled to life . . . something about an auto accident. He listened hard then pushed his chair back. "I better go see what happened. Enjoyed it."

As Otto made his way to the door, Jessie looked at Richard. "Could be there's a visit to the hospital ER in your near future."

Sixteen minutes later, as they lingered over coffee, Richard's pager went off.

Tonight, the ER doc was Neal Amis.

"What have we got, Neal?" Richard asked.

"Female Caucasian with a significant cranial contusion and assorted minor bumps and scrapes suffered in an auto accident. She's a little disoriented and has some anterograde amnesia. Thought you better take a look. We did a CT series after I paged you. They're over here."

Richard followed Amis to the light screen. "Who is she?"

"Name's Holly Fisher. She's from Memphis."

"She tell you that?"

"Her name, but she had trouble with her address. I got that from her driver's license when we looked for her insurance carrier." He flicked on the lights behind the CT scans, illuminating the ghostly images of Holly's brain.

Richard studied the scans briefly, then turned to Amis. "Where is she?"

Amis took Richard to examining room 1, where Holly was already hooked up to a cardiac monitor and a pulse oximeter. Richard nodded to the nurse in attendance, then looked at Holly. "Hello, I'm Doctor Heflin. What's *your* name?"

"Holly Fisher," she said slowly. "They said I was in an accident, but I don't remember it."

"You've got quite a bump on your head, so it might be a little while before it comes back to you."

Richard took the opthalmoscope off its wall holder. "Now Holly, I'd just like to take a look in your eyes."

Finding everything normal there, Richard conducted

a short physical exam that likewise revealed nothing alarming.

"I've got a terrible headache," Holly said. "Could I have something for it?"

"Get her a thousand megs of Tylenol, would you please," Richard said to the nurse. While she went for the pills, Richard turned back to Holly. "Holly, where do you live?"

This time she remembered. Even though Amis already knew her address from her driver's license, if Holly had been more alert, she probably would have been reluctant to personally give that information to a stranger in a town where someone had just tried to kill her. As it was, she answered openly.

"What day is it?" Richard asked.

Holly thought a moment, then said, "Wednesday."

"What month?"

"October."

"Do you know where you are?"

"A hospital?"

"What city?"

This one stumped her.

Richard held further questions while Holly took the pills he'd ordered.

Then he continued. "Who's the president?"

"Of what?" Holly asked.

Richard smiled. "Of this country."

She answered correctly.

"How did your accident occur?"

Holly's brow furrowed as she tried to remember. "I don't know. I was just driving along. . . . There were some lights behind me coming up fast, then . . . For some reason I'm getting the image of snow. It hasn't snowed, has it?"

"Too early in the season."

"I don't know where that came from. Anyway, the next thing I remember is being brought in here."

Richard looked at Amis. "Was she conscious in the ambulance?"

"The entire time, they said."

This added retrograde amnesia to her symptoms.

"Why can't I remember what happened?"

"It's nothing to be concerned about. Your nervous system is dealing with the shock of you being knocked around. After it's settled down, you'll likely remember everything."

Though she hadn't been able to tell him what town she was in, Richard asked the next question anyway. "Is there anyone nearby we should call and tell about your accident?"

"I can't think of anybody."

Holly's CT scan hadn't shown any evidence her brain had been seriously injured, but it was possible there was damage that would show up later. "Holly, I think you're going to be perfectly fine, but to be safe, we need to keep you here overnight for observation."

While she was uncertain about some things, the Green and White Motel was firmly embedded in her memory. With that alternative waiting for her, she didn't have much incentive to argue. Besides, she was too sore and tired to get up. "Whatever you think is best."

"I want to get some fluids into you, so we'll need to start an IV line. It's just a minor inconvenience."

Suddenly sleepy, Holly nodded.

Richard wrote orders for the nurse to give Holly a simple neurological exam every few hours and to administer a 5 percent dextrose half-normal saline solution at 100 cc an hour through her IV. He finished by writing NPO (nothing by mouth) on her chart then went back to Holly's side. "You get a good night's sleep and I'll see you in the morning."

Within minutes after her IV had been rigged, Holly fell asleep. She was awakened thirty minutes later by the nurse.

"Sorry to bother you, but there's someone here who'd like to speak to you."

The nurse stepped aside and was replaced by a large man in some kind of uniform.

"Miss, I'm Otto Christianson, the chief law enforcement officer in this area. Could we talk for a minute?"

"What about?"

Otto had already learned from Neal Amis that there was no evidence Holly had been drinking. "Could you tell me what happened to cause your car to go off the road and roll over?"

"I'm afraid I don't remember."

"Would it help if I told you there were tire marks to indicate another vehicle hit you? Most likely a truck of some sort."

With just that little hint, the ugly details of what happened began to emerge like zombies rising out of the mist. "It *was* a truck, with a big blade on it . . . like a snowplow."

"Did you get a look at the driver?"

"It happened too fast. All I saw was that blade coming at me."

"Were you wearing your seat belt?"

"I couldn't. It was broken."

Drawing on his discovery of the Avis tag on the key ring and the rental agreement in the glove compartment, Otto remarked, "You should have asked for a different car."

"It was working when I rented it."

"Really . . ." Otto grew quiet as his mind examined this shiny new fact from all angles.

With a poorly formed possibility looking for fertile ground in Otto's arid mind, he asked, "Where were you going when this happened?"

"Back to my room at the Green and White Motel."

"And where had you been?"

"A tavern called the Lucy II."

Failing to ask the better question—Where were you before the tavern?—Otto took a slight detour. "I understand you live in Memphis. What brings you to Wisconsin?"

Holly was still far from herself and had not yet realized there was a connection between her investigation and the attempt on her life. But she did remember how the Dallas police had wasted the information she and Susan had given them. Believing that the cops in a much smaller town would be even less competent, she decided to keep the real reason for her visit to herself. "Vacation," she said.

Even to Otto, that sounded odd. "Not really much to see around here," he said. Then, instead of waiting to see what this would elicit, he added, "Unless you were intending to see the corn maze over in Janesville."

"As a matter of fact, that's exactly why I'm here," Holly said.

"Heard about it all the way down to Memphis, did you?"

"On the radio, I think it was."

"Everybody around here thought it was a crazy idea when the folks who made it were first talking about it. But it's been a real popular attraction. Got to hand it to that Hughes family. Do you know them?"

"No. Now if you don't mind, I'd like to rest."

"Oh, sure. I understand." He reached into his pocket and took out a folded document. "You might need this. It's the rental agreement for your car. I got it out of the glove compartment. I'll just put it right here." He set it on the nightstand. "If I can do anything for you when you get out of here, let me know."

At the door, Otto paused and turned. "Should you want to visit your car for any reason, it'll be at the Meinholz salvage yard. Don't think we'll ever see it on the road again."

As Otto stepped into the hall, he was pretty much convinced Holly had been the victim of a drunk driver. It was peculiar though how that seat belt broke just before she needed it. Must be one unlucky woman.

Otto's last comment raised an issue Holly hadn't considered. *Her car was wrecked.* And she hadn't taken out the insurance the company offered. Would her regular car insurance cover it? She vaguely remembered reading somewhere that the credit card she'd used would cover any liability for damages to a rental car. So maybe that was going to be okay. But now she was stuck without transportation.

She brooded over her plight for several minutes, most of that time spent wishing Grant Ingram hadn't turned out to be such a phony, and the rest longing to be home in her own bed. Eventually, even though Otto had reminded her that her situation was worse then she'd realized, she once more fell asleep.

At 2:52 A.M., with Holly still sleeping, a figure dressed in scrubs and wearing a surgical mask, a syringe in one hand, came into her room. Though it was important that he move quickly, he had to wait until his eyes adapted to the dim light.

Soon, when he could see well enough to proceed, he slipped like a spirit across the room to Holly's side, not enjoying the prospect of killing again, but pleased to be on the verge of closing out this assignment.

He raised the syringe and bent down so he could locate the injection port on her IV.

Then, the unthinkable happened.

15

Holly was lying on her back, turned slightly toward the IV so that she saw him as soon as her eyes opened.

Gown . . . surgical mask . . .

Why a mask?

There was no reason for a mask.

"Who are you?" she asked.

Reflexively, he looked at Holly and she saw in his posture and his eyes that he was frightened. And this made her scream.

With no other choice left to him, the man bolted from the room, ran to the custodial entrance, and fled into the night.

Responding to Holly's scream, but too late to see the intruder, the floor nurse ran to Holly's room.

Aware now that her accident had been arranged and that the man in her room had been a follow-up, Holly tore herself free from her IV and all the wires attached to her and leapt from the bed. Forcing her stiff muscles to cooperate, she ran to the room's small closet, hoping to find her clothes.

"What's happened?" the nurse said from the doorway. "What are you doing?"

"Leaving," Holly said, throwing open the closet door. It was empty.

"Where are my clothes?"

"Please get back in bed. I can't let you leave without discharge orders."

"To hell with that. I want my clothes."

"I could lose my job," the nurse whined. "Is that what you want? Let me call Doctor Heflin."

"I don't want you to call anyone. Just get my clothes."

The nurse crossed the room and reached out for Holly, but she retreated. "Stay away from me."

"Be sensible. It's three in the morning. You don't have a car and there's no taxi service after midnight. Let me call Doctor Heflin."

Aware that she was now in a battle for her life, Holly's mind threw off the constraints the trauma of the wreck had imposed on it. Set free, it raced.

The nurse had a point. If she just took off into the night on foot, she'd be an easy target. But was it safe to stay here? Who could she trust? She thought about asking the nurse to call Christianson, the cop, but maybe he was in on it too . . . wanting to know why she'd come here so he could report back on what she knew.

What about Heflin? Could she trust him? If he was involved, wouldn't he have given her some kind of sleeping pill so there was no chance she'd wake up and see what they were trying to do?

Desperately needing a branch to cling to, she tentatively accepted that position.

"All right, call Heflin."

Not sure at all that she had chosen the right course, Holly returned to her bed, where she sat bolt upright until Heflin arrived eighteen minutes later, with the nurse behind him. He was wearing slacks and a wrinkled white shirt, and his long hair looked as though it had been hastily combed. He also needed a shave.

"Holly, what's wrong? Why do you want to leave?"

Now that he was here, Holly had to decide what to tell him. "I'll only talk to *you*," she said.

Heflin politely asked the nurse to leave. When she was gone, he came to the bed and reached out to touch Holly. Without thinking, she flinched.

"What's happened, Holly? Why are you so upset?"

Still concerned that she wasn't making the right choices, Holly sat mutely.

"I can't help you if I don't know what you need," Heflin said, his warm fingers resting gently on her hand.

Then, feeling so utterly vulnerable, she had to take the chance, she said, "Someone came into this room while I was asleep and tried to put something in my IV."

"The nurse, you mean?"

"A man dressed in scrubs and wearing a surgical mask."

Heflin drew his hand away. "I can't imagine who that could have been. Are you sure it wasn't a dream?"

"When I screamed, he ran."

"I don't know what to say."

Holly hesitated. Unsure of how far to go with her story and knowing that her next statement, how she believed the intruder had intended to kill her, would open the door to an avalanche of questions, she tried to enlist Heflin's cooperation in advance. "Before I say more. You have to promise me you won't tell the police what I'm going to tell you."

Heflin's face showed the conflict this created in him. "I can't promise that without knowing what I'm agreeing to conceal."

His answer reassured Holly that he wasn't involved. Otherwise, he would have gone along with her request just to hear what she knew. On the other hand, after hearing her story, he might run with it to that cop.

Not yet ready to take him completely into her confidence, she decided to hold back. "Well, this guy was definitely real," she said. "And clearly didn't belong here. That's why I wanted to leave."

"You put that in the past tense. Does that mean you'll stay?"

Right now, with Heflin there, she couldn't think of a better place to be for the rest of the night. Though she was in no position to bargain, she said, "On two conditions. No IV and you stay with me until dawn to make sure nothing else happens. I know that last part is asking a lot, but I just can't be here alone."

Heflin looked at his watch. Dawn was only a few hours away. That wouldn't be so hard to do. And he found himself intrigued by this woman . . . attractive and involved in something she didn't want to talk about. Telling himself he was doing it solely for professional reasons . . . to ensure that his patient got the best care possible, he said, "Can we reconnect your cardiac leads?"

"Yes."

"And you'll let us make sure you can tolerate solid food before you leave?"

"All right. But in the morning, I'm not staying a minute longer than necessary."

"Deal," Richard said, offering his hand.

After sealing their bargain with a handshake, Heflin called the nurse to reattach Holly's leads. When the nurse had gone, he said, "Do you want the lights on?"

"Not this bright."

He adjusted the lighting then went to the overstuffed vinyl-covered visitor's chair and dropped into it.

"You're a good doctor," Holly said.

"I hope so."

"I'm not saying that just from a patient's perspective. I'm a doctor too."

Heflin sat a bit straighter. "Really . . ."

"Hematology."

"Where did you go to medical school?"

"University of Mississippi in Jackson."

"Ever run into an internist there named Keith Harmon?"

"He was the attending on my medicine clerkship."

"One of my best friends."

With the common ground of medicine between them, Holly and Richard talked easily until dawn.

"Well, I certainly don't think you're the worse for your accident," Richard said finally. "What are you going to do when you leave here?"

"Find transportation. Is there anywhere in town I can rent another car?"

"Sure. I'll run you over there. It's not far. Now let's try you on a little clear liquid. Then, if you do okay with that, some solid food. I'm going home to shower and shave, then I'll come back, and if you've had no problems eating, we'll get you out of here."

"I'm going to take these leads off," Holly said.

"Go ahead. I'll let the floor nurse know it's okay."

Ten minutes after Heflin left, a new nurse appeared in the doorway with a tray. "Good morning. Did you have a good night?"

Obviously she hadn't been briefed. "Oh, dandy," Holly said.

"Doctor Heflin would like for you to eat this broth. Then, if there are no problems, I'll bring you a real breakfast."

She brought the tray over and put it across Holly's lap. Still not ready to trust anyone but Heflin, Holly eyed the broth, then looked at the nurse. "You try it first."

"Why?"

"I have my reasons. If you don't, I won't eat it."

"All right, fine." She picked up a plastic cup from the nightstand, removed the wrapping, and spooned some of the broth into the cup. Then she drank it. "Satisfied?"

"Thanks."

After the nurse left, Holly set the tray aside, slipped from the bed, and carried the broth to the bathroom, where she flushed it. Over the next hour, the nurse checked on Holly several times to see whether she was feeling nauseated. Holly surreptitiously did the same with the nurse. When she was eventually brought a real breakfast of scrambled eggs, bacon, toast, and orange juice by the same nurse, who still seemed to be feeling fine, Holly decided the food was safe.

Though the hospital would never go on her list of the best places to eat in Wisconsin, Holly finished everything on the tray.

Heflin appeared a short while later in a suit and topcoat, looking now like a doctor instead of the vagrant he'd resembled the previous night. For the first time Holly noticed that he was a strikingly handsome man: long brown hair, slightly graying at the temples; sharp yet compassionate eyes; and those thin lips that she'd always felt made a man look as if he'd be competent and cool in a crisis. He was balancing a pile of neatly folded clothes in one hand and had a familiar pair of dark gray running shoes and her handbag in the other.

"I had all your things washed and ironed," he said.

There was something about his expression that made Holly say, "How did you manage that?"

"Actually . . ." he blushed slightly. "*I* did it." Then, to cover his embarrassment, he said, "Consider it a professional courtesy, one doctor to another."

He brought the things over and put them on the bed. He touched a small paper sack on the clothes. "There's a toothbrush and some toothpaste in there. I didn't know what else you might need. I'll be back in half an hour and we'll get you that rental car."

Even though she locked the bathroom door, fleeting thoughts of the movie *Psycho* ran through Holly's head while she showered. As she dressed, she noticed that Heflin had even used fabric softener on her clothes.

She was surprised at how after all she'd gone through seven years ago, she'd forgotten how being a patient and totally under someone else's control took away your dignity, a lot of that coming from those damn gowns that let your butt show, and being barefoot. Invigorated by her shower and once again in her own clothes, Holly felt like herself again.

Heflin returned just as she was about to start looking for him.

"Well, you're a free woman," he said.

"I had a jacket when I came in . . ."

"It's in the ER. We'll go out that way."

It was a clear day, with the sky a seamless blue and the temperature just cold enough to see your breath. On the way to Heflin's car, Holly noticed a variety of birds just sitting quietly, barely moving in the partially clothed trees. After all she'd experienced in the last twelve hours, she was ready to believe that even they were up to something.

Once they got underway, Holly had a strong impulse to tell Heflin everything. But they hardly knew each other. Why should this be *his* problem?

As they drove, Holly became worried that they were heading for an Avis office, the firm that had provided the car she'd wrecked. Wouldn't they check to see if she already had a car out? She certainly didn't want to go through all that now. But finally something went right, for it turned it out be a local outfit.

Heflin hung around until the paperwork was done.

"Sorry you had such a bad time here," he said.

"You made it all bearable," Holly replied. "If you're ever in Memphis, give me a call. I'm in the book."

They exchanged a final handshake and parted, her last words making Heflin think she was going home. But a plan had been forming in Holly's mind since the sun had come up, so that as she drove from the rental lot, she knew exactly what she was going to do, and it didn't include leaving town.

16

Holly's first goal was to check out of the Green and White and find a better place to stay. She got there a little after nine and went inside, where she suddenly felt totally exhausted. Checkout time was eleven o'clock, so she didn't have to leave yet. And she *had* paid for the room. Planning to just rest for a few minutes, she lay down on the bed and closed her eyes.

"It was a real mess," Otto Christianson said, putting his cup down. "Rolled over twice and crushed the top almost flat. But she came out of it okay."

"Who was she?" Charles Hallock asked.

You didn't see many ponytails on men in Midland, but folks figured that being a dealer in rare prints and kind of an artsy type, it was okay for Hallock. He didn't care to be called Charlie, though; it had to be Charles, which once again was what you'd expect from a guy who didn't actually have to work for a living.

"Name is Fisher," Otto said, answering Hallock's question. "Holly Fisher. Up from Memphis. Came to see the corn maze, she said."

"So she doesn't have any relatives around here?"

"Don't think so."

"Where's she staying?"

"The Green and White."

Hallock made a sour face.

"Come on, Charles, some folks just don't want to spend much for a night's sleep."

"Life is too short to waste a minute of it on such a place. What caused her accident?"

Otto was about to spill everything he knew and all he thought about the incident, including his drunk driver theory, when Ted Arneson, the owner of the place, stopped by their table.

"How you boys doin' today?" he asked.

Until about a year ago, Ted had weighed over three hundred pounds. Then, suddenly, it all just dropped away until he was hardly recognizable. At first everyone thought he had cancer, but then word leaked that he'd had his stomach stapled.

"My left knee's been acting up," Otto said. "But otherwise I'm holding my own."

"Well, that's better than holding someone else's," Hallock said.

They all had a good laugh over that and Ted moved on to the next table. The brief interruption gave Otto a chance to see that he was about to lapse into his old habit of talking too much about police business. Reining himself in, he gave Hallock the abbreviated version of the accident. "I think a truck hit her."

"You *think*?"

Unaccustomed to being close-mouthed, Otto had trouble clamming up. "Whatever the vehicle was, it left the scene."

"Hit and run . . . Must have been some reason for *that*. Any witnesses?"

"Haven't found any." Unable to stop himself any other way, Otto stood up. "Charles, you take care now. I've gotta hit the road."

Though his conversation with Hallock hadn't been a great example of self-restraint, it had given Otto an idea.

So he drove from Arneson's over to the *Midland Guardian* and asked Barbara Thorstadt, the owner, to run an appeal in the paper for any witnesses to Holly's accident to contact him. He then returned to his car and went back to the office to work on next year's budget.

Otto hated dealing with numbers. It was by far the worst part of his job. Disliking them so, he found it easy to become distracted. Today, as he worked, the words *seat belt* kept inching into his field of concentration. Finally, after putting together a rudimentary budget, he pushed back from his desk and left his office.

"Claire, I'm going over to the Meinholz salvage yard."

"Say hello to Rubin for me," the dispatcher replied.

The salvage yard was just inside the city limits west of town. As Otto approached, he noticed that two sections of the bamboo screening fixed to its chain-link fence had fallen down, so they were in violation of the Midland eyesore ordinance.

A few minutes later, when he pulled up to the cement block office of the yard, Rubin Meinholz came out with his hands in the air.

"Don't shoot, Otto," Rubin said. "I'll go quietly."

It was the same thing he always said. Originality was never something to count on with a Meinholz.

"Rubin, you look more like your daddy every day."

Rubin was slim and gangly just like his father and he had the Meinholz dimple in his chin. And like every male Meinholz in recent memory, he didn't have a lick of athletic ability.

"How *is* your daddy?" Otto asked.

"Got the best corn crop in years. Two hundred bushels an acre. Course, so does everybody else. You wait for that one great year when the sun is right and the rain is right and when you get it, there's a surplus and the bottom falls out of the market. I don't know why he stays with it. The other day somebody asked him what he'd do if he won ten million dollars in the lottery. And he said, 'Guess I'd just keep farming til it's gone.'"

Otto laughed. "It's a tough life, all right. Say, I noticed coming in that your fence needs some attention; couple places where you can see right in from the road."

"Yeah. Been meaning to fix that."

"Then I'll put it out of my mind."

"That why you dropped in?"

"Actually, I'd like to take a look at the car that was in that wreck last night."

"Come on. It's back here."

Otto followed Rubin through a wide muddy roadway lined with cars that had come to violent ends. About the time Otto was thinking he should have driven in, Rubin said, "There she is."

Holly's car had been so flattened in rolling over that the rescue squad had to cut off the door on the driver's side to get her out. So all Otto had to do to look inside was walk closer and bend over, which he did. He quickly located the seat belt and let it slide through his fingers until he came to the end that was supposed to be anchored to the floor. He inspected the free end carefully then took out his pocketknife and cut off the last eight inches to take with him because it sure looked as though someone had cut the stitches free that held the terminal loop to the eyebolt in the floor.

Holly lurched awake, uncertain of where she was.

Then, she remembered . . . the Green and White. Jesus, she hadn't intended to fall asleep.

Knocking . . . Someone was at the door.

She glanced at her watch. Lord. Three-twenty. She'd slept most of the day away.

She got off the bed and trekked to the door, where she fumbled with the lock. Too stuporous to think of being careful, she pulled the door open.

"Sorry to bother you," the motel owner said. She took a wheezing breath and added. "But checkout time is eleven." Another breath. "Since you're more than four hours beyond that, I need to be paid for an additional night."

Her head clearing, Holly bristled. If the woman had come earlier, she wouldn't be owed any more money and the day wouldn't be nearly gone. Faced once again with a time constraint, Holly decided to just pay up and remain at the motel one more night. She pointed into the room. "I'll get my bag."

Not wanting to take the time for a credit card transaction, Holly managed to dig up the exact amount. Before leaving, the owner gestured at Holly's new rental. "What happened to your other car?"

"It's a long story."

Failing to get the drift of Holly's reply, the woman waited for that story to begin.

"Better told another time," Holly added.

Obviously put out by Holly's evasiveness, the woman trudged back to the office. Holly shut the door and concentrated on what she had to do.

She was wearing charcoal-gray slacks. . . . No good. Too dark. Hurrying to her overnight bag, she pulled out the pair of khaki pants she'd brought, and changed.

Shirt . . . Didn't matter because it'd be covered. But her only jacket was navy. Nuts.

She made a pit stop in the bathroom, then fiddled with her hair so it didn't look slept in. Finally, she was able to leave.

Wishing she could hold back time, she was soon cruising Midland's main street, checking the storefronts. There . . .

She pulled into an angled parking spot, got out, and went into the drugstore she'd seen.

She came out three minutes later carrying a sack bearing a disposable camera loaded with thirty-six-exposure film. While inside, she'd learned that the cheapest clothing store in town was Pederson's, two blocks down on the right. Figuring she wouldn't find a parking spot any closer, she set out for Pederson's on foot.

She emerged from the store as quickly as any customer that day, poorer by the eighteen dollars and fifty cents she'd paid for a khaki jacket that was too lightweight for the weather. But it was all they had in the right color.

Barely able to keep from exceeding the speed limit, she arrived at the dairy with no more than a couple hours of daylight left. The question now was what to do with the car.

She drove past the dairy entrance and kept going until she was well clear of the far property line. Then she began in earnest to look for a good place to park. There was nothing though but narrow, grassy shoulder as far as she could see.

With no other choice available, she pulled as far onto the shoulder as possible. Checking to make sure there was no traffic visible in either direction, she jumped out, pulled off her navy jacket, and put on the one she'd just bought. She threw the extra jacket onto the passenger seat and got the disposable camera out of the little storage compartment in the center armrest.

After a quick look toward the dairy and one in the opposite direction, she locked the car, ran around the front, and dashed down the sloping edge of the shoulder, her movements stiff from muscles bruised when her car rolled over. Using the momentum from her descent, she jumped a small water-filled ditch and ducked into the huge cornfield that flanked the road. The jolt of the jump kicked off a low-grade headache. Ignoring it, she kept moving, her clothing quickly making her invisible among the dead vegetation.

She'd had to leave the car in plain sight, but since it wasn't the one she'd been driving when she'd first visited the dairy, she didn't believe that would be a problem.

The corn was planted in rows perpendicular to the road, so it was a simple matter to follow the path between rows deep into the field. But when she decided it was time to head toward the dairy and began to cut across the rows, she found that the corn formed a tough barrier whose dried leaves raked and cut her hands and face.

After an exhausting trek in which a machete would have been useful, the corn thinned and she could see the chain-link fence of the dairy. But she'd gone too far . . . passed all three barns she'd seen earlier, so she was staring at a ten-foot-tall enclosure of huge concrete blocks filled with silage that bulged the tarp covering it.

From her conversation with Curtis and Gene, the two dairy employees at the tavern, she'd become curious about the new cows and wanted to get a look at them. From the way the place was laid out, she'd guessed that at milking time the cows were herded from the barns into the metal building where she'd seen the milk transport the previous day. The only logical route was along the fence she was now looking through. In fact, down by the barns, she could see another fence parallel to this one on the inside, so the two formed a wide avenue that would contain the cows as they were moved.

Retreating so there were now two rows of corn to hide her, Holly hurried in the direction of the barns. At the tavern, Curtis had said that milking goes on almost continuously through the day. So catching some cows being herded past the fence shouldn't be difficult. With no idea which barn was being used at this time, the best spot to observe the action would be between the first barn and the milking building. That way she'd get a look at any animals being moved.

Upon reaching a suitable location, she pushed back through the adjacent row of corn so only one hid her from view. She then dropped to one knee and carefully removed some leaves so she'd be able to see the animals and photograph them.

There was no real plan behind any of this activity. But something was going on at this dairy that was worth killing her to hide. And she had a strong hunch the new cows were an important piece of the puzzle. Because of that, she wanted to get a look at them. The best approach would be to examine one in an agricultural laboratory to determine just what was so special about them that had made the new owners replace the entire herd. With no hope of that happening, what she was now doing and one other idea were the only things she could think of.

Now that she wasn't moving around, her body quickly lost heat through her light jacket and the contact of her knee with the cold ground. In addition, kneeling like this would have been uncomfortable even if she weren't bruised. After a while, she awkwardly changed position, shifting to her other knee so her slacks now had two cold wet spots on them. Sitting on the ground was out of the question.

It was now four-fifteen. It had taken her about ten minutes to get here from the road. Allowing ten to get back to the car and five to get where she wanted to be at a quarter to five, she could only stay fifteen minutes. Why was she always facing a time problem?

Her plane back to Memphis left tomorrow at three. So if she missed the action today at the other location, she wouldn't get another chance there. But she *could* come back here in the morning.

Consideration of the various options open to her was brought to an abrupt halt as two men swung open the long doors on the back of the metal building and secured them. Cows with camouflage patterns of black and white then began pouring from the opening. By the time the first animals reached her, Holly had the camera ready, correctly anticipating that individual cows would pass by so fast she'd need photographs to get the best look at them.

The fence was about fifteen feet from the first row of corn, but the animals were so big she couldn't fit more than one at a time in the viewfinder. Doing the best she could to get a complete animal in the shot, she clicked off the first picture. The sound of the shutter was not loud, but a half-dozen cows looked in her direction. Ignoring them, she kept shooting.

Three and four abreast, the animals moved quickly

along the fence. Of those she could see clearly, she managed to photograph sixteen.

All the animals were herded into the second barn. With a lot of film left and time to spare, Holly decided to stay put, hoping another group would soon be taken *to* the metal building. Cooperating nicely, another group of animals spilled from the second barn a few minutes later. This time, she managed to get twenty on film. With no exposures left, she headed back to her car, appreciating that for once, she had ample time to get where she was going.

At four forty-two, she arrived at that destination: a small roadside quilt shop with some of its colorful wares displayed outside on stands. She pulled into the gravel parking lot beside the shop and parked so the quilts didn't block her view of Deadfall Road, which led to the dairy's rear gate. Her headache was still present, but wasn't clamoring for attention.

If dairy employee Gene was right, a transport would soon arrive to pick up the calves from the dairy's latest birth cycle. It was possible that if she followed that transport, she might get an opportunity to at least see the offspring of the herd up close. Or even better, she might learn where they were being taken, thereby adding to her minuscule knowledge of how the dairy functioned. Thinking very optimistically, she could even see herself buying a calf . . . and taking it . . . where?

The University of Wisconsin in Madison . . . They had a big agricultural school. *They* could find out all there was to know about the animal. How much would she be willing to pay? And how would she transport it? More significantly, why would the university want to help her?

While her mind played with the various outcomes of what she was about to do, another car pulled into the lot. It parked beside her and two women got out. The driver was maybe forty years old; the passenger, early twenties. Despite the difference in their ages, the resemblance between them was striking. A mother and her daughter, surely. Holly put herself in the mother's place . . . shopping with her daughter . . . all grown up now . . .

The two women remained outside, examining the quilts displayed there, and Holly watched them closely, imagining herself part of every little verbal exchange. What must it be like to know you've brought life into the world?

She was concentrating so hard on the women that she didn't notice the big truck coming from the west until it turned onto the road leading to the dairy's rear gate. It looked like one of those horse trailers with a curved top, but was much larger. Below, the sides were metal. The upper half, including the roof, was covered with canvas. On the cab door she could read *M & J*. Under the initials a smaller word was hard to read from that distance, but she thought it was *TRANSPORT*.

She had no idea how long it would take for the calves to be loaded, but she hoped it could be done quickly. Otherwise, she'd be trailing the truck after nightfall.

Hmmm. Maybe that wouldn't be so bad . . . harder for the driver to see he was being followed.

It wasn't dark when the truck reappeared and headed back to the west, but the sun was so low in the sky that when Holly set out after it, she had to use her car's visor to keep from being blinded. This meant that most of the time she was following something she couldn't even see. Occasionally, she'd peek under the visor just to be sure the truck was still in sight.

At the intersection where Dairy Road met the highway leading to town, the truck waited for an opening then crossed the highway and continued west on what was now called Robertson Road. Holly dawdled at the intersection and did not proceed until the truck had once again opened a comfortable distance between them.

About ten miles from the dairy, it occurred to Holly that the truck's destination could be hundreds of miles away. She had no reason to think otherwise. She had nearly a full tank of gas, but what if she ran out before the truck did?

Then she saw the truck turn right onto another state road. She interpreted this as a sign that maybe this would be a local trip after all.

Six miles down this road, the truck slowed and turned left, into a wide, paved entrance to a sprawling warehouse surrounded by a chain-link fence topped with barbed wire. By the time she reached the spot, the truck driver was loosening a chain that secured the gate.

Maintaining her speed and looking at him only out of the corners of her eyes, Holly drove past. Even without staring, she saw that the site looked as though it had been abandoned for a long time.

Now what?

In the distance, on the right, she saw a farmhouse set well back from the road. Keeping one eye on the rearview mirror, she proceeded to the home's driveway and turned in.

Where it began, the drive was at the same grade as the surrounding cornfields, so Holly lost sight of the warehouse. But as she drew closer to the farmhouse, the land rose, lifting her above the tops of the dried corn. She stopped the car at a point where she could see over the crop, yet most of her car would be hidden to anyone looking in that direction from the warehouse. But the setting sun was beginning to paint the western sky with orange hues. Without light, her fine vantage point wouldn't be of much use.

Then she saw a car come out of the warehouse entrance and head away from her. She waited a few minutes to see what else would happen, but nothing stirred. Unable to wait any longer, she backed down the drive and returned to the warehouse, where she pulled into the entrance and stopped at the gate, which was once more locked.

Through the chain link, she saw no cars or trucks, no activity of any kind. Strange . . .

She got out, approached the gate, and yanked on it.

The chain that was looped through the bars had enough play in it so the gate opened a little. Ducking under the chain, Holly pushed her body into the gap and got caught. She pushed harder. Ignoring the pressure of the metal bars raking her fore and aft, she pulled in everything she could and thrust herself hard sideways. Somewhat compressed and hurting in a half-dozen spots, she popped through.

The warehouse resembled an airplane hangar, though it wasn't as tall. Everywhere, weeds pushed up through cracks in the cement apron. To her right, a cement ramp with rusted metal railings led up to a loading dock. To the left, an opening big enough for a semi to pass through was closed by a folding metal door.

It seemed clear that the transport with the calves must be inside. But why bring them here? Most likely that had been the driver who left. There were no other cars around, so the animals were in there with no one to care for them. Maybe they wouldn't need anything until morning, when the driver would return, feed them, and take them on to their ultimate destination. But why pick them up so late if you couldn't take them to where they were going? It would make more sense to start earlier. Or was *this* the final destination? Surely not. The questions swirled around her like disturbed bees, making her headache worse.

She felt strongly that she needed to see what was going on inside. Considering that the sun was fast fading and she had no flashlight, it was a lousy time to be putzing around here, but if she came back in the morning, the animals might be gone, or the place would be crawling with people. So it had to be now.

Between the dock and the big opening where the transport had surely gone inside, there was a small cement block office with a window and a door.

She walked over and tried the door.

Locked.

She looked through the window, but it was too dark inside to see a thing. The window likewise wouldn't open. She considered breaking it, but it had metal mullions and small panes of glass with chicken wire embedded in it. Looking around, she saw another door at the back of the loading dock.

She pulled herself onto the dock using a rusty metal railing at the near end and checked the door, which was also locked. Aware that she didn't have much more than a few minutes of light left, she retreated down the dock's cement ramp and stepped back for a last look before giving up.

She saw a possible answer above the metal roof over the dock, where there were several banks of small windows. They looked to be of the same impenetrable construction as the window in the office, but in the set on the far left, one whole section was missing, leaving a gaping black hole she thought she could slip through.

But how to get up there?

At the end of the dock near the ramp, the metal roof had caved in so that the corrugated sheet forming that section was dangling, twisted and torn, from one small remaining attachment. The pipe framework for the front of the damaged area had also been torn loose so part of it drooped within easy reach.

Normally, the climb wouldn't have been much of a challenge, but in her current battered state, it taxed every resource she could muster. But eventually, there she was, twelve feet off the ground, staring over a flimsy structure that could never support her weight. But near the wall, the metal frame reinforced the roof so that it should be fairly strong.

Balancing herself with one hand against the building, she stepped onto the frame of the collapsed section and gingerly let it take some of her weight.

So far, so good . . .

She gave it a little more weight, then shifted fully onto it.

One foot in front of the other like a tightrope walker, she crossed the damaged section and stepped onto the part that was still intact. There, with the metal sheeting giving her feet more support, progress was easier. But she'd sure make a great target up here.

Between spates of worrying about being shot, she feared that when she reached the window she'd discover that inside it was a sheer twelve-foot drop to the floor, which would mean all her effort would have been wasted. In fact, that seemed the most likely conclusion to all this.

Three feet more . . . two feet . . .

She was there.

She ducked her head through the damaged window and her eyes strained to penetrate the gloom. Could that be . . . ?

She slid a leg inside and probed the darkness with her foot. Nothing . . . She shifted her balance on the frame so her foot could explore a few inches lower. Her shoe scraped something. She shifted again, lowering her foot a mere quarter of an inch, but it was enough to tell her she'd found a solid floor.

She slipped inside and paused to take stock of her surroundings, which in the deep gloom was difficult. Gradually, as her eyes adapted, she saw that she was in a room littered with metal ductwork. Against the far wall she made out the dim shape of a stairway.

Moving carefully so she wouldn't trip on anything, she made her way to the stairs and followed them down into a cavernous chamber in which the last sunlight of the day filtered weakly in through a bank of windows near the roofline. In the pale light, she saw the truck she'd followed from the dairy.

With the calves right there in front of her and no one around to stop her, she could *take* one. Of course it'd be stealing. But hadn't they stolen from her? She'd have to figure out how to get a door open from inside. Maybe that'd be easy. The gate . . . There was no way she could get one through the gate . . . unless the animal was no thicker than she was, which certainly seemed possible.

Encouraged that she might be able to pull this off, she went down the steps and walked around to the side of the truck facing what light there was. She stepped up on a fender and pulled the canvas aside so she could peer in. Unable to see anything in the dark interior, she pulled her head back and worked on the canvas some more until she had tripled the size of the opening.

She looked into the truck again and took a quick breath, shocked at what she saw.

17

The truck was empty.

How could that be? She'd seen no vehicles leave but that one car, so the animals *couldn't* have been taken away. The only explanation was that there were never any animals *in* the truck.

Why the charade?

In medical school there had been the occasional test question with so little information provided that it was impossible to choose the correct diagnosis. The worst of those paled compared to this. With her head aching from the exertion of her climb to the dock roof and the intractability of the puzzle confronting her, she stepped off the truck and headed for the stairs. But a faint glint of something deeper in the building caught her eye.

She moved that way, her feet sinking in greasy sludge. The object was large, with a broad surface in front that reflected light.

She drew closer.

Lord.

It was another truck . . . *with a snow blade on it.*

It was too dark to conduct an investigation, but Holly

believed that a thorough inspection of the blade edges might find paint from the wrecked Honda.

Keenly aware that she was in a viper's nest, she hurried back to the stairs, took them to the upper room, and moved as quickly as she could through the litter to the window, her heart beating much faster than the exertion alone dictated.

Though she didn't understand the implications of her discoveries, they filled her with excitement and nervous energy so she made the descent from the roof without even noticing the pain when she banged her ankle on a loose pipe.

That was the truck that had collided with her. Trace it to the owner and she'd have 'em by the scrotum. It was a discovery that cried out to be shared. But she had no friends here and the enemy wasn't wearing uniforms.

Or were they?

She was thinking of that cop, Christianson. Logically, he would be the one to tell about the plow. But could he be trusted?

By the time she reached the Green and White, she'd concluded that she was being paranoid to suspect Christianson of complicity. She had no reason to doubt him. So it was settled. She'd call him, and they'd go back to the warehouse together before anything could be moved.

But even as she went inside, she wondered if it would be wise to go back there at all.

No. Let him go by himself.

Then she froze.

Her clothing was strewn all over the room, her suitcase upended.

They'd found her.

Frightened to the core, she grabbed the suitcase, threw it on the bed, and began snatching up her things. When she had them all, she jammed them in her suitcase, latched it, and ran to the door, where she hesitated.

Were they waiting for her outside? *Or,* a tiny voice argued, was someone hiding in the bathroom? That possibility flushed her out of the room and she bolted to the car.

She threw her bag across the console between the front seats and was inside practically before it hit the far door. Concentrating to control the tremor in her hand, she keyed the ignition, pulled it into drive, and headed for Madison, her tires spitting gravel.

It *was* him. She'd told Christianson where she was staying and they'd found her. Well, they win. She was going home, where it was safe.

Otto Christianson walked into the Lucy II and headed for the bar, where, as usual at the end of the day, every seat was taken and Eddie Spears, the bartender, was hopping. Eddie had a glass eye, but you couldn't tell unless you looked real close.

"Hey Eddie. What's the word?"

"Beer. Want one?"

"Maybe later. Did you work yesterday?"

"My wife has needs. I work *every* day."

"Did you notice a pretty blond woman with short hair in here about this time?"

"Hard *not* to notice her."

"She talk to anybody?"

He gestured toward one of the tables. "She sat with Flip and Dip over there for awhile."

"Thanks."

Otto walked over to the two men, whom he already knew. "Hello boys. How's it going?"

"Fits and starts, Otto," Gene said. "Fits and starts."

"Like his truck," Curtis added.

"Understand you two talked to the blond woman who was in here yesterday."

"I did most of the talking," Gene said. "Curtis was too tongue-tied to say much. I hear that's a sign of sexual frustration."

"Who'd know better than you?" Curtis replied.

"What did you all talk about?"

"The dairy," Curtis said. "She seemed real interested."

"She say why?"

"Don't think she did," Gene said.

"And you didn't ask."

"Never occurred to me," Curtis said.

"Me neither," Gene added. "She a wanted woman?"

Knowing that Curtis would never leave a line like that alone, he looked at his friend just as Curtis said, "By every guy in here."

The dairy and Holly remained on Otto's mind the rest of the evening. First thing the next morning he drove over to the dairy to see Don Lamotte. He found him in the parking lot, just arriving.

"Hey, Don. Good morning."

Wearing a worried expression, Lamotte froze, his hand on his car door. "Sheriff Christianson . . . is anything wrong?"

Otto walked over to Lamotte's car. "No, no. I'm just keeping my finger on the pulse of the community. But I was wondering, do you know a woman named Holly Fisher, an attractive blonde with short hair?"

"Sure don't. Why do you ask?"

"Haven't got enough important things to think about, I guess. How's the dairy business?"

"It's a lot of work and milk prices aren't what they should be, but we're doing okay."

"Glad to hear that. Don, you have a nice day."

Otto walked back to his car and got in. He waved at Lamotte and headed for the entrance, wondering if it was just his imagination that made him think Lamotte *did* know Fisher.

Aware that Holly had left the hospital, Otto drove to the Green and White, where he learned that late yesterday, the owner had seen her throw her bag in her car and leave fast, heading away from town.

Figuring she was probably returning to Memphis, Otto decided he wouldn't pursue the case. But that didn't mean he was going to forget it.

•   •   •

"Stop it," Sandy Moore said as her husband, Ryan, cupped her breasts from behind and rubbed his pelvis against her buttocks.

"What's the matter?" Ryan said, nuzzling her ear. "This is foreplay. I thought that's what women want."

"Not while I'm cooking. And besides, neither of us has time for any *after*play. Unless you want us to be late for church."

"The later the better as far as I'm concerned," Ryan said, backing off and leaning against the sink.

"Be careful," Sandy said, taking the eggs to the table. "I hear there's no football in Hell." She gave Ryan his usual three eggs and put two on her plate. "You want to get something hot, make the toast." Smiling at her own wit, she went to the fridge, where she leaned in and got the orange juice.

Suddenly, her nostrils were flooded with the smell of lemon oil and musty antique furniture: her granny's home in Toronto. How she loved to visit her as a child . . . the stuffed bear head in the study, the thick carpets that practically swallowed your shoes. And Granny would make her warm rice and honey with cream for breakfast. . . .

Sometimes the toaster ignored the setting and burned the bread, so Ryan was keeping a close eye on it when he heard a thump and a splash behind him.

Turning, he saw that Sandy had dropped the juice container. And her eyes . . .

Before he could move, her legs gave way and she began to convulse in the spilled juice.

"What's *wrong* with her?" Ryan Moore asked, his whole body pleading for answers.

Though he'd only had time to conduct a neurologic exam on Ryan's wife, Richard Heflin was extremely concerned that the onset and symptoms of Sandy Moore's illness were apparently identical to the Johannsons'. And if this was the same thing, he didn't know how to save her. The immediate question now was what to tell her husband. Rather than lay it on the line, he hedged. "It's too early to say. We've got some tests to do before we'll know."

"Will she be all right?"

"Let's just keep a good thought about that. Now, I've got to make a call to get Sandy an EEG. That's a test of how her brain is functioning."

"Oh God. Her brain?"

Richard gave Ryan's shoulder a supportive squeeze, then called the lab on the wall phone to see if the EEG tech had arrived.

"Ray, sorry to make you work on Sunday. The case I needed you for is on her way down. Give me the usual routine. I'll see you when you get her prepped." He asked the nurse in attendance to take Sandy to the lab, then turned to Ryan, who looked pretty rocky himself. Of course this might have been nothing more than a normal reaction to what was happening to his wife. But thinking of the Johannsons, Richard was afraid that if Sandy was the third case, her husband might soon be the fourth.

"Ryan, if you wouldn't mind, I'd like to examine you."

"Why?"

"Just to be sure you're okay."

"You think I might have it too?"

"At this point, I don't know. But we need to consider the possibility."

Ryan shrugged and turned his hands up in a gesture of helplessness. "Go ahead."

Richard took him to an examining room and gave him a thorough going over, which produced no signs that Ryan was ill. But the course of this disease was so rapid and so strange that Richard remained concerned.

"I'll be in the EEG lab for about thirty minutes. Then we'll talk again. There's a waiting area two doors down where you can find something to read. But why don't you take some magazines back to the nursing station and wait there. I'll tell them you're coming."

Ryan knew exactly why he suggested that. "So you're not convinced I'm okay?"

"It's merely a precaution." Actually, considering how little he'd been able to do for the Johannsons, Richard was aware that if the same disease had hold of Sandy, a nurse wouldn't be much use if it also claimed Ryan.

A half hour later, as Richard accompanied Sandy back to her room, he was deeply depressed, for her EEG was like the Johannsons' in all respects, confirming his belief that she was probably beyond help. Dreading the next few minutes, he went to the nurses' station, where he found Ryan sitting at a desk, his forehead on his folded arms.

"Ryan . . ."

In one motion Ryan was on his feet, still apparently neurologically intact, but obviously under a lot of stress.

"What did you . . ."

Richard took him by the arm. "Come on. Let's go some place quiet."

Richard led him to the empty waiting room and got him seated. Pulling a chair over so he could face him, Richard broke the bad news.

"Ryan, the EEG results were not good. Sandy's brain didn't respond at all to several kinds of stimulation, indicating that the damage is likely irreversible."

Surprisingly, instead of breaking down, Ryan's jaw set in anger and his eyes blazed. "I don't believe you. I want a second opinion." He shot to his feet and faced the door. "I want her sent to Milwaukee . . . to a *real* hospital."

"Of course that's your privilege."

His face still resolute, he turned to Richard. "Then you'll arrange it?"

"Yes."

Several hours later, a medical transport left for Milwaukee with Sandy inside. As he watched it leave, Richard sincerely hoped his prognosis was wrong. But he knew it wasn't. Sandy Moore was going to die. He was less certain about Ryan's fate. Skye's brother, Dennis, was proof that Ryan had a chance, that the disease didn't necessarily claim all members of a household. But either way, it seemed possible that Sandy Moore might not be the last victim.

18

"Doctor Heflin, I just wanted to thank you for what you did," Ryan Moore said. "I couldn't bear the thought of them cutting on her." His eyes were red and swollen and his color was awful. But so far, he had escaped the devil that had killed his wife.

"I didn't really do anything," Richard said. "The decision not to proceed was made by the medical examiner in Milwaukee."

The doctors in Milwaukee had been as puzzled over Sandy Moore's illness as Richard had, so when she'd died the previous day, they referred the case to the ME's office there, preventing her husband from claiming the body. Ryan had then called Richard and asked him to intercede. When the Milwaukee ME heard from Richard that two identical cases had already been processed by the Madison forensic office without finding any support for foul play, he released the body.

Learning from the relevant phone conversations that the neuropathology report on the Johannsons was in, Richard had asked the Madison office to fax it to him. So far, he was still waiting. He'd been about to call them again when Ryan showed up.

"I also want to apologize for doubting your judgment and asking for another doctor," Ryan said.

"You don't owe me any apology," Richard said. "Your reaction was a normal response to the situation. I wish I'd been wrong. I very much wish that."

"This is so hard," Ryan said, running his hands through his hair. "I don't want to go home because it reminds me of her, but I don't have anywhere else to go. I can't even get drunk because I always get sick first."

Keenly remembering his own feelings when Diane was killed, Richard said, "There are counselors who can help. If you like I'll find one for you."

"How can *they* do anything? They can't change what happened."

"Time will be the best healer, but believe me, they can help you over the rough spots."

"Whatever you think."

Richard wondered if it would be callous to ask Ryan a few questions that might lead to the source of the illness that had so far wrecked two families. Deciding that the stakes were so high he had to do it, he said, "Ryan, this terrible thing that happened to Sandy also happened to another couple in town, Ronnie and Skye Johannson."

"I didn't think about that," Ryan said. "We *knew* them. Or I should say, Sandy knew Skye."

This connection between the two families greatly piqued Richard's interest. "Were they good friends?"

"Ever since high school. Four or five times a year they'd spend a Saturday together, shopping, getting their hair done. I didn't much get along with Ronnie though. So we never did anything with them as two couples. But sometimes, when I'd go to Green Bay for the Packer games with my friend Doug, Sandy would spend the day over there. Like two months ago for the Denver game." Then Ryan's eyes teared up. "I never should have done that . . . you know, leave her alone just to see a football game."

This, too, was ground Richard had trod when Diane was killed. But where Ryan was letting grief twist a rea-

sonable absence into a crime, Richard was sure that his
slavish devotion to his Boston practice to the exclusion
of his family was truly culpable.

"You did nothing wrong," Richard said. "It's only the
circumstances that are making you feel that way."

"I don't know how to feel about anything now. It's
all upside down."

"Was that game the last time Sandy visited Skye?"

"Yeah. I'm sorry, but I can't answer any more questions now."

"I understand. I'll get the number of that counselor
and call you."

Ryan nodded and got out of his chair. Richard es-
corted him from the office to the waiting room. At a loss
for a parting sentiment, Richard repeated himself. "I'll
get that number and call you."

"He's feeling pretty low, isn't he?" Connie Persky observed when Ryan was gone.

"Losing your wife can have that effect on you."

Richard returned to his office, where he thought briefly
about the first time he and Diane made love. . . . The rain
and then the crickets. There was probably no one in the
world who appreciated the sound of crickets chirping like
he did.

Then his mind turned to what Ryan had said about
Sandy spending the day at the Johannsons' two months
before her illness. It seemed clear from this that the cause
of the deaths was in the Johannsons' home and that the
incubation period was around sixty days. But what was
it? The plates the health department had put out at the
Johannsons' hadn't grown anything unusual.

Connie stuck her head into the office. "Something's
coming in by fax from the Madison forensic office," she
said, waving the cover sheet from the message.

Richard jumped up from his desk and followed her to
the fax machine, which was chugging out the neuropathology report he'd been waiting for.

Sandy Moore's illness had taken the same course as
the Johannsons', so that she too died within 48 hours of

her first symptoms. And Richard still had no idea what had done it. Hoping that the answer would be in the report, he guided it from the machine and read it fast:

NEURONAL CHANGES IN BOTH BRAINS CONSISTENT WITH RECENT ISCHEMIC DAMAGE IN THE CEREBRAL CORTEX, HIPPOCAMPUS, AND CEREBELLUM. MILD PATCHY NEURONAL LOSS AND GLIOSIS PRESENT IN THE ABOVE LOCATIONS AS WELL AS BASAL GANGLIA AND THALAMUS. ETIOLOGY: UNKNOWN.

"Great," Richard said.

"What's wrong?" Connie asked.

"I don't know any more now than I did before. When's my next appointment?"

"Ten-thirty."

"I'll be in my office."

Richard went to his desk, drew the phone close, and punched in the number at the top of the report, hoping that Maurice Hamblin, the Madison office's neuropathology consultant, had some impressions about what he'd seen that he hadn't put in writing.

"Doctor Heflin calling Doctor Hamblin . . . Yes, I'll wait."

After a few bars of Mozart's *Violin Concerto #5,* Hamblin came on the line.

Richard explained who he was and said, "I just received your report on Ronnie and Skye Johannson and frankly, I'm disappointed. Not at your work, of course, but that we're still in the dark about what killed that couple. I'm calling to ask if you had any feelings about these cases you might be willing to discuss, but didn't want to put on paper."

There was silence on the other end.

"Doctor Hamblin . . ."

"Yes, I'm here. I did have one thought. The lack of

inflammation coupled with neuron loss and gliosis made me think it might be some kind of prion disease."

Richard stiffened in his chair, for the prion diseases were among the most bizarre illnesses known, causing among other syndromes Creutzfeldt-Jakob disease, a usually fatal illness that kills its victims after taking their mind and wrecking their ability to move and speak. The bizarre part was that the infectious particles are unique, consisting of only protein and containing no DNA or RNA, a proposition so scientifically heretical that the study of these particles and the diseases they produce had already generated Nobel Prizes for medicine in two different years.

"I probably shouldn't have even mentioned that," Hamblin continued. "The amount of neuron loss was so small and the reactive gliosis so limited . . ."

"Your report didn't mention any amyloid," Richard said, referring to the plaques that are present to varying degrees in prion diseases.

"There wasn't any. Of course I've seen cases of CJD that didn't look much different than what I saw in those brains."

"I've never heard of any prion disease in which the time between first symptoms and death is so rapid. Usually, it's measured in months."

"You'll have to admit that we don't know if the victims had some minor symptoms they ignored for a few months before they went into crisis. But yeah, you're right. It doesn't fit. I only mentioned it because you asked."

At this point, Richard wondered if they should look at Sandy Moore's brain. "Any chance another case would shed some light on the cause?"

"There was another one?"

"She died yesterday."

"I wouldn't think there's anything more to be learned from her brain. But if you want me to look, and someone will pick up the tab, I will. I'm really swamped with work, though, so if you need a quick turnaround, you might want to send it to someone else. Boy, three cases in two weeks. Makes you wonder."

"Doesn't it?"

Richard hung up and sat with his hand on the phone.

A prion disease. Could Hamblin be right? And this association of Sandy Moore with the two index cases . . . If it *was* a prion disease, or even if it wasn't, she'd almost certainly become exposed through her friendship with the Johannsons.

But prion diseases aren't contagious in the usual sense of the word. In fact, it's thought to be highly unlikely that an infected person could pass it to someone else through any kind of contact. Then he began to think about sexual transmission. He'd never read a word about that for prions. It would explain both Ronnie and Skye being ill, but not Sandy, unless she and Ronnie, or she and Skye . . . But if that's right, why is Ryan okay?

All this made him even more confused. But one thought sliced through that fog. *What if there will be more cases?*

Feeling that this situation should be brought to the attention of the state health department, Richard thumbed through his Rolodex for the number.

He was soon talking to the woman in charge, to whom he explained events of the past two weeks.

"So I thought I'd better let you know about this."

"I'm glad you did, Doctor Heflin. Here's what I'd like you to do, if you would. Write all this up in as much detail as possible and fax it to me, along with the neuropathology report."

As she recited her fax number, Richard jotted it down.

"We'll review the material and get back to you. In the meantime, please follow any leads you feel might be productive in pinpointing the cause of the illness."

He'd barely put the receiver down when the phone rang.

"Doctor Heflin, this is Dale Carlson."

The mayor.

"I just heard there's been another death from the

same kind of thing that killed that other couple. What's going on?"

"A question I've been asking myself."

"Is this going to be the end of it?"

"The latest victim knew the first ones and had often visited them without her husband, who appears to be okay. So for now, it seems to be centered around that first couple. Last week I had a few items from their home analyzed to see if they were contaminated with some sort of toxin, but they were all negative. Right now I don't know what's causing this thing. And without knowing that, I can't say what will happen."

On Richard's phone, the light from the other line began blinking.

"Should we contact the state health department?" the mayor asked.

"I just did. I'm going to send them a complete report."

"Good. Look, I know that Barbara Thorstadt at the *Guardian* is going to call you and ask you the same things I have. It's important that she not come away from your conversation believing that this disease will spread further, because she sure as hell will put that in the paper. I can't tell you who the company is, but I've been negotiating for over a year to get a major manufacturing plant here. And right now, things look good. But if they think there's a health risk in the area, we can forget it. So when she calls, it'd be best if you wouldn't get into too much detail with her and would express your firm belief that this was a brush fire that's now over."

"I can't do that."

"Why not?"

"It's not the truth."

"Doctor, the truth doesn't always set you free. Sometimes it backs you into a corner."

"That's where I'd be if I said it's over and we get another one."

There was a pause on the mayor's end, then he said, "All right, if you can't do what I asked, start your conversation by saying your comments will all be off the record. She'll be mad as hell, but she'll respect the convention. Will you do that?"

"Yes."

"Good man."

Then he was gone. Richard switched to the other line. "Doctor Heflin . . ."

"This is Barbara Thorstadt at the *Guardian*. Do you have a few minutes to talk about those three patients of yours who died?"

Put that way, it sounded as if he were at fault. And if she thought that now, honoring the mayor's request wasn't going to help his reputation. But he had promised. "I have time, but let's be clear on one point. Everything I say will be off the record."

"Why?"

He hadn't anticipated such a response. Well, he wasn't going to lie about that either. But before he could answer, she said it for him.

"It's Carlson, isn't it? He just called and told you to say that. Never mind, I won't put you on the spot. If that's the only way I get to hear the story, I'll take it."

Richard went over it all again and answered each of her questions truthfully.

"Thank you, Doctor. I won't put any of this in the paper, but I am going out back for a smoke, my first since I quit two years ago."

As Richard hung up, the inside line began blinking.

"Yes?"

"Your ten-thirty is here."

In Memphis, Holly Fisher was also on the phone. She'd been trying to contact Susan Morrison for several days, but the fertility clinic director hadn't been at any of her usual numbers. The receptionist at the clinic had given Holly the number of the hospital where Susan's husband was being cared for after his heart attack, but Holly hadn't felt like bothering her there. Nor had she wanted to add to Susan's burdens by leaving a message on her answering machine. Today, she'd found Susan at home.

"How's Walter?" Holly asked, hoping the news was good.

"The hospital discharged him this morning," Susan said.

"That sounds good."

"They said he had a blockage in one of the tiniest vessels that could produce symptoms. All the other vessels were clear."

"Is he moving around?"

"Like nothing happened. He has to stay home, though, for two weeks and avoid any strenuous activity. In a month, he'll start cardiac rehab."

"I'm relieved."

"In a way it was a good thing. It got his attention and showed him he has to eat better and get more exercise, the same things I've been telling him for years. Where are you?"

"In Memphis."

"Did you go to Wisconsin?"

"I was there for three days."

"I feel terrible about canceling on you like that at the last minute."

"You didn't have any choice."

"Was it a worthwhile trip?"

"There's something very strange going on at that dairy." Holly then related all that had happened to her, finishing her tale with her last act in Midland. ". . . so I ran."

"Holly, I am so sorry I wasn't there. If I had been, maybe you wouldn't have gotten hurt."

"Or *both* of us would have ended up in the hospital."

"What are you going to do now?"

"I don't know. If I had any sense, I'd just mind my own business."

"After what they did to you? . . . I'm sorry. I had no right to say that."

"It's okay. I haven't forgotten what they did. It's just

that the situation is so . . . unmanageable. I can't hand it off to the authorities up there because I don't really *know* anything, including who to trust. It's very unnerving to be in a place like that. I felt like everyone was in on it and that I was being watched wherever I went. But I'm definitely not proud of myself for giving up. Of course, it's a lot easier to be critical of past behavior when you're no longer facing the heat."

"Sounds like you've got some thinking to do."

"I guess that's right."

"I'd like to be kept apprised of any new developments."

"Glad to hear it, because I've needed a sympathetic ear."

"I want to be more than that. Call me again."

In Jackson, Susan hung up and sat wondering how she might have influenced what had happened to Holly. Would she have sensed before the truck rammed Holly's car that it was up to no good? Maybe not, but at least there would have been a second pair of eyes and another perspective in the car.

Susan thought about Walter and how much she loved him, how empty her life would be without him. At least once a year they'd make a trip out west to go fossil hunting. On those trips, the change that took place in Walter reminded her of the desert that had come alive with flowers no one had seen in a hundred years after El Niño brought the rain. He walked with a lighter step and he talked faster, showing her bits of bone, pointing out geologic strata, his eyes alert and shining. The older the rock in his hand, the more youthful he seemed.

She had clearly belonged at Walter's side the day Holly had gone to Wisconsin. But if she could have been in two places at once, she'd have taken that plane. Because she'd promised she would and because she'd longed for a crack at the arrogant thugs who had tricked her. And she still did.

• • •

When Richard Heflin was finished with his ten-thirty appointment, he called his grief counselor in Boston and got a recommendation for one in Madison. He left that name and number on Ryan Moore's answering machine, then worked for a while on his report for the health department. At noon he went out front, where he found Connie putting on her coat to go home for lunch.

"I'm booked from one to two-thirty, right?"

She agreed.

"Okay, see you then."

From the office, Richard headed to Arneson's for lunch. As he walked through the door, he saw his sister, Jessie, and her boyfriend, Artie Harris. Artie motioned him to their table.

Walking over, Richard was struck once more by the contrasts between the two. Where Jessie was a dark-haired, olive-skinned beauty with a sophisticated way of carrying herself that scared a lot of men, Artie bore a resemblance to the country singer Glen Campbell, so that seeing them together reminded Richard of the sleek big-screen TV in the Johannsons' early-American living room. A doctor in neuropharmacology and a life insurance salesman . . . What did they find to talk about? But he had to admit, Artie was a likable guy, and sometimes he'd surprise you with what he knew.

"Join us," Artie said.

"You're not going to be holding hands and exchanging adoring glances, are you?"

"We'll try to hold back," Jessie said.

Richard pulled out a chair opposite Jessie and filled it.

"When's Katie coming home?" Jessie asked.

"Not for another week."

"How are grandma and grandpa holding up?"

"I think they're having as much fun as she is."

"She *is* a doll."

Richard turned to Artie. "So how's the life insurance business? Everybody you've written policies for staying healthy?"

"Enough to keep the company solvent."

"I've been thinking that I need some more insurance. The way college costs are rising I want to be sure that if anything happens to me, Katie will be covered. What do you say, want another customer?"

"Sorry, Richard. I don't do business with friends."

"An insurance agent refusing a commission?" Richard said. "Pinch me, I'm dreaming."

"It's just a policy I have," Artie said, grinning at his own joke.

Jessie looked at Richard. "I heard another of your patients died."

"She was actually in someone else's care when it happened," Richard said. "But *I* certainly didn't help her any."

"What's going on?"

"I'm basically in the dark. But the latest case knew the first couple, so there's an association between them that I'm hoping means it's over."

"Is it some kind of virus?" Artie asked.

"I don't think so, at least not one whose behavior I understand. One member of each household where the disease struck appears okay; the wife's brother in the first home, and the husband in the second. Of course, it may be too early to proclaim either one totally in the clear."

Richard interrupted his comments to give his order to the waitress. When she moved off, he said, "A neuropathologist who examined the first couple's brains . . ." He looked at Artie. "Does this bother you?"

"Not at all."

"This guy thought it might be a prion disease."

Being involved in the R&D of depression-altering and other neuroactive drugs, Jessie knew what this was. But Artie said, "What's that?"

"A class of diseases in which neural degeneration occurs because of the accumulation in the brain of an abnormally folded version of a protein that's a normal component of nerve cells. One of the best-known examples is Creutzfeldt-Jakob disease."

"I've heard of that," Artie said. "I thought it was caused by a virus."

"We now know that's wrong. There are several ways someone can get CJD, but all of them depend on the remarkable discovery that each molecule of abnormal protein that makes up the infectious prion particle can convert lots of the normal form into the lethal version. One way this whole process can begin is by a random mutation in the pertinent gene of just one neuron, so that it begins making the abnormal protein. The abnormal molecules then spread over the brain, altering normal ones they encounter."

"And each altered molecule is capable of spreading the effect," Artie said, enhancing his reputation as an astute listener. "So you can die from only one mutation in one cell. You wouldn't think a single little mistake could cause so much trouble."

"Or, the illness can begin by the *spontaneous* folding of a normal molecule into an abnormal one," Richard said.

"Oh, that's encouraging," Artie replied.

"Abnormal molecules can also be acquired by eating an infected animal."

"Is that what they call mad cow disease?" Artie said.

"Yes."

"But nobody here can get it that last way because we've kept contaminated animals out of the country. . . ."

"Exactly," Richard said.

"That's not altogether true," Jessie said.

"What do you mean?" Richard asked.

"Where do you suppose English cows got mad cow disease?"

"I believe it was from meat and bone meal feed supplements that contained infected tissue from other cows and sheep. It's my understanding that prior to the big outbreak in the mid eighties, the disease was almost unknown. Before the outbreak, rendering plants in England used a processing technique that destroyed any prions in infected carcasses. Then, because of new government regulations for the solvents the plants had been using, they switched to a new processing technique that left prions infectious."

"Okay, so that *spread* the disease," Jessie said. "But where did the animals in the infected feed get it?"

Richard shrugged. "I suppose by random mutation of the prion gene in a few animals or by spontaneous abnormal folding of the prion protein . . . like in humans."

"And you really think English cows are more susceptible to that sort of thing than ours are?"

"We don't have mad cow disease here, so maybe that's right."

"Or maybe we *do* have it here, but it occurs at a very low incidence and just hasn't spread for some reason."

"Do you have any data to support that?"

She raised her eyebrows and paused for effect. "In nineteen eighty-five, thousands of breeders on a mink farm in Stetsonville, Wisconsin, died from prion-induced neural degeneration. And the meat in their diet came almost exclusively from fallen and sick cattle within a fifty-mile radius of the mink ranch."

"You're suggesting that my patients ate prion-infected beef?"

"Is that so crazy?"

"In one way it makes sense. The third victim spent the day at the first couple's home, so she probably ate there."

"Surely grocery stores don't sell meat from sick animals," Artie said. "Please, tell me they don't."

Jessie looked at him through the tops of her eyes. "Who knows?"

"Let's not get too carried away with this idea," Richard said. "We're forgetting a huge fact. The onset and course of the illness that killed those people is not like any known prion disease. It has to be something else . . . a toxin."

The waitress brought their food, and for a few minutes conversation flagged. Then Artie said to Richard, "If you really want to know what caused those people to die, why don't you go over to that couple's house and look around?"

"I already did."

"Maybe one of them brought it home from work in their clothes, like asbestos," Artie suggested. "Did both work?"

"She was a bank teller and he drove a truck for . . ." Richard tried to remember who Ronnie's employer was. Oh yeah. ". . . Premier Industries."

"What's their business?" Artie asked.

"They sell dog food," Richard replied.

"No they don't," Jessie said. "They *make* dog food . . . from downer cows."

19

"You said the husband drove a truck for the company . . . Did he pick up dead animals for them?" Jessie asked.

"I don't know. I thought he delivered dog food."

"Suppose he *did* pick up dead animals," Artie said. "Why on earth would anyone eat meat from a cow like that?"

"It's beyond me," Richard said. "But this is all too suggestive to ignore. Especially since I remember seeing a freezer full of meat in their home." He shoved his chair back. "I've got to make a phone call."

Richard went to the cash register, where Ted Arneson had just thanked a departing customer for coming in.

"Ted, may I use your phone?"

Arneson pushed it across the counter.

Richard called information and got the Johannsons' number. While waiting for an answer, he thought about Dennis saying that Ronnie's parents were going to sell the house. Was the meat still there? Surely they hadn't thrown it away . . . or . . . Lord, maybe they took it themselves, or Dennis had given it to the neighbors. "Come on Dennis . . . answer," he muttered.

But no one was there.

"Didn't mean to eavesdrop," Arneson said. "But you trying to find Skye Johannson's brother?"

"Yeah."

"Check the video arcade over on Jackson."

"I will. Thanks. Might as well pay my bill while I'm here. Just put all three on it."

After he'd settled up, Richard went back to the table.

"I have to go."

"Does it have anything to do with those deaths?" Jessie asked.

"I want to talk to Skye Johannson's brother."

"Mind if we go along?" She looked at Artie. "Or would you rather stay here and finish your lunch?"

"After all that talk about prions, I'm not real hungry."

"I might not be able to find him," Richard said.

"We won't hold it against you," Jessie said.

"Let's go then. Everything's paid for here."

Considering that it was the middle of a school day, business was good at the Kaleidoscope and the place was filled with the sound of ray guns, racing engines, and explosions. The clientele was exclusively male, most of them probably from the community college nearby.

"Losers in the making," Artie observed.

"But we'll soon be a country with great hand-eye co-ordination," Jessie said.

Richard spotted Dennis sitting at the wheel of a racing car simulator, trying to keep his virtual vehicle from hitting bouncing tires and the occasional pileup. "There he is."

Jessie and Artie followed Richard to where Dennis was concentrating so hard on the track in front of him, he wasn't aware of their presence. Richard put a hand on Dennis's shoulder. "Hello, Dennis."

Startled, Dennis flinched, sending his racecar into a wall.

"Hi, Doctor Heflin. I didn't know you liked video games."

"I came to see *you*."

"Why?"

"Could we talk outside where it's quieter?"

"Sure."

On the sidewalk Richard introduced Jessie and Artie. Undecided whether he should bow or shake hands, Dennis did both.

"How have you been?" Richard asked.

"I got a job deliverin' papers. And afternoons I clean up around Floramania . . . that's a flower shop."

"Are you still living at home?"

"For now. Ronnie's parents are still plannin' to sell it, but there's been some kind of delay. I don't know why."

"Do you remember all the meat in the freezer at home?"

"Yeah, Ronnie got that."

"Where?"

"At the dairy."

"What were the circumstances?"

"What do you mean?"

"Did he buy a cow from the dairy?"

"Got it free."

"Why was it free?"

"They didn't want it anymore."

"Was it dead when Ronnie picked it up?"

"That's the only kind he carries in his truck."

Richard glanced at Jessie, grimly acknowledging that she'd apparently been right. "So it was supposed to go to the company where Ronnie worked?"

"Ronnie said I shouldn't tell anybody."

"It's okay, Dennis. Nothing can happen to Ronnie if you tell me."

"Are you sure?"

"There's not a doubt in my mind."

Dennis thought about this, then said, "The man at the dairy said it wasn't givin' enough milk to pay for feedin' it. Ronnie figured it was too good for dog food, so he brought it home."

This didn't sound to Richard like the cow was overtly

ill. But its falloff in milk production could have meant that it was, and they'd simply killed it before more obvious symptoms appeared. "When did all this happen?"

"Not too long ago."

"Do you remember what sports were on TV around the time he brought it home?"

Again Dennis lapsed into thought. "Ronnie likes the Packers. So do I."

"Had the Packers played any games before he brought it home?"

Dennis searched his thin mind. "Exhibition game . . . Against New Orleans. They won twenty to thirteen."

So the meat had come into the house around two months ago. "Dennis, do you remember Sandy Moore?"

"Skye's friend."

"Did she ever have a meal with all of you?"

"I remember once."

"What did you have?"

"Everybody else had steaks. But Skye made me spaghetti, on account of I don't eat meat. It plugs me up."

It was all falling together. The cow Ronnie had picked up was the cause. "Is the rest of the meat from that cow still in the freezer at home?"

"I didn't eat any."

"Could we have a package to see if that's what made Ronnie and Skye sick?"

"If you want."

"Do you mind coming with us now to get it?"

"Will you bring me back here?"

"Absolutely."

After picking up the package of meat, it occurred to Richard that Ronnie hadn't butchered the animal himself. To his great surprise, Dennis knew the name of the man who had. Aware that prions cannot be inactivated by soap and water, Richard feared that the butcher's equipment would contaminate everything else he worked on. They therefore, set out to find the man.

Following Dennis's directions, they went to three wrong locations. On the fourth try, with Richard's patience nearly at an end, they found him. Thankfully, he was a retired butcher, who had kept all his equipment and only "put on the apron," as he phrased it, when the odd job came his way. He verified that around the first of September, Ronnie had paid him forty dollars to butcher a "fairly small" cow. To Richard's great relief, the equipment hadn't been used since. Though the butcher didn't fully understand what all the fuss was about, he agreed to let Richard show him how to disinfect everything later that evening.

By this time, Richard was already ten minutes late for his one o'clock. As he let Dennis out of the car back at the Kaleidoscope, he felt his pager vibrating. . . . Connie trying to find him.

"Thanks, Dennis," Richard said. "Good luck with your new jobs and remember, don't do anything with that meat until you hear from me. If Ronnie's parents want to take it or discard it or do *anything* with it, tell them to call me."

When the car door had shut behind Dennis, Jessie said, "I want to do it."

"Do what?" Richard asked, looking across the front seat at her.

She patted the package of frozen beef in her lap. "The animal testing on this to prove it's the source of the illnesses. We've got everything I need at the lab." In response to his blank stare, she added, "That *is* the next step."

"But why do *you* want to get involved?"

"Richard, you said yourself, there's never been a prion disease as aggressive as what you've seen in these cases. If that's what it is, this is huge. Why *wouldn't* I want to work on it?"

"Is it really your call?" Richard asked. "Don't you have to clear this with someone at work if you're going to be using their equipment and supplies?"

"Of course."

"Suppose they refuse?"

"I'll *get* permission."

"Won't it be dangerous?" Artie asked.

"Prions aren't like tropical viruses. A few sensible precautions, everything will be fine. These diseases really aren't easy to transmit."

"What if it's not a prion disease?" Richard said.

"Dennis has lived in the house where it started and he's fine. So is Sandy Moore's husband. Whatever we're dealing with isn't airborne or infectious in the usual sense."

"If you're sure this is what you want," Richard said.

"You bet it is."

In a glass case under the big windows in Zane Bruxton's office sat an "ancient" device for purification of nucleic acids. One of the first of its kind, it stretched ten feet from end to end: two miles of glass tubing bent into repetitious little coils that made it look impossibly complex. Across the room, a Civil War doctor's kit was displayed in another glass case on a French pedestal. Scattered among the leather volumes on the shelves behind Bruxton was his collection of old microscopes. His desk itself was a display case, featuring a couple of original drawings of the circulation by William Harvey, its discoverer. As Jessie sat waiting for Bruxton to finish whatever he was writing, she found herself wondering if he might have a freeze-dried Nobel laureate or two in the closet. She'd been fortunate in getting to see him just hours after acquiring the suspect meat from the Johannsons' freezer.

"Now, Doctor Heflin," Bruxton said, closing the file folder in front of him and putting his pen in the holder on his desk. "What can I do for you?"

"Are you aware of the three people in town who, within the last two weeks, all died of the same illness?"

"This is the first I've heard of it."

"There's a good chance the source of their sickness was a cow carcass that should have gone to the dog food plant but instead ended up on the dinner table of the victims."

"What was the origin of this cow?"

"The Midland dairy. It was supposedly killed because it was no longer producing enough milk. But we think that might have just been the first symptoms of a serious illness."

"We?"

"My brother Richard. You met him at the dedication of the MRI. He was wondering about the pricing of Vasostasin."

"I remember."

"The three people who died were his patients."

"So they were neurologic cases."

"That's right. The neuropathologist who looked at the brains of the first two who died thinks there's a chance they might have had a prion disease."

"Like Creutzfeldt-Jakob."

"Yes and no. Like it in the sense of being prion induced, but very much different in the speed with which death follows the first symptoms."

"What does this have to do with me?"

"I'd like to use the facilities here to test the meat from the cow in question."

"What kind of tests?"

"I want to inject extracts of the meat into mice and see if they get the disease."

"Why would I agree to this?"

"First, it would be a humanitarian gesture to the community in the same spirit that moved you to give the hospital that MRI."

"And?"

"If this turns out to be a new prion disease, the world will forever know that it was discovered at Bruxton Pharmaceuticals."

"And such a discovery would no doubt enhance your résumé immensely."

"No doubt."

"Ambition is a fine thing, but it *can* be dangerous."

"What do you mean?"

He waved at the volumes on his bookshelves. "History is replete with examples of scientists who thought they were the hunters but became the hunted."

"You mean they contracted the disease they were studying."

He nodded.

"There's not much danger of that here. Prions are tough to destroy, but they're pretty safe to work with. I don't think there's a single instance of a scientist who's worked on them contracting a prion disease."

Bruxton got out of his chair, went to the windows, and looked out while Jessie waited for his answer. He had a reputation for making quick decisions. It was said that he usually knew his position on an idea or proposal even before it had been fully presented. This delay seemed like a good sign.

Finally, without turning to look at her, Bruxton said, "Use the empty lab down the hall from yours. The hood there has a HEPA filter. Involve no one else in the work and speak to no one about it. If knowledge of your project gets back to me from any source within the company, I'll terminate it. That's all."

As soon as Jessie was out the door, Bruxton doubled over in pain. He hadn't turned toward her because he was afraid she'd see it on his face. He staggered to his desk and dropped into his chair, sweating profusely.

His life now was a shadow, a spectral alias of what he'd been, but it *was* life and he clung to it. Jessie's belief that his slow response to her request represented indecision was wrong. Nor was the delay related to his pain. He'd known from the instant he'd heard the details that the work had to be done here. But it wouldn't have made sense for him to agree quickly.

To make a fortune, and keep it, required intelligence and a relentless amount of hard work. Bruxton had never underestimated the additional role of luck in his success and had gradually come to view the inability of Vasostasin to control his type of cancer as movement toward a cosmic equilibrium. But now, with the situation Jessie had laid in front of him, whatever force was sending him to his grave and had lately been plaguing him with unexpected crises, wiped his brow and gave him succor.

20

Jessie picked up a Ketamine-anesthetized mouse and began taping it to the oak board she'd found in her garage.

After her meeting yesterday with Bruxton, she'd told Richard the good news, then gone to her computer and combed the prion literature looking for papers that might contain some technical hints on how to obtain the quickest test results. She'd taken a list of promising papers to the company library and located the full articles. The best advice she'd found was rather obvious: inject the test material into the animal's brain.

She'd spent the morning rounding up the things she'd need and arranging them in the lab Bruxton had told her to use. Now, just twenty-four hours after this opportunity had presented itself, she was within minutes of making the first injection.

She wished there were some alternative to the use of animals to obtain the information she needed. But exposing the extract to cells in culture wouldn't tell her enough. She had to see what, if any, neurologic effects were produced by the extracts. Only if the human illness was reproduced in her test animals would she know whether she had found the infectious agent.

The first strip of duct tape went across the animal's snout. The second, she placed well behind its eyes so about half the head was exposed. She took the pinioned animal to the laminar flow hood and flicked off the UV light that had sterilized the work area. She placed the animal inside the hood on the stainless steel work surface, then went to the refrigerator and got the extracts she'd prepared from a small sample of the suspect meat and from a similar sample of meat she'd bought at a grocery.

She placed both extracts in the hood next to the sterile Hamilton syringes she'd use for the injection. Mice are notably resistant to bacterial infection. Even so, Jessie had sterilized everything she'd use, including the extracts, which she'd passed through a bacterial exclusion filter.

Her first objective was simply to prove that the meat was the source of the illness that had killed Richard's patients. Once that was established, she could devise further experiments to clarify the nature of the causative agent. So in this first set of animals, she would inject six mice with an unmodified extract from the suspect meat, and six more with extract from the purchased meat.

She surveyed the contents of the hood to make sure everything she'd need was inside. Satisfied, she sat down, donned a jeweler's headset with magnifying lenses, and reached for a cotton swab, which she dipped in 95% alcohol. After disinfecting the fur on the top of the animal's head with the swab, she made a midline scalpel incision in the skin and pulled the edges back with tiny retractors. It took less than twenty seconds to bore through the bone to the animal's brain using a Dremel Moto Tool in a procedure so bloodless she didn't even need the battery-operated cautery pen she'd had standing by.

With a Hamilton syringe, she carefully injected a tenth of a microliter of extract into the mouse's brain. She finished by pressing a dollop of bone wax into the skull hole, then removed the skin retractors and brought the edges of the cut tissue together. A little Crazy Glue along the incision and she was done.

An hour later, as she put the last animal back in its box, the first one she'd operated on stirred to life. In a few seconds it was mousing around as though nothing had happened. By the time she'd finished cleaning and putting things away, there were three more awake and moving.

Now, it was up to them.

When Holly had returned from Wisconsin she'd wanted nothing more to do with that part of the country. But her conversation with Susan Morrison had brought it all back so that even by the next day it provided a subtext to everything she did, like a weather advisory crawling across the bottom of her perceptions. As a result, she'd remembered that the pictures of the dairy cows she'd taken were still undeveloped. Figuring that since she'd gone to so much trouble to take them, she at least ought to get some prints, she drove straight home from the office at the end of the day and located the camera. She dropped it off at a nearby shop that offered one-hour service, then spent that hour having dinner at her favorite Vietnamese restaurant on Cleveland, an area fast becoming Little Asia.

She'd known even before taking them that whatever made those cows so special might not be obvious from pictures. It was also possible that if there *was* a clue on the pictures, it would take an expert on cows to see it. Nevertheless, upon arriving home with the prints, she turned on the light over the kitchen table and sat down to see what she had.

She'd never used a disposable camera before and was surprised at the quality of the pictures, all of which were bright and clear. She would have preferred that the chain-link fence between the cows and the camera not be there, but she quickly learned to look past it.

By the time she'd gone through the first dozen pictures, the only thing she'd seen of any interest was a cow that had a black spot on its flank that reminded her of the nucleus on a monocyte: a white blood cell whose nucleus is usually shaped like a kidney bean.

A few minutes later, she saw another cow with a very similar pattern. Then, in the next to last picture, another one. She placed this third one on the table and sorted back through the pile to find the other two, which she put beside the third. In all three, the spot on the flank was an oval with its long axis running vertically and the kidney bean indentation facing the tail. But the margins of the spot and the depth of the indentation were slightly different on each animal. With the three pictures in front of her, she saw that the animals had other spots in common as well. In fact, *all* their spots were nearly identical.

Curious about the rest of the animals, she found a distinctive black neck spot on one of the remaining cows, then searched the pile until she found a match. Here again, the other spots on both animals also matched.

Entering into this exercise in earnest, Holly spent the next twenty minutes sorting the pictures into piles of similarly spotted animals. When she was finished, her thirty-six photos lay in twelve stacks—two of them containing five animals each, six with three animals, and four with two animals. She remembered Gene, the dairy hand, saying that he was having a hard time learning to recognize individual cows in the herd. Was this why? If it was, that meant in other Holstein herds the spotting patterns were more variable.

How could she find out about that?

She got up from her chair, went to the cupboard, and took out the heavy ceramic mug she favored.

The Internet . . . She could do a search for Holsteins.

She spooned some powdered hot chocolate mix into the mug and filled it with hot water. After stirring it, she put it in the microwave for twenty seconds. While it heated, she went into her study and turned on the computer.

By the time she returned with her hot chocolate, the computer was booted and ready. She sat down, logged on to the Netscape home page, and selected the AltaVista search engine. In the search blank she typed "Holsteins," then picked up her hot chocolate and sat back to wait.

The search produced 12,179 hits. She scanned the first group and clicked on "Absher Holsteins." The first page that came up gave her a variety of choices: Bulls, Heifers, Embryos, Cows, Contact Us. She chose Cows.

This called up a table listing the names of twenty-three cows along with the name of the bull who sired them. For each animal there was also a pedigree number, some pregnancy information she didn't understand, *and a link to a picture.*

She clicked the picture link for Maria.

An image unrolled itself down the screen, showing a mostly white cow with a black Rorschach spot on its side and some black spatter on its rump.

Would the image print?

She called up the print control panel and clicked the command.

In about a minute, her printer delivered a beautiful picture of the cow on her screen. Over the next half hour, she printed all twenty-three pictures.

The spotting pattern on some of the animals was wildly individual. A few had a pattern that was superficially similar to another animal in the group, but there were always some distinctive differences. She returned to the list her search had produced and chose another entry.

By nine-thirty, she had pictures of ninety-seven cows from five different herds. In all those animals there were no two as similar as the groups she'd found in her own pictures.

What was the deal with those cows at the Midland dairy?

Then she had an idea that would explain things. But how could she know if she was right? Returning to the search engine, she typed "veterinary schools" in the blank.

For the next forty-five minutes she explored vet school home pages, from which she extracted the names of four experts in cow genetics. Figuring that she ought to be able to contact at least one of them in the morning, she shut off the computer and went to bed.

"Susan . . . Holly again. I've learned something. I didn't tell you this in our last conversation, but when I was in Wisconsin, I took some pictures of the cows from that dairy to see if I could determine why they were so special that the new owners replaced the whole herd when they took over.

"Well, I discovered that the pigmentation pattern on those animals falls into twelve groups . . . at least I found twelve on my set of pictures. In every group, the pattern is almost identical. And in looking at nearly a hundred pictures of Holsteins that I printed from the Internet, I saw no such similarity."

"So the animals in each set of your pictures must be genetically more closely related than those in the other herds," Susan said.

"Much closer. I faxed photocopies of my pictures to a bovine geneticist at the University of Texas and he said that the animals in each set had either been bred for many generations to have similar spotting patterns, or to possess some trait that sits very close to the genes that regulate spotting pattern. Or each set of similar animals is a clone."

"Which explanation did he favor?"

"Because the spotting patterns were *so* similar, he thought they were likely clones."

"How many animals does that dairy have?"

"Seventeen hundred."

"If the pictures you took are representative of the entire herd, there could be at least a hundred cows in each clone. What did the geneticist think of that?"

"We didn't get into numbers."

"I could see how it'd be possible to produce a small number of identical animals by separating the first few cells of an embryo and letting them develop independently in surrogate females. That technique has been around for years. But to get a hundred identical animals, they'd have to grow a lot of cells from the desired individual in culture and for each clone, transplant a nucleus from one of the cultured cells into an egg stripped of its own nucleus."

"Like those Scottish researchers made Dolly."

"Right. But it took nearly three hundred attempts to produce her. And the success rate for nuclear transfer is still extremely poor. So if that dairy has twelve different clones with a hundred or more animals in each clone, they either know something about the technique no one else does, or they want those clones badly enough to work like the devil to produce them. I don't know anything about the dairy business, but maybe those animals are such superior milk producers that it's *worth* the time and money to clone them."

"But those two dairy hands I talked with said they're *not* better producers. For the entire herd, the yield is *down*. And they aren't more efficient at converting food to milk either."

"Then why go to the trouble and expense of cloning them?" Susan asked. "And why are there twelve clones instead of just one?"

"Vexing questions, I agree."

21

Jessie wasn't able to check on the mice she'd injected until ten-fifteen the next morning. Looking into the cage containing the first two that had received the suspect extract, she saw a pair of mice that looked active and well, no signs of neurologic problems. She hadn't expected any effects to show up this early, but she was still disappointed. The pair in the second cage were apparently just as healthy. But in the third cage, the wound on one of the pair was gaping, probably the result of a nocturnal scrap with his cagemate. She didn't have time today to fool with this, but that wound *had* to be closed.

After checking the six control animals, which were all doing fine, she loaded a 1-cc disposable syringe with Ketamine and gave the animal needing repair enough anesthetic to knock him out. While waiting for the anesthetic to take effect, she got everything ready for regluing the incision, then took a break for a pit stop.

When she returned, she found the injected animal lying motionless on the bottom of his cage. Donning the jeweler's magnifiers, she carried him to the hood, where she flicked off the sterilizing UV light, placed the animal inside on his belly, and sat down.

Before applying the glue, she had to appose the edges of the wound. As she leaned over and focused on the incision, she saw something inexplicable. . . .

There was no bone wax on this animal's skull. *And no hole.*

How could that be? She couldn't have neglected to drill this animal. She'd done them one after the other, and there were only twelve. It just couldn't happen.

Wondering now about the rest, she got up and went for the Ketamine.

Ten minutes later, she cursed under her breath as she opened the incision of a second mouse and found, like the first, no hole in the skull. She looked at one more, then began to pace the floor, wondering what to do.

Finally, she reglued the incisions on all the mice she'd examined and put them back in their cages. Not wanting to use any phone in the building, she returned to her primary lab, grabbed her coat, and told her techs she had to run an errand.

She drove to Richard's office and burst into the waiting room.

"Is my brother available?"

"He's with a patient," Connie said. "Why don't you go back and wait in his office, and I'll tell him you're here."

Jessie quickly found that she was too keyed up to sit, so while she waited for Richard, she paced. Then she scanned his bookshelves, so distracted that none of the titles there made it to her brain.

She could hear the murmur of Richard's voice in the examining room next door, but couldn't understand what he was saying.

The murmuring stopped.

Was that it? Was he finished?

It began again.

She picked a book from the shelf and flipped through it looking for pictures. After a minute or so, she heard the examining room door open and Richard say, "If that persists, you let me know."

Finally, he came into his office.

"What's going on?" he said. "You can't have results *this* soon."

Jessie shut the door behind him. "While I was looking at the animals this morning, I noticed that the incision on one had come open. When I tried to seal it I discovered there was no hole in the skull."

"What do you mean no hole?"

"I drilled a small hole in each animal's skull so I could inject the extract into the brain. . . . It's the best way. But this animal's skull was intact. And so were the skulls of two other animals I checked. Someone replaced my animals with shams."

"Who?"

"I have to believe it was Bruxton. Not him directly, but on his orders."

"That doesn't seem likely."

"Who else could it be? He's the only one there who knows what I'm doing. He forbade *me* to mention it to anyone."

"It's possible *he* let it slip."

"I don't think he ever says anything he doesn't intend to. But okay, let's say he did. What's the point of the switch?"

"It'd be a good way to make us think that dead cow was harmless. You get no results, we give up the idea. Who has something to lose if that cow *is* the cause?"

"The dairy where it died," Jessie said. "If that cow was sick, others in the herd might be as well. People hear about that, nobody will buy their milk."

"Does this mean that whoever did it knows the cow carried the disease that killed my patients?"

"Or they're just afraid it *might* have."

"On the other hand, maybe this is just a malicious prank by someone at work who doesn't like you."

"I can't imagine who that would be."

"We don't always know who dislikes us."

"I don't think it's that. But right now it's irrelevant. We have to redo the test . . . somewhere else."

"Where?"

Jessie thought a moment. "I can prepare the samples at work, but I'll do the injections and keep the animals in the apartment over my garage. It's empty now."

"What's to keep whoever interfered with the experiment at work from doing the same thing again?"

"I'll put Fitzie on a long chain by the apartment stairs and I'll rig some tricks in the apartment so I'll know if anyone altered anything. I'm going to pretend that I think the replaced animals at work are the ones I started with, so Bruxton won't know I found out. And we're not going to tell *anyone* about the new tests."

"Not that I think he'd spread it around, but it might be hard to keep it from Artie."

"I can do it."

"Where's the meat we got from Dennis?"

"In my freezer at work."

"We can't use that."

"Oh, right. It might have been replaced too. We'll have to get another sample."

"I've got a patient waiting, but if you want to pick it up, I'll see if Dennis is home."

"Call him. Then we have to figure out where to get some test animals and cages. I don't want to take anything obvious from work."

By now, Richard had committed the Johannsons' number to memory. On the third ring, he looked at Jessie. "He may be back at the . . . Dennis . . . this is Doctor Heflin. Are you going to be there for a few minutes? My sister would like to come by and pick up another package of that meat if it's okay."

Jessie saw Richard's mouth gape in a look of surprise.

"What?" she said.

He put his hand over the receiver's mouthpiece. "Dennis had a burglary. They took the VCR and a radio, and emptied the freezer." Removing his hand, he said, "Okay Dennis, thanks. Sorry about your losses." He hung up and looked at Jessie, "Considering what happened to your animals, it's pretty obvious the VCR and the radio were just to cover what they really wanted."

"So now they've got us," Jessie said, glumly.

"It doesn't look good. But I wonder . . ." He drifted away for a few seconds, staring at air. "After a cow is butchered, there's a lot left. I wonder where the remains of the Johannson animal are?"

"Richard, it's been over *two months*."

"I agree, if we find it, it won't be pretty, but if there *were* any prions in the carcass, chances are they'll still be active."

"Oh, we're gonna need a *lot* of luck on this one."

"I don't know what else to do."

Jessie turned her palms up and shrugged. "So call the butcher."

"I think we should talk to him personally. He might need his memory jogged. We can do that better if we're there with him. I can probably go in twenty or thirty minutes. Want to hang around?"

"Hope you've got some good magazines out there."

Buck Lundval, the retired butcher, lived outside of town in a mobile home on a hundred-acre hobby farm on which he raised pigs. The smell from these creatures was so strong, Richard could almost see it enveloping the farm like a giant dome. They found Lundval loading ears of corn from a small picker into a conveyor that carried it up to the top of his corn crib and dumped it inside.

"Mr. Lundval, how are you?" Richard said loudly, extending his hand.

Lundval turned off the conveyor and stiffly shook Richard's hand. Thin and rangy like a mountain spruce growing out of a rock, he was at least sixty with long windblown silvery hair. "I'd be better if I could get my work done."

"This is my sister, Jessie."

Lundval tilted his head. "Ma'am."

"I'm sorry to bother you again," Richard said. "But I've got an important question to ask."

"Could have already done it," Lundval said.

"What happened to the carcass of the cow you butchered for Ronnie Johannson?"

Lundval's already grim face darkened. "If I'da known that animal was gonna lead to this much trouble, I wouldn't have touched it. Hasn't been two hours ago the health department was here asking the same thing."

His hopes of finding the carcass even dimmer now than when they'd come up the driveway, Richard looked at Jessie. "I never told the health department on the phone who butchered the animal and my full report is still on my desk. I was going to go over it one more time and send it today." He turned back to Lundval. "What did these people look like?"

"A woman and two men. She was thin and dark-haired. Had it pulled back in a bun. Kind of a snotty attitude, like I was something she stepped in."

Despite this rudimentary description, Richard looked at Jessie to see if she might know the woman, but she merely shrugged. He turned back to Lundval. "What about the men?"

"I dunno . . . She did the talking. Didn't pay much attention to anybody else."

"What did you tell them?"

"That I'd buried it out back." He turned and pointed to a scrubby field beyond the pigsty. "Next to those two big oaks."

"They took it?"

"Had me show 'em the exact spot and they dug it up. Wore rubber gloves and a mask like they were operating on somebody. Put it all in heavy black plastic bags, packed 'em in the trunk of their car, and drove off without even thanking me."

"What did you do with the animal's blood?"

"Poured it into the hole before I threw the carcass in."

Afraid to hear the answer, Richard asked, "Did they also take the blood-soaked dirt?"

"Every bit of it."

So that was it. Without the carcass there was no way

to prove it was infectious. The best Richard could do was describe in his report how someone had interfered with his investigation and hope the real health department would find that sufficient cause to inspect the dairy's animals. Knowing how bureaucracies function, he had strong doubts they'd move on such circumstantial evidence.

"Well, Mr. Lundval, thanks for letting us interrupt your work. We'll leave and let you get back to it."

"See now, if that woman had been as civil as you are, I might not have let her take the wrong carcass."

22

"Are you saying the remains of the animal you butchered for Ronnie Johannson are still here?" Richard said.

"About thirty yards from where those other people dug," Lundval replied.

"Will you show us the spot?"

"No point in my saying what I did if I wouldn't. You want to dig it up, I'll lend you some shovels."

"Did you leave the brain?" Jessie asked

"Not many folks around here eat brains. Don't care for 'em myself."

"By now, there can't be much left of the brain," Richard said to Jessie. "And it'll be hell to get inside that thick skull."

"But whatever shape it's in, any prions should still be active and that's where the highest concentration would have been," Jessie said. "And we can go in through an eye with a long needle and wash out the cranial cavity."

"There's already a hole in the skull," Lundval said.

"What kind of hole?" Richard asked.

"Bullet."

"That hole will be easier to use than an eye," Jessie said. "But I've got to gather up some materials first."

"And we should change clothes," Richard added.

"Do you remember where the head is?" Richard asked.

"About right there," Lundval said, pointing.

"How deep?"

"Ain't easy digging a hole big enough to hold the leftovers of a cow."

Seeing that this was all he was going to get, Richard pulled his surgical mask up over his mouth and nose and walked to the edge of the burial scar in the earth, where he drove the blade of his shovel into the ground with his foot.

When Jessie figured out that his intention was to dig a semicircular trench around the plot's periphery, she joined in at the opposite end of the arc.

Fifteen minutes later, when they had produced a continuous trench a foot deep, they paused to catch their breath.

"Didn't have any help when *I* dug that hole," Lundval observed from the folding chair he'd brought out from the house. He seemed to have lost interest in getting his corn into the crib.

The human sense of smell is generally able to adapt to noxious odors so that with continual exposure, the intensity fades. This did not apply to the stench from Lundval's pigs, which easily penetrated Richard and Jessie's surgical masks and filled their lungs with each labored breath they took. And it was a cool day. Had it been summer, they'd have needed scuba gear to breathe.

Wanting this to be over, Richard returned to work and began scraping dirt from the center of the plot into the trench. With Jessie's help, they soon uncovered a white ear. A little more work brought the top of a mangy black head and snout into view. The cool temperatures of fall had slowed the decomposition process so that the flesh on the head was pretty much intact.

Now that he knew exactly where things were, Richard

drove his shovel into the earth next to the cow's massive head and levered it upward, raising two sunken sightless eyes to the surface, like some weird land crocodile looking for prey.

"We could use a broom," Jessie said to Lundval.

"Don't have one I'd want to use on that," he said. He got out of his chair, took a jackknife from his overalls, and walked over to a tall stand of dried grass, where he harvested a fistful and brought it to Jessie. "Don't have to buy everything you need from a store."

With the grass, she whisked the dirt from the cow's head, looking for the bullet hole.

"Wasn't on that side," Lundval said after she'd worked a while without finding it.

After moving to the correct side, she located it in about two minutes: a dirt-filled depression just behind the cow's ear. She moved her box of supplies in close and cleared the dirt and tissue debris from the bullet hole with the wooden handle of a cotton swab. Then she reinserted the handle and slid it deeper into the hole, feeling around for the brain. But the skull seemed empty.

There was no way to know the exact condition of the cow's brain after two months in the ground. It had probably been reduced to a liquid or had dried into a shriveled little ball like the orange Jessie had once mistakenly left in her high school locker the entire year. Either of these possibilities would explain why she hadn't felt it with her probe.

With her money on the liquid possibility, Jessie wedged the female end of a long, large-bore needle into a length of plastic tubing. She attached the other end of the tubing to the tip of a turkey baster she'd added to her supplies from her kitchen at home. She inserted the needle into the bullet hole until only a small amount of the shaft was still visible. Then she pumped the rubber bulb on the baster.

This drew nothing from the cranial cavity but air. So, if the brain was still liquid, there wasn't enough volume for her to find it. But that was easy enough to fix.

From her box of supplies, she took out a large plastic bottle of saline solution and unscrewed the top. She put the needle into the saline, filled the baster, and discharged the contents into the cow's cranial cavity. She did this twice more, then tried again to collect fluid from the skull. This time when she pumped the rubber bulb, a dingy liquid moved up the plastic tubing into the baster. To make sure she was getting a well-mixed sample, she discharged the captured brain soup back into the skull, then again drew as much of it into the baster as she could get.

She put this material into a series of plastic vials and screwed on their blue caps. In the interest of safety, she slipped each of the capped vials into a larger vial, which she also sealed. The contaminated needle was treated the same way. Needing larger containers for the baster and the plastic tubing, she used double zip-top plastic bags for those. After wiping the outer vials and bags with a prion-inactivating solution, she carefully removed her rubber gloves and dropped them into a plastic bag that Richard held out for her. This too, was double-bagged.

She and Richard then held a short conference, speaking quietly so Lundval couldn't hear.

"What should we do with the carcass?" Jessie asked.

"Do you have all the sample you're ever going to need?"

"I've got a lot, but I'd hate to do something irrevocable here and not be able to get more."

"Then let's just cover it up."

"Suppose the people who were here earlier discover they've got the wrong carcass?"

"I don't want to dig this whole thing up and then have to hide it somewhere. They won't even look at what they got. They'll just dispose of it."

"Then for now, we leave it."

Assuming for the sake of safety that the carcass truly was infectious, while Richard reburied it, Jessie explained to Lundval that he shouldn't disturb it and should stake a plastic cover over the spot so nothing further from the site could leach into the groundwater. Before leaving, Richard wiped the shovels down with inactivating solution.

When they were back in the car, Jessie said, "Now we need some animals and cages."

"How about the pet store on Lincoln?" Richard said.

"Someplace in Madison would be better. Can you take care of that? I have to get back to work."

"What do you need?"

Without the Bruxton vivarium backing them up, Jessie decided to buy a few more mice than she'd used the last time. "Get sixteen mice and eight cages." She picked her handbag off the floor and fished around in it until she came up with a set of keys. She removed one from the ring and handed it to Richard. "This opens the door to the apartment over my garage. When you get the animals, put them in the kitchen. Leave the key under the flowerpot at the foot of the stairs."

"I think she'd like that one," Otto Christianson said, pointing at an old print showing two apples on a branch and another split in half. His wife's birthday was coming fast and he'd asked Charles Hallock to bring over some prints that would look good in a kitchen.

"There's a matching one in here somewhere," Hallock said, flipping through his pile.

As he worked, Otto noticed that Hallock's left little finger stuck out at an odd angle. The old Otto, before he'd embarked on his efforts at self-restraint, would have asked Hallock what had happened. But the new Otto kept quiet.

"Here it is." Hallock pulled out another apple print with the same colors in it, but with the fruit arranged differently. "If you have the room, these complement each other nicely."

"How much for the pair?"

Hallock cited a price that made Otto wince, but Frannie was hard to buy for and he'd never find anything *else* in the time left.

"Does that include framing?"

"Sorry, framing's extra."

"You're a hard man."

"It's a hard world, Otto."

"Will you take care of the framing?"

"Do you know what you want?"

"How about you come to the house, take a look at the kitchen, and you decide. And tell me if I picked wrong."

"When?"

"She'll be at bingo tonight. Come over around seven-thirty."

"I'll be there."

"Can it be ready by Tuesday?"

"Jesus, Otto, you waited kind of late to do this, didn't you?"

"I thought the customer was always right."

"Oh, you're doing the right thing. I just could have used a little more time. But I'll get it done."

Hallock gathered up his prints and left. With that out of the way, Otto felt that even if he didn't do another constructive thing all day, he'd have had a good one. But there was one other important thing on his agenda.

"I'm sorry, but Doctor Bruxton has left for the day," his secretary said.

"Is he at home?" Otto asked.

"I'm not free to say. Would you care to make an appointment?"

"That's okay. Thanks for your time."

Otto left Bruxton's office and headed for the exit. He could have saved himself the wasted trip by calling Bruxton and asking him the questions on his mind, but he always felt dissatisfied with any conversation that wasn't face to face. He probably could have intimidated Bruxton's secretary into telling him where Bruxton was, but that might have gotten her into trouble. So, he'd just drive over to Bruxton's home and see for himself if he was there.

Twenty minutes later, Otto pulled up to the wrought-iron gates across the entrance to Bruxton's estate and pressed the button on the speaker mounted on a pole at window level. High on the cut-stone column supporting the left gate, a TV camera stared down at him.

"Yes?" a cold voice said from the speaker.

Forty years ago, Otto would have given in to the thought that flashed through his head at that instant and he'd have said, "I'd like a Big Mac and a large order of fries." But the acquisition of responsibilities and two arthritic knees takes the impishness out of a man. So he just said, "Sheriff Christianson here to see Doctor Bruxton."

After a short wait, the gates swung open and Otto went in. He had read once that there were two levels of society whose homes were largely unseen: the poorest because they live in sewers and cardboard boxes in dark alleys, and the richest because they can afford enough land to ensure their privacy. He thought of that now as he proceeded up the cobblestone drive, toward a house set so far into the property he couldn't even see it.

Finally, after a three-minute winding trip, it came into view: a tall sprawling structure with many wings and elevations in which the cobblestones of the drive seemed to continue up the walls to a slate roof. It looked to Otto like a very solid home, but one that would cost a lot to heat.

As he drew near the front door, he saw a man come out and get into a white van with some lettering on the side. When the van pulled away, he could see that the lettering said: *A & M Communication and Electronics*. Taking the van's parking place, Otto concluded that Bruxton had probably just had some kind of new security system installed.

Even on the short drive over here, Otto's knees had locked so it took him twice as long to get out of the car as it would most people. And his first few steps were stiff and slow. But by the time he reached the front door and rang the bell, he was pretty well oiled up and moving fine.

The door was answered by a man with long blond hair, a prominent nose, and soft skin. Boone, Otto thought he was called. Whether that was his first or last name, Otto didn't know. Boone was wearing a tan suit that seemed too casual for his position. *But what the hell do I know about people with this kind of money,* Otto told himself.

"Please come in," Boone said, stepping back.

Otto had never been in Bruxton's home before, so he was eager to see it. Stepping inside, he entered a reception hall with a ceiling so high it didn't seem like it could fit in the house he'd seen from the drive. The floor was two shades of tan marble laid like a checkerboard but with the squares at an angle. A staircase with complicated black and gold wrought-iron railings led to a landing with a big stained-glass window. It then cut back and went up a few feet more to a balcony. The center part of the staircase steps were covered with a continuous carpet the color of a Guernsey cow but with gold striping on the edges. The walls were cream-colored and must have had at least three coats on them to look that good. Next to the stairs was a weird sofa that looked as though it had been made by somebody who'd gone right from an all-day bender at the Lucy II to his workshop. The seat kind of ran along okay for a while, then just curled to the floor and went under the damn thing. Weird. But it had a pretty fabric on it; cream like the walls, but with Guernsey-colored stripes.

"Doctor Bruxton is in the study," Boone said, leading the way.

Seeing him in here, Otto wondered if Boone had picked out his suit so he'd blend with everything else.

"Doctor Bruxton . . . Sheriff Christianson."

"Thank you, Boone. Come in Sheriff."

The study was so unusual that Otto found himself cranking his head around trying to see it all at once, like a tourist at the Vatican, or at least what he thought that might be like having never been there.

The ceiling here was a series of domes and arches all

painted with heads like the cameos his wife collected. Against the walls were a dozen columned bookcases with glass doors. In them, all the books looked as old as Methuselah. Bruxton sat in a portion of the room partially separated from the rest by two columned room dividers that served as pillars for a ceiling arch painted with more cameos. He was working at a gold table supported on the corners by black and gold statues that looked Egyptian . . . or maybe they weren't.

"Have a seat," Bruxton said.

Otto couldn't see Bruxton very well because there was a window behind him with white curtains that spread the light from the sun so it was like looking directly into a flashlight.

Otto crossed the room, entered the alcove where Bruxton waited, and pulled the offered chair from directly in line with the window, to the left, where he could see Bruxton's face. Otherwise, he might as well have just called.

"May I get you something?" Bruxton said. "Coffee, soft drink . . ."

He was dressed in a dark suit with a thin gray stripe and wore a tie with a bold pattern of blue and yellow diamonds. The tip of a handkerchief poked from his breast pocket. Classy. But he still looked old and weak.

"No thanks. I'm fine. I just wanted to ask you a few questions about Henry Pennell."

"You're lucky I was available," Bruxton said. "That wouldn't normally be the case. What I'm suggesting is that it would be better in the future if you would make an appointment instead of just driving up to the gate like that, or appearing at my office unexpectedly as you did last time." In the next room, just a pair of doors away, was Bruxton's beloved art collection. To have a law enforcement official, even one with the limited abilities of Christianson, this close to it was exciting for Bruxton, even beyond the risk of discussing Henry Pennell.

"I guess I should apologize," Otto said. "But making

an appointment just doesn't seem like the way the police should work."

"As you wish," Bruxton said. "But don't be surprised if the next time you do this, you are turned away." Bruxton knew he shouldn't antagonize Christianson, but he wasn't going to let this bumpkin think he was dealing with some farmer.

"I'll remember that," Otto said.

"What is it you wanted to know?"

"I forgot to ask you last time we talked . . . What exactly was it you wanted to say to Pennell the night you had the guard at the company gate stop him?"

After a lifetime of practice, Bruxton was a consummate liar. Because of his deteriorating health he didn't have the skills he once possessed, but felt he could still handle Christianson with ease.

"Earlier in the day, Henry stopped me in the hall and asked if we could talk. I told him to set up an appointment with my secretary, but that I probably couldn't get to him for three or four days because the next morning I was leaving for France to set up a better European distribution system for Vasostasin. He seemed so disappointed that later, after I'd finished the work I'd taken home for the evening, I decided to talk to him if I could locate him.

"He worked late most nights, so I called his office, but got no answer. I then checked with the guard at the gate to see if he'd left for the night. I learned from him that Henry was still on the premises. So I told the guard that if he saw him within the next hour, to have him call me."

Even as Bruxton wove his tale, he could see difficulties with it. The answering machine in Pennell's office . . . Why hadn't he left a message there for Pennell to call?

"Why didn't you talk to Pennell when the guard called and said he was right there?"

"I was in the middle of another more important call and couldn't talk."

"I see." Otto dropped his eyes and looked at the floor, trying to think if that was everything he wanted to know.

More than ready for this to be over, Bruxton said, "Well, Sheriff, if that's all . . ."

"Why didn't you leave a message on the answering machine in Pennell's office that night telling him to call you if he got back by a certain time?"

Bruxton almost said, "I did." But the way Christianson had phrased the question made it sound as though he already knew there was no message.

Of course.

The day Christianson had been allowed to look around Pennell's lab and office he must have checked the answering machine. All the notebooks and computer files dealing with Pennell's project had been removed, but Bruxton had never thought about the answering machine. He really *was* losing it. But he was still more than a match for this oaf.

"When Henry didn't answer, I thought he might have gone home. After the guard said he was still around, I figured the message I left at the gate was enough. Now I really have some things to do . . ."

"Sure, okay," Otto said, getting up. "Thanks for seeing me."

After Christianson was shown out, Bruxton reviewed their conversation. He couldn't find any fault in his performance, but it bothered him to be questioned. Finally, he decided that Christianson hadn't come there because of any suspicions. The man was just blundering around trying to act like a cop. He thought of the fat fool looking right at the white van that had been by the front door. He'd no doubt been curious about it, but couldn't have any idea what it meant. But one day he'd certainly be aware of the results.

Bruxton got up and walked to the double doors that led to his picture gallery. He went inside, turned on the lights, and paid quiet homage to the evidence of genius on his walls, knowing that now he could keep the entire collection until he drew his last breath and it would never betray him.

At the end of Bruxton's driveway, as Otto waited for the big gates to let him out, he decided he didn't like Zane Bruxton much. All that talk about appointments and not just dropping in. In his experience the only people who get upset when you just knock on their door are folks who have a messy house or something to hide. And Bruxton's place sure looked clean.

23

The brain soup Jessie had taken from the buried carcass created certain problems for her. It was surely loaded with bacteria as well as numerous toxins they had produced. She couldn't inject something like that into a test animal. After some thought about how to clean it up, she decided on a simple approach. She'd autoclave it—heat it to sterilizing temperature. This would not only kill the bacteria but likely inactivate any toxins. The neatest part of this approach was that prions were known to be resistant to autoclaving so that if the injections gave a positive response, it not only would prove that the suspect animal was the source of the disease, but at the same time would implicate prions as the infectious particle.

Since very little of the soup would be required for her experiment, she autoclaved only a small portion of what she'd collected. After what happened to her first set of animals, she stayed close to the autoclave for its full cycle to make sure that what she put in was what came out. And she kept the rest of the soup nearby on ice.

When the autoclaved sample had cooled, she concentrated it to make sure there would be as many prions as possible in the tiny amount she would inject into each animal. At the end of the day, she left work with all the tubes of the sample material and everything she'd need to test it packed in her briefcase.

On the way home, Jessie stopped at the grocery and picked up two bags of frozen corn, two of green beans, and a roll of magic tape. She then drove to Shell's hardware for some plastic sheeting.

Upon arriving home, she carried everything to the back yard where Fitzhugh, her black Labrador, came bounding out of his igloo-shaped doghouse to see her. Though she was eager to get upstairs to the garage apartment and start work, she took Fitzie off his chain and played Frisbee with him for a while. She then hooked him back up and gave him his dinner from a bag of Ol' Roy in the garage. Free now to pursue her own interests, she picked up her briefcase and the things she'd bought and went up the wooden stairs to the garage apartment.

Earlier that afternoon, as she'd prepared the sample for testing, she'd been worried that Richard might call her at work and tell her he had the animals she'd need. Considering that the phones there probably weren't secure, that could have been a mistake. To his credit, he hadn't called. However, that meant she didn't even know if he was back yet from Madison. But as she went inside, she saw eight small cages on the floor by the dishwasher.

Richard had dropped the mice and cages off at Jessie's apartment around four forty-five. He'd then gone back to his office and proofed the report he'd been trying to get finished for the health department. He'd briefly considered adding the events that had unfolded today, but decided to file that in an update after he had the results of the tests Jessie would do at home. He faxed the report to the department at five-ten, then went to his car and headed for Jessie's house.

Turning into her driveway now, he saw that she was

already home. He pulled in behind her car, got out, and walked toward the backyard.

Even before he came around the corner of the house, Fitzie shifted to alert status. At the first visual sign of Richard, the dog went on a barking tear. Why the animal had never learned to accept him was a mystery.

"Hush, Fitzie. It's me, remember?"

The noise brought Jessie out of the garage apartment to see what was going on.

"Richard. Stop bothering the dog."

"Does he bark at Artie like this?" Richard said, starting up the stairs.

"He loves Artie."

"The dog is confused."

"You're just in time to give me a hand."

"You can't request applause," Richard said. "It has to be spontaneous."

"Come in here and spontaneously help me rig an operation tent."

Inside, after Jessie described what she had in mind for the plastic sheeting she'd bought, they draped it over the Formica-topped kitchen table. Richard pulled the plastic up in the center and twisted it so they had a tongue Jessie could tie to the hanging light fixture directly overhead. She cut a slit in the side of the tent for access, then lightly misted the inside with alcohol. She also gave the table an alcohol wipedown.

"It's probably not a sterile field," she said, surveying their work. "But it has to be better than operating without *any* precautions."

Within an hour, eight animals had been injected with the prepared sample and eight with saline.

"Where's the rest of the material we collected from that carcass?" Richard asked.

"In the fridge."

"I don't think we should leave it there."

"At least not right out in the open."

"What do you mean?"

Jessie got the samples from the fridge along with the

frozen vegetables she'd bought. She went to the countertop near the sink and laid it all out. She banged a bag of vegetables on the edge of the sink to loosen the contents. With the scissors she'd used to slit the plastic tent, she made a small cut in the end of the bag, then slipped one tube of the brain soup inside. She did the same with the other two bags. The last bag also received the small tube of autoclaved sample. She put this bag in the freezer then explained the rest of her plan.

"One of those other bags goes in my freezer in the house. The third, you're taking home. That last tube, I'm going to bury in the yard. Okay?"

"I can't think of any better way to hide them."

"Now let's fix the cages." To show Richard what she meant, Jessie went to the cages and put one on the countertop. She bent over next to the cage and ruffled her hair with her fingers. She then cut a small piece from the roll of magic tape she'd bought and used it to pick up one of the hairs she'd shed. She taped that end of the hair to the cage and secured the other end to the lid.

"I get it," Richard said. "If anyone opens the cage, the hair will break and we'll know the animals have been tampered with."

Working together, they spent the next few minutes rigging the other cages. When they were finished, Jessie took a last look around and said, "That's all we can do up here. Let's bury that last tube, move Fitzie to the foot of the stairs, and drop your bag of veggies off. Then let's get something to eat."

After dinner, Jessie checked on the animals and found that they'd all recovered from the anesthetic and were acting like mice should. She took a quick look Saturday morning, another that afternoon, and again that evening. Each time she went to the apartment she made sure all the hairs they'd rigged on the cages were still intact. After each visit, she called Richard and gave him a report.

There was no way to predict how long a latent period there might be before the animals showed any symptoms.

In the three people who had died, their seizures had appeared about two months after eating the suspect beef. But ingestion of prions was known to produce a much longer latent period than direct introduction into the brain. Of course, she wasn't working with humans. The whole time course could be different for mice. Or they might even be refractory to this strain of prion. This last possibility was one Jessie tried not to think about.

The mice looked fine all day Sunday and were still that way on Monday morning. That afternoon Jessie ran into Bruxton in the hall.

"Hello, Jessie. How's that new project going?"

The only new project she was involved with was the prion testing. So he had to mean that. It was the first time she'd seen him since discovering that her animals at work had been replaced. This made her look for any hint to suggest he already knew the answer to his question. But his manner and expression conveyed only sincerity.

"Nothing yet," she said.

"Well, it's only been a few days."

"That's true."

"You let me know if anything develops."

"Yessir, I certainly will."

Bruxton had seemed so confident that Jessie began to wonder if he knew about the second set of animals and had somehow compromised them.

He couldn't have. . . . The hairs were all intact. And Fitzie would never let a stranger up those stairs.

These arguments should have given her comfort, but they didn't. So when she left work for the day, she wanted to get to the apartment and take a really hard look at everything. She gave this such a high priority, she hurried past Fitzie with just a quick pat on the head and dashed up the stairs.

Key in the lock . . . And she was inside.

She flicked on the lights and surveyed the kitchen. The cages were on the floor lined up along the cabinets just as she'd left them. And there was a feeling of undisturbed continuity in the room. Of course, when the final note of a piano concerto fades, who can tell when the instrument was last played?

The cages were arranged so that the one nearest the door and the next three held saline-injected animals. All these mice were normal, just as they should be.

The short interval since she'd begun this test along with her concern that someone might have tampered with the experiment led her to believe that the animals injected with brain soup would likewise be fine. But this time her expectations were turned upside down.

In the first cage beyond those that held the saline control animals, one mouse was lying immobile on its side. The other was in the corner having a seizure.

24

"They're *all* sick," Richard said, checking the last cage. "I need to call the health department."

"It's almost six o'clock," Jessie said. "No one will be there."

"Probably not, but I should try."

They went to Jessie's house and Richard called information for the number. As Jessie predicted, he got only a recording, reciting the department's regular business hours.

"Nobody home," Richard said hanging up. "But they need to know about this as soon as possible. I've got to get back to the office and write an addendum to my original report. What are these results going to do to your relationship with Bruxton? If he was behind the animal switch at work, what's he going to think when it gets back to him that you got positive results from a second set of animals? Won't that tell him you know what he did?"

"He asked me to keep him informed. So I'll tell him about the results myself. I just won't mention the second experiment. If he *was* involved in the switch, he won't dare let on that he knows the first animals couldn't be sick. He might even think whoever was supposed to make the switch screwed up somehow. Let him wonder what happened. If he *wasn't* involved, the issue of two sets of animals is irrelevant."

"Hello, Doctor Patterson, this is Richard Heflin. Hope I'm not bothering you, but I was hoping you could give me an update on how the department is handling that situation here in Midland." He hit the button for speakerphone so Jessie could hear.

After leaving Jessie the night the animals became ill, Richard had spent the evening writing up a detailed addendum to his original report to the health department, omitting any reference to the interference they'd encountered with their first experiments. Expecting that the department would want to take possession of the carcass on Buck Lundval's property and believing that Lundval might mislead them about its location, he included a description of exactly where to dig. He'd faxed the report as soon as he'd finished so it would be there whenever the director arrived for work the next day. To make sure she was aware of it, he'd called her yesterday morning and learned she was just moments away from starting on it. Enough time had now elapsed for them to have taken some action.

"We picked up the carcass of the infected animal yesterday and all the dirt that had soaked up blood," Patterson said. "Mr. Lundval didn't seem happy to see us."

"I'm not surprised," Richard said. "Have you sent someone to the dairy?"

"I talked to the manager, Mr. Lamotte, by phone and he said that animal was killed because it had a seizure. They intended to incinerate the remains on the premises, but their incinerator was broken. Rather than consulting with his superiors about disposal, the employee who killed the beast called Premier Industries to take it away. He apparently didn't make it clear to their driver that it was a sick animal. The important thing is, they haven't had any other cases. So it was just a sporadic incident."

"What about the milk the sick cow produced?"

"It was in a dry cycle and hadn't been in production for several months. Even in England, where they've had such a problem with mad cow disease, there was never any indication it could be transmitted to humans in milk. Besides, any milk that cow produced has long ago been consumed. So there's nothing to recall. In your three patients, the latent period was only two months. If there had been any contamination in milk from the dairy, we should have seen some additional cases by now. So I believe we're in the clear."

"You don't think their herd should be inspected?"

"As I said, it was an isolated incident."

"You know this is a very aggressive and very different prion strain than anything previously known."

"That's very clear."

"So isn't it possible that there are some other cows out there in the early stages of prion recruitment that might be showing no signs of disease but be dumping abnormal prions into their milk?"

"That apparently didn't happen with the index animal."

"Who knows why that was true?"

"What makes you think other animals at the dairy might be ill? Prion diseases aren't contagious."

"I don't know what caused the index animal to get sick. Maybe it was an isolated incident, maybe not. I just think a thorough investigation is warranted."

"I appreciate your concern, Doctor Heflin. But our resources here are already spread thin. And I just don't feel that we can waste them on pursuing this. Again, thank you for keeping us so well informed."

Then she was gone.

Richard hung up and looked at Jessie. "I can't believe they're treating this so casually."

"It could just be bureaucratic ineptitude," she said. ". . . or something more."

"You think whoever was behind the animal switch got to them?"

"It would have to be someone with a lot of influ-
ence."

"Bruxton."

"He's the obvious choice."

"If it is him, he must have some connection with the
dairy."

"Maybe he owns it. That would explain his involvement in the animal switch. He didn't want us to find out
they had a sick cow out there because of the bad pub-
licity. If people knew about that, they'd stop buying the
dairy's milk."

"That wouldn't hurt him. Compared to his take from
Vasostasin, the amount of money the dairy's making has
to be insignificant. It either isn't Bruxton, or the dairy
is important for some other reason."

"It *has* to be Bruxton."

"What the hell is going on out there?"

Then, a seed that had been germinating a couple of
inches below conscious thought in Richard's brain pushed
to the surface. "That woman . . . Holly Fisher . . . the one
who was run off the road. Otto said her seat belt looked
as though it had been cut and that just before her accident she was in the Lucy II asking a couple of guys who
work at the dairy a lot of questions about the place. I
wonder what that was all about?"

"Call and ask her."

Richard reached for the phone and punched in the
number for hospital records to find out what contact numbers Holly had given them.

After copies of *Hustler* magazine had been found in the
rooms of several boys at St. Peter's Orphanage in Mis-
sion Viejo, California, Father Lucius Graham had scheduled an assembly for the next afternoon, at which he spoke
for forty-five minutes on the dangers of impure thoughts
and masturbation. Returning now to his office after the
assembly, his secretary informed him that the mail was
on his desk.

"If it wouldn't be too much trouble, Mrs. Lang, could

you make me a cup of tea? I believe I strained my voice speaking to the boys."

"Of course, Father. I'll bring it to you in a few minutes."

Hormones, Lucius thought, opening the door to his study. Quite possibly the one aspect of God's handiwork that had caused him the most trouble in his life . . . his own as a young priest and now those of his boys. He thought of Jesus' plea when he was sorely afflicted with the burden God had placed on him: "Let this cup pass from me." It was a plea Lucius had made frequently over the last year about the orphanage. But so far it was a prayer unanswered.

The mail was sitting on his desk, already opened with the envelopes clipped to the contents, exactly the way he wanted it. Once again the mail reminded him of Mrs. Kirk, his previous secretary, who had done a beautiful job for him the first few years, then had an episode where her blood pressure went so high it caused tiny hemorrhages in her eyes. Her doctors got it under control, but she was never the same after that. Her work became riddled with mistakes and she developed a relentless disregard for his wish that after opening the mail, she not discard the envelopes. When he called this or any other of her errors to her attention, she cried. And he couldn't fire her. She needed the job to put food on the table. So he simply lived with her mistakes, month after month, year after year. It was such a terrible situation that two weeks ago, when she'd had a major stroke, his first thought had been that she would no longer be able to work and he'd finally be rid of her. His reaction was a sin he had prayed daily about ever since, so that as he sat behind his desk and started on the mail, he was in a penitent mood.

The first three items were orphanage bills. The fourth was a credit card solicitation addressed to Mr. Father Lucius Graham. But the next was something quite different; a crisp hundred-dollar bill clipped to a sheet of paper. On the paper there were just five words: *In Memory of Henry Pennell.*

In the last few years Lucius had received a number of new hundreds for the orphanage, always given in someone's memory. After the third one arrived, he'd become curious about the sender. But of course, the envelope bearing the benefactor's return address was never with the money and the note. He probably could have found it in Mrs. Kirk's wastebasket as he had other envelopes he'd wanted, but he'd never given the issue that kind of priority. Now, the envelope was right here.

He unclipped it and checked the upper left corner.

No address.

And the postmark was blurred, so he couldn't read it.

Looking at his neatly typed name, he was struck by the fact that his title, Father, was underlined.

Underlined.

The face of Billy Lynch, the only psychopath he'd ever had at the orphanage, popped into his head. Billy had arrived as a six year old after his missionary parents had been killed by bandits in South America. To all outward appearances he was a fine boy; polite and intelligent. But he had a dark side that caused him to do the most heinous things.

Once, he piled all the clothing of another boy on the floor and set it afire. Another time, while an older boy was washing his hair in the shower and had his eyes closed, Billy had turned off the cold water so the boy was badly burned. And each time he was caught, he was so apologetic and so sorry he would weep and offer to do anything to make up for what he'd done. The strange thing was that the psychologist they called in said he truly *was* sorry. It just didn't stop him the next time.

Billy ran away from the orphanage when he was twelve. And for the next eight years, Lucius had no idea if he was alive or dead. Then, one day a long letter arrived from Billy, describing in detail what a difficult time he'd had in the last eight years and thanking Lucius for all he had done for him. Three more letters had followed at about six-month intervals. Since this was well before Mrs. Kirk's disdain for saving envelopes, Lucius had seen that each was postmarked from a different city and, like the first, bore no return address. More importantly, on the envelopes of all four letters, Billy had underlined Lucius's title. Then the letters stopped.

Billy Lynch . . . The hundred-dollar bills were from him.

Suddenly, Lucius had a thought that chilled him down to his toes.

He pulled out the drawer in his desk where he kept things that he didn't want to throw away but weren't important enough to file. He was sure that when the last hundred dollars had arrived just a few months ago, he'd kept the . . .

There it was: *In Memory of Chester Sorenson.*

Dread filling his heart, Lucius reached for the phone. He punched in the number of one of his boys who had made something of himself and he waited for an answer.

"Detective Clark, please. . . . Hello, David. Lucius Graham . . . I'm fine. The boys? They're keeping me on my toes. Say David, I have kind of an odd question for you. If I gave you two names, is there a way you could determine if they were murder victims anywhere in the country?"

25

"Doctor Fisher, you have a phone call from Doctor Richard Heflin."

"Tell him I'll be right with him." *Heflin. What could he want?* Holly wondered. Was he in Memphis? Or was he back *there*? As she remembered how she'd been stalked in Wisconsin, her heart quickened.

"Is anything wrong, Doctor?" her patient asked.

"That's supposed to be *my* line," Holly said brightly, trying to cover her feelings. "I'd like to see you again in one month. The nurse at the front will set a date for the labs; then, a few days later, when I have the results, we'll talk again."

Holly ushered her patient out of the examining room and pointed him in the right direction. Then she headed for her office and picked up the phone.

How to answer? "Doctor Fisher" didn't seem right. "Richard, this is Holly."

"Sorry to bother you in the middle of the day. Do you have a few minutes?"

"Yes. Where are you?"

"In Midland. How's your head?"

Surely he didn't call just to ask her that. "No

headaches and I still remember everything I used to know."

"That's good. Excuse the abrupt segue, but we've got a situation here where three people have died after eating meat from a sick cow that was picked up at the local dairy and mistakenly butchered for human consumption. I think this warrants a full investigation of the dairy by the health department, but they don't agree. For some other reasons, I think the department might have been influenced to look the other way. I don't fully understand why and I was hoping you might be able to enlighten me."

Holly was thrilled to hear that Heflin knew some things about the dairy she didn't. At the same time, she realized she had never spoken to him about her interest in it. "What makes you think *I* know anything?"

"Otto Christianson, our sheriff here . . . You remember him, he talked to you in the hospital the night you were hurt."

"I remember." How could she forget Otto? The only one in town who knew where she was staying, and the guy who had either rifled her room himself, or had helped his friends find her.

"Otto told me that the night you were hit by the truck, you had been in the Lucy II asking questions about the dairy."

Holly viewed the fact that Christianson knew about her conversation in the tavern as further evidence of his duplicity. She definitely hadn't wanted to give up her investigation, and for days had been thinking it was time to pick it up again. But fear had caused her to do nothing. Now, with an ally at hand who lived in the town, she could help her cause without risk. "I do have a lot to tell you, but it's an involved story. And I don't have enough time at the moment to talk about it."

"This is a conversation we should have face to face anyway. If I can arrange to get a flight into Memphis tomorrow can we meet somewhere?"

"I'm booked pretty heavily, so it might have to be after five."

"I'll see what I can put together and give you a call later at home."

"Do you have the number?"

Heflin recited the number he'd obtained from hospital records.

"That's it. I'll expect your call."

Holly parked in the upper outside level of the short-term parking area and headed for the terminal. It was three-eighteen and she was cutting it close. She'd cleared the latter part of her afternoon so she could pick Heflin up at the airport, but with each patient after one o'clock, she'd fallen a little further behind schedule.

Inside the terminal she checked the TV monitors for the arrival gate and hurried that way. She got there just as the first-class passengers were coming in. She spotted him a few minutes later and felt an unexpected flutter of pleasure that had nothing to do with the purpose of his visit.

Picking her out of the crowd, he smiled and waved. Her memory of him was that he had a mane of dark hair that was graying at the temples and he wasn't bad looking. Seeing him now, coming toward her in dark gray slacks and a light-gray V-neck sweater over a beige dress shirt, he registered much higher on her approval scale. She hadn't remembered that his features were so finely drawn, masculine for sure, but making him look like a guy who would rather finesse his way around an obstacle than crush it.

"Hi, have a good trip?"

"You know the old saying: 'any flight you can walk away from . . .'"

Holly gestured at his briefcase. "Is that all you brought?"

"I'm going back at seven-thirty tonight, so I don't need much."

"First time in Memphis?" Holly said, starting for the terminal.

Richard fell in beside her. "I've gone through here a few times on trips elsewhere."

"With only four hours before you leave, you'll hardly have been here this time."

Twenty minutes later, they were sitting across from each other at Holly's kitchen table, each with their hands lightly wrapped around a cup of hot chocolate.

"I've read the material you faxed to me last night," Holly said, referring to the two reports Richard had drawn up for the Wisconsin health department. "Why do you think the health department is being influenced from outside?"

Richard told her about the first animal experiments, the theft of the meat from the Johannsons' home, and the obviously phony personnel who picked up the carcass at Buck Lundval's. "It seems likely that Zane Bruxton was behind all that, so it doesn't seem unreasonable to believe he also got the health department to ignore the potential danger in the situation."

"He must have a financial interest in the dairy."

"That's what we thought at first. But his pharmaceuticals company is making a fortune from a drug called Vasostasin. You've heard of it?"

"Who hasn't?"

"With all he's making from that, why get involved in a coverup for a business whose profits by comparison have to be minuscule?"

"The dairy is apparently important to him in a way we don't understand."

Richard's face fell. "You said *we*. So you don't have an answer either?"

"I know some things. But I don't see how they fit into the picture you've drawn."

"May I hear *your* story now?"

Holly found it hard to begin because it would reveal something to Heflin she'd rather he didn't know: that she was not a whole woman, that she could never have a child of her own. But there was no way out of it, so she simply started. "When I was in medical school I was diagnosed with acute myelocytic leukemia . . ."

Sympathy and horror fought for control of Richard's face, precisely the emotions she didn't want to incite. But she went on.

Later, when she'd wound her way to her discovery that someone had been in her room at the Green and White Motel, she said, "That's when I left town. You may think I overreacted, but after what had already happened to me, I couldn't stay."

"Of course you couldn't."

"And the only person in town who knew where I was staying was Otto Christianson."

"You don't think *he* was in your room?"

"Or someone he tipped off."

"I know Otto pretty well. He's a good man."

Thinking of her former boyfriend, Grant Ingram, Holly said, "People only reveal the sides of themselves they want us to see. The rest is hidden. You don't really know Christianson."

"Holly, he told me that the day after you were run off the road, he went to the salvage yard where your car had been taken to find out why the seat belt had stopped working. And he found that it had been cut."

"Damn it. I should have figured that out myself. He never told *me* that."

"The point I'm trying to make here is that if Otto was in on what happened to you, why would he examine your car? He'd already be aware of what he'd find."

"How do you know he really looked at the car?"

"I guess I don't. But why would he tell *me* about your seat belt?"

"I don't know . . . maybe to divert suspicion from himself. Whatever the reason, I don't trust him. I might even be making a mistake talking to *you* like this."

"Believe me, you're not."

"Obviously I don't think so either. But I can't be certain. Nor can you vouch for Christianson. Given the facts, I think there's reason to seriously doubt him. In any event, I don't want you to tell him anything I've said."

"That might be difficult."

"You *have* to promise."

Reluctantly, Richard said, "If that's what you want."

"Say it."

"I promise I won't tell Otto anything you've told me."

"Or anything I may tell you in the future."

"You should have been a lawyer. . . . Or anything you tell me in the future." Richard shook his head. "But even with what you've said, I still don't see the big picture. Your story does raise the ante though. I mean, they tried to *kill* you. What could be worth that? Oh oh."

"What?"

"About three months ago a dairy employee was found floating in a nearby pond. It's not generally known, but the forensic findings showed that it was clearly murder."

"I heard about him from the two dairy workers I spoke to in the tavern," Holly said. "Chester . . . somebody."

"Sorenson. I wouldn't be surprised if his death was part of all this."

"The guys at the tavern seemed to think it might have been a suicide. How did *you* hear it was murder?"

"I serve as the local coroner, something I should have considered before promising I wouldn't tell Otto what you've said. He spread the word around town that it was either an accident or suicide because he thought it would make it easier for him to conduct an investigation if the killer believed they were in the clear. Everything you've told me is germane to that case. As coroner, how can I keep what you've told me to myself?"

"You're still assuming Christianson isn't involved. If you're wrong and you tell him what I said, you'll just be putting yourself in danger. "And you *did* promise."

Richard ran his fingers though his hair. "All this just gets better and better."

"And there's more," Holly said. ". . . something that

bears on your concern that the herd may be harboring additional sick animals. Be right back."

Holly went to her study and got the pictures she'd taken of the dairy animals and those she'd downloaded from the Internet. Returning to the kitchen table, she spread out the twelve piles of photographs. "These are the thirty-six pictures I took of animals in the dairy's herd. First, notice how different the pigmentation patterns are in the top picture on each pile."

Richard stood up so he could study the pictures. After a minute or so, he looked at Holly. "Okay . . ."

"Now look through each stack separately."

Richard picked up the first pile and returned to his chair. When he'd seen all four pictures he said, "They're very hard to tell apart."

"And it's the same for the other groups. Each set is quite different from the others. But within a group, the patterns are as similar as those you've seen."

Richard looked at a second set, then Holly slid the stack of Internet pictures toward him. "Here are ninety-seven animals from other herds I found on the Internet. No two are as similar as the ones within a set from the Midland dairy. I talked to a bovine geneticist about it and he thinks the animals within each group of my photos may be clones."

Richard immediately saw the health implications of this. "If that sick animal acquired its illness from a spontaneous conversion of normal prion protein to the abnormal form and other members of its clone are still in the herd, they're likely to be making conversion-susceptible protein too. How convinced was the geneticist you talked to that the similar animals were clones?"

"He hedged a little."

"If we knew with absolute certainty that they *are* clones, the health department would *have* to inspect the herd. There must be a test to prove animals are clones."

"We could call the geneticist and ask him."

"Let's do it."

"Come on." Holly led Richard to the second bedroom she used as a study. "Have a seat."

She found the phone number in her Rolodex and was soon waiting for someone to pick up.

"Doctor Weichmann's office."

"This is Doctor Fisher. May I speak to him please."

"I'm sorry, but he's in a lab meeting."

Richard could see from the expression on Holly's face that they weren't going to get an answer right now.

"May I tell him . . . Oh, wait a minute. Here he is now."

Holly nodded to Richard and hit the button for speakerphone.

There was a short interval of silence, presumably while Weichmann went to his office. Then he was on the line.

"Yes, Doctor Fisher. What can I do for you?"

"A few days ago when we spoke about Holstein pigmentation patterns, you expressed the opinion that the animals with patterns as similar as those I faxed to you could be clones. Would it be possible to determine with certainty, say from a blood sample, that they *are* clones?"

"Absolutely."

"Is that something *you* can do?"

"My lab does have that capability."

"Would you be willing to test the blood from three or four animals for me?"

"I'm really not in a position to take on outside work."

"What if I told you that the health of thousands of people could depend on the results of those tests?"

"Then I suppose I'd have to reconsider. What people are we talking about?"

"I'm sorry. I know this is going to sound odd, but I can't tell you that. In time, perhaps. But for now, I can't. And there's one other complication. The blood I'll be sending may contain prions capable of causing an aggressive neurologic disease in humans for which there is no cure."

Holly knew that when she got to this part, it wasn't

going to sound good, but hearing it aloud, it was even more chilling. Partly for Richard's benefit, as she waited for Weichmann's response, she closed her eyes and winced as though expecting a painful blow.

"Well . . . that certainly makes this all sound hugely attractive," Weichmann said. "Actually, that's not a problem. Our procedures generally include precautions that assume all the blood we handle might have safety risks."

"Then you'll do it?"

"Yes."

"Could you also determine if there's abnormal prion protein in the blood?"

"That's way out of my area of expertise."

"Assuming that the animals *are* clones, will you be able to tell why they were cloned?"

"That's a huge question I don't think any lab in the country could answer."

"How much blood will you need?"

"We can work with just a drop. But as long as you're drawing blood, let's say one cc."

"Where's the best place to get it?"

"There's a big vein under the tail where it attaches to the rump. Or you could use the jugular . . . in the neck. That'd be easier to get to and you'll be less likely to get knocked unconscious from a flying hoof."

"How long would it take to get the results?"

"A few days."

"Where should we send them?"

Holly jotted down the address Weichmann gave her. "I really appreciate this."

"I'll just put it on my CV as public service."

"We're in business," Holly said, hanging up. "Or we will be as soon as we figure out how to get the blood samples we need."

"That question you asked him . . . about why they were cloned. I hadn't thought of that."

"The new herd is producing less milk and they aren't cheaper to feed. So what makes them worth cloning, especially when, as Susan Morrison told me, the cloning process is very inefficient, and therefore has to be costly?"

"I don't know," Richard said. "But if they were being cloned for some desirable trait, wouldn't all the animals have the same pigmentation pattern? I mean, the simplest way to get the trait into all the animals would be to clone one animal that has it."

"But then it would be obvious the herd was cloned. This way, with twelve clones, it takes some study to realize that. Even the dairy employees who work with the animals every day aren't aware they can be grouped into a dozen different patterns. One of the men I talked to at that tavern had a vague feeling that individual cows were hard to recognize but he didn't know why."

"I'll have to give this some thought," Richard said. "Meanwhile, how are we going to get those blood samples?"

They sat in silence mulling this over, then Richard said, "This is a tough one. I could sneak into one of the barns at night and do it, but if we're going to send four samples, two should be from one pair of animals with similar pigmentation and two from a different pair. Finding the right animals and getting the blood drawn by flashlight could be difficult. And we have no idea what kind of security they have at night."

"I know a dairy employee who might do it."

"One of the guys you talked to at the tavern?"

"One that I didn't: Chester Sorenson's brother. He was there that night drinking alone. The two guys I was with said he was still very despondent over his brother's death and didn't believe it was a suicide. I'll bet you could get his cooperation by telling him that by helping us, it could ultimately clarify what happened to his brother. Of course, he'll have to agree to keep quiet about everything."

"I dislike bringing in someone we don't know."

"Sound him out. And proceed only if you get a good feeling about him."

"And if I don't like what I hear?"

"We'll come up with another way."

"He's not going to know how to take a blood sample. But I know a vet who could show him. We could just say he's curious and wanted to tag along on a couple of calls. The health risk could be a problem. I'd have to tell him about that."

"Agreed."

"Hope you don't mind if I get my sister, Jessie, in on this. She's already involved. And I might have her approach Sorenson's brother so he doesn't think I'm investigating the dairy in my capacity as coroner. He might also be more inclined to help a pretty woman than he would me."

"I think he'll be *very* motivated regardless of who approaches him. Call me and tell me what he says as soon as you can. Your idea that we should have him take blood from two pairs of animals with different patterns is a good one. Before you go home, we need to make copies of some of my pictures so he can see what you're talking about. But first, how about I take you out for dinner? Do you like ribs?"

"How did you know?"

They arrived at Corky's famous Bar-B-Q just before the equally famous line of people wanting to be fed began spilling out the front door.

Holly gave their names to the hostess and joined Richard at the end of the line, where they queued up next to autographed pictures of Farrah Fawcett, Ryan O'Neal, and Dennis Quaid. Over the next fifteen minutes, entertained by top 40 hits from the fifties and sixties, they slowly moved past signed photographs of an array of movie stars, politicians, and pro athletes, some of whom had scribbled a few words on their pictures about the food. Finally, with Roy Orbison singing "Pretty Woman," they were seated at a rustic booth with a sleek painting of a white '57 Cadillac hanging on the wall.

The waiter took their drink orders and left them so they could study the menu.

"What do you recommend?" Richard asked after looking it over.

"The dry ribs are fantastic."

"So be it." Richard closed his menu and took a look around. "I like this place, particularly the music. It reminds me of simpler, happier times."

"You're not happy now?"

"Before this prion thing I was relatively happy, considering . . ."

"Considering what?"

Richard held his reply while their waiter set two glasses of iced tea and a basket of hot buttered rolls in front of them. After they'd ordered and the waiter left, he said, "I don't want to burden you."

"If I were concerned about being burdened, I wouldn't have asked. But if you feel I'm prying . . ."

"Not at all." Staring at his iced tea, Richard told Holly what had happened to Diane and why he'd moved to Wisconsin.

"Did you go through a period where you felt as though God or whatever controls things had chosen you to dump on?" Holly asked when he'd finished.

"The *why me* phase? Sure."

"Me too. When I got sick I thought I was the only one in the world with such troubles. But the fact is, life is an obstacle course with all kinds of traps and dangers where we can get hurt. But we have to just get up and push on. It's not always easy, but what choice do we have?" Holly blushed and covered her face with her hand. "I'm sorry. That was stupid. You didn't need to hear that."

"Don't apologize. Since I lost Diane I've felt isolated from everyone I meet. Like there's a partition between us. They're all on one side and I'm on the other. It's not a good way to live. But with you, I feel like we're in the same place. I don't think it's because of what you went through with your illness. At least I hope it isn't. Mutual misfortune seems like a poor basis for a friendship."

"Did you and Diane have any children?"

"One little girl, Katie. Without her I'd have been totally lost."

"How old is she?"

"Five and so smart it's a wonder to see."

"I'd like to meet her."

"She's visiting my parents in Arizona. When she comes home, we'll have to arrange something."

Richard and Holly walked out of the restaurant at sixten. In the McDonald's parking lot next door, Billy Lynch flicked on the ignition and pulled his rental car out so he'd be in position to follow them whichever way they went. He didn't understand why Richard Heflin was here, but it couldn't mean anything good.

After the failed attempts to kill Holly in Midland, it had been decided that it would draw too much attention if they succeeded on a third try while she was still in town. So when Billy had entered her room at the Green and White, he'd merely thrown her clothing around to scare her back to Memphis. When she'd lit out for Madison after discovering what he'd done, he'd tailed her to the Hampton Inn. It wasn't until the next day, when she'd dropped her rental car off at the airport, that he'd finally returned to Midland. After giving her a little time to settle down, he'd come after her. But why the hell was Heflin here?

He followed their car west on Poplar, then over to Union, where they stopped briefly at a Kinko's to copy something. From there they went to the riverfront, drove past the stainless steel Pyramid sports arena, and circled back to Beale Street, a happening kind of place with lots of blues clubs. Apparently she was giving Heflin a tour.

After Beale, they headed away from the riverfront and took the expressway south. A short while later, they turned into the airport, where Billy hoped Heflin would get his ass back on a plane and let a man do his job.

Billy followed them into the short-term parking area and stayed with his car while they went inside. It was after seven-forty when Holly came back alone. Now, Billy thought, he needed to get serious.

He didn't have it all worked out yet, but he was sure of one thing. This time there'd be no one to force him into some half-baked scheme that was as likely to fail as succeed. He'd do it his way, without haste and with complete certainty that, as Father Lucius was fond of saying when speaking of the dead, her race would be fully run.

26

"Susan . . . it's Holly. How's Walter?"

"He's doing great. His doctor said if he was going to have another attack, it would probably be within the first two weeks. And we've just passed that point."

"Terrific. I know you're relieved."

"I was sure from the start he wouldn't have any more trouble, but it's good to have the most dangerous period behind us."

"I just had a visit from Richard Heflin, the neurologist who treated me in Wisconsin after I was forced off the road."

"Business or pleasure?"

"Business, mostly. He told me some things that make the question of whether the dairy herd in Midland are clones extremely important."

Holly relayed everything Richard had told her, then said, "If we can get blood samples from the animals, the geneticist who thought they were clones has agreed to analyze them so we know for sure. But he won't be able to tell us *why* they were cloned."

"So we won't know much more than we do now."

"Establishing that they *are* clones will mean the health

department will have to inspect the herd. *Then* we might find out why it was done."

"I find the involvement of Zane Bruxton extremely interesting."

"Why?"

"Because it adds a pharmaceutical house to the equation. I don't know what it means, but I believe he's the key to everything. This Heflin fellow . . . you like him?"

"Yes."

"Single?"

"Widowed."

"That can be a problem for future relationships."

"Come on, Susan. You're rushing things."

"And being nosy too. This is all very exciting and important."

"I wish I knew more, but that's all I've got to tell you for now. Stay tuned for future developments."

"I'll be waiting."

After Susan hung up, she went into the family room and watched Walter sitting in front of the TV, channel surfing. It was good and right for her to be here, but it was also vexing to hear secondhand how the investigation was going. It made her feel old and useless and irresponsible.

She went into the kitchen, got a handful of potatoes from the pantry, and put them on the chopping block. Armed with a cleaver, she began whacking at the potatoes, sending pieces flying.

Old . . . *whack*.

Useless . . . *whack*.

Irresponsible . . . *whack*.

"What are you doing?" Walter asked from the doorway.

"Cutting up potatoes."

"Why? We already had dinner."

"Because they deserve it."

During the first leg of his flight home, Richard tried to read an article in *Scientific American* detailing how Mars could be converted into a habitable world, but he couldn't concentrate on it for more than a few seconds at a time, his attention fractured by a collage of thoughts about mad cow disease, his daughter, and Holly.

Holly ... There was something about her ... something more than looks and intelligence. She was strong and capable, but still very feminine. And it felt so good to have a partner again, trading ideas, working toward a common goal.

A wave of remorse for his murdered wife suddenly crested out of nowhere and washed over him, exposing as it receded, a bright feeling of guilt for the thoughts he'd been having about Holly. Chastened, he raised his magazine and gave the red planet another try.

When Richard got home, he went directly to the phone book and flipped to the listings for all the Sorensons. He didn't remember the name of Chester's brother, but recalled that during the early days of the investigation into Chester's death, Otto had mentioned that the two brothers lived together. Hoping the brother hadn't moved, he ran his finger down the listings until he found Chester's number.

His hand reached for the phone.

Wait a minute ... What time is it?

He checked his watch. Eleven thirty-three. Pretty late to be calling someone.

Finally, worried more over what might be brewing at the dairy than he was about disturbing Chester's brother at this hour, he made the call.

It rang a couple of times, then someone picked up. "Yeah, I'm here. Who's this?"

"Richard Heflin. I'm a local doctor. We've never met, but I'd like to talk to you about your brother's death."

"What do you mean? Talk about what?"

"I'd rather not get into the details over the phone. Could we meet somewhere tomorrow?"

"What's wrong with tonight?"

"Nothing. I just thought, since it was so late . . ."

"You know Mecklin's Trailer Park?"

"Yes."

"Come in the main entrance and bear to your right until you come to Pitty Pat Lane.... I know it's a shit name, but it ain't my fault. I'm the fourth trailer on the left down that street. You'll see two Harleys out front. How long will it take you to get here?"

"About twenty minutes."

Richard broke the connection with his finger then called his sister. "Jessie, it's me. Are you dressed?"

"I just got out of the shower."

"Well, throw on some clothes. We have to meet somebody in twenty minutes."

"Who?"

"Chester Sorenson's brother. I'll explain on the way."

Mecklin's Trailer Park had been there about fifteen years. In all that time, no one had thought about planting any trees, so it sat stark and ugly in the cold moonlight. Most of the inhabitants had already gone to bed, but at the Sorenson trailer, the lights were on.

Richard pulled onto the parking pad behind two motorcycles shrouded so fully in green tarps that only a little of the wheels showed.

"You still haven't said why you need *me* to do this." Jessie said.

By making the initial contact himself, Richard had ruined his idea that he might let Jessie take the lead in the negotiations with Sorenson's brother. But he felt he still needed her. "You're the bait," he replied, shutting off the engine. "So don't act too smart and scare him off. Just sit there and look pretty."

"Just what I've always wanted out of life."

Richard's knock on the trailer's front door summoned a young man in jeans and a University of Wisconsin sweatshirt. Even this late, there was a Packers baseball cap perched on his head.

"I'm Doctor Heflin. This is my sister, Jessie."

"I'm Buddy Sorenson. Come on in."

The trailer wasn't large, so with all three of them inside, it seemed quite crowded.

"There's a place you can sit," Buddy said, gesturing to a ratty sofa.

Richard took one end and Jessie the other.

"Either of you want a beer? Buddy asked. "I only got regular, no lite."

"We're fine," Richard said, glancing at Jessie to see if she agreed.

Buddy dropped into a rocking chair with soiled upholstery and leaned forward, elbows on his thighs, his hands folded. "So what about my brother?"

Buddy's heavy face was mostly chin, bringing to mind the phrase *big palooka.* But he didn't have a palooka's body. Hoping that he likewise didn't possess the brain of a palooka, Richard said, "Do you believe Chester committed suicide?"

"No fucking way." He glanced at Jessie. "Uh . . . sorry." Then, returning to Richard, he added, "It really torques me to hear people say that, like he was mental or something. He wouldn't do that. And I don't see how it could have been an accident either. He couldn't swim, so he was afraid of the water. He never would have gone into that pond."

"What do you think happened?"

"I don't know. He wasn't the kind to make trouble. Some guys get a few beers in 'em and they get aggressive and start saying things they shouldn't, getting people upset. You hear they're found dead, it wouldn't surprise you much. But even when he was three sheets to the wind, which wasn't often . . . I don't want you to think he was an alcoholic or anything. Chester was just a sweet guy. We were saving up to buy our own dairy farm. Nothing big, forty cows maybe. It was kind of our dream." Buddy leaned back in his chair, crossed one leg over the other, and held it with his hands. "But it's not gonna happen now."

Watching the thin muscles around Buddy's mouth twitch as he tried to control his feelings, Richard felt em-

barrassed at being the agent who had so pointedly reminded Buddy of his loss.

"In fact," Buddy continued, "I wouldn't have a dairy
farm now if you gave me one. I'm so sick of wading in
cow shit I can barely go to work in the morning." He
shook his head. "I'm sorry. You didn't come here to listen to me complain. But why *did* you come?"

Richard had heard enough to realize that Buddy was
no dummy. His alienation with dairy farms was also a
good sign. "Buddy, we share your view that your brother
didn't commit suicide. And we're here to ask you to help
us obtain some information that could ultimately uncover
the complete story of his death."

"I don't understand. You said you were a doctor. Why
are *you* interested in Chester's death?"

Richard had wanted to keep his duties as coroner out
of all this, but he now saw that he had to use it to le-
gitimize his interest in the case. "In addition to my neu-
rology practice I also serve as the local coroner, which
means I have responsibility for making sure that the circumstances surrounding every death in this area are completely understood."

"I don't know anything about the circumstances."

"But you can help all the same."

"Through your employment at the dairy," Jessie added.

"I'm not following you."

"Before I explain, you'll have to agree that whatever
we tell you will remain just between us, at least for a
while. If you agree but then break our trust, we may
never know exactly what happened to Chester. So there's
a lot riding on your complete cooperation on this issue."

"If I tell you I'll do something, you can take it to the
bank. I'll do whatever you want if it'll help Chester."

"Good. Now, what I'm about to ask of you may not
make much sense, but it does have a bearing on Chester's
death."

"Okay, okay. Get to it for God's sake."

"We want you to get us blood samples from four cows
at the dairy where you work."

Buddy looked bewildered. "You're right. I don't get it, but go on. . . ."

"Obviously this will have to be done without anyone seeing you do it."

"Obviously," Buddy echoed.

"Now here's the nasty part." Ready to explain the health risks associated with the blood Buddy would be collecting, Richard decided that in the young man's best interests, he should overstate the danger. "You must be sure none of the blood comes into contact with any part of your body. If it does, you could die."

A look of incredulity crossed Buddy's face. Then he grew angry. "What is this, some sick joke? Who put you up to this?"

"I'm quite serious about what I said."

"Die? I could die?"

"So you'd have to wear rubber gloves and some sort of face protection, which we'll provide."

"What's the matter with those cows?"

"Maybe nothing. That's why we want the blood . . . to find out."

"What *could* it be?"

"I'm sorry, but I can't say."

"Shit . . . If it was a matter of stepping in front of a bullet for Chester, I'd have done that without thinking. But . . ." He rubbed his nose, then let his hands drop into his lap. He looked at Jessie, then at his hands. After a long minute, he let out a deep breath. "So I just won't get any blood on me."

"Would you be free sometime tomorrow for a lesson on how to draw blood?"

"My uncle's a vet over in Dodgeville. When I was in high school I wanted to be a vet too, so I used to go around to the farms with him all the time. I've taken blood from lots of cows."

"It's not just any four cows we want sampled," Richard said. He reached into his jacket and produced the pictures he and Holly had copied in Memphis. "Two of the

samples should be from cows with this spotting pattern."
He gave Buddy the two pictures on top.

"They almost look like the same animal," Buddy said
after examining the pictures. "We got nearly two thousand animals out there. How the hell am I gonna find
those two?"

"It doesn't have to be them. Just find two that resemble their spotting pattern. There should be lots of
them. The other two should resemble these." Richard
gave Buddy the remaining pictures. "There should be lots
of those as well."

"And we'll give you a disposable camera to photograph the animals you choose," Jessie said. "The sample you label number one should be the first animal on
the film; number two should be the second."

They'd never discussed this, but Richard saw the wisdom in Jessie's idea. This way they'd have a record to
show that Buddy had correctly picked similar animals.
"When can you do it?" he asked.

"When can you get me the supplies I need?"

"It's too late tonight. Can we meet somewhere on your
lunch break tomorrow?"

"About a mile down Pike Road from where it comes
off Dairy Road there's a black mailbox riddled with bullet holes. Go up the driveway and I'll meet you by the
burned-out house back there around eleven-fifteen. I'll
get the blood tomorrow afternoon. You can pick it up
here when I get home."

"For a moment there I didn't think he was going to do
it," Jessie said a few minutes later, as Richard back-
tracked his way out of the trailer park.

"Remember when he glanced at you just before he
agreed? He didn't want you to think he was a coward."

"Oh, come on."

"That wasn't the only reason, but it helped."

"I don't like being bait."

"Sorry, kid. But the way you look, it can't be helped."

"Will he keep quiet?"

"If I weren't convinced of that, I wouldn't have gone forward."

Richard was so excited to have successfully enlisted Buddy that when he got home, he called Holly even though it was now well after midnight. Her voice when she picked up sounded as though she'd been asleep.

"It's Richard. . . . We got him. Chester's brother will draw the samples for us tomorrow."

"How'd you do it so fast?" Holly said, now sounding completely awake.

"It just all fell together. I can probably have the samples off to Weichmann . . . Oh-oh."

"What?"

"Tomorrow's Friday, which means if I send them overnight express, they'll arrive on Saturday. There probably won't be anyone at his university to receive them. And I'd like to get them in his hands as soon as possible."

"I'll call him tomorrow and see what we can arrange."

"Okay. Good deal. Sorry to have called so late, but I just wanted to tell you the news."

"I'm glad you did."

"So we'll talk again tomorrow."

"Yes."

Their conversation was clearly over, but Richard didn't want it to end. Not knowing how to prolong it without appearing needy, he simply said, "Good night."

"Good night, Richard."

With all he'd done that day, Richard should have been worn out. Instead, he felt energized, fueled by the feeling that his life was on the verge of moving from the siding where it had been parked back onto the main track. And this time, when guilt rose, threatening to impede that transition, it seemed paper-thin.

In Memphis, the last thing Holly thought of before she returned to sleep was Richard's face.

27

"Oh yes, cheating on a test is definitely a sin," Father Lucius said, towering over the little boy.

"But it's not in the Ten Commandments," the boy said.

"Of course it is. 'Thou shalt not steal.'"

"What did I steal?"

"You attempted to steal a grade you were not entitled to."

"I never thought of that. But who was I stealing it from?"

Because the boy seemed sincere in his questions and was so young, Father Lucius was willing to continue this dialogue. He did not however, have a ready reply for this last point. He was therefore relieved when his secretary's voice came over the intercom.

"Father, Detective Clark is on line two. Will you take it or should I ask him if there's a message?"

Lucius looked at the boy and whisked the air with his hand. "Wait for me in the outer office. We're not through."

When the boy was on the other side of the door, Lucius pressed the button for line two. "Hello, David . . ."

"Father, I've got some information on one of those names you gave me. Henry Pennell is a missing person.

He was driving home from work late one night about two weeks ago, but never got there. His car was found a quarter mile from his home, sitting in the middle of the road with its lights on and the engine running."

"Do you think he's dead?"

"That's certainly a distinct possibility."

"What about the other name?"

"Don't have anything for you there. Came up with Pennell because the case was so odd and people are still looking for him."

"Where did Pennell live?"

"Midland, Wisconsin."

Richard did not have to wait long before hearing from Holly the next day. The call came into his office forty minutes before he was to meet Buddy and give him the supplies to draw blood.

"It's all set," she said. "You're to send the samples to Weichmann's home. Here's the address . . ."

She rattled off the destination, then said, "If he gets them tomorrow, he'll put someone on them Monday morning."

"When he sees the shipping bill, isn't he going to know where the diseased cows are located?"

"I'd suggest you put my name and address as the sender, but I don't think they'll accept it if you do, and it isn't worth the delay to send everything to me and let me forward it. So let's just ship it from there and not worry about it. Actually, Weichmann won't know for sure where the cows are. They could be in any of the towns around Madison. Anyway, he's got enough to do without worrying about that."

"Weichmann said he needed one cc per sample, right?"

"That's what he said, but have Buddy get two cc's."

"Why two?"

"I'd like to take a look at the samples through the microscope."

"Looking for what?"

"I don't know. I'm just curious."

"Do you know about cow blood?"

"I took a comparative hematology course once, so I've studied it some."

"I'll send your samples the same time I send Weichmann's. To your home address?"

"That'd be best."

"If everything goes right, they should get there before noon tomorrow. I'll call you tonight and let you know what happened."

Otto Christianson stepped back and looked at the left front tire of his cruiser . . . still a little flat. Compressing his belly, he bent down and put the nozzle of the air hose on the tire's valve stem and gave it another shot. As he stood up to check the results, the radio affixed to his shirt spoke to him.

"Sheriff, Claire here. Come in . . ."

Otto pressed the Talk button on the radio. "I'm here. Go ahead."

"You've got a phone call."

"Is it important?"

"I think so."

"I was about to head in anyway. Get the number and tell 'em I'll call back in a few minutes."

When he walked past Claire's station five minutes later, she handed him a piece of paper with the caller's number on it.

"It's long distance," he said, concerned about the cost. "You should have asked him to call back."

"That's not what you told me to do."

"I didn't know then it was long distance."

"Now I see why Frannie doesn't want you to retire. She'd rather have *me* put up with you all day."

Hoping this would be a short conversation, Otto went into his office and called the number. "Father Lucius Graham, please . . . Father, this is Sheriff Christianson in Midland, Wisconsin, returning your call."

"Thanks for getting back to me so quickly. Sheriff, do you know a man named Chester Sorenson?"

"He was a resident here until his death a few months ago."

"I understand that another man from your town, Henry Pennell, is missing."

"That's right. How do you know all this?"

"Sheriff, I think you've got a psychopathic killer living there and I believe I know who it is."

Otto listened hard to everything Father Lucius said, all thoughts of what the call was costing forgotten. When Lucius had finished his tale, Otto said, "I don't know anyone around here named Billy Lynch. So if he's here, he's changed his name. How old would he be now?"

"Thirty-two."

"Can you think of any distinguishing marks or features that would help me identify him?"

There was a brief pause while Lucius considered this. Then he said, "I can't think of any."

"What color hair did he have?"

"Brown."

"Do you remember the color of his eyes?"

"As often as I looked at his face in my office, I should, but I don't. I'm not sure how much good it will do, but I could send you a picture of him taken when he was here."

"I'd appreciate that."

Otto gave Lucius the office address, thanked him for the information, and hung up.

Billy Lynch . . . Thirty-two years old and using a different name . . . Someone who moved here relatively recently and who would have a great interest in the investigation of Chester Sorenson's death and Henry Pennell's disappearance . . . Someone like Jessie Heflin's boyfriend, Artie Harris.

The dirt driveway leading from the mailbox Buddy had described on Pike Road was heavily rutted so that as he traversed it, Richard's head jerked and bobbed, threatening to strain his neck muscles. Finally, the burned house came into view: a charred husk with several pieces of partially burned upholstered furniture around it. But no Buddy.

Wincing at all the broken glass around the site, Richard backed the car onto an apparently safe piece of ground littered with used condoms so that he was facing the drive. Then he cut off the engine to wait.

It was certainly a good meeting place for two people who didn't want to be seen together. But as he sat there, it occurred to him that it would also be a good place for an ambush. At that instant, very close to him, there was a gunshot. Instinctively he threw himself sideways, jamming his rib cage painfully into the console between the seats. Realizing after the damage was done that the sound had just been the engine cooling, he pushed himself up and resumed waiting.

After a long six minutes, he thought he heard the sound of a motorcycle. He lowered the passenger window.

Yes. And it was getting closer.

Seconds passed and then, astride his Harley and wearing a black leather jacket, but no helmet, Buddy shot out of the mouth of the driveway. He made a tight turn and parked in front of Richard's car. Richard popped the trunk lid and got out.

"Sorry I'm late," Buddy said. "But you know the saying, 'shit happens,' especially when you work with 1700 factories that don't do much else but make it. You got everything?"

"Back here."

Buddy followed Richard around to the trunk, where Richard reached in and brought out an old, oblong, black lunchbox that had once belonged to his father.

"That's great," Buddy said. "I was worried about carrying something suspicious-looking."

Richard opened the lunchbox and inventoried the contents aloud, adding safety tips and instructions as he went. When he finished, he said, "We'll need two cc's of blood from each animal."

"No problem."

"What time do you get off?"

"Six."

"Is there any way you can get the samples to me earlier? I need to send them off for testing, but that won't give me time to pack them and get them to the Fed Ex pickup."

"I could get sick after I collect them, leave early."

"That'd be a big help."

"How long will it take before you know what happened to Chester?"

"Hard to say."

"I've decided to quit the dairy. I'm going out to California. See what life is like where there's no snow. Ever been there?"

"Only to visit."

"Maybe I'll just quit today."

To have Buddy far away from the dairy after he'd delivered the samples was an appealing prospect. If he wasn't around, he *couldn't* talk. But if anything went wrong with the samples, they might need him again. "How about waiting a few more days? Getting sick is okay, but if you quit in the middle of the afternoon, it's going to look odd. Better not to draw that much attention to yourself with the samples in your possession."

"Yeah, okay, that makes sense."

Buddy put the lunchbox in a compartment on the back of the Harley, waved to Richard, and left, fishtailing and throwing dirt.

28

Saturday morning, a little after eleven o'clock, the assistant manager called Holly from the apartment house office to tell her a package had arrived for her by Federal Express. She hurried down to claim it and took it back to her apartment where, nestled in shredded paper inside an insulated container kept cool by a reusable cold pack, she found four plastic tubes of blood inside four larger tubes held together with a rubber band. There was also a note:

"Enjoyed my brief visit. Hope when things settle down, we can get together again. Richard."

Holly put the lid back on the insulated container, grabbed her handbag, and headed for the elevator.

Approximately fifteen minutes later, she was standing at the distribution counter of the hospital hematology lab filling out the orders for the lab to make and stain blood smears from the samples Richard had sent. She didn't need to mention any possible health risks from handling the blood because, as in Weichmann's lab, these people also assumed all blood was infectious.

"How long do you think it'll take?" Holly asked.

"About an hour," the clerk replied.

"Along with the slides I'd like the remaining blood returned."

"Can do," the tech said, noting that on the order.

With an hour to kill, it seemed like a good time for lunch. Since she was in the building, Holly decided to eat in the hospital cafeteria.

She arrived in time to queue up behind a guy whose scalp bristled with EEG electrodes and wires. Off to her left, under a big banner advising the cafeteria's patrons to EAT HEALTHY, was a help-yourself taco bar containing lots of sour cream, ground beef, and guacamole. She'd once thought the banner meant the food under it was specially prepared from low-fat, healthy recipes, but was now aware that the banner was simply an admonition that had nothing to do with *any* of the food. To fully follow the advice, you'd have to eat somewhere else.

Ignoring the fried catfish, the fried chicken, and the seafood primavera with its high-fat sauce, she chose a vegetable plate and took it to the observation deck, which was cleverly situated right over the emergency room entrance so that in return for a little sun you had to watch a constant flow of ambulances arriving.

Pleasant as all this was, Holly finished her meal well before it was time to pick up the slides. To occupy herself while waiting, she wandered down to the vending center, bought a *USA Today,* and read it at one of the tables.

Finally, when it was time, she went up to the lab and got the slides, which they gave to her in a small cardboard holder. Using the hallway that ran under Madison Avenue, she took the slides directly to her office.

Now . . . what kind of blood cells do these animals have? she thought, putting the first slide on the stage of her microscope. She started with the 10X objective, which didn't allow her to see much, but permitted her to find a good area of the smear to study. She then switched to 40X.

A little adjustment of the fine focus and there they were: a sea of bland erythrocytes with the much more interesting white cells dispersed across the field like little jewels.

But something was wrong.

The white cells were too small.

Or . . .

Switching to an ocular with a micrometer in it, she checked the size of the erythrocytes.

Jesus, this was strange.

She examined all the other slides, then reached for the phone and called Richard at home. But she got only his answering machine.

"Richard, this is Holly. Give me a call at home as soon as you get in."

When she arrived home and put her key in the lock, she could hear the phone ringing. She dashed inside and caught it before it stopped.

"Richard?"

"It's Grant," her former boyfriend said. "Who's Richard?"

"What do you want, Grant?"

"I've been thinking, . . . I'm willing to forget the damage you did in my office and the irrational way you acted and take you back."

"Oh Grant, don't forget it. Remember it. Cherish it. I know I do."

"Who's Richard? It's not Richard Forrest, is it? Because I happen to know he's involved with a huge malpractice suit in which the damages sought far exceed his insurance coverage. If he loses, you'll be supporting him the rest of your life."

Hearing the signal for another call coming in, Holly said, "I have to go." She cut Ingram off with her finger on the disconnect, then let the other call in.

"This is Holly."

"It's Richard. What's up? Did you get the samples?"

"I got them and that blood is weird. When I first looked at it, I thought the white cells were too small, but then I measured the red cells and discovered that *they're* too big."

"I'm not following you."

"In cud-chewing animals, the erythrocytes are smaller than in humans, so when you're accustomed to looking at human blood, the white cells of cows seem unusually large. But it's only because of the smaller red cells. The red cells in these samples are the same size as in humans."

"All four samples are like that?"

"Every one."

"So these cows really *have* been genetically manipulated. What the devil can be gained by increasing the size of their erythrocytes?"

"Each cell would have more hemoglobin. So they could carry more oxygen."

"What does that accomplish?"

"We need someone like the health department to examine the dairy's animal records."

"I'm tempted to use your erythrocyte observations as proof to the department that the animals are clones."

"It doesn't really prove that. It shouldn't take Weichmann long to finish his tests. Let's wait for him."

"Okay. There probably wouldn't be anybody at the department today anyway."

Tuesday night it was Billy Lynch's turn to make a pickup at the airport. He'd worked with Bobby Fowler a half-dozen times over the years and for the most part, they understood each other. But when Bobby entered the concourse, Billy didn't like what he saw.

"How they hangin', man?" Bobby said when he'd made his way to where Billy was waiting. Knowing that Billy didn't like to be touched, he didn't offer his hand.

"That mustache has to go," Billy said, starting for the terminal.

"Why?"

"It doesn't match what you'll be wearing. And you should have told me you'd gained weight. I hope the clothes I bought for you fit."

"Yeah, I'm fine. Thanks for askin'."

If you had told Father Lucius the day that Billy had scalded Bobby in the orphanage shower, that someday the two of them would be working together as assassins, he would have thought that assassin was a reasonable prediction for Billy, but not Bobby. And working together? God's ways are mysterious to be sure, but such an alliance would strain even that premise. But there they were.

"Who's the pigeon?" Bobby asked.

"A doctor named Holly Fisher."

Bobby stopped walking. "Aw c'mon . . . A woman? Not a woman."

"To the rest of the world she's a woman. To us, she's an assignment, nothing more."

"I have trouble thinkin' that. And you know how you get afterwards. . . . It'll be worse with a woman."

Billy fixed him with a steely glare. "How I get afterwards? What do you mean?"

Bobby had instantly regretted his comment. He'd known for years that shortly after a hit, feelings of remorse would practically make Billy a zombie. And then a few days later, he wouldn't remember any of that part. It was like at the orphanage when you choked your chicken and then felt so ashamed you told yourself you'd never do it again. But you did. That was normal. But this deal with Billy wasn't. What the hell, if he didn't want to remember how bad he'd feel later, screw it. "Nothin', man. Forget it."

"If you can't handle this, get on a plane and go home," Billy said. "And don't expect to ever work with me again."

"I was just sayin' . . ."

"Are you in or out?"

"Well, shit . . . I guess I'm in."

"Don't guess."

"All right. I'm in."

Before opening the manila envelope that had just arrived, Otto got a Zagnut bar from the stash in his desk and quelled the rumbling in his stomach by eating all of it. He washed it down with a Diet Coke from his little refrigerator, then picked up the envelope and opened it.

Inside was a group photo of a bunch of kids. Father Lucius had circled one of the boys with a black marker. Even after using his hand magnifier on it, Otto couldn't make out much about the child. Putting the picture aside, Otto wondered what that priest was thinking—that he had access to the equipment NASA uses to clear up the pictures from that big telescope they got up there? Even if he did, Billy Lynch would certainly look a lot different now.

There was a knock on the door and Claire, his dispatcher and secretary, came in. "Here's that report you wanted from Missouri motor vehicles." She looked at the Zagnut wrapper still on his desk. "I thought you were on a diet."

"If I wasn't, I'd have eaten *three* of them."

"What do you expect me to say when Frannie asks me if you're being good?"

"Tell her I don't tolerate spies in the office."

"We're just trying to do what's best for you," she muttered as she left.

Otto looked at the report she'd handed him. Sure enough, there it was.

When his interest was first aroused in Artie Harris, Otto had Claire call up Artie's Wisconsin driver's license on her computer. Looking at it, he'd noticed something out of order. Artie had once told him he'd lived in Pennsylvania all his life, yet the first three digits of his social security number were those reserved for residents of *Missouri*. And here was proof he'd lied: Artie's Missouri driving record showed a previous St. Louis address. It was time he and Artie had a talk.

Otto looked up Artie's number and made the call.

No answer. Come to think of it, he hadn't seen Artie in days.

Otto looked up the number and called Bruxton Pharmaceuticals.

"Jessie Heflin, please."

A short selection from the Carpenters ensued before Jessie answered.

"This is Otto. Is Artie out of town? I need to talk to him about something."

"He went to visit some friends and was then going on to an insurance convention his company wanted him to attend."

"Did he give you a number where he could be reached?"

"Sorry. If he calls me, I'll tell him to get in touch with you."

"Okay, thanks."

Even more curious now about Artie, Otto turned to the insurance listings in the Yellow Pages to see what company he represented. There he was: Arthur Harris, Metropolitan Life.

Otto got up and opened the door of his office. "Claire, will you see if you can find me the number of the main office of the Metropolitan Life Insurance Company?"

Using the Internet, Claire had the number in under five minutes.

"Someday you're gonna have to show me how you do that," Otto said, taking the slip of paper from her with the number on it.

When a woman at Met Life picked up, Otto said, "I hope you can help me. I need to get a message to one of your agents who's attending that insurance convention you sent him to. Could you give me the location of that event or maybe a contact phone number?"

There was a long quiet interval while the woman on the other end did some checking. With nothing to occupy his mind, Otto began to think of the remaining Zagnut bars in his desk. As he bent to get one, the woman came back on the line. "I'm sorry, but no one here knows of any insurance convention taking place at this time."

29

"Doctor Fisher, we've discovered some interesting things about those samples you sent us," Weichmann said. "To determine whether animals are clones, we normally compare several segments in the part of the genome involved with the immune system—those regions that make each animal a distinct individual immunologically, because that's where no two animals are ever alike. . . . Unless they're identical twins or clones. Well, all four samples you sent were identical in the regions we checked."

"Wait a minute," Holly said. "I don't understand. Two of those samples were from animals that had the same pigmentation pattern. The other two were from a pair with a *different* pattern. How can all four be clones if they don't even look alike?"

"You're sure about the pigmentation?"

"I didn't personally witness the drawing of the blood. But the plan was for the samples to be taken as I've described. And I have no reason to believe the plan wasn't followed."

"If the samples truly *are* from two sets of animals with different pigmentation patterns, there's only one explanation for the results we obtained. Someone must have taken cells from each of two different cows and in both, replaced a long stretch of DNA with a sequence from another source. They then produced cloned individuals from the progeny of those altered cells."

"Why would someone want to make all the animals in a large herd immunologically identical?"

"Don't misunderstand me. I'm not saying the four animals that provided the blood are identical at *all* their immunology-related sites. We only analyzed a few of them. They may be the same at all those sites, they may not. We just don't know. Either way, I can't think of a reason for doing such a thing. But I can tell you that this kind of manipulation isn't simple. So if there's a large number of animals involved, those responsible must have a compelling purpose. Do you know who that was?"

"Not really."

"Too bad. If you did, you could just ask them about it."

"I wish it was that easy. Well, you've given me a lot to think about, Doctor Weichmann. I'm in your debt. If I can ever . . ."

"I haven't told you the other thing we discovered— quite by accident, as it turns out. But then that's how penicillin was discovered, isn't it? Some of my regular work here involves genetic analysis of animals that have had genes inserted from a variety of sources. One of my students mistakenly included samples of the blood you sent in an analysis she was running. Doctor Fisher, those cows of yours have some human DNA sequences in them."

Shocked at this revelation, Holly's mind struggled to make sense of it. "Are you saying those immune sequences that match in all the animals are human?"

"Again, that's taking the data too far," Weichmann said. "The probes we use to determine whether there are human inserts present can't answer that question. But I can tell you that the human DNA and the matching sequences are in the same chromosome."

•   •   •

"How sure are we that Buddy followed your instructions when he chose the animals to sample?" Holly said into the phone.

"My sister, Jessie, suggested we have him photograph the cows he picked," Richard said. "I've got the pictures right here. He did it correctly."

"I never thought of that. Good for Jessie."

"What's going on?"

"All four cows have identical sequences in regions of their DNA where no two animals would normally ever be the same—sites involved in immune function." Holly explained the implications of this for their cloning question, then said, "And get this . . . In a separate test, Weichmann found evidence that all the animals have stretches of human DNA in the same chromosome as the matching sequences he found. He couldn't say that the common sequences were human, but it seems pretty likely to me that they are."

"That's wild. Cows with human DNA. But these animals aren't the first. I know that other drug companies are putting human genes into cows, trying to get them to synthesize human proteins in their milk. But there'd be no reason to make the cow's immune system more like humans to do that."

"Could they be planning to use cow organs for human transplantation?"

"There are programs hoping to do that with pig organs, but I've never heard of cows being candidates for that kind of thing. Whatever they're doing, those animals are all genetically similar enough that somebody needs to make sure they're not all making abnormal prion protein. With the genetic meddling that's been done on them, the prion gene might have inadvertently been altered too so it produces a form of the protein that's more susceptible to spontaneous conversion. I've got to call the health department."

•   •   •

"What do you mean, this information doesn't change anything?" Richard said to the director of the state health department.

"As I've tried to explain, Doctor Heflin, the management of the dairy has been watching very carefully for neurologic disturbances in their animals and they've seen nothing. That one case was simply an isolated incident."

"Come on . . . To let the dairy decide the extent of the problem is like . . ." Richard searched his mind for a devastating analogy but couldn't come up with anything. "Well, it's just foolish."

"Doctor Heflin, I didn't get where I am by being a fool."

"Then there must be some other explanation for your refusal to listen to me. What is it?"

"I think you're focusing too much on this."

"And you're not focusing at all."

"I don't have time for further debate on this matter. Please don't call me again about it."

Then she hung up.

With several patients waiting, Richard didn't have time to think about his next move.

Two hours later, just as he finished discussing her options and prognosis with a patient in the early stages of Parkinson's disease, Connie informed him that he had a phone call.

Thinking it might be Holly with more news, and wanting to tell her about the health department's ridiculous stand, he took it eagerly.

"Doctor," a male voice said. "I have some instructions for you."

"What kind of instructions?"

"Give up your interest in the Midland Dairy. Nothing there concerns you. Do not discuss it with anyone again."

Richard bristled with anger. "I don't respond well to threats."

"You should learn, for the sake of Katie. Imagine how you and her grandparents in Mesa would feel if anything happened to her."

The caller's reference to Katie hit Richard like a fist in the face, making his legs rubbery. *Katie . . . They knew where she was.*

"There are many other areas in the country that need a neurologist," the voice said. "Find one. We'll expect to see a For Sale sign on your house within seventy-two hours. Don't take this lightly."

At the other end of the line, Zane Bruxton's aide, Boone, hung up the pay phone and went back to the car where Bruxton waited.

"How did he react?"

"Defiant, before I mentioned his daughter."

"And after that?"

"He didn't say anything."

"Let's go home."

As they drove, Bruxton wondered again whether he was doing the right thing by simply warning Heflin. It was a risky strategy, but it seemed like having him killed would be worse. That dimwit Otto Christianson was already too curious. He settled back in his seat and rubbed his eyes, feeling that he was on the edge of a great vortex that was slowly pulling everything associated with him toward it, trying to swallow who he was and all he had built. And he saw now that the vortex had always been there. But his strength and intelligence had kept him so far from it, he hadn't known of its existence. Now that he was old and weak, the sound of it roared in his ears. But his brain still worked and as long as it did, he would fight the currents that wanted to drag him down.

After the threatening phone call, Richard immediately called his parents in Arizona.

"Pop . . . This is Richard. Is Katie there?"

"Sitting right here in your mother's lap."

"May I speak to her?"

There was a pause then Richard heard Katie's sweet voice. "Hello . . . Daddy?"

A tide of relief surged through him. "Hi, cupcake. Are you having a good time?"

"I went swimming this morning. Well, not actually swimming . . . but I waded."

"I'll bet that was fun."

Richard spoke to Katie for another couple of minutes. Then, hugely relieved that she was intact, he asked her to put her grandfather back on the line.

"Pop, I have to talk to you about something. But I can't do it right this minute. Don't go anywhere until I call back. It's important."

Richard hung up and sat there, at a loss for what to do. He couldn't put Katie at risk and he couldn't ignore what he knew about the dairy. The threat alone suggested there was a lot *more* to know.

What to do?

He sat for several minutes, bent over, his head in his hands as though trying to squeeze out an answer. He didn't want to leave Midland. He liked it here. And the thought of having his life manipulated again by thugs was repellent.

No, by God. He wouldn't run. He'd fight. He didn't know how exactly, but he'd show them they couldn't get their way by force. But first, he had to make sure Katie was safe.

How to . . .?

Struck by an idea, he reached for his Rolodex and thumbed through it. Finding the number, he paused. *It's one o'clock here, it'll be seven there.*

For the next six minutes, he spoke to Peter Galbreath, the man who would either make or break his plan. At the end of that conversation, he called his parents back.

"Pop, I need for you to do something for me."

"Sure. What is it?"

"I'm involved in something here that has caused some people to threaten Katie. And they know she's with you."

"What are you talking about? Threaten her?"

"If I don't do what they want, they implied they'd hurt her."

"Son, what have you gotten yourself into?"

"I can't explain now. It could be nothing more than a threat. But I can't take that chance. Do you remember when I did that year in London with the group specializing in head trauma? One of my patients was the child of an inspector for Scotland Yard. Diane and I became good friends with him and his wife. They've agreed to keep Katie until this is resolved."

"You're going to put her in the hands of strangers?"

"They're only strangers to you, Pop. And it's the safest place for her. They've got a little girl Katie's age, so she'll have someone to play with."

"Why don't you just do what these people want?"

"I can't. If you were in my place, you'd see that. I want you and Mom to take Katie to London as soon as possible. Will you do it?"

"If it means keeping her safe, of course. When?"

"Can you leave tomorrow?"

"That's not much notice."

"We need to move fast. It'll be tiring, but you can go tomorrow and come back the next day, unless you want to stay longer."

"How long will it take to resolve this problem?"

"I don't know."

"I'm sure your mother won't want to leave Katie in another country. She'll want to *know* she's okay."

"Then stay there a few days until I can sort this out. Let's say a week. I'll find a hotel for you near the people who'll be taking care of her."

"Why can't we just keep her with us?"

"The people who threatened her might find you there. Peter Galbreath, the fellow who agreed to protect her, is a professional at dealing with things like this. Let him handle it."

"You're right. I just hope I can explain that to your mother."

"I'll call you back in a few minutes and let you know the flight arrangements."

Richard hung up and reached for the phone book.

Within ten minutes, he had three seats on a Delta flight that left from Phoenix the next morning for a connecting flight in Cincinnati. Since it was out of season, there were plenty of seats available and they were relatively cheap.

He then called his father and gave him the pertinent flight information and told him the tickets would be waiting at the Delta counter. He then placed another call to London.

"Peter, this is Richard again. It's all set." He told Peter the flight number and arrival time at Gatwick, then said, "I hate to keep piling things on you, but would you have time to make reservations for a week for my parents at a hotel near your home? Under the circumstances, they're reluctant to leave Katie."

"As all good grandparents would be," Peter said. "I'll take care of it. In fact, I'll have someone look out for them too, just in case."

"I don't know how I'm going to repay you for all this."

"Hey, I'm not footing the bill for the hotel, am I?"

"Of course not."

"I was just having you on. Considering what you did for Megan after her accident, it's my great pleasure to do this for you. Don't worry. She'll be safe here."

"I hope this doesn't put you or your family in any danger."

"Anybody tries to get to any of us, *they're* the ones who'll be in danger."

"I'll try to resolve this quickly. Take care. And thanks again."

Richard then set about wondering how he was going to resolve the situation at all, let alone quickly.

30

Holly meant to pick up some toothpaste on the way home from the office, but for hours everything Weichmann had told her filled the gaps around her patients' needs, leaving no room for the mundane. She remembered it a little after 7 P.M. when she went into the bathroom and saw the empty tube in the wastebasket.

Did she really want to go out just for toothpaste? No. Could she live with water brushing for just one night? Also no. The jeans and cross-trainers she was wearing were fine for going out, but she needed more on top than a T-shirt. So before leaving, she slipped on a long-sleeved french terry-knit pullover.

She drove to a small shopping center near her apartment, where the only two places open were a Rite Aid drugstore and, way across the vast parking lot, a Megamart grocery store.

She was inside the Rite Aid for less than five minutes. When she emerged, she noticed casually that a blue van had taken the empty parking space on the store side of her car. With streetwise curiosity, she looked to see if it was occupied as she approached, but saw no one behind the wheel or in the passenger seat.

When she passed the van, she was shocked to see a
priest sitting on the pavement, his back leaning on her
car, hand over his heart, his flushed face contorted in
agony. Behind her car, sprawled on its side, was a bicycle.

"Pills . . ." the priest groaned. He pointed at the pavement between him and the bicycle. There Holly saw a
prescription bottle. Realizing he was probably having a
heart attack, she rushed to the bottle, scooped it up, and
returned with it to the priest's side, where she looked at
the label.

Nitroglycerin.

She unscrewed the lid, tapped a pill into her hand,
and leaned forward. "I have your medicine, Father. Open
your mouth."

His face a canvas of pain, the priest did what she
asked. When Holly's fingers were an inch from his lips,
he suddenly grabbed her arm with his right hand and
yanked her off balance. At the same instant, his left hand
came from under his leg and he shoved an electric stun
gun against her.

The jolt of electricity ripped through Holly's body,
short-circuiting her brain and stiffening her muscles before they failed her and she sprawled limply across the
priest's body.

The van's door slid open and Billy Lynch jumped out.
He pulled Holly off Bobby Fowler and dumped her in
the van, where they'd removed the back seats.

Bobby grabbed up the prescription bottle Holly had
dropped and stuffed it in his pocket. Leaving the bicycle, which they'd handled only with gloved hands, Bobby
jumped into the van and shut the door as Billy got them
moving.

In the back, where Holly was still too stunned to
realize what was happening, Bobby stuffed a washcloth
they'd stolen from their motel into her mouth, then covered her mouth with duct tape, which he ran twice around
her head. He added two courses from under her lower
jaw to the top of her skull so there was no way she could

open her mouth even a slit. He covered her eyes with another length that circled her head, then bound her wrists and ankles.

Holly was lying between two long pine one-by-fours her abductors had screwed to the van's floor shortly after they rented it. Bobby pulled a short length of tape from the roll and nailed the free end to one of the boards at a point opposite Holly's head. He ran the tape across her forehead and nailed the other free end to the opposite board, making sure it held her head tightly. He then ran similar strips across her chest, thighs, and calves. As he carried a final strip across her hands, he looped it twice around her wrists before nailing it. Satisfied that she could now neither sit up nor lift her legs, Bobby unfolded the long cardboard box they'd constructed, and put it over her. He tacked the edges to the pine boards and joined Billy in front.

"You sure she can breathe?" Billy asked.

"I'm sure."

Though they were going to kill Holly, Billy had no intention of having her die in the van where they could be in an accident or a cop might stop them for some obscure traffic reg they'd violated. He was positive the grab had been squeaky clean, but if by some weird chance they *had* been seen and the cops would soon be looking for them, there was no way he was going to be caught with a body. The sentence for kidnapping was no picnic, but a murder conviction could put a permanent dent in a man's future.

That same kind of foresight was why he'd ignored all the potential wilderness dump sites across the river in Arkansas. That would have made it a federal offense. And he sure didn't need the FBI complicating his life.

"I feel like a Lilliputian," Bobby said.

"What do you mean?"

"The way we've got her strapped down; it's like the Lilliputians did to that guy, Oliver."

"It was Gulliver."

"Oh, yeah."

"How can you remember *Lilliputian* and forget *Gulliver*?"

"How do we remember any of that crap they taught us at St. Peter's? . . . Do you think about the place much?"

"Sometimes."

"Do you hate them? I do."

"I don't hate anybody."

"Then why am I dressed as a priest? That wasn't some slap at Father Lucius?"

"It just seemed like a good way to get her attention without making her suspicious."

"What about the people who killed your parents? If they were here now, would you kill them?"

"I already did. Five years ago."

"Well?"

"Not out of hate. But because they took something from me, something I needed very badly at that time in my life. If you don't stand up for your rights, you'll always have someone trampling on them. Hate just clouds the mind. Always retaliate, but never with hatred."

"Why are we workin' so hard? We could have just hit this woman in the parking lot."

"Too chancy. When we walk away from this, I want to know for sure it's over. No lingering in a hospital, no possibility of recovery."

"When the time comes, *you're* going to do it, right?"

"I'll do it. Now that's enough talk. She can hear."

Bobby was about to ask what difference that made if they were going to kill her, but Billy was acting so nice toward him, he didn't want to risk setting him off.

In the back, Holly had recovered to the point where she had indeed heard Billy's remark about no chance for recovery. Though she was weak and felt as if there were a beehive in her head, she struggled against her restraints. But she could accomplish nothing.

The man who sounded as though he was in charge was almost certainly the one who had been in her hospital room that night in Midland. And this time, she could see no escape. She'd faced death before when her bone marrow had turned against her, but then there had been options . . . treatments . . . a chance for a reprieve. Now she had no options.

No. Don't think that way, she told herself. There was always hope. No matter how bleak the outlook, you have to have hope. Maybe someone had seen what happened, had taken down the license number of the vehicle they were in. And even now there was a call going out to every patrol car on the streets. Help could be just minutes away.

But no one had seen what happened. There was no call going out. In fact, the bicycle her abductors had left in the parking lot had already been stolen, so that the only evidence of what had taken place there was a few scattered white pills on the asphalt.

From the time Billy had spent learning the city, he knew that the most direct route to the river from where they'd picked Holly up was Poplar Avenue. But that would take them directly past the Justice Center, which would be crawling with cops. He therefore, took a less direct route to Second Street, which he followed north, through a part of the city that would never appear on a tourist brochure.

Shortly after he crossed the Wolf River bridge, he turned onto a dirt road and followed it, fighting the wheel as ruts and potholes made the headlights jitter over the scrubby landscape. Eventually, the main track ran down a hill and ended in the black water of the Mississippi.

Billy took a much fainter path to the left and eased the van through the scrub about thirty yards before braking and putting it in park. Leaving the headlights on, he said, "Okay, let's get her out."

Billy left the driver's door open when he stepped from the van so Bobby would have the overhead light to help him see what he was doing. In the back, Bobby pulled the cardboard box off Holly, folded it, and put it out of the way. He then cut the straps holding her down.

As Bobby worked, the tiny flame of hope that Holly had been clinging to while they drove to this spot flickered and died. She could tell by the way the van had bounced around that they had left the paved road. With the door open, her nostrils were filled with the wet smell of the river. There was no way the police could find them now.

In desperation, Holly swung her bound hands through the air, hitting Bobby in the temple. She squirmed and pivoted on her back, bringing her legs around to where she felt him against her feet. As she lashed out, pushing him hard, Billy opened the van and Bobby tumbled out.

Calmly reaching into his jacket, Billy got his stun gun and climbed into the van.

Holly was clawing at the tape over her eyes when she felt him get in. Still unable to see, she kicked in that direction, but he merely swatted her legs aside and pressed the stunner against her.

The jolt of electricity immediately took Holly's will and ability to resist. But it brought a gift too. With her mind scrambled, she was no longer able to grasp the peril she was in. If her abductors moved quickly, she would be spared the terror of waiting for death.

Billy pulled her out of the van. With Bobby's help he carried her past the front of the vehicle and dumped her on the ground about ten feet in front of the headlights. There, he reached into his jacket for the nylon cord he would use to strangle her. Straddling her, he wrapped the cord around her neck. Bobby turned to look away.

The mental effects of the electric shock had worn off too soon. Horribly aware now of what was happening, but with tape still over her eyes so she couldn't see him, Holly tried to buck Billy off her. But she hadn't the strength. He tightened the cord, constricting the flesh of her neck, and leaned close to her. "This is an ugly world full of disappointment and heartache," he whispered. "I'm doing you a favor."

But then, over the purr of the van's engine and the faint eerie moan of protest coming from Holly's throat, Billy thought he heard something else. He allowed the cord to slacken and listened hard. Suddenly he jumped up and bolted for the van, where he cut off the engine and the lights.

Puzzled, Bobby was right behind him. "What's wrong?" Then he heard it too.

"Get down," Bobby hissed.

The two men scattered, finding cover that allowed them to see the dirt road. Within seconds a pickup pulling a boat trailer bounced into view. It stopped at the top of the approach to the river and flicked its headlights three times, then sat with its engine running and its lights shining steadily.

Across the river, on the Arkansas side, Big Eddie Burkhalter fired up the outboard and headed for home, aiming the bow of the boat for the twin beacons formed by the headlights of his brother's pickup. In the bow, Little Eddie, Big Eddie's twenty-year-old son, swept the water ahead and upstream with a big flashlight, watching for floating logs. They'd had a good trip and were bringing back ten wood ducks each, far over the legal limit. Ignorant of gun safety, both had their pump Remington 12-gauges propped on the middle seat fully loaded. Ernie, their golden retriever, sat on the middle seat enjoying the feel of the wind on his face.

Even if Billy couldn't have heard the sound of the approaching boat, it would have been obvious that the truck had come to pick up someone on the river, meaning there would soon be even *more* activity here.

The van was deep into the scrub and the night was moonless, so it was distinctly possible that it would never be noticed. He decided to just wait the situation out.

Holly too, heard the boat and hope returned.

When Big Eddie's boat was forty yards out, his brother, Ben, left the pickup and walked down to the water. "How'd you do?"

"Got a bunch," Little Eddie shouted back.

The bow of the boat struck land and Ben pulled it a few feet on shore so they could unload. The dog jumped out, shook himself, and tested the air for interesting smells. There was a slight breeze coming from upriver, which meant that he picked up nothing from the direction of the van.

The usual clatter and conversation of men returning from the hunt ensued. From the tone and content of the talk and their attention to the work as they ferried items from the boat to the pickup, it was obvious to Billy that they had no idea anyone else was around.

Holly too could tell that the hunters hadn't seen the van. She'd been trying to get the tape off her mouth so she could remove the washcloth Bobby had used to gag her, but with her wrists still bound, she'd only been able to roll the upper margin of the tape down a little. She tried now to scream, but the gag muffled what little sound she could muster. With her ankles also still bound, and still suffering muscle weakness from the stun gun, there was no way she could stand. All she could manage was to squirm on the ground, trying to find something she could kick to make a little noise.

She was lying a few feet from the edge of the hill that dropped to the river. In the spring, the spot where the van was parked was regularly under several inches of water. When it receded, it always left a lot of debris behind. As Holly squirmed and tested her surroundings with her feet, she found a clump of dry twigs caught in the low branches of some scrubby bushes. With her third kick at them, she caught a good sized one just right and it broke with a sharp *CRACK*.

At the pickup, the dog's head swiveled in Holly's direction and he began to bark. Coming up the hill with a bag of ducks in one hand and his shotgun in the other, Big Eddie walked to the dog and looked into the darkness. "What is it boy?"

• • •

Sensing that this could be big trouble, Billy drew his automatic from his shoulder holster. Behind him, Bobby did the same, only *he* started to sweat.

Hearing that she'd attracted some attention, Holly kicked again at the debris, but couldn't generate a significant sound. Casting around to find something else to kick, she rolled to the edge of the hill, then tumbled off it, making the noise she sought as she crashed into another tangle of dry twigs.

"What's going on?" Little Eddie said, bringing the rest of the ducks and the second shotgun up from the boat.
    "There's something out there."
    Little Eddie looked hard into the darkness. "Is that a car?"
    Big Eddie dropped his ducks. "Get the flashlight."

At that moment, Billy considered opening fire, but the two men were thirty yards away, too far for accuracy with a pistol even in good light. But it was a perfect distance for a shotgun. Could he bluff his way out of this? Not likely, especially if the dog picked up the girl's scent and led them to her.

While Little Eddie went for the flashlight, which he'd stowed in the pickup, Bobby Fowler panicked. He could see the next few minutes clearly in his mind. Billy was going to make a stand. There was going to be a gunfight, pistols against shotguns: a piss-poor matchup. He looked behind him. He could run for it, hide in the brush. Or . . .
    Not fully realizing the consequences of his decision, Bobby bolted for the van, jumped into the driver's seat, and twisted the key in the ignition. Without bothering to turn on the lights, he dropped it into reverse and sped toward Big Eddie, who was outlined in the pickup's headlights. If Eddie had remained where he was, Bobby would

have hit him. But at the last moment Eddie retreated, allowing Bobby to make an unobstructed tight turn that got the van pointed toward the highway. Punching the gas hard, Bobby fled.

Ignoring for the moment the treachery in Bobby's act, Billy believed that it might have defused the situation. If the hunters thought everyone associated with the van was in it when it departed, they might just go on about their business and leave without investigating.

But then he heard Ben say, "What the hell was *that* about? He almost *hit* you."

"They must have been up to something bogus," Little Eddie said.

"Somebody laying a little pipe maybe," Ben said.

"Then what was that noise I heard?" Big Eddie said. "Let's take a look."

The three men and the dog started toward Billy. But only two of the men had shotguns. Fight or run. . . . He could stay hidden and hope they passed . . . kill them from behind. But the dog would probably give him away before he could gain the advantage.

Lying a few feet below the crest of the hill, Holly had heard the van leave, but she didn't know if both her abductors had been in it. If their leader was still around and she made any noise, he might find her before the other men. So she decided, for now, to stay quiet.

Billy too, had made his decision. He holstered his automatic and began to crawl deeper into the scrub.

When the hunters reached the spot where Billy had been hiding, the dog began to bark. Little Eddie played the flashlight in that direction.

Fifteen feet off the track, Billy slipped his gun out and got ready. If the dog came after him, somebody was going to die.

•   •   •

Hearing the dog and the men so close, Holly decided it was safe to reveal her location, and she began kicking at the bushes around her and making what sounds she could in her throat.

The dog turned and ran to the edge of the hill. The men followed.

"What the hell's that?" Little Eddie said, finding Holly with his flashlight.

"It's a woman, you dope," Ben said.

Billy again weighed his options. Now that the hunters were focused on Holly, he might be able to take them. But once more, the advantage the shotguns gave them was cause for concern. If one of them just got off one round, even poorly aimed, he could lose an arm. His heart began to pound in his chest as he considered making this his last stand. He'd often dreamed of death. The details were never clear, but there was always smoke and explosions, so he knew his would be a violent end. Why not go for it, try to take them and see what happens? What he'd told Holly was true: this *was* an ugly world full of disappointment. Look at what Bobby had done to him. Of all people.

Thinking of how Bobby had betrayed him, he began to see things differently. If he charged those hunters and was killed, Bobby would never have to pay for what he'd done. And the woman . . . He'd be leaving *that* job unfinished as well. Finding these loose ends too untidy to accept, he once again holstered his gun and crawled deeper into the brush.

31

None of the three men who had rescued Holly could say how many people were in the van when it left the river, so the police brought in a helicopter and extra men to search the area. They were still looking when Holly was taken to the precinct house to tell her story one more time.

In all her exchanges with the police, she gave as full and complete an account as she could in her responses to their questions, *until* they asked if she knew the men who'd abducted her. She said they were strangers. While this was literally true, it was the obvious time to tell them about everything that had led up to her abduction. But she'd kept all that to herself—mostly because she felt it would be too complicated and nebulous for them to grasp, or care about, especially since the rotten heart of it was in Wisconsin.

With all she'd been through, she'd lost her handbag. Miraculously, the cops found her keys on the ground where they'd fallen out of her jacket pocket when she was squirming around trying to find something noisy to kick. A little after 1 A.M., two detectives drove her to her car, which was sitting where she'd left it in the Rite

Aid parking lot. There, the detectives meticulously gathered up the scattered nitroglycerin pills that hadn't been crushed and put them into an evidence bag. Then they asked her one more time if she could give them any part of the van's license number. After she explained yet again that she never saw the license plate, they released her, promising that they'd see her safely home.

Despite having a security guard at the gate and another in the lobby of her building, as well as a deadbolt on her apartment door, Holly let the detectives come with her and check out her apartment to be sure no one was hiding there.

She'd lost one credit card along with her purse. After they'd looked around, the detectives asked her if she knew the number to call to report it stolen. When she said she did, they asked her to make the report right then so they could give the bank a number to call if any information came in about someone using the card.

She'd been holding up marvelously all evening, but the moment she shut the door behind the detectives the adrenaline that had been powering her ran out, leaving her depleted of all emotion and feeling as though she couldn't move another step. Even so, she managed to drag herself to the bedroom and fall across her bed, where sleep quickly took her.

Billy Lynch waded into the cold Mississippi. Behind him he could hear the rasp of patrol car radios and the *whup, whup* of the police helicopter as it made ever-widening circles over the scrub, looking for him with a big searchlight. He'd come to the river because there was no other escape available.

But what now? In only to his calves, he could already feel the treacherous current trying to pull his feet out from under him. And he was a poor swimmer.

It was so dark he could see nothing around him, but coming upstream was a lighted barge that looked as if it would pass only about fifty yards from shore. If he could reach that, he could hitch a ride and say "so long suckers" to all those cops.

He waded in a little deeper to test the current and was almost swept downstream. Retreating toward shore, he knew that reaching the barge was out of the question. But that current . . . if he could just ride it somehow.

Yeah, but with what? He could never stay afloat without help.

Behind him the helicopter made a wider swing that brought its searchlight within twenty yards of the riverbank. With the next pass, they'd likely see him even if they weren't expecting him to be in the river.

Think, Billy.

Wait a minute. . . . He'd once heard of a woman from a capsized sailboat staying afloat by tying the legs of her slacks together and trapping air in them. What about that?

But she was in the ocean. Would it work in fresh water? And would his pants actually hold air? Though he did not believe his life would end by drowning, the thought of trusting such a flaky idea held little appeal.

He looked over his shoulder and saw that the helicopter was starting its next pass.

By now, the barge was directly across from him and its lights dimly illuminated his surroundings. The sound of the helicopter grew closer.

Heart in his throat, he searched along the shore upstream for an answer, but there was only thin scrub, lined at the water's edge by a narrow mat of driftwood twigs and a couple of beer bottles. He turned and looked downstream. A few feet away, where the ground abruptly rose much steeper than where he stood, the river had undercut the bank, gouging out a deep recess. With the helicopter almost upon him, he sloshed toward the undercut.

The water quickly deepened again to mid-calf and then to his knees. Feeling twin pulses beating behind his eyes, he pushed on, fighting the currents that tried to spin him around and drag him deeper into the river.

He reached the recess and ducked inside just as the world exploded in light from the helicopter.

Had they seen him?

Back pressed against cold dirt, he got out his gun and waited.

Seconds passed with no new cop sounds . . . then minutes. He could still hear the helicopter, but now sounding far off. Was that because he was in a cave or because it was going away? Gun ready, feet braced against the current swirling around his legs, he waited in the dark to see what would happen.

Maybe they'd sent for a police boat and any second it'd pull up and rake the recess with a searchlight. What chance would he have then?

So he waited . . . and waited, unable to see an inch in front of him, the cold from the river seeping through his body until he began to shake.

It had been quite a while since he'd heard the helicopter. Maybe they *were* gone . . . Or just waiting for him to *think* so.

Suddenly, the current changed.

No . . . something was pressing against his legs, something *muscular.*

What the hell *was* that?

He kicked out and his foot hit a heavy smooth object that sluggishly yielded to the pressure and moved away. With only one leg supporting him, he was pushed sideways by the current and he danced downstream for several feet until he got his balance.

It was too dark to read his watch, so there was no way to judge the passing of time. But two more barges passed without any sign of a cop boat.

God it was cold.

Long ago, Billy had discovered that the secret to tolerating discomfort or pain was to mentally put himself in a different place. He went now to his favorite refuge; his mother's arms, his mouth on her full breast. Many believe it isn't possible to have memories of events that take place when people are so young. But Billy remembered. There, enveloped in her love, the smell of her powdered skin filling his nostrils and her milk giving him strength and comfort, the cold left him and time passed.

When he returned to the river, it was still dark. And another barge was coming upstream.

How long had he been here? Were the cops still waiting?

As the barge drew closer, its lights permitted a limited look at the river, where a few yards upstream he saw a dim shape in the water: a big plank of driftwood, barely ten yards from shore.

Seizing the opportunity and keeping his gun high in the air so it wouldn't get wet, Billy waded deeper into the river, which quickly rose to his thighs, then to his waist, raising gooseflesh on his arms and neck.

Fighting to stay on his feet, Billy could see the driftwood passing by just out of reach. He struggled forward one more step and threw himself at the plank. But he reached it with only the fingertips of his left hand. Having badly missed his target, Billy disappeared beneath the black water.

He fought to the surface two seconds later, coughing and disoriented, inhaled river water draining from his nostrils, his gun lost on the river bottom. Something tapped his head and slid by, raking his skin.

The driftwood plank . . .

His lunge and miss had spun it around so it was now on the shore side of him. He reached up with his right hand and cradled it in his arm. Holding on as tightly as he'd ever held his mother, Billy was carried downstream.

When the thin rays of the sun filtered through the filmy curtains of Holly's bedroom the next morning, she woke having had no resources even to dream. During the night, her muscles and joints had gone on strike, so it took some coaxing to get them working. On stiff legs she limped to the bathroom, where a hideous apparition inhabited her mirror.

Her eyes were bloodshot and had dark circles under them, and her face was crisscrossed with inflamed scratches. Luckily, it was Saturday and she didn't have to see any patients. Still too tired to be frightened, she stripped off her clothes and took a long, hot shower.

Feeling better, she put on fresh clothes and made herself a cup of hot chocolate. As she sat at the kitchen table, the events of the previous night skittered around in her head, moving too quickly to be examined. But then a nasty little thought rambled onstage and was slow to leave. At the precinct house, the cops had asked her if there was someone they could call for her, but she couldn't think of anyone, at least not in Memphis. She'd gone through hell and had no one to call when it was over, no one to hold her and stroke her hair and tell her everything was all right. And even now, when she needed moral support, she was sitting all alone in her kitchen.

For the next few minutes, Holly brooded over the emptiness of her life. Gradually that phase passed into gratitude that she still *had* a life. She'd believed that when she fled Midland the night someone had been in her room at the Green and White, she could leave all that behind, come home, and be safe.

But they'd followed her.

And if the cops hadn't caught them by now, they could still be out there, waiting for *another* chance. Suppose they *were* caught. Whoever had hired them could send someone else.

It was like her leukemia, when her bone marrow was pouring out assassins. But this malignancy was dispatching its killers from Midland, Wisconsin. And the only way to treat it, for her to be safe, was to do just what her doctors had done to her marrow: *destroy it.*

With that decision made, her mind sharpened. Maybe it was the two jolts of electricity she'd received to subdue her. Whatever the explanation, the events that had taken place during her three-day visit to Midland stood at attention for inspection, so that she was able to recall her conversation at the Lucy II in minute detail. They'd talked about the cows, how the new owners had replaced the whole herd and how the new animals didn't seem to be better than the old. Of course the workers didn't know that the new cows were carrying human genes.

She ran through the rest of that conversation and moved on to being forced off the road . . . the hospital, the attempt to add something to her IV, taking pictures of the cows, following the transport to the abandoned warehouse . . .

The transport that carried nothing.

Her mind flashed back to her conversation with the workers at the Lucy II: *The cows are divided into groups* . . .

When had she arrived in Midland?

She thought back. It was a Wednesday. So she saw the transport on Thursday. And the dairy workers had said that the transport always arrived to take the calves away three days after . . .

Which Thursday of the month was that?

She went to her study and looked at the calendar. Of course, it was the third Thursday of the month. Which meant that the next cycle . . . she ran her finger down the calendar and flipped the page . . . would be this coming *Monday*.

That didn't give her much time.

She located her emergency Visa card and looked up airlines in the Yellow Pages. A short while later, her flight arrangements made, she put a few things in a handbag she didn't like nearly as much as the one she'd lost, and left the building.

Still wet, Billy trudged up the foot of Union Avenue, intent on finding a cab. He'd spent the night in a grove of riverbank willows in his mother's arms. But he couldn't be there and look for a cab too, so he was now cold and miserable.

If stopped by any cops, he'd show them one of his

fake IDs and tell them he was a copier machine salesman in town to drum up some business and that he'd
gone down to look at the paddle-wheel riverboats and
had fallen in the river. Sure, it was risky, but it was the
best he could do short of riding that driftwood to
Natchez.

Like most cities, the other pedestrians on the street
were so accustomed to bums and misfits among them
that no one paid Billy any attention. He was pretty sure
he'd find a cab at the Greyhound station just across from
the new baseball park, and he did, reaching it without
either of the two patrol cars that passed even slowing
down. The cabbie, though, wasn't as blasé as the rest
of the city about Billy's appearance, and was reluctant
to take him anywhere until he saw some money.

Billy and Bobby were sharing a room at a twenty-
nine-dollar-a-night motel on the other side of the expressway. On the way there, Billy had the cabbie make
a detour past a McDonald's takeout window, where he
bought a cup of coffee and an Egg McMuffin that drove
the river from his bones and filled the hollow in his
stomach.

Upon reaching the motel, Billy had the driver cruise
the parking lot so he could get a feel for the situation.

Then he saw something he couldn't believe. *The van.*
Bobby hadn't even bothered to ditch it. And the car Billy
had rented before Bobby had arrived in town was there
too.

Were the vehicles just bait? Were the cops waiting in
the room? Without his gun he couldn't even defend himself.

He tapped the front seat. "Where's the closest pay
phone?"

"Gas station on the corner, I'd guess," the cabbie
replied.

"Take me there."

The cabbie drove to a large Exxon station half a block
away. With the cab waiting, Billy went inside for some

change. He came back and called the motel, letting information dial the number.

"Room two thirty-one, please."

It rang just once and Bobby answered.

"You should have dumped the van," Billy said.

"Billy, are you okay? Man, I'm glad to hear your voice. I was really worried, you know? Hope you're not mad. I dunno what happened back there at the river. I just lost it."

"I'm not mad. Are you alone?"

"Yeah, of course. Who else would be here? Where *are* you?"

Billy surveyed his surroundings. "I want you to leave the room and walk down to the Xpert Tune shop. It's about two blocks to your left as you leave the motel. Wait for me there."

Billy hung up and got back in the cab.

"Where to now?" the cabbie asked.

"Nowhere. We're just going to sit here for a few minutes."

Soon, Billy saw Bobby come down the sidewalk from the motel and cross the street. He walked to the Xpert Tune and waited out front.

Over the next five minutes, Billy saw no sign that Bobby had been followed or that there were any cars hanging around that might contain cops also watching Bobby.

Billy tapped the front seat. "See that guy standing across the street . . . let's pick him up."

"I'll have to go around the block."

"So do it."

When they pulled up in front of Bobby a few minutes later, Billy threw the door open. "Get in and don't say anything."

Wearing a puzzled expression, his complexion paler than usual, Bobby did as he was told.

"Take us to the Blue Monkey," Billy said to the cabbie, naming the restaurant where he and Bobby had eaten lunch yesterday. While the driver headed that way, Billy frisked Bobby for a wire.

"What are you doin'?"

"Making sure it's just you and me in here," Billy said. "Don't talk."

Having verified that Bobby was clean, Billy watched all the way to the restaurant to see if they were being followed. Seeing no evidence of that, when they reached the restaurant, Billy asked the cabbie to take them back to the motel, where dry clothes, and hopefully no surprises, were waiting.

Billy paid for the ride with a soggy twenty and a ten, and he and Bobby went up the motel's metal staircase to the second floor. As Bobby unlocked the door to their room, all Billy's instincts told him it was probably safe. But the slight margin of doubt made his heart beat faster.

Bobby opened the door and went inside. Hesitating for only a fraction of a second, Billy followed.

The room was a mess: the bed unmade, Bobby's clothes thrown on the chairs, a bag and some greasy papers from the nearby Tops Bar-B-Q littering the table with the phone. But there were no cops.

"What are we gonna do now?" Bobby said. "I mean about the woman?"

"Nothing we *can* do, at least not for awhile. She's very spooked at the moment and will be extremely alert. We'll have to wait until she calms down."

Bobby reached out and ran his hand down the sleeve of Billy's jacket. "I'm real glad you're not mad at me. I was afraid you would be. I knew right away when I left you at the river that what I did was wrong, but by then it was too late." His expression brightened. "But I did wait for you. That counts for somethin', doesn't it?"

"Of course." Billy hit Bobby affectionately on the shoulder. "We all occasionally do things in the heat of the moment that we regret later." Billy gestured to his suitcase. "Now, how about getting me some dry clothes?"

"Sure thing," Bobby said, grinning.

Happy that Billy was so understanding, Bobby put

Billy's suitcase on the bed and reached for the zipper to the main compartment. As he did, Billy stepped up behind him, his hand reaching in his pocket for something he *hadn't* lost in the river.

Afraid that her kidnappers might be following her, Holly kept one eye on the rearview mirror all the way to the medical center. Even though she saw nothing suspicious, she remained watchful even inside the parking garage, moving quickly from her car to the walkway connecting the garage and the medical building concourse.

She reached the office without mishap and turned on the computer that had the appointment calendar in it. When it was booted up, she set about contacting every patient she was scheduled to see on Monday or Tuesday, apologizing to them and asking them to call the office on Monday to reschedule. Finished with office business, she put down that phone and went to the one on her desk, where she soon had Richard Heflin on the line.

"I was just about to call *you*," he said before she could say anything. "The health department couldn't care less about what we discovered. And a few hours after I talked to them someone called me and threatened to hurt my daughter if I didn't forget about the dairy. They gave me seventy-two hours to put my house up for sale."

"It's getting rough here too. Last night, someone tried to kill me."

"Oh my God. What have we stumbled onto? Are you okay?"

"I was very lucky to get out of it with only a few scratches and bruises. Some duck hunters rescued me. We can't let this continue."

"How do we end it?"

"Do you still want to be involved?"

"Of course."

"What about your daughter?"

"For the time being, she's safe. You sound as though you have an idea."

"Remember me telling you about that transport truck I followed from the dairy, the one that was supposed to be taking calves away?"

"Only it was empty."

"I have the strong feeling that if we knew what that was all about, we'd understand everything."

"And you're proposing what?"

"The dairy workers I spoke to said that the herd is divided into groups in which the delivery dates are controlled by artificial insemination and drug-induced labor . . . if that's the right term for cows. It's arranged so that a group is induced every other Monday. One of them supposedly delivered the week I was there, which means the next is scheduled for this *coming* Monday."

"So you want to . . ."

"It's all done at night. There should be some way to get a look at what's going on. There are cornfields all around the dairy. We can use them as cover, get to the fence, and cut an access with a bolt cutter."

"How would we know where to go if we did get in?"

"When I was in the manager's office the day I first came to Midland, I saw an aerial photograph of the place with labels on all the buildings. I know where the calving area is."

"Holly, this could be dangerous."

"We're already in danger. I've booked a flight to Madison on Monday, but I won't get there until six-fifteen in the evening. That's later than I wanted, but I didn't have any choice. It should be okay though."

"You're sure you want to do this?"

"We have to. And remember, not a word to Christianson, not to *anybody*."

"That's not good. If we get jammed up, what are we going to do?"

"Bring a cell phone. We get in trouble, call the state police."

"I don't know if that's good enough."

"Do you own a gun?"

"Yes."

"Bring that too."

"Holly, I don't know . . ."

"Think about it. Will you meet me at the airport?"

"Of course."

She gave him the flight number and the airline and said, "See you then."

Holly had talked to Richard as if she were totally confident they could pull this off. In truth, she had no idea if they could even get on the dairy property. With her patients taken care of and Richard alerted to her plan, she turned her attention to getting a replacement driver's license.

Tears welling up in his eyes, Billy arranged Bobby's head on the pillow of the motel bed so he looked comfortable. He pulled the covers up to Bobby's chin, hiding the ugly ligature mark on his neck. He'd miss Bobby. Except for that one mistake, he'd been a reliable ally and a good friend. Billy stood for a moment, taking a last look at the man he'd known for most of both their lives. Billy wiped at his eyes with the back of his hand then placed his palm gently on Bobby's head.

"Goodbye, old friend."

It was time now to go home and tell Bruxton he still had a problem.

"Some things have happened since we last talked," Holly said, speaking by phone to Susan Morrison. "Richard Heflin's daughter has been threatened because of his interest in the dairy, and someone tried to kill me here in Memphis. I'm sure that was related to the dairy too."

"Were you hurt?" Susan asked.

"No. But these people have to be stopped. Before we can hope to do that, we have to know the whole story. I think there's a good chance that if Richard and I are at the dairy tonight, we'll understand everything, or at least be a lot closer to a full understanding."

"Why's that?"

Holly quickly explained her reasons for wanting to

be present at the next calving and gave Susan a thumb-nail portrait of her plan, which was sketchy at best. "As soon as I hang up, I'm leaving for the airport. I wanted you to know where I was going so if anything happens to me, at least you'll know what I was doing. Wish me luck."

"*Gei zaigezunt un kum gezunt,*" Susan said. "Go in health. And come back in health."

32

Richard was waiting at the Madison airport with an attractive brunette. Puzzled as to who this was, Holly went to meet them.

"Holly, this is my sister, Jessie. She did the test proving that dairy animal was infectious. She's going to help us tonight."

Holly accepted Jessie's extended hand. "It's good to finally meet you," Jessie said. "Richard told me what happened to you in Memphis. You're a courageous woman."

"They didn't leave me any choice." Believing that there wouldn't be time to change before they'd have to be in position at the dairy, Holly was wearing black denim jeans, a black cotton canvas shirt, and charcoal hiking shoes. In her carry-on, in addition to a more feminine outfit, she had a black L.L. Bean three-season jacket she'd be wearing when she went through the dairy fence. Richard and Jessie were also dressed in rugged dark clothing, so as the three of them headed for the terminal, they looked as though they all belonged to the same club—which, in a way, they did.

When they reached Richard's car and were settled inside, Richard asked Holly if she was hungry.

"Not really. I don't think we should stop for anything. It's already dark and I don't exactly know what that dairy worker meant when he said the calving is done at night. Does that mean seven o'clock, midnight, 2 A.M.? I just don't know. So we need to get there."

"Exactly my feelings," Richard said, starting the car.

When they were through town, Holly said, "We should talk now about what we're going to do when we get there. You brought the bolt cutter?"

"It's in the trunk. Jessie and I drove past the dairy yesterday to get a feel for the place and I hate to tell you this, but the cornfields you were counting on to hide us have all been harvested."

"That's terrible. What are we going to do now?"

"The field on the dairy side of the fence must be some kind of experimental corn because it's still a little green," Jessie said. "That'll provide cover on the inside."

"It's going to be a moonless night," Holly replied. "Without the corn to hide us, how are we going to get close? I brought some flashlights, but we can't use them if the fields are bare."

"About two hundred yards from the dairy's rear gate, there's a good-sized woods where we can park," Richard said. "Cutting through that woods is a ravine with a small creek in it. The ravine leads right to the dairy fence and continues on the other side, angling across a corner of the property and out the other side. The ravine is deep enough so that if we stay low and keep our flashlights directed at the ground, we can get there without being seen."

"That sounds good."

"Your feet are going to get wet."

"I've been through worse."

"We picked up a couple of handi-talkies at an electronics store," Jessie said. "Richard thought that I should stay at the car with one of the talkies and the cell phone. If you and Richard get in trouble, he'll call me and I can contact the state police. I'm not crazy about being so far from the action, but I'll do it."

"I can't think of a better plan," Holly said. She looked at Richard. "You brought a gun?"

"I've got it, but if it comes to the point where we need it, we're going to be in deep trouble."

They reached the dairy a little after seven and Richard turned down the road that led to the rear entrance. They could see at the top of a distant hill on the property that the complex the aerial photograph identified as the calving area was awash in lights.

"They've already started," Holly said, excitedly.

Richard stepped on the gas and they were soon at the woods, where he shut off the headlights. Using only the running lights, he eased the car down a path so narrow that bushes and weeds on each side tickled the paint. He stopped twenty yards in, shut off the engine, and popped the trunk lid.

Though many of the trees stood gaunt and bare, the oaks remained fully clothed and there were enough small ones that the lights from the dairy were totally obscured.

They all got out of the car and gathered at the trunk, the chill in the air quickly creeping through Holly's shirt.

"You're going to need a jacket," Richard said.

"I have something." Holly got her jacket from her bag, slipped it on, and zipped it. She then produced the flashlights she'd packed. "I didn't know Jessie was coming so I only have two of these."

"We've got extras," Jessie said.

Richard unzipped the gym bag he'd brought and gave Jessie a flashlight from it. He returned to the bag for the handi-talkies. "Holly, give me some light here, would you?"

Holly directed the beam of her flashlight onto the handi-talkies.

"They can communicate on several frequencies," Richard said. "We tested them yesterday and left them both on the same setting. I just want to be sure . . . Yeah, they're still the same."

He handed one of the talkies to Jessie, then fished a
.38 from the bag and slipped it into a deep pocket in his
jacket. He returned to the bag for the bolt cutter, a hefty
model that looked as though it would have no trouble
with chain link. He slipped one of the handles through
a metal ring attached to his belt and looked at Jessie.
"There's nothing secure about communication on these
talkies. So we should use them only when absolutely necessary. And don't speak openly. Use veiled language. I'll
just identify myself as twenty-two. You'll be twenty-
three."

"Why can't *I* be twenty-two?" Jessie said.

Richard grinned and looked at Holly. "When we were
kids, she always wanted what *I* had. Now, where's that
second flashlight you brought?"

Appreciating that he'd asked for hers instead of using
one of those that were likely still in his bag, Holly handed
it to him.

"Everybody ready?" Richard asked.

The women nodded.

"You two be careful," Jessie said. She kissed Richard
on the cheek and then Holly.

"When we're about ten yards away," Richard said,
"I'll call you on the talkie and we'll make sure they're
working."

As the first step in the plan started to unfold, they all
knew that if Richard and Holly got into trouble, by the
time the state police could respond to a distress call, it
could be too late. But it was more on the minds of Richard
and Jessie than Holly, who was so excited to be on the
verge of learning one of the dairy's pivotal secrets that
she wasn't thinking much of the danger.

It was so dark that by the time they were ten yards
from the car, neither of them could see it. Richard stopped
walking and raised the talkie to his lips.

"Twenty-two calling twenty-three."

"Twenty-three here," Jessie answered.

Satisfied that everything to make this a successful ven-
ture was in place, Richard resumed walking.

For nearly five minutes they moved quickly along the path, their flashlights illuminating oval patches of the ground in front of them. It was so quiet that the sounds of their breathing and their feet pressing into the moist leaf litter were all they heard.

Finally, the chuckle of flowing water reached Holly's ears.

Within minutes they were standing at the edge of a deep ravine about twenty feet across. Holly played her flashlight along its sharply sloping walls and saw that it was thick with brush and small trees. At the bottom, in a creek as wide as one lane on a country road, black water rippled and chortled around slippery-looking rocks.

"How deep is it?" she whispered.

"In most places about four inches," Richard said, his voice muted. "But there are holes much deeper. The trick is not to step in them. Ready?"

"Let's go."

Picking a spot relatively free of bushes, Richard started down, using a small tree for support. Deploying the beam of his flashlight in advance to find suitable footing, he edged down the slope and stepped into the water.

"Ah! It's cold. Come on."

Still sore in spots from her tumble down the hill the night she'd escaped from Billy Lynch, Holly followed the route Richard had taken and joined him in the water, which went over her low-cuts.

"Are we having fun yet?" Richard said.

"It's going to be worth it," Holly said, having to raise her voice so it could be heard over the sound of the flowing water. Eagerly, she took the lead.

It was difficult to walk quietly and they splashed a lot, but the noise mingled naturally with the sounds of the creek, so neither of them worried about it. In just a few minutes, the ravine emerged from the woods. Between the trees, Holly could see, off to the left, the lights from the dairy.

The ravine was about five feet deep, so that if they walked standing erect, it wouldn't fully hide them.

Though it was extremely dark, they proceeded from this point in a bent-over stance to prevent detection.

After a short stint of this awkward gait, their thighs began to ache. Powered by her intense need to have her many questions about the dairy answered, Holly ignored the pain and pressed on. But Richard faded.

"I need a break," he said. Using a tree for cover, he rose to an erect stance and took a look. Holly did the same.

The fence was now only about seventy yards away. Except for the rise and fall of their chests, they stood motionless behind their respective trees for another minute until the aching in their thighs subsided and they caught their breath.

"Ready for the final push?" Richard asked.

For an answer, Holly dropped into the stance they'd adopted and resumed walking. Ten yards later, she stepped into a hole and went into the water up to her knees. With Richard's help, she struggled out of the hole and kept going. But now she was *really* cold.

About the time Richard thought he was going to need another break, they negotiated a turn and there it was: the chain-link fence, constructed so that it went down into the ravine and crossed it with its lowest links under water. The webbing had caught a significant amount of debris, forming a dam that made the water higher on their side of the fence than beyond.

Leaning close to Richard so she could speak softly, Holly said, "Do you think it's electrified?"

"Wouldn't we be feeling it standing in the water like this?" Richard said.

"I suppose."

Richard climbed out of the water and approached the fence. Knowing that it could be a bad idea, but without any other way to test it, he ticked the fence lightly with his index finger. He didn't feel anything.

Rejoining Holly, he said, "It seems okay. But they might have some kind of surveillance mechanism to tell if it's been cut. I think we should cut one link, then fall back and see what happens."

He shut off his flashlight and stuffed it in his pocket, then slid the bolt cutter from the holder on his belt. With Holly at his side providing the light, he approached the fence, clamped the cutter's jaws on the fence at waist level, and severed the test link.

In the dairy security center, Giuseppe Palagio looked at the computer screen where the entire fence perimeter was schematized. In the region of the ravine, one small red dot was blinking.

"I've got an anomaly on sector three," he said in Italian to Franco Leonetti, the chief of security.

Also in Italian, Leonetti said, "Let's take a look."

Palagio flicked a switch activating the infrared system on the TV camera, atop what appeared to be nothing more than a flagpole. He skillfully guided the camera so that a ghostly green image of the ravine section of the fence appeared on the monitor next to the screen displaying the blinking red dot.

They watched the monitor for fifteen seconds then Palagio said, "Must be a malfunction."

Leonetti held up his hand. "We'll see."

In the ravine, out of range of the TV, Holly said, "Nothing's happened."

"Yeah, it seems okay," Richard said. "But let's wait a bit longer."

They held their positions for another minute, then another, until Richard said, "That's long enough."

They both waded back to the fence and Richard began cutting in earnest.

"Doctor Bruxton's residence," Boone said.

"This is Leonetti. We've got a problem over here."

"I'll tell him."

Boone went into the study, where Bruxton was sitting

in front of the fire reading an article about his company in the *Wall Street Journal.*

"Sir, Leonetti's on the line. He says they have a problem."

Bruxton picked up the phone beside him. "What kind of problem?" he said to Leonetti.

"There are two people in the ravine behind the dairy cutting a hole in the fence."

"Show me."

Bruxton went to the bank of monitors on the other side of the room and waited for the transmission. The screen flickered and a green image came on in which he could see exactly what Leonetti had described.

"I want to see their faces."

He watched intently as the image of the two intruders steadily grew larger. Being illuminated by infrared, it wasn't the clearest picture in the world but there was no doubt who it was. Richard he recognized from having met him, Holly from the set of candid photos Billy Lynch had sent him.

"Let them in," Bruxton said. "Then take them . . . alive. I want no shots fired. The man has a sister who may also be in the area. I want her too. Give them no opportunity to communicate with her or allow her to communicate with anyone else. Do *not* foul this up. Call me on my cell phone when you have her."

Bruxton hung up and rang for Boone.

Anticipating that he might be wanted, he was nearby.

"Bring the car around. We're going to the plant. And hurry up. I want to be back here in twenty minutes."

Richard made a final cut and removed a section of fence. Not knowing whether he might need it again, he slid the cutter back into the holder on his belt.

"You know the lay of the place," he said. "So you lead."

Holly nodded and slipped through the opening. She held her flashlight so Richard could come through. Then they looked for a suitable place to climb out of the ravine.

Finding one about ten feet away, they moved to the spot and Holly flicked off her flashlight. Carefully and mostly by feel, they climbed up and ducked into the dairy's cornfield.

The calving area was in front of the cornfield and about a hundred and fifty yards to their left. The field was planted in rows that ran perpendicular to the ravine, so it was easy to move in that direction. And the corn was so tall they could walk erect.

The source of the lights in the calving area couldn't be seen over the corn, but they illuminated the sky enough that Holly was able to accurately judge when she and Richard were directly opposite the action. Pulling Richard close, she whispered, "Now it gets tougher. Try to jostle the corn as little as possible." Again taking the lead, she stepped through the closely spaced row of cornstalks in front of her.

It took nearly ten minutes to work their way across the field. Finally, with just one row of corn left to hide them, they could see, on the other side of a paved road and a well-used cow trail from the barns, an eight-foot-tall wooden fence that surrounded the calving area. Inside the fence and no more than a few feet from it was a white brick building.

"How are we going to get inside?" Richard whispered.

"Give me a lift and I can go over that fence," Holly said.

"Then we'll be separated."

"We can't stop now. We're so close."

"How will you get out?"

"I can use the fence stringers on the inside as a step."

"I can't let you go in there alone."

"It's not for you to say what I do," Holly said gently.

"I know. I just . . ."

"Will you help me or not?"

Shaking his head in resignation, Richard said, "I suppose. But you should take the gun."

"You keep it."

"I have a bad feeling about this."

They moved into the open and darted across the narrow road. They vaulted the two split-rail fences that flanked the cow trail and melted into the shadows of the tall wooden fence where it ran along the right side of the white building.

"How do you want to do this?" Holly whispered.

In response, Richard braced himself and laced his fingers together, forming a stirrup. Holly stepped into his hands and grabbed the top of the fence. With a minimum of scuffling, she was over it more quickly than Richard thought possible.

Seeing a window in the white building, Holly went to it, but found it too high to look through. She stepped onto the lowest fence stringer, which raised her to the right level, but now she was too far away.

Stepping down, she looked in both directions for something she could put under the window. There was nothing. She went to the side of the building facing the rest of the dairy and saw nothing useful there either.

Then she got an idea.

Hurrying back to the window, she stripped off her belt and tied a knot in the end without the buckle. She stepped onto the lowest stringer and slipped the belt between a crack in the fence boards so the knot was on the outside. Using the belt as a tether, she leaned toward the window and looked in.

33

Through the window, Holly saw a single huge room with walls and floor of gleaming white tile. Along the left wall, ten cows stood in stanchions that kept them from moving. Behind each animal was a stainless steel cart curved to cup the cow's rump. A dark-complexioned man in a black rubber apron over a white jumpsuit paced the line of cows, watching the carts. He stopped at the second animal from the far end and tugged gently on three pink strands dangling from her vagina. He did the same with the strands hanging from the cow beside her. None of the others had these things.

Suddenly, the man moved quickly to the third cow from the end nearest Holly, where something was oozing from the animal's vagina. With rubber-gloved hands, he caught the object and lowered it into a curved pan on the metal cart. Holly had no direct experience with calving, but she'd seen on TV that newborn calves were covered with hair and were a lot bigger than this one. Being pink and so small, it had to be *very* premature.

Another similar calf appeared from the same cow. Without difficulty, it slid wetly into the world and was deposited in the pan on the cart. This was followed by yet another. When this calf had joined the others, the man cut the three umbilical cords tethering them to the placentas and, without clamping them, let them drop into the pan. Apparently he didn't care if the calves bled to death. Of course, they were so premature, they probably couldn't have survived anyway.

At the other end of the line of animals, a small placenta emerged from one of the animals with the dangling pink strands, which Holly now knew were umbilical cords, and it plopped into the cart.

The man she'd been watching picked up the pan containing the three calves he'd just helped deliver and carried them to a circular stainless steel island in the middle of the room. There, he put the pan on the counter next to two others, each of which contained a similar mound of glistening pink tissue.

In the center of the island, a woman with dark hair and dressed like the man was working with her back to the cows. Directly in front of her in the island was a sink. The left section of countertop was pierced with three large oval holes along its outer rim. To her right were the curved containers.

The woman turned on the water then reached into the container nearest the sink and grabbed a handful of the pink tissue. As she lifted it out, two legs and two arms flopped into view.

Holly nearly gagged.

It wasn't a calf at all. It was a human fetus—with a monstrously large head.

The woman washed the fetus under the faucet, then threw it onto a wooden cutting board to her left and picked up a meat cleaver sitting nearby. With one expert stroke, she severed the fetus's head, which she dropped into the hole in the countertop nearest the sink. The body went into the adjacent hole.

By now, the cow Holly had seen deliver a placenta had delivered the other two she carried. A man who'd been working at a sink on the far side of the room took hold of that cart and pushed it along the outer rim of the circular island until he reached the hole in the counter the woman hadn't used. There, he gathered up the placentas and dropped them into the hole, which, like the others, undoubtedly had a large bucket or something similar under it.

Now Holly knew why there were no calves in the transport that supposedly took them away each week, and why the dairy's animals had human genes. They were genetically engineered to bear human monsters. But for what purpose?

"All right, miss. You've seen enough," a voice suddenly said from beside her. "Step off there."

As she looked down and was blinded by a flashlight, she heard another voice . . . from the right. "Stand exactly where you are and don't move."

At first she didn't understand why she was being given conflicting commands. Then she realized, the second one was meant for Richard. They were *both* caught.

Unable to even see what she was up against, Holly had no choice but to follow orders. She stepped down and was told to put her hands behind her.

After they bound her wrists, she was spun around and pushed toward the corner of the building. She still hadn't gotten a look at her captors, but there seemed to be two of them. Staying behind her, the men herded her around the corner toward all the lights and the sound of agitated cows.

They soon emerged into a large service area where ten cows were waiting in a small split-rail enclosure. Across a paved apron, a half-dozen vehicles were parked in front of another white building much smaller than the first. As Holly's captors prodded her toward the building, the wooden gate to the compound swung open and two men pushed Richard inside, also with his hands cuffed behind him. With both of them caught, it was up to Jessie to save them. But had Richard been able to alert her?

She gave him a questioning look.

Understanding what she wanted to know, he shook his head.

But there was still hope. Eventually, Jessie would realize something was wrong and would bring help. And they needed it badly. Holly had seen their secret. And while she still didn't understand the point of it . . .

Wait.

Oh my God.

Of course.

The details still danced just out of reach, *but she knew.* Oh my God. It was *huge.* No wonder they'd tried to kill her and had threatened Richard's daughter.

It was all up to Jessie now. *Soon, Jessie,* Holly said silently. *Bring help soon.*

Holly and Richard were pushed and prodded through the door of the small building, into a room half full of surveillance equipment. The other half contained a dinette table and chairs, a sink, and some cabinets.

"Go on . . ." Holly was pushed forward. As she stumbled further into the room, she saw something that took her breath away; Jessie, bound and gagged on the floor.

"We got them all," Leonetti said. "What should we do with them?"

Leonetti's call had found Bruxton still en route back to his home from the plant. "For the moment, nothing," Bruxton said into his cell phone. "I'll let you know."

Bruxton was as good at concealing anger as he was pain. So he'd given Leonetti no hint that he was seething inside over how Holly and Richard had compromised him. And Billy Lynch had to share a good part of the blame.

He punched Lynch's number into the phone. Well aware that it was an insecure transmission and that Lynch would recognize his voice, he didn't identify himself when Lynch answered, but got right to the purpose of his call.

"Your failure has come back to hurt me. Security has

her under control at site two. I want you to pick her up and bring her to my home."

"I don't think that's a good idea," Lynch said. "It'd be safer for you to go to her."

"I didn't ask for your opinion. Do what I tell you."

"I'd rather not."

"Are you refusing?"

"Just expressing my strong opinion that this is a mistake."

"Do it."

"You're the boss."

"How nice that you remembered. Get someone from security to drive you. I want her in the back with you beside her so it just looks like three friends going somewhere."

"Why are you micromanaging me?"

"Because when you manage yourself, *I* get burned."

As Boone slowed and turned into the entrance to Bruxton's estate, Bruxton touched the vial in his pocket. Before he had the woman killed she was going to suffer—not physically, but mentally, which he believed could be far worse.

She would certainly realize she was to be killed, but a woman like that would never give up hope that something would save her. Just as *he* still hoped for a cure. And he would use that hope against her.

On the way over, she would talk to Lynch, and he would come to see that she was a person, not a thing. When the time came, that would make it hard for Lynch to kill her. He'd do it, but it would hurt him. And that would be *his* punishment.

Accompanied by Ricky Blake, one of the night deputies on his payroll, Otto Christianson knocked on the door to Artie Harris's apartment. Artie's car was in the parking lot, so Otto was pretty sure he was home.

The door opened.

"Otto, this is a surprise," Artie said.

"Mind if we come in? I'd like to ask you a few questions."

"Can it wait? I was just on my way out."

"I'd like to talk now."

Artie stepped back from the door. "If it's that important, come in."

It was the first time Otto had ever been in Artie's apartment and he was taken aback by the furniture, which was all made of driftwood.

Accustomed to people being startled by his unusual tastes, Artie noticed Otto's reaction. "I know it's kind of offbeat," Artie said. "But I like it, because it shows that nothing is intrinsically worthless. That no matter how tortured the history of an object or how rough it appears, if you can imagine what *can* be instead of what is, you'll be rewarded."

If Otto had any doubts about Artie actually being Billy Lynch, this veiled reference to orphanage children who were never adopted erased it. He shifted his feet so if Artie tried anything, he'd be ready. He glanced at Blake and tried to let him know by eye contact that he should be prepared as well.

"I get the feeling this isn't a friendly visit," Artie said.

"Oh, it's really nothing," Otto said, trying to get Artie to relax.

"And 'nothing' can't wait until tomorrow?"

"I was just wondering . . . You once told me that before you moved here you lived all your life in Pennsylvania."

"So?"

"Why do you have a social security number that's issued only to residents of Missouri?"

Otto could tell from the look on Artie's face that he knew he was had.

"My family only lived in Missouri less than a year and things didn't work out with my father's job, so we moved back to Pennsylvania. I got my social security card during that year. It was such a small part of my life, I just never mention it."

"Just a year?"

"That's all."

"You were issued a driver's license in Missouri and three years later had an accident that went on your permanent record there."

Artie's face turned ashen. "What else do you know?"

"That the company you work for didn't just send you to an insurance seminar. Where *have* you been?"

"Why are you asking all this?"

"I have information that you may actually be a man named Billy Lynch, who grew up in an orphanage in California."

"Well, I'm *not*."

"This man is responsible for the deaths of at least two people."

"Christ, Otto. You know me. I couldn't have done that. I'm *not* this Billy Lynch."

"Then why did you lie when you told Jessie Heflin where you were going on this trip you just took?"

"Jessie . . . Does she know about this Lynch guy?"

"I didn't tell her."

Artie stared at Otto, apparently trying to think up a lie Otto would believe.

Finally, he said, "I was taking care of my father in Milwaukee. He was beaten and robbed on the street there. When the police called and told me he was in the hospital, I had to go."

"Why didn't you just tell Jessie that instead of lying to her?"

"Because he's homeless . . . an alcoholic who sleeps in doorways or in cardboard boxes. I've tried to get him help, but he doesn't want it. And he refuses to live here with me. He's the reason I don't want people to know we ever lived in St. Louis. The cops there had to come and stop him from beating on me or my mother two or three times a month. Before he started drinking, he was a terrific father. But after he found the bottle, it was all different." Artie shook his head and his shoulders slumped. "And he can't stop. It destroyed our family and it's killing him, but he just keeps drinking."

Then he firmed up, eyes flashing. "But he's *still* my father. How could I not go to him when he needed me?" His voice softened. "Someday I'll figure out how to get him to stop. Then he'll be the man he was. But at the same time, I'm sorry to say I'm ashamed of him. I don't want people, especially Jessie, to know about this. Don't tell her. . . ." He reached out and touched Otto's arm. "Please, Otto, don't tell." He looked at Blake. "Or you either, Ricky."

This, at last, sounded like the truth and even explained what Artie had said about his driftwood furniture. But Otto needed to be sure.

"What hospital treated your father?"

"Saint Luke's."

"How is he?"

"He's back on the street. He shouldn't be, but I couldn't stop him."

"What's his name?"

"Frank."

Otto pointed to the phone. "May I?"

"Sure."

Otto called information and had them connect him with St. Luke's Hospital in Milwaukee. After being routed through a couple of departments, he learned that Frank Harris had indeed just been released after a week's stay.

Otto hung up and looked at Artie. "I'm sorry I had to do this, but . . ."

"I know," Artie said. "Please don't tell anybody what you've learned."

"I won't." Otto looked at Blake. "Neither will Ricky. About the cost of that call . . ."

"Forget it."

As Otto and Blake left, they both wondered if Otto would be able to keep his promise. Of more immediate concern for Otto was that Billy Lynch was still out there and up to God knows what.

34

Unable to dislodge the weight of Billy Lynch from his mind, Otto couldn't go home, but instead went to his office and got out the photograph of Lynch that Father Lucius had sent him. Sitting with it at his desk, he examined the boy Lynch once more with a magnifying glass, trying to see some identifying feature that had so far eluded him. But it was a futile gesture, born from his feeling that he had to do *something* to catch the man.

Disgusted and disappointed, Otto leaned back in his chair and flicked the picture toward his desk. It hit the stem of his desk lamp and flipped over.

What the . . .

He rocked forward and grabbed the picture.

There was writing on the back that he hadn't seen before because he'd never turned the photo over. It was a note from Father Lucius:

> *Just remembered. Billy broke his left little finger while he was here and it didn't heal properly so it stuck out at an angle from the rest of his fingers. Hope this helps.*

Oh Father. does it ever, Otto thought. Because he now knew that Billy Lynch was Charles Hallock, the print dealer.

Otto lugged out the phone book, looked up Hallock's number, and gave it a try. If he was home, Otto would just hang up and he and Blake would go over there and bring him in for some tough questioning.

But there was no answer.

Otto hurried into the outer office, where Doris, the day dispatcher's sister, was working the night shift. In keeping with his belief that computer skills were inherited, she was as good as Claire in that area.

In just a few minutes, she had accessed the state motor vehicle records and had a description of Hallock's car and his license number.

Otto handled the call to his night shift deputies himself.

"All cars be on the lookout for Charles Hallock . . ." In case they didn't know what he looked like, Otto added, "Thirty-two-year-old white male with brown hair worn in a ponytail. Believed to be driving a maroon Toyota Camry, license number HSR-642. If sighted, please advise."

Otto had no idea if Hallock was even in town. But if he was, they'd stand a good chance of finding him, especially if Otto got out there and helped his men look.

While he went to his car, the dispatcher informed the night shift that he was in service. Otto first cruised Arneson's parking lot to see if Hallock might be having a late dinner. He then drove by his townhouse on the chance that he'd come home. While Otto was wondering where he should look next, his radio spoke to him.

"Car three to car one, come in."

Otto picked up the mike for his radio and thumbed the Talk button.

"Car one here. Go ahead."

"Sheriff, I've spotted our subject going east on Dairy Road. What should I do?"

Deciding that it might be useful to see where Hallock

was going, Otto said, "Car one to car three. Keep subject in sight, but stay back and try not to attract his attention. Report in every two minutes."

Otto made a U-turn and headed for Dairy Road, wanting to be in the area, but planning to stay far enough out of the way that Hallock wouldn't see two cruisers behind him.

Two minutes later, car three reported that Hallock had turned onto Deadfall Road and gone into the rear entrance of the Midland dairy. Otto thumbed his mike. "Car one to car three. Stand by."

Otto thought about the area. There was really no good place to park on Dairy Road where you could look down Deadfall Road and monitor both directions from the dairy's rear gate. That meant . . . "Car one to car three. Proceed down Deadfall Road to Delany woods, cut your lights, and watch the dairy's rear entrance until I get there."

Unfortunately, this plan left the dairy's front entrance unobserved. After checking with the other cars on duty and learning that he was the closest to the dairy, Otto stepped on the gas, already knowing that when he got there, he'd take up a position in the parking lot of the abandoned Tastee Freeze about fifty yards from the dairy's front entrance.

With Otto still six minutes away, Susan Morrison pulled into the Tastee Freeze parking lot and tried to figure out what to do.

After Holly's phone call in which she said she was planning to sneak onto dairy property tonight to get a look at their calving operation, Susan had become so worried about the danger Holly might face that she'd asked her sister to care for Walter for a day or two. Susan had then packed her Beretta, her Randall survival knife, and a change of clothes and had taken a Southwest Airlines flight to Chicago. There, she'd rented a car and headed for the dairy. Before she'd left home, she'd tried to call Holly and tell her she was coming, but by the time Susan was sure she could get there, Holly had already left for the airport.

Assessing the situation, Susan saw all the lights in the calving area. Figuring that she might be able to get a closer look by going down that road she'd passed around the last bend, she put the car in reverse, backed up, and was about to return to Deadfall Road, when she saw a maroon car inside the dairy drive up to the front gate and wait for it to open. The car then pulled onto the highway and headed east, away from where Susan was parked.

She hesitated.

Deciding that she'd take a quick look at the passengers in the car then come back, she stepped on the gas.

Holly sat in the backseat, on Billy Lynch's left. One of the Italian security men was driving. She still had her hands tied behind her, but her feet were free. Billy had a stun gun in his hand, ready to zap her if she got out of control. He was also carrying the backup automatic he'd put into service after losing his other one in the river.

Billy was nervous. It was only a short drive to Bruxton's estate, but every second they were on the road like this they were exposed. And if they were stopped by a cop now, it was going to be ugly.

From his voice, Holly had recognized Billy as the leader of the two men who'd tried to kill her in Memphis. The driver hadn't spoken, so she didn't know if he was the other one. Whoever he was, they *could* be taking her somewhere now to be killed. But she didn't think so.

"Where are we going?" she said, looking at Billy.

"You'll know when we get there," Billy replied. He reached over and pinched her face between his fingers and turned her head forward. "Don't look at me."

Keeping her eyes forward, Holly said, "How many people have you killed?"

Billy didn't answer.

"How can you do that . . . take a life?" Holly said. ". . . end an existence?"

Billy knew he should just tell her to shut up, but something made him reply. "It's just a job. I don't enjoy it."

"And you think that makes it okay?"

"You're a hematologist, right?"

"Yes."

"So you treat people with diseases of the blood."

Wondering where this was going, Holly agreed.

"And some of those diseases are fatal. I mean sometimes, despite everything you do, a patient dies."

"That's true."

"What percent of your patients die?"

"I don't know."

"It doesn't have to be accurate. Guess."

"Five percent maybe."

"So for every hundred people who come to you for help, you fail five of them."

"That's not . . ."

"You do. Don't fool yourself. You fail. I *never* fail in *my* work. I've never made a commitment I didn't honor. And don't think you're the exception. The first time with you, I was forced into an approach I didn't like. The second time, at the river, you were just lucky. But tonight, that ends. How many people can say they've never failed? You can't. So why are you looking down on *me*?"

Remembering what she'd heard in the van when Billy had kidnapped her, Holly said, "Does your mother know what you do for a living?"

"She was killed when I was just a kid."

"That must have been rough."

"Don't patronize me."

"I'm not. To have someone you love ripped away from you, never to see her again, or hear her voice, or feel her touch, is a terrible thing."

Billy's eyes glistened as he thought about his mother.

"So every time you take a life and destroy one of the most complex and wonderful things ever created, you also destroy the people who love them. And nobody ever paid you to do that."

Seeing that letting this woman talk was just going to make his job later more difficult, Billy said, "Be quiet now."

Holly took sustenance from the gentle way he'd silenced her. Maybe she'd gotten to him and somehow that would make a difference.

"Car three to car one. Come in."

"Car one. Go ahead."

"Sheriff, I'm at Delany Woods and there's a parked car in the path that leads to Rock Creek. The keys are in the ignition and there's no one around. I think it belongs to that neurologist, Doctor Heflin."

"What's the plate number?"

The deputy recited the tag number.

Speaking to the dispatcher, Otto said, "Doris, check that, will you?"

"I'm on it."

She quickly verified that the car did belong to Heflin. Sensing that there was something important going on here, Otto ordered the closest car on duty to the Tastee Freeze. He sent the next closest to the woods and had several others start for the dairy as fast as they could travel.

Already heading that way, he arrived in the area first. He parked at the ice cream stand and watched the dairy's front gate until his replacement arrived. Even with that delay, he reached the woods before the other car he'd called.

"It's weird, Sheriff," Deputy Calvin Erickson said as Otto got out of his car. "I checked back into the woods all the way to the creek, but didn't see anybody."

"You were supposed to be watching the dairy gate."

"Sorry. I just got sidetracked wondering about this car here."

"Well, get yourself to a spot now where you can see it."

While Calvin headed for the road on foot, Otto walked

past Calvin's cruiser to Heflin's car, opened the door, and looked inside. Seeing nothing of interest, he pulled the keys from the ignition and went to the trunk. Aided by the lights from Calvin's car, he opened the trunk. Relieved not to see Heflin's body, he looked in the empty gym bag Richard had left behind, then picked up Holly's carry-on.

When he saw her name on the ID tag, his mind slowly began to turn, almost making an audible clanking sound.

There was a flash of light as the other car he'd called to the woods pulled onto the path. Joining him, Deputy Del Brice said, "What's goin' on, Sheriff?"

"I'm not sure. Calvin hasn't been able to find either Doctor Heflin, the owner of this vehicle, or the woman I think might have come here with him."

"Maybe they don't want to be found," Del suggested, grinning at his sexual innuendo.

"These aren't kids," Otto said. "If that's what they wanted to do, they wouldn't be doing it in the woods."

Suddenly, the machinery laboring in Otto's mind delivered the product it had been constructing. He pressed the Talk button on his shoulder mike and ordered the car at the ice cream stand and one other in service to proceed to the dairy's front entrance and block it so no one could leave. He sent two more cars to do the same at the rear gate, and called a pair to join him.

"Jesus, Sheriff," Del said. "We've never used more than two cars on anything. Why are we mobilizing against the dairy?"

Choosing to ignore the question, Otto called Calvin on his radio.

"Sheriff to Calvin."

"Calvin . . . Go ahead."

"Del and I are going to take a look around. Let me know when the other cars arrive."

Del already had a flashlight with him. Otto got his and they headed down the path into the woods, checking thoroughly on either side of the path as they went. When they reached the creek, Otto played his flash-

light over the sloping side of the ravine. The fresh foot-
prints and broken shrubs he saw convinced him that for
some reason, Heflin and Fisher had come here to spy on
the dairy.

Heflin could have left the keys in his car because he
was excited about what they were doing. *Or,* something
had gone wrong. Otto shined his light down the ravine
toward the dairy. While he was thinking about what he
should do, the two cars he'd ordered to the front gate
reported that they were in place. Thirty seconds later, the
other two were also in position at the rear entrance.

Otto had never been involved in an operation like this,
so there was a lot to think about. If Heflin and Fisher
had been caught and were in danger, as seemed likely
by Hallock's arrival and his probable involvement in the
attempt on Fisher's life during her first visit to Midland,
then he had to move fast.

This realization made him panic inside, because he
couldn't see the best course of action. He was standing
there appearing so lost that Del thought he might have
had a stroke.

"Sheriff . . . are you okay?"

"Quiet. I'm thinking."

Otto's mind became a sandstorm, everything blowing
around, nothing visible.

Through the grit he saw that the quickest way to protect Heflin and Fisher was by letting the people in the
dairy know that he and his men were out here. They
might have already noticed the cars at both entrances,
but in case they hadn't . . . His hand went to the Talk button on his shoulder mike and he called the office.

". . . Doris, I want you to call the Midland Dairy and
tell whoever answers that I have men at both their gates
and we want to look around immediately. If no one answers, call Don Lamotte, the manager, at home."

Then he received a call from Calvin. ". . . Sheriff, the
other two cars are here."

He asked Calvin to stand by. If Heflin and Fisher had
already been harmed, then any delay in getting in there

would allow Hallock to cover up evidence. He glanced at the ravine. If they had gone to the dairy this way, they must have been carrying a cutter for the fence. And if they'd been caught after they got inside . . .

He knew the area well enough to recall that just on the edge of the woods, a tributary joined Rock Creek. And that stream was in a ravine with steeper sides than this one, forming a significant hindrance to approaching the dairy through the woods and across the field behind it.

Otto thumbed his shoulder mike. "Sheriff to Calvin."

"This is Calvin. Go ahead."

"All of you get back here to the creek on the double. And get my bullhorn from my car."

He looked at Del. "Let's go." Without waiting for the others, Otto started down the bank of the ravine, hoping his gimpy knees wouldn't fail him.

35

After his conversation with Holly, Billy's mind worked to repair the breach she had made in his emotional armor. By the time the car pulled up to the gates to Bruxton's estate, he'd recovered to the point where he'd definitely be able to do what was required of him and keep his record of successes intact. He *had* to. It was all that made him special. But for the first time in his life, he thought of the penance for an act before he'd committed it. A single hundred-dollar bill wasn't going to do the job this time.

Seeing the ornate capital letter B woven into the wrought iron of the gates, it wasn't difficult for Holly to correctly guess who lived here. But she still had no idea why she'd been brought.

When they pulled up in front of the house, Billy got out, went around to Holly's side, and helped her out. With Billy propelling her forward with his hand in the small of her back and the driver behind them, they stepped up to the front door, which opened at their approach.

"He's in the study," Boone said.

He led the group to the study's big double doors and

turned to face them. "He wants to see only Mr. Lynch and Doctor Fisher." Looking at the driver, he added, "While you wait, I can offer you the use of the billiard room, the bowling alley, or our theater."

The driver expressed an interest in the theater.

"If you'll just wait here, I'll return and show you the way." Boone opened the study doors and Billy pushed Holly inside.

Bruxton was standing in front of his desk in a three-button gray suit, a blue-and-white striped shirt, and a micropattern tie as though he were about to preside over a board meeting. Holly was struck by his small stature and luminous pink complexion.

"Doctor Fisher, we meet at last. I'm Zane Bruxton. But I suspect you've figured that out already, you're such a clever woman."

Bruxton's talents at camouflaging his feelings were being greatly tested as anger and pain fought for control of his face and mind. He looked at Billy. "Turn that chair toward me and put her in it."

When Holly was seated, Bruxton turned a matching chair toward hers. He sat and put his pink hands in his lap.

"My security chief said when he caught you, you were looking through the window of our collection area. What did you see?"

"Something that made me sick to my stomach," Holly said.

"Do you understand what it means?"

"I think that's where you get Vasostasin. You extract it from some part of those fetuses."

"The brain," Bruxton said. "It's a substance normally produced in very small amounts in the developing brain. But we've inserted a promoter in the genome of each fetus we create that drives the production of huge amounts of the material. This overproduction causes the brain, and therefore the head, to be abnormally large. It's worked out extremely well."

"Creating human babies to be harvested . . . it's obscene," Holly said.

"They're hardly human," Bruxton said. "At least not in the usual sense of the word. The abnormal brain development is incompatible with life outside the womb. So each fetus is stillborn, which means we aren't killing them because they never really lived."

"But they had the *potential* to live. They're stillborn because of what you did to them. You *made* them monsters."

Fighting off the pain that was as bad as it had ever been, Bruxton said, "In my experience, potential is a vastly overrated commodity with little significance."

"Pardon me for also pointing out that what you're doing is a federal crime. So obviously, the legislature of this country feels the way I do."

"Only because they had no idea what they were doing when they created that law. At the time, the issues involved were all abstractions to them. I know of three senators and a dozen congressmen and women who voted for that bill who are cancer-free because of Vasostasin. And there are scores of legislators whose spouses or parents are still alive because of me. Do you think any of them would vote the same way now?

"You're morally outraged over this, but when you were diagnosed with leukemia . . ." Noticing the surprised look on Holly's face, Bruxton said, "Yes, I know a great deal about you. When that happened, it wasn't a hopeless situation. There was an effective treatment available. But suppose your own bone marrow couldn't have been cleaned. And the only place where marrow to save you could be obtained was from a genetically engineered human fetus like those I'm producing. Would you have said, 'No thanks, I'd rather die'? What would you have done? Be honest with yourself."

He waited for Holly's answer, but none was forthcoming because she wasn't sure what she'd have done. She'd been so frightened of dying. . . . Would she have compromised her moral beliefs just that once?

"Not such an easy decision, is it?" Bruxton said. Now that he'd educated her, it was time to hurt her.

"And you have put it all in jeopardy. Your disappearance alone will focus a great deal of attention on this community. But you brought Richard Heflin and his sister into it as well. When they vanish too, it will be extremely difficult for us. But the program *will* go on. It must. Actually, you should feel proud of the integral part you've played in our success."

"What do you mean?"

"The ability to drive the production of Vasostasin to the abnormally high levels necessary to make the program economically feasible requires a genome that contains a particular combination of coding sequences in a number of genes. We don't fully understand why, but it does. Before we could begin, we had to find a woman with that rare combination of coding sequences."

"And that was me?"

"You came to our attention through the relationship we had with various hospitals across the country in which they sent us a small sample of blood from each of their female patients along with the patient's name and address. Through genetic analysis of those samples, we found you."

"That's why I was approached to become an egg donor?"

"Exactly. At the time, we were unaware of your medical history. After your refusal to participate, our investigators discovered your connection to the fertility clinic in Mississippi. That made it all so easy.

"We fertilized one of your eggs with the appropriate sperm and when the resulting embryo had divided several times, we separated the cells and established a number of cell lines in culture. We then inserted a special promoter for Vasostasin into those cells and established another line so that we now have millions of such cells. The next step requires a steady supply of human eggs that don't have to be special in any way. I like to think of these as 'starter' eggs.

"I hired a man named Henry Pennell to develop a method to use bovine eggs for this step, but that didn't work out. Until that's possible, we will continue to operate our traveling clinic and our program to buy starter eggs from willing donors."

As Bruxton explained things, Holly's mind was racing ahead of him. And she saw with horror where his story was heading.

"Each fetus we produce is made by removing the nucleus of a starter egg and replacing it with the nucleus from one of the cells we have in culture. We allow the starter eggs to divide four times then we separate the resulting sixteen cells and culture them individually until each one has formed an embryo. They are then implanted into the cows we have genetically manipulated to support human gestation. Our level of success with this is far superior to any other group in the world, approaching a hundred percent, so that fairly routinely, we ultimately get sixteen fetuses from each starter egg we buy. But as I have indicated, the starter eggs merely provide the right environment for development to begin. Any human egg can suffice. It's the genome that's the key. *Your* genome.

"So you see, Doctor Fisher, if I'm the father of the program, *you* are the mother."

36

Mother . . . She was the biological mother of every fetus Bruxton had produced. The thought was so impossible Holly's mind couldn't grasp it. How many had there been? Hundreds? Thousands? All carrying her genes . . . harvested . . . their heads removed . . .

The impact of all this was so emotionally staggering that to protect Holly from it, her brain began shutting down. Bruxton was still talking, but his voice sounded far off. He was reaching into the inside pocket of his jacket.

"And we were able to accomplish this using only three of the eleven eggs you left at the fertility clinic." He produced a vial containing a pink liquid. "The other eight are here, still viable I'm sure, even though I've let them thaw."

Her eggs . . . He had her remaining eggs in his hand. Holly's senses snapped back, heightened. She started to get up, but Billy put a firm hand on her shoulder. Fearing the stun gun, she remained seated. Muscles coiled, she watched Bruxton through slitted eyes.

He unscrewed the cap on the vial and alarms began to clang in Holly's head.

"All my professional life, I have rewarded loyalty, and where possible, punished those who work against me," Bruxton said. "What I do now, I do, not for pleasure, but out of necessity."

As he tipped the vial and poured the contents onto the floor, Holly erupted from her chair, a primal cry of anguish coming from a part of her she'd never known. Hatred seething behind her eyes, she lunged for Bruxton, but Billy intercepted her with the stun gun.

The electrical shock took her legs and she crumpled to the floor, her head grazing Bruxton's pants as she fell.

Suddenly, a repetitious buzzing sound filled the room. A calm female voice said, "There is an intruder on the property."

Considering the size of the house and grounds, Susan Morrison shouldn't have been surprised when the security system began switching on the outside lights. But she was.

When she'd approached Billy's car from behind as it left the dairy, she'd recognized Holly through the rear window. Considering all that Holly had told her, it seemed possible that she was being taken somewhere against her will. Then, when Billy turned Holly's face forward with his hand, a rude gesture at best, she'd come to believe that even more.

She couldn't follow them onto Bruxton's estate, but the B in the wrought iron gates told her, too, who lived there, a further cause for worry. At that point, she had to make a quick decision—go for help or try to do something herself. Afraid that any delay might allow them to harm Holly, she'd driven fifty yards past the front gates, then veered onto the lawn that ran along the iron fence surrounding the estate. She'd managed to get over the fence by climbing onto her car. Now that she was inside and lights were popping on all around her, she at least had their attention. That alone should give them something to think about besides Holly. Caught in the open, she ran for a cluster of spruce trees that would provide cover.

"It's a woman," Bruxton said, watching Susan on one of the monitors in his study, ". . . in street clothes." He leaned closer. "And she's carrying a pistol." He glanced at the other monitors that served different parts of the grounds. "She seems to be here alone." He turned to Billy. "Get rid of her. If you go out through the kitchen, you'll see those trees she's in off to your left. Boone will show you the way."

He went to his desk and called Boone on the intercom, which served the whole house. He then called the sheriff's office in Midland.

"This is Doctor Bruxton. The alarm you've just received from my house was a malfunction. Please ignore it." He gave them the code number that proved his identity and hung up as Boone answered his call.

"Take Mr. Lynch to the kitchen exit." Realizing as they departed that he was being left alone with Holly, who was only partially restrained, Bruxton stepped into the reception hall and called out, "And get some rope or tape and come back here and secure this woman's legs."

Returning to his study, Bruxton looked at Holly, still on the floor recovering from the stun gun. What a fool he'd been to bring her here.

From her position in the small group of spruce trees, Susan considered her next move. Toward the rear of the house she saw a conservatory. There had to be a door there, most likely with a lot of glass in it, so if it was locked, she might be able to break it and let herself in. But there was a lot of open lawn between the spruces and the conservatory. And if she took a direct route, it would allow her to be seen through a bank of windows on the side of the house.

About ten yards from the spruces, on a line roughly parallel to the house, was a large curved flower bed backed with a line of huge rocks and a double row of thick junipers. Beyond that, separated by another stretch of open lawn, was a similar curved bed, so the two beds formed a discontinuous arc facing the house. Susan saw that if she approached the conservatory from the second flowerbed, she'd be screened from the house by a stand of hollies on the edge of the conservatory patio. She took a deep breath and sprinted for the first line of junipers.

The exit Billy used was behind the conservatory so even if Susan had been watching instead of running, his emergence would have been hidden from her by the tropical plants inside. But as he came around the conservatory with his automatic drawn, he saw her running. Instinctively, he raised his gun and fired two rounds.

Susan heard two gunshots from her right. At nearly the same instant, one slug passed so close she could hear it whisper her name. The other ticked the back of her jacket.

She dove the last three feet to the flowerbed and hit the ground so hard it knocked the wind out of her. Gasping for air, she rolled to her knees, making sure she stayed low so the rocks in front of the bushes would shield her. There was no doubt now. She'd been right to follow that car and go over the fence. These people were desperate.

It had been forty years since her military training, but it all came back in a rush along with her breath. That damn light in the tree behind her . . .

She turned and fired once. The light source exploded, and blessed darkness collapsed around her.

Billy heard the shot and saw the light shatter, but he didn't connect the two, mostly because his adversary was a woman and therefore easy pickings. He ran for the flowerbed that Susan had been planning to use as a cover before approaching the conservatory. He was exposed and a little apprehensive for the five seconds it took him to cross the open lawn, because even a woman could get off a lucky shot.

•   •   •

In the ravine behind the dairy, Otto's flashlight illuminated the freshly cut hole in the fence. Completely convinced now that Heflin and Fisher were inside and in trouble, he finally revealed that to his men.

". . . And they're probably in the area with all the lights," he said. "The quickest way to that point once we get inside is to climb out of the ravine and proceed along its edge to the road. Okay, let's get in there."

Otto had twisted his left knee slightly on a slippery rock just before they saw the hole in the fence. But he was so excited he didn't even feel any pain as he moved through the hole with the agility of a man much younger and a lot thinner.

In the security center, where Richard and Jessie were still bound and gagged on the floor, all the remaining security men except their apparent leader were drinking coffee: two at the table and the one who seemed to have responsibility for the surveillance control panel standing with his back to the monitors. Though Richard and Jessie didn't know it because the men had been speaking only in Italian, they'd been discussing who would go and get Richard's car, which they thought belonged to Jessie. With her car—and by association, Jessie herself—the topic of conversation, one of them looked at her and said in English, "You are too beautiful to die. Why did you have to come here?"

Richard and Jessie had tried to keep from thinking that their captors were prepared to kill them. After the security man's comment, they could pretend otherwise no longer. And it seemed likely that it *would* happen because no one in the security area was aware yet of the police at the gate.

Richard's thoughts were mostly for Katie. His parents would take care of her, but what would happen to her if they fell ill? The prospect of not even being able to say goodbye to her just like when her mother was taken was unfathomable. She was just a little kid. She didn't deserve this.

Sandwiched between his concern for Katie, Richard was also worried about Holly. He had no idea where they'd taken her or why. She might already be dead.

Beside him, Jessie was wondering about her dog. Would he be taken to the pound and killed? People don't adopt old dogs. She also thought about her work . . . what she'd leave behind . . . what impact it would have . . . if the few notes and the one experiment she'd done on the soup from the diseased cow would ever be acknowledged. She decided that she'd done too little in everything. She'd die and except for her mother and father and maybe Artie, would quickly be forgotten.

Suddenly, Leonetti burst into the room, his cell phone at his ear. He glanced at the monitor that was still showing an image of the hole in the fence, only now cops were pouring through it.

He cursed in Italian and pointed at the screen. The man who should have been watching it turned and cursed as well. The others kicked their chairs back, unholstered their weapons, and ran to look too.

Neither Richard nor Jessie could see what had upset the room, but whatever it was encouraged them greatly. While the security men waited for orders, Leonetti entered Bruxton's number into the cell phone.

As Bruxton watched the scene outside his home unfold on his monitor, Boone tied Holly's ankles together with an Ace bandage he'd found. As he finished, the phone rang. Boone answered, listened a moment, and said, "It's Leonetti."

Irritated at having his attention diverted from the intruder outside, Bruxton took the call and told Boone he could leave. Keeping his eyes on the monitor, Bruxton put the receiver to his ear. "What's the problem?"

"There are cops all around us here and they're coming in. What should we do?"

With the light out of commission, Susan turned her attention to Billy and she peeked through the junipers just as he disappeared behind those in the next flowerbed. He obviously planned to come around the near end of that bed and "surprise" her.

Scrambling to her feet, Susan stepped around the end of her flowerbed that was farthest from Billy's, got in a good stance, and fired five rounds in his direction, spreading them evenly from left to right.

In thinking that just because he couldn't be seen he was safe, Billy had made a silly mistake. Susan's second round ripped through the junipers hiding him and shattered one of his ribs before tearing through his left lung and exiting through his back. As blood spurted into his collapsed lung from a major pulmonary vessel, he couldn't believe a woman had done this to him.

He coughed and sprayed bloody froth into his hand. His head felt as if it were bobbing on the end of a string and he was definitely going to throw up. Aware that he was dying, his only regret was that even if someone else killed Holly, he had for the first time in his life failed to complete a contract.

Billy toppled into the junipers, fell through the branches, and came to rest draped over the rocks in front of them.

Seeing Billy fall and hearing that the police were at the dairy, Bruxton realized it was over. Just like that . . . all he had worked for . . . gone. His picture and stories about the monsters he'd produced would soon be in newspapers all over the world. Tasting blood, the media would tear him apart, forgetting in their zeal all the people he'd cured. "There's nothing that *can* be done," he muttered into the phone to Leonetti.

Otto and his men stood in a line across the front of the wooden gates to the calving area, their weapons drawn. Otto raised the bullhorn he'd owned for three years but had never used. Still breathing hard from the trek there, he took a calming breath, pressed the Talk button, and said the kind of things he'd always longed to utter.

"This is the sheriff. I have men at both entrances. Open this gate immediately."

Inside, Palagio moved the camera on the flagpole so Leonetti could see what they were up against.

He wasn't impressed. Only five men, led by a sloppy old *grassone* and lined up in the open. He spoke sharply to his best marksman, Tony Manzione, who grabbed his Fara assault rifle and left the room.

In two minutes, Manzione reported by radio that he was on the roof of the calving building and had the *grassone* in his sights. Whenever Leonetti gave the word, they were all dead.

37

Lips pinched, eyes flinty with rage, Bruxton looked at Holly.

Recovered now from the stun gun and having seen on the security monitors what had happened outside, Holly could tell from Bruxton's expression that the phone call had brought further unwelcome news. "Having a bad day?" she said.

"Not as bad as you're going to have." He snatched a cell phone off his desk, crossed the room, and locked the study doors. As he hurried past Holly, she tried to trip him, but missed. Reaching the far side of the room, he disappeared through a small door decorated to look like part of the wall.

On the other side of the door, Bruxton urged his tired and pain-racked body up a flight of stairs that led to the roof. Whatever happened in the next few days or weeks wouldn't affect his foreign bank accounts. He'd still be able to live well in some other part of the world. But he'd never be remembered as a great and good man, as he wished. And he was being driven from his home and country like some refugee. Even alone on the stairs he could feel the heat of humiliation on his cheeks.

But in all this dross, there was a glint of gold. Because he still had the power to make the one responsible for his troubles pay dearly.

Boone listened hard.

The helicopter on the roof . . . The cough of its engine . . .

Immediately realizing the implications of this, he bolted for the front door. In the soundproofed theater upstairs, the driver who'd brought Billy and Holly had no idea what was taking place.

Boone darted into the night, leaving the front door open. Afraid of being shot by whoever was out there, he ran awkwardly, his hands over his head.

Seeing him, Susan gave chase. When she'd closed to within ten yards, she ordered him to stop running.

Boone turned, the shadows exaggerating the fear governing his face.

"Where's the woman with short blond hair?" Susan asked, her Beretta pointing at Boone's head.

"It doesn't matter. She'll be dead in a minute and so will we if we don't get away from here."

Susan jabbed the air with the Beretta's muzzle. "Would you rather die right now? *Where is she?*"

"In the study."

"Who else is in the house?"

Forgetting the driver in the theater, Boone said, "No one. Doctor Bruxton is on the roof, leaving in his helicopter."

"Show me where she is."

"I can't."

Susan fired a shot over Boone's head. "The next one will make a mess of your hair."

Whimpering like a whipped dog, Boone started for the house. "You're going to kill *both* of us."

"Hurry up."

Boone started running, Susan close behind. When they reached the reception hall, Boone pointed across it. "In there."

"Go over and open the door."

"Lady, you're insane." Boone ran to the door and tried to open it. "It's locked. And I don't have a key."

"Holly, it's Susan. Are you in there?"

"I'm here," Holly called out. "But I'm tied up so I can't move."

"We've *got* to get out of here," Boone said, tears filling his eyes.

On the roof, with Bruxton at the controls, the helicopter lifted off. On the seat beside him was his cell phone. To prevent the discovery after his death that he possessed many stolen works of art, the house had been rigged with plastic explosive attached to large canisters of propane, wired to detonate when he called a special phone number and entered a five-digit code. He'd believed when he'd conceived the plan to hide his larcenous soul that he'd be making the call as his last act, from a hospital bed. Even then it would have hurt to destroy his things. Coming now, with life still throbbing within him, it was going to be much worse. But ledgers have credit columns as well as those for debits. In just a few seconds, the death of Holly Fisher would substantially offset his losses on this transaction.

Susan pushed a thirty-thousand-dollar Chinese vase to the floor, shattering it. "Help me here," she said, motioning to the short Corinthian column on which the vase had rested. "We're going to use this as a battering ram on those doors."

Susan had to keep one hand free to hold the Beretta. Hers was therefore a one-armed contribution to their effort. Aiming the column at the line where the two doors met, Susan said, "On the count of two. One . . . two . . ."

Susan and Boone charged the doors and they splintered the door open. The impact tore the column from Susan's curled arm. Unable to hold it on his own and with no need to try, Boone dropped his end as well.

Seeing Holly on the floor, Susan ran to the spot, knelt

beside her, and put down the Beretta. Drawing her knife from the sheath strapped to her ankle, she went to work on Holly's restraints. Taking advantage of the moment, Boone fled.

Leonetti stared at the monitor where the five policemen were still waiting for his response. The warrior in him wanted to show them how stupid they were to stand like that, but he saw the futility in it. If those men were killed, the ones at the gates would radio for help and there would be a massive mobilization against him and his men. Better to let them in and take his chances with the American judicial system, which could easily be manipulated by money and clever lawyers. And what had he and his men really done? It was all Bruxton's doing. Even if the woman had been killed by now, they had no part in that.

He ordered Manzione to come off the roof and be prepared to surrender his weapons. He told the others the same and ordered them to give the impression that they spoke only Italian. They all went outside, where they met their countrymen from the special projects section, who'd left the harvest to see what was happening. Leonetti quickly explained the situation and sent a man to let the policemen in.

Seeing the gates begin to move, Otto's heart, already beating faster than it had in his entire career, set a new record. When he saw the eight Italians, all with their hands in the air, and he realized there would be no skirmish, he was greatly relieved and a tiny bit disappointed.

Otto moved forward, his men close behind him. They entered the compound and Otto ordered those inside to lay down their weapons.

The Italians all acted puzzled. Leonetti uttered a few lines of Italian to show Otto they didn't understand.

Ricky Blake pointed at his gun and then at the Italians. He mimed laying his gun on the ground and pointed at them again. When everyone who was armed had complied, Otto waved them away from their weapons. Leaving three men to watch them, he sent Del Brice to the calving area to look for Richard and Holly while he checked the security building.

When Otto found Richard and the woman he at first thought was Holly, and saw that they were still alive, he was thrilled. He quickly realized as he began to remove her gag who the woman was.

"Otto," Jessie gasped when she could speak. "How did you find us?"

"You practically left a road map," he replied, turning to remove Richard's gag. "Where's Doctor Fisher?"

"We don't know," Richard said slowly, his mouth dry and his tongue stiff. "They took her somewhere."

"Sheriff."

It was Del Brice, at the door, obviously excited. "You gotta see this."

When Holly's feet were free, Susan grabbed the Beretta and helped her up. "I think there's a bomb in the house. We've gotta go."

Holly's first couple of steps were gimpy and she moved far too slowly for the situation.

Hovering a safe distance over the house, Bruxton entered the last digit of the detonator code into his cell phone. In the mansion's wine cellar, the locked relay box emitted a barely audible click as a switch was activated and electrical pulses were sent along twenty-three wires to their destinations.

"What are they?" Otto said, bending to look at the slippery objects still attached to the cow's uterus by their umbilical cords.

As he spoke, a convulsive shudder rippled along the cow's flanks and a third object oozed wetly from the cow's vagina and plopped into the stainless steel tray on top of the others.

"They're . . ." Almost unable to utter the words, Richard's parched mouth, now arid out of horror, said, "human fetuses."

Then, in a moment none of them would ever forget, the eyes of the one that had just entered the world blinked open, stared at them longingly for a moment, and closed.

Suddenly, from far off, they heard the whump of a tremendous explosion.

The blood pumping into Holly's vessels from her racing heart lubricated her muscles so as she burst from the house behind Susan, she was moving at near peak speed. When they were twenty yards from the house, it blew, producing a flaming shock wave that threw both women off their feet and set their clothes on fire.

The blast erupted through the floor of the mansion's theater, blowing out the walls. Along with twisted seats, pieces of framing lumber, and a hailstorm of plaster, the theater's lone occupant, his legs severed at the knees, his head crushed, was thrown from the wreckage onto the front lawn, where his body became just another lump of smoldering debris. Because of the smoke and dust, Bruxton was unaware that Holly was outside the house when it exploded. His distress at the loss of his belongings was therefore mitigated by the belief that her debt to him was now paid.

While reflecting on the devastation he'd created, he was startled to see a piece of gilded picture frame fly past the helicopter's windshield. Realizing that he was in some danger here, he decided it was time to leave. The helicopter had moved barely ten feet when a silver candlestick hurtled out of the smoke below and hit the main rotor blade.

The copter shuddered and went into a sliding dive, slipping toward the flaming wreckage below. Bruxton fought the controls, trying to save the situation. But his efforts were fruitless.

A scant second before impact, he closed his eyes, took his hands off the controls, and let the vortex have him.

FIRE . . .

As Holly rolled across the grass to put out the flames

eating their way to her flesh, the word blinked behind her eyes in neon letters higher than the sulfurous smoke plume that boiled from the mansion's remains into the night sky. Focused on her own survival, she was barely aware of the additional explosion as Bruxton's helicopter disintegrated, adding to the flames and producing a second wave of shrapnel that whistled and twittered in all directions.

Almost as though Bruxton were trying one last time to kill her, a jagged piece of the helicopter's control panel that had been thrown from the wreckage dropped from the sky and impaled the lawn where Holly's head had been a millisecond earlier. She continued to roll until she hit one of the theater seats, then reversed direction.

Finally, the flames were out.

Struggling to a sitting position, she could smell singed hair and fabric, but her skin didn't feel as though she was burned anywhere.

Where was Susan?

Oh God.

The explosion had knocked out all the security lights, but in the hellish glow from the raging fire in the mansion's ruins, Holly saw that one of the flaming objects on the lawn was Susan. And she wasn't moving.

Holly scrambled to her feet and hurried to her fallen friend, pulling off her own charred jacket as she ran. When she reached Susan, she fell to her knees and smothered and beat at the dancing flames feeding on her. It seemed as if it took much longer, but in less than a minute the fire was out.

Holly crawled around to Susan's face and leaned close. "Susan . . . can you hear me? Susan . . ."

There was no response.

Holly lifted Susan's hand and applied a finger to the older woman's wrist. Her pulse was weak but steady. She needed an ambulance. Surely the explosion and fire had been reported by someone. . . .

Suddenly Holly heard a sharp *crack* behind her. The flaming wreckage was to her left, so she thought the sound was probably from a burning tree or piece of the house blown onto the lawn. But when she turned to look, she saw Billy Lynch lumbering toward her, one hand holding his side, the other aiming a gun at her.

He fired again and the bullet slapped into the ground at Susan's side. Which of them was he after? Probably both of them: Susan for having wounded him and her to keep his record intact. If she ran, that would leave Susan unprotected.

The Beretta . . .

She was sure Susan had it in her hand when they'd run from the house, but it wasn't there now. Where was it? Holly frantically searched the ground nearby.

Where was it?

Billy fired again and Holly felt the slug drill into the calf of her left leg. She couldn't just stay put and be shot. Hoping that Billy would think Susan was already dead or would realize he could come back for her later, Holly ran.

But there was nowhere to hide and every time her left foot hit the ground, white pain ran up her leg and exploded in her skull so that she wasn't able to move much faster than Billy.

He fired again and the slug tunneled through her hair. Still running as well as she could, she glanced back to see where he was.

He appeared to have ignored Susan and was coming after her, at a steady, plodding rate.

Where could she go?

There was lots of debris on the lawn, but nothing she could use for a shield. And the flames from the house were burning so brightly that the darkness had been banished for at least a hundred yards in all directions.

Billy fired again. How many rounds did that damn gun have?

Then she saw the grisly remains of the driver who had brought her to the house. So filled with terror there was no room for any other emotion, she at first viewed the legless corpse as simply another consequence of the explosion. But just as she was about to lurch off in a different direction, she saw that the body could be her salvation.

She gimped her way to the grisly corpse and stepped over it. Ignoring the blood on the grass from the raw stumps of its legs, she dropped to the ground beside it. The driver had removed his jacket in the theater so that his Glock and shoulder holster were visible.

She removed the weapon from the holster and with both hands pointed it at Billy, who was still trundling forward, but was now weaving slightly. And his arm was shaking. Whether he did so because he saw the gun in Holly's hand, or just figured he was close enough now, he began firing rapidly.

With slugs slapping the ground around her and stuttering into the body in front of her, Holly pulled the Glock's trigger again and again and again, firing before she'd fully compensated for the way the gun was bucking.

She was firing so fast she couldn't count the rounds, but he kept coming. Finally, one of her shots found its mark, staggering Billy. He reeled to the side as another hit him. She kept firing even as he fell, unable to stop, her mind screaming at him to die.

Finally, the magazine was empty. Still pointing the weapon at him, Holly watched Billy with wide eyes, her ragged breathing drowning out the sounds of the burning mansion. She watched and watched him for the slightest movement. But Billy would never move again.

Finally, in the distance she heard a siren coming closer. Suddenly, the Glock was too heavy to hold and she let it fall from her hands. Forcing herself to her feet, she gave Billy's body a wide berth and hobbled toward Susan.

38

When Otto learned from Holly that the creation of human fetuses for commercial use was a federal crime, he informed the FBI, so the investigation became a federal, state, and local effort. Susan Morrison suffered a concussion and second-degree burns over most of her right arm and the back of her neck. Following a night in the hospital, she was fit enough to answer questions. After hearing Susan and Holly's account of how Billy Lynch died, the attorney general's office decided that both women had acted in self-defense. Though they weren't pleased with Susan's "commando raid" to save Holly and could have filed some charges against her, they didn't. So within twenty-four hours after that wild night, Susan and Holly were free to leave the state.

The bullet that had struck Holly's calf had removed some tissue and temporarily left her with the need for a cane. Otherwise, like Susan, she was travelworthy. Afraid that Walter might have another heart attack if she told him what had happened to her, Susan didn't mention it when she called him. With their work in Wisconsin finished, the two women booked themselves on the same flight to Chicago, where they would then take separate planes home.

Accompanied by Richard and Jessie, Holly and Susan had barely reached their gate at the Madison airport when a newswoman on TV said, "And now more on the story from Midland, Wisconsin, where yesterday, it was learned that, in violation of federal law, the anti-cancer drug Vasostasin, a product of Bruxton Pharmaceuticals, was being purified from human fetuses carried in cows genetically engineered to support human gestation. At about the time authorities were making this discovery at the dairy where most workers thought the animals were ordinary milk cows, Zane Bruxton, CEO and founder of Bruxton Pharmaceuticals, was killed when his helicopter crashed after taking off from the roof of his palatial home in Midland. For more, we take you to CNN correspondent Bob Rains in Midland, Wisconsin."

The scene switched to an overweight man wearing a trench coat and standing in front of the Midland Dairy.

"Bob, do we know what caused Zane Bruxton's helicopter to crash?"

"Liz, apparently the initial report we had blaming the explosion and fire that destroyed Bruxton's home on the helicopter crashing into it, was wrong. The house exploded first and it's believed that the aircraft was brought down by flying debris."

"Do we know why the house exploded?"

"Not yet. There's speculation that Bruxton's long-time aide, Phillip Boone, knows something about it, but he's not talking."

"Is he a suspect in that explosion?"

"No. There was a clause in Bruxton's will stating that as long as Boone never speaks about Bruxton's private life and what went on in the home while Boone worked there, his salary will continue, paid from a trust fund set up years ago. That's apparently why he's remaining silent."

"There have been reports of three people in Midland recently dying from a form of mad cow disease after eating meat from one of the dairy's cows. Have you learned any more about that?"

"Phillip Boone may not be talking, but the dairy manager, Don Lamotte, in return for prosecutorial immunity, is saying plenty. According to what he's told FBI investigators, after one of the dairy's animals was put down for aborting the fetuses it was carrying, Lamotte discovered that the dairy's incinerator, where they disposed of all their biological waste, was broken and couldn't be repaired for two weeks. Needing to dispose of the carcass, he called the local dog food plant to take it away. Instead of being used for dog food, meat from the animal found its way onto the dinner table of three townspeople, all of whom died. Fearing that he was seeing the start of an epidemic, a local neurologist, who traced the disease to the dairy, tried to get the state health department to inspect all their animals. But Bruxton allegedly paid the director of the health department to look the other way because he was afraid the special nature of his animals would be discovered. She's been suspended pending a full investigation of her actions."

"Wasn't Bruxton worried about spreading mad cow disease in the milk the dairy was selling?"

"The herd of seventeen hundred cows was composed of clones generated from genetically altered cells of twelve animals. When Bruxton learned that it was one of his animals that had caused the deaths of those three people, he had all the other animals from that clone put down and their carcasses disposed of in the dairy's incinerator. Investigators have seized all the sacks of bone and ash from that incineration to make sure they're not infectious. And of course, the dairy is now closed."

"Bob, there's speculation that two other people from Midland were killed by an enforcer Bruxton hired. Are any details available regarding that aspect of the story?"

"Two bodies in addition to Bruxton's were found at his home. Don Lamotte has identified one as a member of the dairy's security force and the other as Billy Lynch. Lynch was apparently the enforcer you mentioned. Lam-

otte has told investigators that Lynch was responsible for
the deaths of Midland residents Chester Sorenson and
Henry Pennell, who had both learned the real source of
Vasostasin. It's believed the security man died in the explosion. But Lynch had been shot repeatedly. Two as yet
unidentified women were apparently taken from the scene
to a local hospital. So far, their role in all this is un-
clear."

"An amazing story, Bob. Thanks."

The newswoman looked at the camera. "In a related
development, earlier today the FDA withdrew its approval
of Vasostasin. Later, a distinguished panel of religious
leaders and physicians will discuss the ethical dilemma
posed by the use of engineered humans for commercial
purposes. Stay tuned."

"Well, we certainly figured prominently in *that* report," Jessie said. ". . . Local neurologist, unidentified
women. *I* wasn't even mentioned."

"The anonymity suits me," Holly said. "I just want to
forget the whole thing, though I doubt I ever will. Think
they'll close the pharmaceutical plant too?"

"If they do, it shouldn't be for long. The company
was profitable even before Vasostasin. And there's a board
of directors that can elect a new CEO. Be interesting to
see if they change the name to make people forget this
mess."

"Probably wouldn't have to," Richard said. "The public has a very short memory." He looked at the clock on
the wall. "We better get to the other gate."

Given the all clear, Richard's parents had immediately
brought Katie back from England and caught a connecting flight to Madison, which would arrive in just a few
minutes. Knowing they were coming and wanting to see
Katie, Holly had chosen a flight that would allow her to
meet that other plane with Richard and Jessie.

"I'll be back in a few minutes," Holly said to Susan.
"Will you be okay?"

"I'll be fine." With her good hand, Susan waved the

paperback she'd bought at the airport newsstand. "I'll just sit here and read."

"Can you turn the pages?" Holly asked, referring to Susan's bandaged right hand, where only her fingers were visible.

"Stop hovering," Susan ordered. "And get out of here."

Richard stepped over and put his hand on Susan's shoulder. "Susan, it's been a privilege meeting you. I hope we'll see you again and that you'll have a quick recovery."

Jessie added her good wishes and Richard and the two women headed for the other gate.

"She's a tough woman," Jessie said.

"I wouldn't want to get on her bad side," Richard said.

Their destination was not far away and they reached it just as the plane taxied up to the gate. When the passengers began filing in, Holly spotted an older couple with a little girl. Seeing Richard and Jessie, their expressions brightened.

With her oversized glasses, she looked like a retired librarian. He was the only man on the flight in a tie and jacket. His clothes and his well-groomed silver hair and mustache made him look as if *he* could run Bruxton Pharmaceuticals. If Richard aged as well as his father, he'd have no complaints.

Katie was a beauty: long reddish-brown hair and perfect features. She was wearing a ribbed black turtleneck under a red-and-black plaid jacket and skirt, and red lace-up boots on her little feet.

"Daddy . . ." She ran to Richard and he snatched her into his arms. "I've been to . . ." Katie looked at her grandmother.

"London," her grandmother said.

"London," Katie repeated. "That's in England. I had a good time, but I missed you so much."

Jessie and Richard hugged and greeted their parents, then Richard introduced Holly.

She was surprised when they both hugged her too.

"I'm so sorry you had to go through what you did," Richard's mother said.

"But you handled it damn well," his father added. "I'm proud of you."

"Don't swear, dear," his wife cautioned sweetly.

"And this is Katie," Richard said.

"Hello, Katie. I've been wanting to meet you for a long time."

"You're pretty," Katie said. Then her little brow furrowed with concern. "Why do you have a cane?"

"I hurt my leg."

"Will it get better soon?"

"I think so."

The most genuine expression of relief swept Katie's concerned look aside. "I'm so glad," she said.

Impulsively, Holly kissed Katie on the cheek and the child put her arms around Holly's neck.

Holly returned Katie's hug, then disengaged herself. "It's been lovely meeting you all, but my plane is about to board."

"You all go on," Richard said to the others. "I'll catch up."

Jessie wiggled her fingers at Holly. "Goodbye kid. Take care of yourself."

"Katie likes you," Richard said as the others moved off.

"She's a sweetheart."

"And so do I. Wish you didn't live so far away. We could use a good hematologist around here."

"It's worth thinking about."

"Really?"

"Meanwhile, there's always the phone and airplanes."

"Poor substitutes," Richard said. He leaned close and Holly tilted her face upward. Their lips met in a soft kiss that neither wanted to end. But it *was* a public place and a plane waited.

"I'll call you," Holly said, easing away.

Richard watched her until she turned the corner.

Holly arrived at the gate for her flight just as the first-class passengers were boarding. Since she and Susan would be sitting in the middle of the plane, Susan had not yet joined those in line. Taking the seat beside her, Holly said, "Remember that story you told me about the women who kept the children they brought home from the hospital even though it was later discovered each had the other's baby. . . . When we get settled on the plane, I'd like to talk about that some more."

Epilogue

A week after the FDA had disapproved Vasostasin because of its source, two independent studies reported
that patients who had received Vasostasin therapy were
showing delayed onset of extensive and irreversible kidney damage. Thus Congress was spared the difficult task
of deciding whether the vast benefits of Vasostasin out-
weighed the moral imperative against its production.

Following considerable debate, the pregnancies of all
the dairy's animals were terminated. Across the country,
church services were held for those fetuses and all the
others Bruxton had created. Bruxton was so vilified by
the pro-life movement that those who supported the use
of fetal tissue or tissue products for the treatment of cat-
astrophic diseases largely found it best to keep their views
to themselves. After closing for a month, Bruxton Pharmaceuticals reopened under a new name.

Author's Note

At the time of this writing, a number of substances that act by denying blood vessels to tumors were either in or about to enter clinical trials. To my knowledge there is no member of that group called Vasostasin. If one should appear bearing that name, it should not be confused with my fictional creation.

COMING SOON IN HARDCOVER

Uncommon
Justice

TERRY DEVANE

PUTNAM